BLESSINGS

'What is it? What's happened?'

'No, no,' the voice on the telephone said quickly. 'Nothing bad. I'm sorry I frightened you. It's just this. I represent a service for adoptees. We're called Birth Search. You've probably heard about us.'

'I don't believe so.' She was puzzled. 'Are you in need of an attorney?'

'Oh, no. This isn't a legal matter. It's this way –'

She seemed to see the man settled back for a lengthy explanation, and so she interrupted quietly. 'I'm an attorney, so since it's not a legal matter, I really don't have time to talk. I'm sorry –'

Now it was he who, with equal quietness, interrupted. 'If you'll just give me a minute or two, I'll explain. You're aware, I'm sure, of the numbers of adoptees who are now seeking their natural parents. So many organizations have sprung up to help, of which ours is just one, and we –'

A long sigh quivered in Jennie's chest. 'I give as much to charity as I can afford. If you'll send me a brochure describing your work, I'll read it,' she said.

The man wasn't about to let go. 'This isn't a call for charity, Miss Rakowsky.' There was a long pause. When he spoke again, it was almost in a whisper. 'You gave birth nineteen years ago.'

Also by Belva Plain
and available from Coronet Books

Evergreen
Random Winds
Harvest
Treasures
Whispers
Daybreak

About the author

Belva Plain is one of the world's best-loved writers. Her first novel, *Evergreen*, was published in 1978, and she has since entranced an international audience with nine further best-sellers, including, most recently, *Harvest*, *Treasures, Whispers* and *Daybreak*.

Blessings

Belva Plain

CORONET BOOKS
Hodder and Stoughton

First published in Great Britain in 1990
by New English Library Hardbacks
A division of Hodder Headline PLC

New English Library paperback edition 1991
Coronet edition 1995

10 9 8 7 6 5 4 3 2 1

British Library C.I.P.

Plain, Belva *1918–*
Blessings
I. Title
818.54 [F]

ISBN 0 340 64011 1

Printed and bound in Great Britain by
Cox & Wyman Ltd, Reading, Berkshire

Hodder and Stoughton
A division of Hodder Headline PLC
338 Euston Road
London NW1 3BH

The human heart has hidden treasures,
In secret kept, in silence sealed;
– CHARLOTTE BRONTE

1

The day on which the sky cracked open over Jennie's head had begun as gladly as any other day in that wonderful year. It had been the best year of her life until then.

At noon she had been standing with Jay on the lip of the hill that overlooked the wild land called, by the town to which it belonged, the Green Marsh. It was one of those Indian summer intervals, when, after two weeks of rain and premature gray cold, everything suddenly burns again; the distant air burns blue and the near oaks flare red; in the marsh, cattails and spreading juniper glisten darkly after the night's rain. Canada geese come streaming, honking their long way to the south; and ducks, with a great flapping racket, splash into the pond.

'You see, it's not all marsh,' Jay explained. 'There's meadow and forest at the other end. Over a thousand acres, all wild. Been here for Lord knows how many thousands of years, just as you see it, untouched. We're trying to get the state to take it over as part of the wilderness system. That way it'll be safe forever. But we've got to hurry before the New York builders put their bid through.'

'Do you suppose they'll be able to?'

'God, I hope not. Imagine ruining all this!'

They stood for a little while listening to the silence. Totally at ease, accustomed as they were to quiet hours with each other, they felt no need for a continuous flow of speech.

A small sudden wind blew a dry shower of leaves, and at the bottom of the hill Jay's children came into sight, running with the wind They made themselves fall, the two girls rolling their little brother in the leaves. They shrieked, the dog barked; and the wind, carrying the sounds back up the hill, shattered the Sunday peace.

'Darling, Jay said.

Turning to him, Jennie knew that he had been watching her while she watched his children.

'I'm happier than anyone has a right to be,' she murmured.

He searched her face with such intensity, such love, that she felt an ache in her throat.

'Oh, Jennie, I can't tell you ... You give me ...' He threw out his arms to encompass the whole bright scene in one characteristic, generous gesture. 'I never thought ...' Not finishing, he put his arms around her shoulders and drew her close.

Into the curve of his arm she settled, feeling a perfect happiness. Memory ran backward to the beginning of this miracle. A year and a half before, when they had first met, Jay had been a widower for two years, his young wife having died most terribly of cancer. He had been left with two small girls and an infant son, a rather grand Upper East Side apartment, and a partnership in one of New York's most prestigious law firms, a position not inherited as sometimes happens, but earned through merit and hard effort. One of the first things Jennie had observed about Jay had been a strained expression that might signify anxiety, overwork, loneliness, or all of these. Certainly if loneliness was a problem, the city had enough desirable young women to fill a man's vacant hours, especially those of a tall young man with vivid eyes and a charming cleft in his chin. When she knew him better, she understood that he had been very, very careful about involvements because of his children. Some of his friends had asked her whether she didn't find his devotion to the children a bore or a hindrance; on the contrary, she admired it, was glad of it, and would have thought less of him if he had not felt a loving, deep responsibility toward them.

She turned her face up now to see his. Yes, the look of strain was definitely gone, along with that nervous habit of pulling a strand of hair at his temple, and along with smoking too much and sleeping too little. Indeed, this last month he had stopped smoking altogether. Smiles came easily now, and certainly he looked much younger than thirty-eight.

'What are you staring at, woman?'

'I like you in plaid shirts and jeans.'

'Better than in my Brooks Brothers vest?'

'I like you best in nothing at all, since you ask.'

'Same to you. Listen, I was thinking just now, would you like to have a little summer place up around here? We could build something at the far end of my parents' property, or somewhere else, or not at all. You choose.'

'I can't think. I've never had so many choices in my life!'

'It's time you had some, then.'

She had never been one who craved choices. In her mind she stripped things bare to the core, and the core now was just her pure need to be with Jay always and forever; houses, plans, *things* – all were unimportant beside that need.

'Have you decided where you want the wedding? Mother and Dad would be glad to have it at their apartment. Mother said she's already told you.'

A woman was supposed to be married from her own house. But when the home consisted of two cramped rooms in a renovated walk-up tenement, even the simplest ceremony presented a problem. Obviously Jay's mother understood that, although with kindest tact she had not referred to it.

'Yes. It was a lovely offer.' But in Jay's apartment, Jennie thought, it would seem a little bit like her own home. 'I'd like your place. Would that be all right? Since that's where I'm going to be living?'

'I'd love it, darling. I was hoping you'd want to. So, now that's settled. One thing more and we'll be all settled. What about your office? Do you want to stay where you are or come to my firm's building? There's going to be some available space on the fifteenth floor.'

'Stay where I am, Jay. My clients would be intimidated, scared to death on Madison Avenue. All my poor, broken-down women with their miserable problems and their shabby clothes ... It would be cruel. Besides, I couldn't afford a move like that, anyway.'

Jay grinned and ruffled her hair. 'Independent cuss, aren't you?'

'When it comes to my law practice, yes,' she answered seriously.

She supposed that his practice must mean as much to him as hers did to her. After all, why else would he have chosen it and stayed in it? But she couldn't imagine anyone, certainly not herself, caring as deeply about wills and trusts and litigation over money as about people – the battered wives, abused children, dispossessed families, and all the other pitiable souls who came asking for help. Yet no one could be more kind and caring than Jay. And money, after all, did grease the world's wheels, didn't it? Obviously, then, somebody had to take care of it.

At the foot of the hill they could see the setter's tail waving above dead weeds. The children were now stooped over.

'What on earth are they doing?' Jay asked.

'Collecting leaves. I bought scrapbooks for Sue and Emily to take to science class.'

'You think of everything! They're going to love you, Jennie. They do already.' He looked at his watch. 'Hey, we'd better call them. My mother's having an early lunch, so we can get back to the city by their bedtime.'

The two-lane blacktop road passed dairy farms and apple growers' wide, level spreads: little old houses with battered swings on front porches stood close to big red barns; horses in their shabby winter coats drooped their heads over wire fences; here and there a glossy white-painted house at the end of a gravel drive bordered with rhododendrons and azaleas proclaimed ownership by some local banker or, more likely still, by some city family who enjoyed its two or three summer months of rural peace.

'I can't believe my noisy little rooms in New York are only hours away,' Jennie said.

When the winter-brown fields gave way to the town, they entered the main street. Here chain stores, gas stations, a bowling alley, a pizza parlor, a redbrick consolidated high school, a Ford dealership, a dingy movie theater, and three or four new, low office buildings reflected modern times, while a saddlery, a volunteer fire department, and a feed store with a sign above the front entry – FOUNDED 1868 – spoke of a life that had been and was now changing.

'As I remember it, the town was half this size when Dad bought our place,' Jay remarked.

'Do you think of this as your true home?'

'Not yet. Maybe someday when I'm my parents' age. You know, I wouldn't be surprised if they were to give up their New York apartment and stay here all year, now that Dad's selling the factory and retiring.'

Mrs Wolfe was spreading compost over a rose bed at the side of the house when they drove up. She straightened, took off her gardening gloves, and spread her arms to the little boy, who ran into them.

'Did you have a good ride, Donny? Did you see the horses?'

The girls interrupted. 'We went to the academy, but Donny didn't want to get on the pony.'

'Daddy promised us chocolate bars, but the stores were all closed.'

'A good thing, too, or you wouldn't eat any lunch. And we've a beautiful chocolate cake for dessert.' The grandmother smiled at Jennie. 'I hope we haven't tired you out this weekend.'

'No, Mrs Wolfe, I could walk ten miles a day through these hills.'

'Well, I'm sure Jay will take you up on that sometime. Let's go in, shall we?'

Jennie stepped aside to let the other woman precede her into the house. She must be careful to remember every little nicety. . . .

It was only natural to feel unease in the presence of one's future husband's parents, wasn't it? Especially when this was her first visit after only two previous meetings, and those in the impersonal setting of a restaurant. Enid Wolfe, for all her welcoming manner, possessed an elegance that easily could be daunting. Even in her gingham shirt and denim skirt, she had it without trying.

The whole house had it. Its very simplicity told the story of people who were above any effort to impress. Through a white-paneled door one entered into a low-ceilinged hall; people were shorter two hundred years ago, so Jay had explained, when this farmhouse was built. Now worn old Oriental scatter rugs lay on the wood-pegged floors. Mixed fragrances of pine logs, furniture wax, and flowers hung in the air. On the coffee table in the living room lay a mound of splendid, blood-red roses – the last of the year, someone said. A pair of chintz-covered sofas faced each other in front of the fireplace. The cabinets looked antique, and there was a handsome baby grand piano at the far end of the long room. Two small paintings of blurry skies above a river stood on the pine mantel. They looked like the Turners Jennie had seen in the museum, but knowing so little about art and fearful of making a foolish mistake, she refrained from saying so. Really, she must make an effort to learn more about these things, for Jay knew and cared about them.

She suspected that the taste here was faultless, and undoubtedly expensive. Yet the room, the whole house, said: 'I don't pretend, I am who I am.' Fat, homemade needlepoint pillows lay about. Books stood in piles on tables, with a tumbling stack on the floor. Photographs cluttered another large round table: there was a 1920s bride in a short skirt and a long train; there were children and a graduation picture and one of a pug dog. Tennis rackets were propped against a wall in a corner. A tortoise cat had wrapped itself in an afghan on one of the easy chairs, and now the setter came bounding in to flop in front of the fire.

Jay's father got up from the wing chair in which he had been sitting with a drink in hand. He was craggy, with a beaky, aristocratic nose, and taller than his tall wife. Jay would look like him someday.

'Come on in. Daisy is just about to put things on the table. Where've you people been all this time?' he inquired as they went to the dining room.

'Oh, around,' Jay said. 'I wanted to show Jennie the neighborhood. We finished at the Green Marsh. What's new with the situation since I talked to you?'

Arthur Wolfe gave the table a startling thump. 'They've been up from New York, thick as thieves all over town these past weeks. Made a big offer, four and a half million.' He made a grim mouth. 'It'll tear the town apart, I predict, before we're through.'

'What's happening with the state? The park negotiations?'

'Oh, politicians! Red tape! Who knows when they'll get around to it in the legislature? In the meantime the developers are on the move, and fast. I'm disgusted.'

Jay frowned. 'So what are you doing about it?'

'Well, we've got a committee together, Horace Ferguson and I. He's doing most of the work. I'm too old to do much –'

'Arthur Wolfe, you are not old!' his wife protested.

'Okay, let's say I'm doing enough. I've been talking to the people who'll be sure to see it the right way, especially on the planning board.' The old man took a spoonful of soup, then laid the spoon down and exploded again. 'Good God, the whole nation will be paved over before you know it, with nothing green left alive!'

'Hmm,' Jay reflected, 'that marsh is an aquifer. They'll wreck the water table if they start to tinker with it. It'll affect every town in the area, and all the farms. Don't they know that?'

'Don't who know it? Developers? What do they care? Come up from the city, pollute the place, make a bundle, and leave.'

'Arthur, eat your dinner,' his wife said gently. 'The soup's getting cold. We're all very conservation-minded in our family,' she explained, turning to Jennie. 'But you've probably noticed.'

'I agree with you all,' Jennie answered. 'It's high time we cleaned things up – the water, the air, the strip mines, everything. Otherwise there'll be nothing left for people like Emily and Sue and Donny.'

'Jennie's an outdoor girl,' Jay said. 'Last summer in Maine we took a thirty-mile canoe trip with portage a good part of the way, and she held up as well as I did. Better, maybe.'

The old man was interested. 'Where'd you grow up, Jennie? You never said.'

'Not where you might think. In the city, the heart of Baltimore. I guess maybe I was a farmer's daughter in another incarnation.'

Now, as the meal progressed, the conversation was diverted. Donny's meat had to be cut up for him. Sue had complaints about her piano teacher. Emily spilled milk on her skirt and had to be dried off. Enid Wolfe inquired about tickets for a new play. They were having dessert when Arthur returned to the subject of the Green Marsh, making explanations for Jennie's benefit.

'It's almost fourteen hundred acres, including the lake. The town owns it. Was willed to it . . . oh, it must be close to eighty years ago. Let's see, we've been summering here since our first son, Philip, was born, and he's going on fifty. At first we rented, and then after I inherited a little money from my grandmother I bought the place for a song. Well, so the town has the land and it's understood that it would be kept as is. It's full of wildlife, you know, beaver and fox. And, of course, it's a sanctuary for birds. Some of the oaks are two hundred years old. Local kids all swim in the lake. Then there's fishing and nature trails for the schools, everything. It's a treasure, a common treasure for everybody, and we can't let it go. We're not going to.' He balled his napkin and thrust it from him. 'Our group – concerned citizens we can call ourselves, I guess – is pooling our money to hire counsel and fight this thing hard.'

'You really expect a hard fight?' Jay asked.

'I told you I do. I hate to be a cynic – good liberals aren't supposed to be cynical – but money will talk to a lot of folks around here. They won't care about natural beauty, not even about the water table, poor fools. There'll be promises of jobs, increased business, the usual short-sighted arguments. So we'd better be prepared.'

'I see.' Jay was thoughtful for a moment. 'Hiring counsel, you said. Somebody in town?'

'No. The lawyers around here aren't on our side. They all hope to get business from the developers.'

'Got anyone in mind, then?' asked Jay.

'Well, your firm's diversified, isn't it? Would somebody take it on? Of course, there won't be much of a fee. It'll depend on what Horace and I and a handful more can raise among us.' As Jay hesitated, the sharp old eyes twinkled. 'Okay, I know your fees. I'm only teasing.'

'That's not it at all! You know I'd do it myself for nothing if you asked me to. The fact is, I was thinking of Jennie.'

'Me!' she cried.

'Why not? You can do it beautifully.' And Jay said to his parents, 'I never told you that the first time we met, Jennie had just won an environment case. I had happened to read an article about it in the *Times* that morning, and so when somebody at this party pointed her out, I asked to be introduced.'

'How did you come to do that, Jennie?' Arthur Wolfe wanted to know. 'It's not what you generally do, is it?'

'Oh, no, I almost always take women's cases, family problems. It happened that I defended a woman with four children against a landlord who wanted to evict them. Well, she was very grateful, and later she asked me to help some relatives on Long Island who had a land-use problem. I had never done anything like it before, but it appealed to me – the justice of it, I mean – so I wanted to try it.' She stopped. 'That's it. I don't want to bore you with the details.'

'You won't bore us. I want the details.'

'Well.' Suddenly aware that she was using too many *wells*, she stopped and began again. 'It was a working-class neighborhood. Blue-collar, without money or influence. At the end of the street on the cross avenue there was a vacant tract that was zoned for business and bought by some people who wanted to build a small chemical plant. There would have been noxious odors and, quite probably, carcinogenic emissions. It would have blighted the neighborhood. We had a very tough fight because there were political connections – the usual thing.'

'But you won,' Jay said proudly. 'And you haven't mentioned that it was a test case and set a precedent.'

His father was studying Jennie. 'Do you think you'd be interested in our case?'

'I'd need to know more about it. What do they want to do with the land?'

'They want to build what they call a recreational subdivision. Vacation homes. Corporate retreats. It would be high-density condominiums one on top of the other. You see, the new highway makes it accessible, there's skiing only half an hour away, and after they dredge the lake they'll double its size and –' He stopped.

Enid interjected, 'And incidentally, if we should have a wet season, flood all the fields south of town. Oh, it makes me sick! This is one of the most beautiful areas in the state – in the East, for that matter. I see it as a symbol. If this falls victim to greed, then anything can. Do you see what I mean, Jennie?'

'Oh, greed,' Jennie said. 'I deal with it every day. It's the ultimate poison, whether it's rat-infested tenements or polluted oceans or mangled jungles –' Again she stopped, feeling still the slight unease of being there under observation, and was conscious of her voice, which tended to rise in her enthusiasm, and of her hands, which she had been training herself to keep in her lap. 'It will destroy us all in the end,' she finished more quietly.

Jay smiled. He approved of her enthusiasm. 'Not while there are people like you to fight.'

'I take it that you accept,' said Arthur Wolfe.

She thought, So I shall be defending the rights of a piece of land to exist! A curious change for an urban person who'd never owned a foot of land. And yet, ever since she had been a child, taken for an occasional Sunday ride in the country, she had felt a pull toward the land, as if the trees had spoken to her. Later, reading Rachel Carson's book, or the Club of Rome's, and watching the *National Geographic* programs on television, she had felt a stronger pull, with greater understanding.

'Yes, I'll do it,' she said, and felt a warm surge of pleasurable excitement.

'Great! If Jay says you're good, you're good.' Arthur got up from the table and stood over Jennie. 'We've already had the first reading of the proposal before the town council, and the matter's on the way to the planning board. They'll be hearing it in two or three weeks, so you'll be coming back up here pretty soon. Jay can fill you in on the town government. I won't take up your time now, but it's the usual thing, nine elected council members, one of whom is the mayor.' He shook Jennie's hand, pumping it. 'Before you leave now, I've a mile-high stack of papers for you to take back, reports from engineers and water experts, a survey, the petition to the legislature, and of course the developer's lousy proposal.' He pumped her hand again. 'We're on the way, I think.'

'It's a challenge,' Jennie told him. 'I'll do my best.'

Jay looked at his watch. 'Time to get started. Let's get our bags, Jennie, and go.'

Jennie was in the guest room collecting her coat and overnight bag when Mrs Wolfe knocked.

'May I come in? I wanted one private minute with you.' She was carrying a flat maroon leather box. 'I wanted to give you this. Quietly, upstairs here, with just the two of us. Open it, Jennie.'

On a velvet cushion, curved into a double circle, lay a long strand of pearls, large, uniform, and very faintly, shyly, pink. For a second Jennie went blank. She knew really nothing about pearls, having owned only a short string bought at a costume-jewelry counter, so as to seem less strictly tailored in the courtroom. The instant's blankness was followed by an instant's confusion.

'They were my mother-in-law's. I've been keeping them for the next bride in the family,' Enid Wolfe said, adding after a second's hesitation, 'I'd already given away my own mother's necklace.'

Jennie's eyes went from the pearls to the other woman's face, which was subdued into a kind of reverence. She understood that the gift had deep meanings.

'Oh . . . lovely,' she faltered.

'Yes, aren't they? Here. Try them on.' And as Jennie leaned forward, she dropped the necklace over her head. 'Now look at yourself.'

From the mirror above the chest of drawers a round, young face, much younger than its thirty-six years, looked back out of a pair of unusually sharp green eyes. 'Cat's eyes,' Jay teased. At this moment they were rather startled. The cheeks, which were naturally ruddy so that they had never needed to be rouged, were flushed up to the prominent cheekbones.

'Pearls always do something for a woman, don't they?' Enid said. 'Even with just that sweater and skirt.'

'Oh, lovely,' Jennie repeated.

'Yes, you don't see many like them anymore.'

'I'm . . . I'm speechless, Mrs Wolfe. That's not like me, either.'

'Would you like to call me Enid? Mrs Wolfe is too formal for someone who's going to be in the family.' Enid's austere face brightened suddenly. 'Believe me, I don't say lightly what I'm going to say now. One doesn't watch one's son give himself and his precious children over to the care of another woman without thinking very, very carefully about her. But you've been so good for Jay. We've seen it, and we want you to know . . .' She laid a hand on Jennie's shoulder. 'I want you to know that Arthur and I are most happy about you. We admire you, Jennie.'

'Sometimes I think I'm in a dream,' Jennie said softly. She stroked the pearls. 'Jay and I and the children . . . and now you. All of you being so wonderful to me.'

'Why shouldn't we be? And as for Jay, I surely don't have to tell you how loving he is. You'll have a good life with him. Oh,' said Enid, smiling with a mother's indulgence, 'he has his faults, of course. He can't stand to be kept waiting. He likes his hot food burning and his cold food icy. Things like that.' Perched now on the bed, she was confiding, intimate. 'But he's a good man, a good human being. The word *good* covers so much, doesn't it? Total honesty, for one thing. Jay says what he means and means what he says. He's entirely open, easy to read. And I see the same in you. Of course, Jay's told us so much about you that we felt, before we even met you, that we already knew you.' She stood up. 'My goodness, I'm talking my head off. Come, they're waiting for you. You've got a good three-hour drive ahead.'

On the way home Jay remarked, 'I haven't seen my father so worked up about anything since the days when he used to fight in the city for public housing and better schools for the poor.'

They were talking in low voices while the children dozed in the backseat.

'I hope I can handle the case. And I guess I won't be able to think of anything else until I've done it.'

'Are you that nervous about it already? I don't want you to take it if you're going to be. I want my bride to be relaxed. No worry lines around the eyes.'

'I have to do it now. I said I would.'

'Come on. Don't let Dad foist it on you if you feel any hesitance. I'll get one of the young guys in the office to do it, that's all.'

She answered with mock indignation, 'What? Turn it over to a man, as if a woman couldn't handle it? No, it's just that – it's your father, your family. I so want them to think well of me.'

'For Pete's sake, they already do. You know that. Do you need more proof than having my grandmother's pearls in your lap? My mother would as soon part with her teeth as see those in the wrong hands. Seriously, though, for such a feisty lady, you shouldn't be so unsure of yourself around my family.'

'Am I? Is that the impression I give?'

'A little. Don't worry about it.' Jay reached over and squeezed her hand. 'More seriously, hang on to that box until I can get it insured in the new name tomorrow.'

It was dark when they drew up in front of the apartment house. Two handsome brass coach lamps gleamed at the entrance under the green awning. Down Park Avenue, a double row of parallel streetlights shone on the white limestone and the brick and granite fronts of the fine solid structures that stretched all the way to the low facade of Grand Central Terminal, with the Pan Am Building behind it, at the base of the avenue. It was one of the most famous views in the world, as typical of the city as London's Trafalgar Square or Paris's Place de la Concorde.

Jennie stood a moment to take it all in while Jay helped the children out of the backseat. Her life seldom brought her to this part of the city; in fact, she had never even been inside a building like this before knowing Jay.

'Is the nanny back yet?' she asked now.

'No, she comes early Monday morning in time to get them ready for school.'

'Then I'll go up and help you put them to bed.'

'No need to. I can manage. You've got a big day tomorrow, you said.'

'You've got a big day too. Besides, I want to.'

Upstairs, while Jay undressed his little son and settled him in bed among a mound of assorted teddy bears and pandas, Jennie supervised the girls.

'It's late and you had a shower this morning, so I think we'll skip baths tonight,' she said.

Sue clamored, 'A story? Do we get a story?'

Jennie looked at the clock on the table between the two ivory-enameled beds. 'It's too late for stories. I'll read you some poems instead.' Becoming more and more accustomed to and accepted by the children, she felt competent, equipped to mother them. 'How about A. A. Milne? Good? All right, into the bathroom with you.'

They brushed their teeth and washed their hands and faces. They dropped their soiled clothes into the hamper and put on their pink cotton nightgowns. Lastly Jennie unwound their braids and brushed their long, straight tan hair. Jay and his family were dark-haired. Probably the girls were like their mother.

Emily touched Jennie's hair. 'I wish I had black curls like yours.'

'And I wish I had hair like yours. Mine gets all frizzy when it rains. It's a nuisance.'

'No, it's beautiful,' Sue said. 'Daddy thinks so too. I asked him.'

Jennie hugged her. They were so sweet, these children, with their fragrant skin and moist, sloppy kisses! Oh, they could have nasty tantrums now and then – she had seen a few – but that was natural. She felt a surge of something that, if not love – how easily one tosses the word *love* around! – was very close to it. Back in the bedroom, she got out the beloved book and read about Christopher Robin.

'They're changing guard at Buckingham Palace;
Christopher Robin went down with Alice.'

She read about water-lilies.

'Where the water-lilies go
To and fro,
Rocking in the ripples of the water –'

She closed the book – 'Now, bedtime' – and drew the embroidered curtains against the night.

In the rosy, lamplit room, all was orderly and clean. This peace did something to Jennie's heart. So much did she see of life's other side, of the abuse and hurt and ugliness that human beings inflict on one another! Taking a last look at the two little girls, she felt waves of thankfulness that they, at least, had been spared. Complicated feelings these were, almost prayerful.

She turned off the light. 'Good night, darlings. Pleasant dreams. That's what my mother used to say to me. Pleasant dreams.'

Jay was standing at the door of the master bedroom. 'I know you said you don't want to change anything in the apartment,' he began.

'It would be awfully extravagant when everything's in perfect condition.'

The thought of redecorating all these rooms was distressing. She wasn't prepared with the right knowledge to do it, and moreover, she wasn't really interested. She looked down the corridor now into the long living room, over a sea of moss-green carpeting on which stood islands of mahogany and chintz in pleasing, quiet taste, and then across into the dining room, where she surprised herself by recognizing that the table was Duncan Phyfe, and the chairs, with seats of ruby-flowered silk, were Chippendale.

'But the bedroom, at least,' Jay said. 'We'll want a new bedroom.'

Yes, she would concede that. She didn't want the canopied bed in which he had slept with another woman. Also, she would replace the armoire and chests in which Phyllis had kept her clothes. She would take time next week and attend to that.

On a tall chest, which she supposed was Jay's, stood a silver-framed photograph of a young woman wearing a spreading ball gown and the other grandmother's pearls. Her eyes were large, with traces of amusement in them; her face was round, with prominent cheekbones. Why, Jennie thought, except for the straight, light hair, she looks like me! She wondered whether Jay was conscious of the resemblance. Probably he wasn't. It was said that people unconsciously made the same choice over and over. She paused, examining the face and comparing.

Somewhat anxiously Jay said, 'That won't stay, of course. I should have put it someplace else.'

'Why shouldn't it stay? You wouldn't be much of a man if you were to forget her.'

Poor soul, dead of cancer at thirty-two, leaving all this life, these beloved people behind!

'There's nobody like you, Jennie.' Jay's voice was rough with emotion. 'Not one woman in fifty would say that and mean it, as I know you do.'

And she did mean it. Strange it was that, alone with Jay, she felt no insecurity, not the least dread of invidious comparisons with anyone else. Alone with him, she was absolutely certain of her own worth. It was only the family, the parents, the setting that caused a wavering, a dread of not belonging in spite of all their welcome. But she would get over that....

He put his arms around her and laid her head on his shoulder. 'I'm in such a damn hurry to get this wedding business over. Couldn't sleep together this weekend at my parents' house, can't sleep together here because of the children and the nanny. It's hell.'

'My place again any night this week,' she murmured, then raised her head to look into his face. She ran her finger down his nose. 'Have I ever told you that you remind me of Lincoln? If you had a beard, you'd be a dead ringer for him.'

Jay burst out laughing. 'Any man who's tall and thin and has a narrow face and a long nose is supposed to look like Lincoln. For a hardheaded young lawyer, you're a romantic,' he said.

'Hardheaded I may be, but softhearted too.'

'Darling, I know that well. Now listen, you need your sleep. I'm going to put you in a taxi. And phone me when you get home.'

'I can put myself in a taxi, Jay. I've never been so pampered! You don't think the taxi driver's going to kidnap me, do you?'

'No, but phone me, anyway, when you get back.'

The flat in the renovated walk-up near the East River was a different world. Here lived the singles and the live-together couples, young people from the theater, the arts, and business, either on the way up or hoping to start on the way up soon. Their homes ranged from empty – futon on the floor and a standing lamp – to half furnished

– raw wood painted over in brave black enamel or scarlet, with Victorian wicker rocking chairs from the secondhand stores – to the furnished, complete with rugs, books, records, and plants. Jennie's was furnished.

The moment she turned the key in the lock, the door across the hall was opened.

'Hi! How was it?' Shirley Weinberg, in a chenille bathrobe with a wet head wrapped in a towel, wanted to know. 'I was just drying my hair when I heard you. How was it?' she repeated. 'All right if I come in?'

'Sure, come on.'

They had been neighbors for five years and hadn't much more than neighborliness in common, that and friendly goodwill. Shirley, secretary to a theatrical producer, thought in terms of Broadway and what she saw as glamour, certainly not in terms of battered wives and dingy courtrooms. She sat down on Jennie's sofa.

'Was it gorgeous, their place?'

Shirley's vision, no doubt, was of marble floors and gilded wood.

'Not really. It's a farmhouse, a hundred fifty years old or more. I liked it, but you wouldn't.'

'They're terribly rich, though, aren't they?'

Questions like this were offensive, yet one should take them from where they came. Shirley was blunt and kind. But why did so many people ask such questions? From somewhere a memory stirred, a voice asking, 'Who? When?' The memory dissolved. . . .

'I don't suppose they are "terribly rich." But they're not poor, either,' Jennie replied patiently. 'Somehow one doesn't think of them that way.'

'*You* may not. But you're a funny duck,' Shirley said affectionately. 'What's in the box?'

'A necklace. I'll show you.'

'My God, will you look at that!'

'You scared me. What are you shrieking about?'

'These, you idiot. You've got ten thousand dollars' worth of pearls here, don't you know that? No, what am I saying? More than that. Pearls have gone way up again.'

'That's not possible,' Jennie said.

'I'm telling you what I know. I used to work on Madison Avenue at a jeweler's, didn't I? They're nine-millimeter. Do you know what that means? No, of course you don't. Put them on.'

'Now I'm afraid to touch them. I'm afraid they'll break.'

'They won't break. Put them on.'

'I feel silly if they're really worth that. Where will I wear them?'

'Lots of places. They're gorgeous. Look.'

'I never knew about things like these,' Jennie said wonderingly. 'I mean, why would anybody want to hang all that money around her neck?'

'You *are* a funny duck,' the other repeated. 'They really don't matter to you at all?'

'Well, in one way they do. They're very beautiful, of course, but what matters to me is what they stand for, that I'm wanted in their family, and I'm very, very happy about that. I just never craved things like this. And a good thing I didn't, because I never could have afforded them.'

'Well, it looks as if you'll be able to afford them now. You're really mad about him, aren't you?'

Jennie raised her eyes to the other's face, on which a certain tenderness was mingled with curiosity. 'Yes,' she said simply. 'That's about it. I am.'

'I've never seen you like this about anyone before.'

'I haven't felt like this about anyone before, that's why.'

'You're lucky. Do you know how darn lucky you are?'

'Yes, I know.'

'To be in love with a man who wants to make it forever. God, I'm sick of guys who don't want to promise you anything except that they'll never interfere with your freedom. I'd like to give up a little freedom – not all of it, just some of it – to have a home and a kid. Two kids. The men you meet these days are all kids themselves,' Shirley finished, grumbling.

Jennie, hanging up her coat, had no answer. She remembered how, not much more than a year ago, Shirley, like most of her contemporaries, including Jennie herself, had gloated over total independence, being able to experience the adventure that had once belonged only to men. And then the biological clock, as they called it these days, had begun to tick very loudly.

'The biological clock,' she said now.

'Yeah. Well, I'm glad for you, anyway.' Shirley stood up and kissed Jennie's cheek. 'Couldn't happen to a nicer gal. Listen. Be sure to get a piece of flannel and wipe those every time you wear them. And have them restrung every couple of years. I'd go to Tiffany for that, if I were you.'

When she went out, Jennie stood for a few moments with the pearls draped over her arm. Thoughts flooded her mind. She looked around the little room. You certainly wouldn't call it a handsome room, but it was comfortable and pretty, with its prints, Picasso's doves and Mondrian's vivid geometrics. Sometimes she thought what fun it would be if Jay could just move in here with her, instead of the other way around. She had painted the yellow walls herself, bought the homemade patchwork quilt from Tennessee mountain craftspeople, and nurtured the tall palm that stood in the brass container at the window. The books, which were her extravagance, and the first-rate stereo equipment all were the fruits of her own labor, and that was a good feeling; probably there was no better satisfaction.

Indeed she had come far. Now, having confronted the

world and proven that she could survive in it alone, she was ready, willing, and glad to relinquish some of her independence to Jay.

They had met at one of those big, fancy gatherings of disparate people in a fancy, renovated loft filled with abstract sculpture, stainless-steel mobiles, sushi, white wine, and buzzing talk. Somebody had made a remark about Jennie's Long Island environment case, and somebody else had casually and hastily introduced Jay. Almost at once they had drifted away by themselves.

'You're a lawyer too?' she asked.

'Yes. With DePuyster, Fillmore, Johnston, Brown, Rosenbaum and Levy.'

'Very different from me.'

'Very different.' He smiled. His eyes held a twinkle of amusement. 'Are you thinking that I'm a wicked defender of wicked corporations?'

'I'm not stupid enough to think that corporations are all wicked.'

'Good. Because I'd like you to approve of me.'

'It's just something I could never imagine myself doing.'

'Fair enough. But I do pro bono work also, you know.'

'That's good too.' She smiled back.

'You're not enjoying this,' he said. 'All the pop sociology and psychology. You know what it boils down to? "Look at me, I'm here, listen to me." When it's all over, you've nothing but a headache to show for the whole evening. Let's leave.'

In a quiet bar downtown they sat half the night telling each other all about themselves: their politics, their families; their taste in music, food, books, and movies; their interest in tennis. They liked Zubin Mehta, Woody Allen, Updike, and Dickens. They hated golf, buttery sauces, zoos, and cruises. Something clicked. Afterward they both agreed that they had known it right then, that very night.

The next day he sent flowers. She was touched by the old-fashioned gesture, and expectant as she had never been before. Suddenly it was clear to her that she had never known the possibilities of loving, never known what lay at the core of things. She had only thought she knew.

So it had begun.

She had come a long, long way since the row house in Baltimore and Pop's delicatessen. A long way from the University of Pennsylvania and its tuition, so painfully eked out. About the time she had graduated from the university, her father became ill with a degenerative kidney disease. When he died, she was already twenty-five. Her mother sold the store and with the small proceeds of the sale, plus Pop's small insurance, went to live with her sister in Miami, where the climate was benign and living was cheaper. Then, having saved enough for law school, Jennie went back to Philadelphia and enrolled again at the university.

She had no time to waste, for she had lost four years. She was all purpose, working hard and seldom playing. At twenty-nine, she graduated with an outstanding record, enough to provide her with a prized clerkship for the following year. The clerkship would have led to a position in an esteemed Philadelphia law firm, if she had wanted it to. But during the intervening hard years, a distinctive character had been formed and a point of view had been taken. The times were ripe for what she wanted to do, and the logical place to do it was, in her mind, New York.

In a modest neighborhood downtown near Second Avenue, she established an office, two rooms sublet in space belonging to a striving partnership of three young men who were just barely out of law school themselves and eager to get a footing in criminal law. Having no interest in family cases or the particular problems of women, they were glad to refer all such to Jennie. So she began and gradually was able to build a reputation as a dedicated, caring, tough defender of women's rights, especially those of the poor.

And the years went by then in the style of the times and the place. She went to consciousness-raising groups, learned something from them, and left them behind. Like Shirley, she had her share of men, who were bright and fun but wanted no permanence. She fell briefly in love – or thought she did – with a nice young man who finally, half in tears, confessed that he had tried hard, but he really preferred nice young men, after all. She was pursued by one or two decent men who would have married her and whom she would have married if only she could have loved them. She met a charming man who adored her but had no intention of divorcing his wife. Somehow nothing worked out. So she was thankful to have her work and all the good things that the city afforded, the ballet and opera at Lincoln Center, the first-run foreign movies, jogging on Sundays in the park, Fifth Avenue bookstores, Italian trattorias in the Village, and courses at the New School.

A busy life it had been, a productive and useful one, but it had led nowhere in particular, and when all was said and done, there had been a coolness at its heart.

Until Jay had come into it. Almost two years it was now, and here they were.

Her reflections ended, Jennie wiped the pearls as she had been advised to do, laid them carefully on their velvet cushion, and hid the box under her nightgowns. Undressed, she regarded herself in the full-length mirror on the bathroom door. Not bad. She had never had much trouble keeping her weight down, which was a blessing because she loved food, good rich pastas and lots of bread. No flab, either, thanks to tennis and running.

Humming to herself, she whirled and did a little dance in front of the mirror. Happy, happy –

The telephone rang.

'Is this Janine Rakowsky?' Janine. Nobody except her mother called her that anymore.

'Yes,' she answered cautiously.

'My name is James Riley.' The voice was courteous and refined. 'I know that what I'm going to say will startle you, but –'

Mom. An accident in Florida. Mom's hurt. In the flash of a second, brakes yelp. Rain glitters on the highway. Sirens. Police converge. An ambulance comes racing. Red lights revolve.

'What is it? What's happened?'

'No, no,' the man said quickly. 'Nothing bad. I'm sorry I frightened you. It's just this. I represent a service for adoptees. We're called Birth Search. You've probably heard about us.'

'I don't believe so.' She was puzzled. 'Are you in need of an attorney?'

'Oh, no. This isn't a legal matter. It's this way –'

She seemed to see the man settled back for a lengthy explanation, and so she interrupted quietly. 'I'm an attorney, so since it's not a legal matter, I really don't have time to talk. I'm sorry –'

Now it was he who, with equal quietness, interrupted. 'If you'll just give me a minute or two, I'll explain. You're aware, I'm sure, of the numbers of adoptees who are now seeking their natural parents. So many organizations have sprung up to help, of which ours is just one, and we –'

A long sigh quivered in Jennie's chest. 'I give as much to charity as I can afford. If you'll send me a brochure describing your work, I'll read it,' she said.

The man wasn't about to let go. 'This isn't a call for charity, Miss Rakowsky.' There was a long pause. When he spoke again, it was almost in a whisper. 'You gave birth to a girl nineteen years ago.'

Seconds passed. The second hand jerked and ticked on the desk clock. Small crackling sounds came over the wire, or maybe they were the sounds of blood rushing in the arteries.

'She's been searching for more than a year. She wants to see you.'

I'm going to be sick, Jennie thought. I'm going to faint. She sat down.

'I called you at home rather than at your office, since this is so personal.'

She couldn't speak.

'Are you there? Miss Rakowsky?'

'No!' A terrible sound tore out of Jennie's throat, as if she had been cut without anesthesia. 'No! It's impossible! I can't!'

'I understand. Yes. Of course this is a shock to you. That's why your daughter wanted us – me – to call first.' A pause. 'Her name is Victoria Miller. She's called Jill. She's here in the city, a sophomore at Barnard.'

Cold fingers ran on Jennie's spine. Her leaping, crazy heart accelerated.

'It's impossible.... For God's sake, don't you see it's impossible? We don't know each other.'

'That's the point, isn't it? That you ought to know each other?'

'It's not the point! I put her in good hands. Do you think I would have let them give her away to just anybody? Do you?'

Now Jennie's voice squealed and ended with a sobbing breath.

'No, I certainly don't think you would, but –'

'Why? Is there something wrong with her? Has something happened to her?'

'Not a thing. She's quite happy and well adjusted.'

'There! You see? I told you! So she has a family, they're taking care of her. What does she want with me? I never even saw her face. I –' Clutching the phone, Jennie sank to the floor and leaned against the desk for support.

'Yes, she has a family, a very good one. But she wants to know you. Isn't it natural for her to want to know who you are?' The voice was quiet and reasonable.

'No! No! It's over, it's ancient history. Everything was settled. When things are settled, leave them alone. I couldn't have taken care of her then! You don't know what it was like! I had to give her away. I –'

'No one is saying a word about that, Miss Rakowsky, it's well understood. We're all professionals here, psychologists and social workers, and we do understand. I understand you. Believe me, I do.'

Sweat poured on Jennie's palms and all over her body. The sweat, the racing heart, and the weakness in her legs were terrifying in themselves. She had to pull herself together, had to; she couldn't collapse here, have a heart attack alone –

'Jill is a delightful young woman, very intelligent,' the voice coaxed. 'You would –'

'No, I said! There's no sense in it! We can't just – just start up after nineteen years. Oh, please!' Now she wept. 'Please tell her it's impossible. Tell her to be happy and to leave me alone. Forget this. It's better for her the way it is. I know it's better. Please. For God's sake, go away and leave me alone! Oh, please!'

'Miss Rakowsky, I won't bother you anymore now. Take a few days to think it over. I believe, if you try, you'll understand it's not such a bad thing, not a tragedy. I'll talk to you again.'

'No! I don't want to talk to you again. I –'

The connection was broken.

She laid her head back against the desk, holding the dead phone in her lap. Her heart still hammered so fiercely that she could hear it in her ears.

'Oh, my God!' she said aloud. 'Oh, my God!' She closed her eyes and put her head down between her knees.

'I'm going to vomit, I'm going to faint. . . .'

When she opened her eyes, the pattern on the big chair was spinning. Brown, white, and black circles, squares, dots, and stars flickered and flashed. She closed her eyes again, squeezing the lids against the eyeballs.

All these years. I didn't want to remember her. I had to forget her, didn't I? And sometimes I did forget her. But other times? I don't dare think of the other times . . .

'Don't you see?' she cried out into the silent room, cried out to no one, to everyone, to the world, the fates. 'Don't you see?'

'Oh, my God . . .' she sobbed. With her hands over her face, she rocked and sobbed.

After a long while then, her mind began to click. She summoned it now, the little machine in her head, to take control lest she fly apart and scatter in broken pieces.

Think, Jennie. You can't afford to panic. There's an intelligent way of handling everything, isn't there? You always tell other people so. Now tell yourself. Think.

The phone rang again. Muffled in the folds of her bathrobe, it sounded far away.

'You didn't call me,' Jay said.

She went blank. 'Call?'

'Your line was busy.'

'Yes, it was a client.'

'Must they bother you on Sunday too?'

'Well, it happens sometimes.' She began to babble. 'The landlord's been harassing the woman. It's awful. And Shirley was here, so I couldn't use the phone, anyway. She just left this minute. I couldn't get rid of her.'

Jay laughed. 'She'll miss you, that one. Oh, wasn't this a perfect day? I'm just sitting here thinking about it.'

'A perfect weekend. Yes, it was.'

'We still haven't gotten your ring. Can I pin you down one afternoon this week?'

How can I just suddenly produce a child? If I had told him the first day –

He spoke again, interrupting her thoughts. 'We'll go to Cartier's. It won't take long.'

'Jay, I don't need such an expensive ring. Really I don't.'

'Jennie, don't be a nuisance, will you? Don't argue with me. Go to sleep. I'm half asleep already. Good night, darling.'

She hung up and cried out loud into the room. 'My God, what am I going to do?'

Walk into the family all of a sudden with a nineteen-year-old daughter, dropped down from nowhere . . . Jay's babies . . . the wedding just a couple of months away . . . the Wolfes, that decorous, trusting, honorable pair. Liberal. Decent. But never fool yourself, the code behind the pleasant surface is a rigid one. And Jay . . . I've lied. . . . Concealment like this, all this time, is a lie and nothing but. Yes . . . yes.

An intelligent girl, the man had said. Jill, they call her. Why should she want me? I'm the one who gave her away. Poor baby. Given away. She came out of me, out of the very core of me. I heard the newborn squall of protest, and that was all, one pitiable, helpless cry, and then they carried her out, a small wrapped bundle carried out of the room, out of my life. Does she look at all like me? Would I feel any recognition if I were to meet her someplace, not knowing who she is? But I did right. You know you did right, Jennie. And she can't come back into your life now. She can't. It won't work. Think, I told you. But I can't think. I haven't got the strength. I'm drained.

After a while she got up from the floor, turned off the lights, and, still huddled in the bathrobe, lay down on the bed. She had begun to shiver. For a long time she lay with the quilt drawn over her head. Absolutely alone . . .

Alone, just as she had been on that bus heading back east from Nebraska. It felt the same. She could smell the exhaust again and swallow the threat of nausea as the bus swung, lurching too fast through all the monotonous small towns, passing the supermarkets, used-car lots, and malls, going back to pick up a life. Going back . . .

2

It begins in the Baltimore row house, in the kitchen over a cup of tea after the supper dishes have been washed and put away. Sometimes, rarely, perhaps on the Sabbath, the tea is drunk in the cluttered front room where dust gathers on the paper flowers. The sofa and chairs are covered with plastic sheets except when there's company, and the blinds are darkly drawn to keep the meager north light from fading the carpet. 'Blue is the most perishable color,' Mom says.

Actually, the story begins even farther back than Baltimore, for is not each of us only the latest link in a long, binding chain? It begins in Lithuania, in a town with an unpronounceable name, near Vilna, the city of great scholars. Mom's parents, who were not scholars, peddled horseradish for a living. 'If you can call it a living,' Mom says. It is a simple story that she tells, and yet with each repetition she has something with which to embellish it, some comical or pathetic anecdote. The part when the family leaves for France is dramatic, with the pathos of departure and the adventure of novelty. There is new scenery, another language, and for the little girl, Masha, a new name: Marlene. She goes to school wearing a pinafore, like any little French girl. It does not take her long to feel French, to lose all but the vaguest graying memory of the muddy road to Vilna. Then the Germans come, and the girl learns that she is, after all, not French. Her parents are taken away back east again, to be consumed in the fires. And she, in some miraculous fashion, is swept up into a group of fleeing refugees and brought to America.

'We came across the Pyrenees. You wouldn't believe – I can't believe it myself – how we did it, Janine.'

Janine, the name she has given to her daughter in memory of Jacob, her father, is the last, wistful, prideful memento of her short-lived Frenchness.

'There were German patrols and observation planes. We had to hide among the trees, we had to climb above the treeline, climb through the rocks in the terrible cold. A man had a heart attack and died there. . . .

'Well, I got here, anyway. I was sixteen. I had no money at all, and not nearly enough education to do much. But then I got lucky. I met Sam.'

Sam, too, has a story to tell. Unlike his wife, though, he refuses to tell it. It is through her mother that Jennie learns how Pop survived the concentration camp: An expert tailor, he was put to use making uniforms for the Germans. He has unspeakable memories, and now he will not touch a needle, except that once in a long while he will copy a suit or coat from *Vogue* for his wife or daughter. He is more or less cheerful in his delicatessen, making sandwiches and ladling salads, while Mom takes the cash.

Jennie is an only child. Her parents' labor is for her alone. Their savings, the things they do not buy for themselves, and the vacations they do not take are all for her. They never say so, but she knows it. She is aware that they are giving her 'good values': work, family, respectability, and education. Their daughter must have the education they missed. The world's evil must not touch her. They keep her safe.

Pop is the more religious parent. Orthodox, he closes the store on Saturdays, even though it could be the busiest day of the week. He is clean-mouthed; she has never once even heard him swear. She thinks she will remember him best at the table on Friday nights, washing his hands before prayers, while her mother holds the basin and the little white towel, and the flames waver in the brass candlesticks.

Jennie doesn't share all their beliefs, but she respects their beliefs and them. They are gentle parents, overworked, grateful for what they have, disappointed over what they missed, and sometimes remote; lost, she understands, in their remembered experiences. And while, even when she was still in high school, she knew she would leave their world, she also knows that in spirit at least she will always be part of it.

'So he lives in Atlanta?' Mom says. Her hair is in curlers. She looks chubby, even in her envëloping housedress. Now she frowns a little, trying to decipher the letter's smart-looking backhand script. It is a woman's writing on thick gray paper. The envelope is lined and the paper is engraved in navy blue. Mom runs a finger over the raised letters. 'Nice that the mother writes to invite you.'

'Mom, it's proper. She's supposed to.'

'Atlanta – it's far?'

'Only a couple of hours by plane.' Jennie feels delightful excitement. 'They live in the suburbs. They'll meet us at the airport.'

'They're rich people, I suppose.'

Now, for some reason, Jennie feels embarrassment and irritation. 'Mom, I never asked.'

'Who said "asked"? Of course you didn't. But a person can tell.'

'I don't care. That doesn't interest me.'

'Doesn't interest her, she says!' Mom leans on her

elbows and holds the teacup between both hands. Her eyes, glinting green-brown over the cup's rim, are reflecting and amused. 'What do you know? You've never been without money, thank God. Do you know what it is to wake up at night where you're hiding in your bed, and you look at the clock and in a few hours you have to face the landlord and the butcher – they want their money and you haven't got it? No, you don't. So it doesn't interest you. Tell me, what will you wear?' And without waiting for an answer, she says, 'Listen, your father will make you a spring suit, a traveling suit.'

'Don't bother Pop. He's tired. I can find something.'

'One suit won't hurt him. A few nights and he'll finish it. What color do you want? I'll tell you, it should be gray. Gray goes with everything. A nice suit so you'll look like somebody when you get off the plane. He's a nice boy, Peter. Why do they call him Shorty?'

'Because he's six-feet-three.'

'He's a nice boy.'

And Mom, wearing her familiar, warm little smile, pours another cup of tea.

It had begun even earlier than that, soon after the start of Jennie's first year of college. Having skipped lunch to study for a test, she had stopped for a sandwich in the middle of the afternoon at a luncheonette off campus.

'Do you mind if I sit with you?'

She looked up at the tallest boy she had ever seen, with a head of the reddest hair she had ever seen.

'No, of course not.' In a new school and a new city, one needed to keep meeting people. And she moved her books aside on the table.

'I've been wanting to talk to you. I watched you here every day at lunch last week.'

A fast talker. A wise guy? She answered, revealing

neither surprise nor pleasure, 'Why didn't you, then?'

'You were with a crowd. There wasn't any good way to begin.'

She waited. She wasn't going to help him without knowing more about him. He had friendly eyes, but he'd begun too fast and had made her wary.

'I like the way you look. And your voice was something else I noticed. You don't have a shrieking soprano.'

'I'm noticing your voice too.' His accent was full of soft vowels. 'You from the South?'

'Atlanta. My name's Peter Mendes.'

'Jennie Rakowsky. From Baltimore.'

He put out his hand. People didn't do that on campus. Maybe it was a southern custom. Southerners were supposed to be more mannerly, more formal.

'I'd like to know you better, Jennie.'

She'd heard that before. Drinks and then bed, taken for granted, without having known each other more than a couple of hours. Well, he'd have a surprise in store for him if he was counting on that.

'Would you have dinner with me tonight? Do you like Italian food?'

'Everybody likes Italian food.'

'Okay, then. I know a great place. It's not fancy, but it's all home cooking. What time can I pick you up, and where?'

'I didn't say I'd go. I said I liked Italian food.'

'Oh.'

She saw a flush almost as bright as his hair rise on his cheeks and was instantly sorry. He wasn't a wise guy. He was straight and simple.

'Please.' She reached out to touch his hand. 'I was only teasing. I'll go with you, and thanks. I'm in the new dorm, and six would be fine if it's all right with you.'

There was a tenderness about his mouth as it widened

into a smile. In that instant she knew that she liked him, and all the way back to the library she hummed to herself.

What did they talk about over the ubiquitous checked tablecloth, the candle, and the tomato stains? On the college campuses of 1969, one didn't hold a ten-minute conversation without reaching the subject of Vietnam. Jennie said she'd wanted so much to get to the convention in Chicago the year before, but she still had been in high school and her parents had been adamant. Peter's experience was the same.

'It's not that they don't think it's all horrible, what's happening in Vietnam,' Jennie said. 'But, well, they think kids shouldn't go out in the streets. It doesn't accomplish anything. They think Chicago was just a wild scene. You know how it is.'

Peter nodded. 'Everything's a mess. Sometimes I think the whole world's going to rack and ruin. Sometimes I have so much angry energy, I think I'll really be able to change things when I get out into the world.' Earnestly he drew his brows together, and as suddenly relaxed into a laugh. 'The funny thing is, here I am ranting about fixing things in the future, and do you know what I'm going to study? Archaeology! Crazy, wouldn't you say?'

'Not if that's what you like. Why do you?'

'It started one summer in New Mexico when I saw the Indian reservations and read about the Anasazi, the Ancient Ones. They have a wonderful philosophy, all about their place in nature, about how things are joined, all things with one another – trees, animals, and people – and we have to live in harmony.'

Oh, she liked his face, his generous thoughts, his long, clean hands, his freckled neck and arms, and his clean white shirt! She liked the fact that his middle name was Algernon and that he could laugh about it.

'They say, "My mother the earth, my father the sky." Have you ever heard that?'

'No. It's a beautiful idea,' she acknowledged, but what she was seeing was the head of thick russet hair, the eyes like opals: gray shot through with lavender light.

'So that's what got me started. Now what about you?'

'I want to go to law school if I can afford to. I'm on a partial scholarship here, so I have to keep my grades up.'

Their talk bounded then from topic to topic. Music. Disco. Tennis. He was a seeded player. They had a tennis court in their yard, he said, so he'd always had lots of practice time. She had never known anyone who owned his own tennis court.

Had she ever ridden out to the Amish country? he asked. No, she hadn't, although she'd read about them. So had he; he hadn't spent much time in the North until now, and one of the places he'd wanted to see was the Amish country. Would she like to go there with him some Sunday? They could rent a car and take turns driving, if she liked to drive.

'I haven't got a license. I'm only seventeen,' she told him.

'I'm eighteen. You're young to be here.'

'I skipped a year in junior high.'

'I'm impressed.'

She flirted now, looking downward, then sideways, then upward, in a movement she had practiced before the mirror years ago. It revealed her thick black lashes and a curve of black curl across her temple. She thought of it as her piquant look.

'You needn't be. I'm really not all that smart. I just work hard, for the reasons I told you.'

'You have amazing eyelashes,' he said.

'Really? I never noticed.'

'Well, they are. Gee, I'm glad I saw you this afternoon.

I'd been thinking, this place is so big, maybe I wouldn't ever see you again – or not for months, anyway.'

'I'm glad you did too.'

'I thought at first you didn't like me.'

'I was only being careful.'

'So how about what I was saying, renting a car next Sunday?'

'I'd love to.'

They walked back across the campus, gone dark and almost vacant in the chill of early fall. Peter left her at the door.

'It's been great, Jennie. Let's start early Sunday and have the whole day. Good night.'

'Good night.'

He didn't even make an attempt to kiss her. Ordinarily she would have felt this to be an insult, a rejection, even by someone whose kiss she didn't want. Now she felt only that there was something serious in the quiet 'Good night.' Odd, she thought, and hard to explain, even to herself.

They took their ride to Lancaster County, the first of many rides together. At an inn they ate seven sweets and seven sours, shoofly pie, and cider. They drove and walked past rich, rolling farms, fields of winter rye, and herds of dairy cattle in thick winter coats.

'No electricity, no machines,' Peter said. 'They milk by hand.'

'You mean you can milk cows by machine?'

'Of course. That's how it's done these days.'

'How do you know so much about farms and animals?'

'Oh, we have a place in the country. I spend a lot of time there.'

'I thought you lived in the city.'

'We do, but we have this other place too.'

As fall turned to winter they began to see each other

every day in their free time. They went to the zoo, the airport, and the waterfront. They sat on a bench in Rittenhouse Square and talked for hours. They took the train to New York and saw a French movie in Greenwich Village, where he bought her a silver bracelet.

'It's too expensive,' she protested. 'You spend too much, Peter.'

He laughed. 'You know what? Let's go back to the store.'

'What for?'

'To get the necklace that matches. Don't look so shocked. It's okay, I said.'

She looked up into his face while he fastened the silver chain around her neck. Happiness showed in his smile, in the fit of his fine lips, curved and upturned at the ends.

She loved his cheerfulness. It was contagious, in the same way that Mom's worrying was contagious. At home she felt an underlying anxiety, even when conversation was pleasant enough; she felt a vague fear that things – what things? – might at any minute crumble, that there were no supports. It felt good to be with a person who was happy. Happiness made you strong.

Toward the middle of their second month together Peter kissed her. Afterward she remembered her first thought: *This* kiss, unlike any other, means something. It was late one afternoon and raining, so that there were hardly any people out to see them. She was holding an umbrella when he took her in his arms; letting the umbrella drop, she reached around his neck, and they stood like that for a long time in the soft rain.

For another week or two there were more such fervent, innocent embraces, becoming each time more and more disturbing, as they pressed against each other with the heat of their bodies flaming through all the layers of heavy cloth. When he let her go, her nerves were alive. When she trudged upstairs to her room, she felt as if part of her had been torn away. Not enough, she thought. It's not enough.

'It's not good like this,' Peter said one day. 'We have to do something about ourselves.' And as she did not answer, he said, 'We need each other, Jennie. Really need. Do you understand?'

'I know. I understand.'

'Then will you leave it to me to plan everything?'

'I leave it all to you. I always will.'

'Oh, darling Jennie.'

All that week before the great change was to come, she could think of nothing else. She had always slept in pajamas, but now she went out and bought a pink nightgown trimmed with ruffled lace. Her moods fluctuated. Sometimes she felt the excitement catching in her throat; then she read poetry or turned the radio to splendid music, something that soared in triumph, like Beethoven's Ninth. She felt like crying. Then she felt like laughing. As the weekend came closer, a thin strain of fear crept into her spirit, and she was afraid of the fear, afraid that it would be there to spoil the joy.

But he was very gentle, and she need not have been afraid. When the door to the motel room closed, he turned toward her with an expression so reassuring, so loving and protective, that all fear vanished. Tactfully he dimmed the strong glare of the overhead light, leaving only a lamp in the corner. With none of the haste or roughness that others had described, or about which Jennie had read, he took off her clothes.

'I'll never hurt you,' he whispered. 'Never in any way.'

And she knew it was true. He would never willfully hurt anyone. The beating heart under the hard male chest was soft. So she came to him willingly and gladly.

She never got to wear the fancy nightgown. In the morning they laughed about that. They took a last look around the drab room and laughed about that too. It had been warm and clean, and that was enough. They would be back.

How exquisite was the world! The way a sparrow left its tiny arrow-shaped prints on the snow. Pyramids of apples, sleek as red silk. The smile of a stranger holding a door for her to pass through. All were beautiful.

Yet sometimes – rarely, it is true – before falling asleep or while dreaming over a textbook, Jennie wondered whether these marvelous feelings could last through four more years. Four years! It was forever. And a little chill would shake her.

'Don't leave me, Peter,' she said aloud into the darkness.

He told her gravely one day, 'This is forever, you know.'

'We're very young to know our own minds,' she answered, testing, waiting for his denial.

And it came: 'Only a couple of generations ago people married at sixteen. They still do, in some places. We'll just postpone it, that's all. Get there a little later, when we graduate.'

'That's true.'

Best not to think about it too hard. If you don't think about a good thing, it will happen.

'I have to visit some people in Owings Mills next weekend,' Peter said one day. 'That's near you, isn't it?'

'Not far. We never go there.'

'They're old friends of my parents. Mr Frank went to the U of P with my dad, and he's been sick, had some sort of awful operation on his neck. They've invited me, and Dad wants me to go.'

'Well, as long as you're not going to be here, I'll go home this weekend. Mom's been at me to come. Do you want to have dinner at my house before you go out to your friends?'

'Sure. I'll take the train to Baltimore.'

'You'll have to take a taxi to my house. On Saturday my father doesn't drive.'

'That's okay.'

She wanted to make sure that everything would be really nice. Sometimes, when Mom had been working in the store all day, things were a little hurried and careless. Today, however, because it was Saturday, Mom was setting the table in the dining room.

'Oh, darling, I've one little job for you. Take the silver from the drawer and give it a good wash, will you, while I finish the stuffed cabbage? I hope he likes it.'

'He's not a fussy eater. You needn't go to so much trouble.'

'You must be serious about him, Janine. You never invited a boy to have supper here before.'

She wished her mother would stop saying 'boy.' Peter was a man. But she answered quietly, 'Please don't jump to conclusions, Mom. You'll embarrass me.'

Perhaps it had been a mistake to invite him. Yet it would have been more embarrassing not to invite him, when he was going to be right in the area.

'Don't worry, I understand. Play it cool, isn't that what you young people call it? Go, give the silver a wash, will you?' Her mother picked up and weighed a fork. 'It's good silver plate, the best. Wears as long as sterling. Put a towel in the sink so you won't scratch it.'

From the window over the sink one looked directly into the Danielis' kitchen, across the concrete strip that divided the yards. In the summer when it was too hot to eat indoors, everybody moved card tables to the back porches. You could smell the pungent gravy that was always simmering on the back of the Danielis' stove.

'Yes, they all chipped in where I worked and gave me that set when I got married. So generous. I remember I cried . . .'

Pop, curious about the preparations, came into the kitchen. 'Why does he call you Jennie?'

'At school everybody does.'

Mom, who was energetically chopping onions, joined in. 'Why do you let them change it? Your name is Janine, such a beautiful name.'

'It doesn't go with Rakowsky.'

'Sam, do you hear? So it's Rakowsky she doesn't like. A good thing your grandfather – may he rest in peace – can't hear. He was proud of the name. He was a hero. That time there was a fire, you remember –'

'Mom, I know about Grandpa.' Jennie spoke with affection. 'How many times have I heard it?'

'Well, so you'll change the name,' Mom said cheerfully. 'You'll pick out a man with a beautiful name.'

Jennie moved toward the dining room, where the best plates lay on the best cloth and the plastic covers had been removed from the chair seats. Her father's voice followed her.

'Mendes. What kind of a name is that? Mendel, I know, it's common, but Mendes –'

'It's Spanish or Portuguese.'

'Spanish! Well, Jews are everywhere. Even in China, I read someplace. Yes, even in China.'

Everything went well, so Jennie needn't have worried. Peter brought a bunch of daffodils and she arranged them in a low bowl on the table. It was surprising what a few flowers could do for a room. Mom's dinner was delicious. She was her usual talkative self but made no remark more personal than when, bringing the ketchup bottle to the table, she patted her husband's head and declared that Sam would soon be putting ketchup on ice cream too.

Pop did more talking than he usually did. Peter and he were both enthusiastic about baseball. It surprised Jennie to know that her father knew so much or cared so much about the Orioles. Probably, living in a house with two women, he hadn't felt the need to talk baseball.

She could see that he liked Peter. 'Janine tells me they call you Shorty.'

'She doesn't, but a lot of people do.'

'If you were any taller, you wouldn't get through our front door,' Pop said. 'Have you heard the one about the dwarf and his brother?' And he went on to tell a joke in Yiddish.

When Peter obviously didn't understand, Jennie explained it as best she could. Pop was astonished.

'You don't understand Yiddish?'

'I'm sorry, I never learned it,' Peter apologized.

'Learned it! It's something you don't learn, you just know it. Your people come from the other side, don't they?'

'From Europe, yes, but a while ago.'

'Your grandfather came?'

'No, before that.'

'How long?' Pop persisted.

Jennie hoped Peter would understand that he wasn't being rude but merely interested and curious.

'Well,' Peter said, 'they came to Savannah from South America sometime in the 1700s. Before that, they'd been in Holland.'

'Two hundred years in this country?' Pop shook his head in wonderment. Probably he thought that Peter didn't know what he was talking about.

When jokes – in English now – were exhausted, they came inevitably to politics. They were all concerned and angry over the Vietnam war and the American role in it, which they believed to be senseless and wrong. While the talk went on, Mom filled Peter's plate again. Then came warm apple pie, merging the smell of cinnamon with the sweetness that came from the narcissi. Peter ate and argued and was, Jennie saw, at home. She had good feelings.

Of course, if they had any idea about Peter and herself, that would be something else. . . . But these were other times. Mom and Pop weren't out in the world enough to know, except from reading the papers and being shocked by what they thought of as exceptional behavior, how different these times really were.

So the evening wore on, until Peter said someone would be coming at nine to take him out to Owings Mills.

'Too bad you can't stay here overnight,' Mom said. 'We can put a cot in the front room. It's a very comfortable cot.'

'Thank you, I'd like that, but they're expecting me.'

The man who came for Peter drove a station wagon. When the front door was opened, they could hear barking and see three terrier heads in the back of the car. Peter peered out and signaled that he was coming.

'Tell your friend to come in and have a cup of coffee with us,' Pop urged. 'And there's plenty of pie left too.'

'I don't think he can, on account of the dogs. He won't leave them in the car even for a minute. They're show dogs, very rare, Tibetan terriers. They've a wall hung with blue ribbons in their house,' Peter explained.

Then he thanked the Rakowskys, was careful to be casual with Jennie, and went down the steps.

Pop and Mom watched the station wagon drive away. 'Blue ribbons,' Pop muttered. 'What was he talking about? But he's a nice fellow, all the same. Very nice, Janine, even if he does call you Jennie.'

Peter said, 'I liked your parents. They're good people.'

'I'm glad. They liked you.'

'I hope you'll like my family too. Will you come for a

few days over next spring vacation? I'll have my mother write next week if you want to.'

He had never said much about his people, except that he had one sister, age fourteen. His father was in some sort of investment business, which, Jennie supposed, you would call 'banking.' She imagined a fair-sized house with a tennis court, the sort of prosperous white house that one saw on Sunday drives through the suburbs.

'He wants his parents to meet you, and if they like you – why shouldn't they? –' Mom fancied, 'then he will ask your father if he can marry you.'

'Mom! This is 1969. People don't ask fathers anymore. Besides, for Pete's sake, neither of us is ready for marriage. We're too young.'

'So you'll wait a year or two. I was nineteen,' Mom said positively.

A long dark blue car driven by a black man in a dark blue uniform met them at the airport in Atlanta. Jennie assumed it was a hired limousine, and, never having ridden in one before, was impressed.

Then the black man said, 'Good to have you home, Mr Peter. Seems like a long time between visits.'

'How's everybody, Spencer? Mother? Father? Aunt Lee?'

'Your folks are all right, and your Aunt Lee, she's still the same salt of the earth. Isn't that what you call her?'

'That's what she is, the salt of the earth.'

This was their own car and chauffeur! Jennie smoothed her skirt. She smoothed and smoothed the good gray wool that Pop had made.

'Hand-stitched,' Mom had marveled. 'You know what this would sell for in the stores? Golden hands, your father has. Now you need a yellow blouse, black patent-leather pumps, and you can go anyplace.'

Peter put his hand over hers. 'You're nervous.'

He saw everything and felt everything, as if his nerves were connected to hers.

'Yes. Do I look all right?'

'You look beautiful.'

She couldn't say 'It's this car that's done something to me. Riding in this car. I'm scared.'

Somebody had left an umbrella on the floor, a Burberry plaid. A girl at college had one, with the raincoat to match. 'Cost a fortune,' Mom would say.

They turned off the highway into city streets and then onto a wide road bordered with old trees, now in full leaf. Then there were lawns, hedges and fences, and houses set back at the end of long driveways. Soft air, much milder than it was at home, poured in at the window, cooling Jennie's hot cheeks.

'Jennie, my parents won't eat you. They aren't ogres.'

Peter's parents. It's absolutely stupid to feel like this. So what if they have their own car and chauffeur? So what?

The car slowed down, swung into a long drive, and moved up a slight slope under a ceiling of pink blooms.

'Dogwood. Atlanta's famous for dogwood,' Peter said.

At the top of the rise the car turned around an enormous circular bed of scarlet tulips and came to a stop. It flashed through Jennie's mind that they must be stopping to call for somebody at a country club or a private school. Two-storied columns blazed white against red brick; a short double staircase curved and joined the veranda under the columns. She had a second's vision of *Gone with the Wind*, or perhaps the Parthenon. When she saw people standing in the white doorway, she understood in a second flash that this was the home, Peter's home.

She had to say something. Trivial words came from her mouth. 'Oh, all those tulips!'

He was already out of the car and running up the steps. The driver helped Jennie and took her suitcase. She went up the stairs to where, with a welcoming gesture, Peter had already turned to her.

'Mom, Dad, this is my friend, Jennie Rakowsky.'

Jennie put her hand out to a blur of a woman, a symmetrical, pale blur with elderly pale skin and keen, quick eyes.

'How do you do, Jennie? We're always glad when Peter brings another of his friends,' said Peter's mother.

The father was a large man, white-haired and powerful, like someone you see on the television news, a senator or a general. She felt small beside these tall people, under these tall columns.

Inside there was a lofty, two-storied hall with a crystal chandelier on a long golden rope, and more curving double stairs that united with a landing halfway up and under a bright window.

'Here's Sally June,' Peter said.

A young girl was coming down the stairs, wearing a short white tennis dress and swinging a racket. She had her brother's red hair and freckles.

'Hi,' she said, not smiling, and went on past them out the front door.

You don't even hug your brother? And you're supposed to smile when you greet someone, Jennie thought, with her own smile unacknowledged. The girl had made her feel foolish.

'Let me show you to your room,' Mrs Mendes said.

Jennie followed her up the stairs. It was pleasant to climb on such wide treads and low risers. But the straight, narrow back ahead of her looked in some way forbidding. There had been a vice principal in high school, a formidable, correct woman with dark, gray-streaked hair in a French twist, who had walked like that.

They entered a room at the end of a wide corridor. 'Dinner's in half an hour,' Mrs Mendes said. 'You needn't bother to change, after all that traveling. Just make yourself comfortable and join us downstairs whenever you're ready. There'll be drinks in the library. Oh, yes – if there's anything you need, just ring. Press the button next to the light switch.'

I shall be careful not to press it by mistake, Jennie thought, and said, 'Thank you. Thank you very much, Mrs Mendes.'

Mrs Mendes closed the door. It clicked neatly, letting silence fill the room. Jennie stood at its center, circling it with her eyes. A mahogany four-poster bed was covered with a print of miniature lemons and green leaves on a dove-gray background. Full draperies of the same print were looped back from the windows. The carpet was a gray sea on which stood plump yellow-and-white chairs; a pair of dark, gleaming wooden chests; and a round table that bore a bouquet of the red tulips she had seen outside.

Change. You needn't bother to change. Change into what? I'd have thought my suit would do for supper ... dinner. Then my dark blue silk in case we go to the movies or someplace tomorrow – The thought broke off and she went to the window. Automatically she always went to a window to see where she was.

The room overlooked the front of the house. Over to the left was a corner of lawn, very green. There was no other house in sight, nothing but grass and thick trees. The late afternoon lay in deep quiet.

Here, indoors, it was also completely quiet. At home one always heard things: a flushed toilet, voices from the yard next door, trucks passing, or footsteps going up the stairs on which there was no carpet. 'It wears out too fast on stairs,' Mom said.

Now she opened her door and looked down the corridor into the face of a grandfather clock. No, you were supposed to call it a 'tall clock,' she remembered, having read that someplace, maybe in *House and Garden*, which she sometimes picked up at the beauty parlor when she went for her occasional haircut. Another piece of random information, she thought, that I seem to collect without trying to or wanting to. The clock struck: Bong! Bong! Come downstairs whenever you're ready. She'd better wash her hands and go.

Her room had its private bath, all pale yellow tiles. The towels were thick and white with yellow monograms, the same monogram that had been on Mrs Mendes's notepaper: a large *M*, flanked by a small *c* and a small *d*. *C* for Caroline, *M* for Mendes, of course, and the *d* must be for her maiden name. That's the way you did a monogram. Another piece of useless information that sticks on me like flies on flypaper, she thought, beginning to laugh. She felt silly. Shall it be when – if – we are married, shall it be Janine Rakowsky Mendes? Monograms! Mom buys our towels at Sears when they wear out, and they're good enough.

She ran a comb through her hair, her good, strong, curly hair, so easy to maintain, which meant one less worry and expense. A fresh comb had been provided on the dressing table. On the bedside table were a carafe of ice water and some magazines, *Town and Country* and *Vogue*. If the guest were a man, the magazines would probably be *Time* and *Newsweek*.

Peter, I never imagined you lived like this. You never said. But why should you have said? How could you have?

Jennie, we're very rich, we live in a mansion.

Idiot! she thought. My cheeks are so hot, they'll think I have a fever.

She went out, closing the door without a sound. Across the hall, through an open door, she saw another bedroom, this one decorated in a vivid ink-blue. There were at least eight bedrooms on the floor. All the doors were open, so you were supposed to keep them open. She went back to open hers, then went downstairs to find the library. First there was a large room with a bow window at one end, and great cabinets filled with books to the ceiling. She wondered whether the presence of these books meant that this was the library, but there was nobody there.

'This way, miss,' someone said.

It was the same black man who had driven the car. Now he wore a white jacket and carried a silver tray. Through several rooms she followed him, treading on almond-green velvet carpet and Oriental rugs and once on a carpet flowered in pale peach and cream. At the other end of the house people were gathered in a long, wood-paneled room lined with bookshelves. There were leather chairs, some models of sailing ships, and over the mantel a portrait in oil of a man wearing a gray uniform. All this she saw through peripheral vision as she walked in.

The men stood up and introductions were made. There were Peter, his father, a grandfather, and an uncle. Mrs Mendes and an aunt made room for Jennie on the sofa before which, on a low table, the man had set a silver tray holding bottles and glasses. Peter offered Jennie the glass.

'You haven't asked your guest what she wants,' his mother said.

'I always know what Jennie wants. She drinks ginger ale.'

Jennie sipped while the men went on with whatever they had been talking about. She remembered to keep her ankles neatly crossed. 'With a straight skirt,' Mom said, 'you have to be careful. It rides up when you cross your knees.' Mom knew about things like that. Jennie smiled inwardly. Sometimes, but not always, it paid to listen to Mom.

'I suppose,' said Mrs Mendes, 'your garden can't be as

advanced as ours? They tell me you're at least a month behind us up north.'

Your garden. Jennie was careful not to look at Peter.

'Oh, no, it's still pretty cold at home.'

'How nice to have a house full of young people,' the aunt remarked. She could have been a clone of Peter's mother, even to her silk shirtwaist dress and ivory button earrings. 'I understand Sally June has a guest for the weekend too.'

'Yes, Annie Ruth Marsh from Savannah.'

'Oh, the Marshes! How nice! So the girls are friends?'

'Yes, we got them together last summer at the beach, didn't you know?'

'I didn't know. How lovely. So many generations of friendships.'

Meanwhile Jennie was examining her surroundings, and recalling a fascinating book for Sociology 101, with a chapter about house styles and ethnic backgrounds. Some Anglo-Saxons were supposed to like old things even if they weren't inherited, because they like to make believe they were inherited; they want to proclaim that they're not new immigrant stock. Some Jews go in for modern to proclaim that they *are* new immigrant stock, and see how far they've come! These people were Jews who were as 'old-family' as any Anglo-Saxon. And all of it so foolish ... But it was none of her business. The room was handsome, with so many wonderful books.

'You're looking at the portrait, I see,' said Mrs Mendes, suddenly addressing Jennie.

She had not been looking at it, but now saw that the gray uniform was indeed a Confederate one. The man had side-whiskers and held a sword.

'That's Peter's great-great-grandfather on his father's side. He was a major, wounded at Antietam. But' – this spoken with a little laugh – 'he recovered to marry and father a family or we all wouldn't be here.'

The grandfather echoed a little laugh. 'Well, let's drink to him. He stood, flourishing his glass, and bowed to the painting. 'Salutations, Major. He was my grandfather, you know, and I can remember him. I'm the only one left who can. I'll tell you, I was five when he died, and all I remember, to be honest about it, is that he kept bees. Hello, here's our Sally June.'

A second girl in a white tennis dress came in with her.

'Annie Ruth Marsh, Jennie Rakowsky. Thank you so much for the cake, dear,' Mrs Mendes said. 'Annie Ruth remembered how we all adored that Low-Country fruit-cake their cook makes.'

'Mother thought they'd be a nice house gift for this time of year,' said Annie Ruth, 'because you can keep adding brandy all summer and they'll be perfect for the holidays.'

House gift. Then you were supposed to bring a present? Why hadn't Peter told her? He should have told her. But how could he have said, 'Listen, you're supposed to bring something, Jennie.'

It was cold here, cold and foreign. She was relieved when dinner was announced. Eating would take up the time. There wouldn't be a need for conversation.

The table was polished like black glass. On each linen mat stood a glittering group of objects: blue porcelain, silver, and crystal. For a moment Jennie had a recollection of her mother bringing the ketchup bottle . . . Dinner was served by the same black man, Spencer, in the white jacket. Talk was easy, chiefly carried on by the men, who spoke about the local elections, golf, and family gossip. The food was delicately flavored and included a soup that Jennie learned from someone's casual comment was black turtle, roast lamb fragrant with rosemary, and beets cut into rosebuds. She ate slowly, seeing herself as a spectator, observing herself as she observed and listened.

Suddenly came the inevitable subject of Vietnam, with a report of yesterday's battle and body count. The grandfather spoke up.

'What we need is to stop pussyfooting, once and for all. We need to go in there and bomb the hell out of Hanoi.'

Peter's father added, 'We're the laughingstock of the world. A power like this country allowing itself to be tossed around like' – he glanced indignantly around the table – 'like, I don't know what. These young people marching, this rabble protesting! If any son of mine did that ... Believe me, if this war is still on – and I hope it won't be, that we'll have trounced them by then – but if it should still be on when Peter's through with college, I'll expect him to put on a uniform like a man and do his duty. Right, Peter?'

Peter swallowed a mouthful. He looked past Jennie to where his father sat behind the wine decanter.

'Right,' he echoed.

She was aware that her astonishment was showing on her face, and she wiped the expression away, thinking, But you told me, whenever we spoke about it, you told me that you would never go, never; that it was an immoral, useless war. All the things you said, Peter!

'And most of your friends, what's their attitude, Peter?' the grandfather inquired.

'Oh, we don't talk about it that much.'

Not talk about it that much! That's what everybody talked about most – in class, after class, in the cafeterias and half the night. You might even say that's all we talk about!

The grandfather persisted. 'But they must have some opinion.'

Peter's face was reddening. 'Well, naturally some think one way, some another.'

'Well, I hope you speak up like a man, unlike these whining cowards, and defend your President. You just can't let them get away with defeatist talk. That's what weakens a country. I certainly hope you don't sit silently and let them get away with it, Peter.'

'No, sir,' Peter said.

Mrs Mendes interrupted. 'Oh, enough politics! Let's talk about happier things, like Cindy's birthday party tomorrow.' She explained to Jennie, 'Cindy's a cousin, actually a second cousin, who's turning twenty-one, and they're having a small formal dance for her at home. I do hope it doesn't rain. They're planning to dance outdoors. It should be lovely.'

A small formal dance ... He didn't tell me that, either. Maybe he didn't know. But I have no dress ... Jennie thought. Never had she felt so much a stranger.

The talk continued. 'Have you heard what Aunt Lee gave her?'

'No, what?' asked the uncle.

'A horse!' said Mrs Mendes. 'A colt, to be accurate. You've met our Aunt Lee,' she reminded Annie Ruth, 'the one who has the horse farm.'

'She's such a queer! A regular skeleton in the closet,' said Sally June.

'Sally June, what a dreadful thing to say!'

'Well, it's true, isn't it?'

'I don't know what you mean,' Mrs Mendes answered stiffly.

Sally June giggled. 'Mother! You do know.'

'My sister has always been a tomboy,' Mr Mendes said, probably for the benefit of Jennie, the stranger in the room.

'A tomboy!' the girl persisted. 'She's over fifty. Everybody knows she's a –'

'That will do,' Mr Mendes said, and repeated sharply, 'That will do, I said!'

In the silence one heard the clink of silver on china. Sally June hung her head, while a fearful flush spread up her neck. She looked frightened.

Peter broke the silence. 'Speaking of horses, it reminds me that when I was at Owings Mills that weekend, I saw Ralph out riding. We passed him in the car. I didn't know he's at Georgetown now.'

How gracefully Peter drew the new subject out of the old! Of course, he had felt the tension in the room. He continued, 'He may be going into the diplomatic service like his brother.'

'And get killed like his brother,' the aunt said, explaining politely to Jennie, 'These are old friends of our family's. Their son was killed during a riot in Pakistan.'

'Fifteen years it must be,' said Mrs Mendes. 'And his mother still mourning. It's ridiculous.' She spoke briskly, addressing the table. 'I have no patience with people who can't face facts.'

'It was a terrible death,' Peter reminded her gently.

'All the same, she ought to shape up,' his mother said. 'People can, and they do.' Unexpectedly she turned to Jennie. 'Peter tells us that your father was in a concentration camp in Europe.'

So he had talked about her here at home. 'Yes,' she answered. 'He was very young and strong, one of the rare survivors.'

'What does he do now?'

Peter hadn't told them that. 'He has a store. A delicatessen.'

For an instant the other woman's eyes flared and

flickered. 'Oh. Well, he got through it all right. He picked himself up and survived.'

'Yes,' Jennie said. *Survived. His nightmares. His silent spells*. And for the second time that day she found herself staring at the cuff that was finished with the skill that had kept her father alive, the skill he couldn't bear to remember.

She glanced back at Mrs Mendes, who had begun on another subject. You have no heart, she thought.

The servant was placing before her a plate on which lay a doily and a bowl of ice cream; on either side of the bowl were a spoon and an implement that she had never seen before. It seemed to be a cross between a fork and a spoon. Having no idea what to use, she was hesitating when, without changing his expression, the man placed his forefinger almost surreptitiously on the handle of the curious implement. All at once she remembered having heard about such a thing as an ice-cream fork and knew that was what it must be. She wished she could thank the man and decided to do so if ever there should be an opportunity. He had seen her bewilderment. She thought, He knows more about me than does anyone else in this room except Peter. I do not like it here. It's colder than the ice cream.

But the ice cream was different from any she had ever had, with possibly a trace of honey in it, and some sort of tart liqueur. She ate it slowly, finding an odd comfort in its smoothness, as if she were a child with a lollipop.

After dinner Peter showed her the grounds. Beyond the tennis court lay an oversize pool shaped like an amoeba and seeming as natural as a pond. A pretty, rustic poolhouse faced it. Groups of pink wrought-iron chairs and tables under flowered umbrellas stood about on the perfect grass. Peter turned on some lights so that the pool shone turquoise out of the dusk. Jennie stood quite still, looking into the gleam, past it to the shadowy shrubs, beyond them to the distant black trees, and heard the silence.

'I didn't know you lived like this,' she said at last. 'I don't know what to feel, what to think.'

'Think nothing. Does it matter how I live? Does it?'

'I suppose not.'

'Is it important?'

He was standing so near that she could feel, or imagine that she felt, the warmth of his beloved body. Of course it wasn't important. What mattered was Peter, not what he owned or didn't own. Yet there was something...

'You agreed with them about Vietnam.'

'I didn't, really. I just didn't disagree.'

'It's the same thing.'

'No. Think about it.'

'I'm thinking.'

'Well, it's to keep the peace, and I hate arguments. What would have been the point in starting a long one that would only end as it began? We'd all keep our opinions. And you saw how it was in there.'

She considered that. Yes, it was true. At home there were subjects better left alone. No quarreling with Pop, for instance, about the old-fashioned custom of separating women from men in the synagogue. Pop knew it was right because it had been ordained, and nobody was going to change his mind, so there was no point in trying. Yes, Peter was right. He had peaceable ways, as when he had turned the subject away from Aunt Lee when his father was so angry. It was one of the things she loved about him.

'I wish we could sleep together,' he said. 'The pool-house would be so great. There's a sofa.'

'Peter! We can't. I wouldn't dare.'

'I know. Oh, well, we'll be back home soon.'

It pleased her that he spoke of school, the place where they were together, as 'home.' Then she thought of something else.

'You didn't tell me there was going to be a dance. I would have brought a dress.'

'I didn't know. I have this ridiculous cousin. . . . For God's sake, who gives formal dances these days?'

'Apparently people still do.'

'I hate them.'

'But what'll I do? I've nothing to wear.'

Peter looked at her doubtfully. 'Nothing?'

'Only this suit, my good dark blue silk that I always wear, and some skirts and shirts. I don't even want to go. Do we have to? I suppose we do.' Her voice trailed away.

'We'll ask my mother. She might have something to lend you.'

'I can't do that.'

'I'll ask her. Come inside. Come on in now.'

'Oh, dear,' said Mrs Mendes, 'you're sure you haven't brought a thing?'

Jennie shook her head. As if there were some secret compartment in her suitcase from which, if she looked hard enough, she could turn up a formal gown and slippers!

'I hate to be such a bother,' she said.

'No bother at all. Let me go upstairs and see what Sally June has in her closet. Of course, you're taller than she is, but still – Oh, dear,' she repeated.

Sally June and her friend were sprawled on the twin beds. Mrs Mendes opened the closet where hung a long row of clothing and racks of shoes. 'We'll have to borrow one of your dresses, Sally June. Jennie hasn't brought one.'

'Not the blue eyelet. I'm wearing that.'

'Of course not.'

Mrs Mendes regarded Jennie with a measuring eye and took a dress from the closet. 'This is floor-length on Sally June. It will probably be ankle-length on you. Try it and let's see.'

She felt naked, with the three others watching her in silence as she got out of her suit and into the dress. It was white cotton, soft as a handkerchief, with a deep ruffle off the shoulders and another one at the hem. The short puffed sleeves were laced with ribbons and bows. It was a little girl's party dress, just barely passable for a girl of fourteen. On Jennie it was ridiculous. Dismayed, she regarded herself in the full-length mirror.

'A charming dress,' said Mrs Mendes. 'We had it made for Sally June's birthday. But she's been gaining weight.' She wagged a finger at her daughter. 'It fits you perfectly, though,' she said to Jennie. 'Pretty, isn't it?'

'Very,' Jennie said, and thought, Mom would laugh her head off if she could see me in this.

'Your bra straps show, but you can pin them back. And shoes. What size do you wear?'

'Seven and a half.' What will she bring out, Mary Janes?

'Oh, dear, Sally June wears six.' The shoes, white kid slippers with low curved heels, were acceptable, except that they were a size and a half too small and set up an instantaneous shock of pain.

'Do they hurt?' asked Mrs Mendes.

'Yes, some. Yes, they do.'

'Well, my feet are even smaller, so I guess you'll just have to manage.' At the door she remembered something else. 'I have a bag I can lend you. Fortunately it's unseasonably warm, so you won't need a wrap.'

Jennie, emerging from under the ruffle, caught sight of the girls lying on the twin beds and silently giggling. Sally June's eyes slid away as soon as she met Jennie's. Strange that the same beautiful eyes, which were so kind and mild in her brother's face, could be so cold and mocking in hers!

She put her suit back on and folded the dress over her arm. 'Thank you,' she said quietly. 'I'm sorry to have bothered you with this.'

'I don't mind at all,' Sally June told her.

They despise me. I don't look queer, I have manners as good as theirs, and a hell of a lot more heart, Jennie thought. But they despise me all the same.

The cousin's home out in the country had ample land around it, fields, and a brook with a bridge, but the house was very like the Mendeses', even to the portrait of the same ancestor over the mantel.

Mrs Mendes, standing next to Jennie, whispered, 'You recognize the portrait? He's their great-grandfather, too, but this is a copy. Ours is the original. Somebody allowed them to have a copy made, which I thought a mistake. However . . .' She shrugged and moved on.

Jennie, barely hobbling on her tortured feet, was on her way to the powder room. They were three hours into the party; if her feet hadn't pained so much and she hadn't felt so conspicuous in the foolish dress, she would have enjoyed the spectacle. To her it was just that: a spectacle. The enormous house, the servants, the lanterns on the terrace, the flowers in stone jardinieres, the orchestra, the girls in their beautiful dresses were all theater.

For someone who hated these affairs, Peter was having a surprisingly good time. He had introduced her all around and danced with her so often that she had told him he must pay attention to someone else, certainly to the cousin whose birthday was being celebrated. She had had many partners herself, neat young men with neat faces and neat haircuts, very different from the men she knew at home. Their conversation was different, too, mostly courteous banality. Over their shoulders, as she whirled and turned, she kept glimpsing Peter's laughter and high spirits. But why not? These were his people, and he hadn't seen them since Christmas. So she kept whirling and turning until her feet could tolerate no more and she had to excuse herself.

The powder room was really a little sitting room with mirrors, a couch, and two soft chairs. In one of the chairs an elderly woman sat reading a magazine. Jennie took the shoes off and groaned, rubbing her feet.

'Your heel's blistered,' the woman observed. 'It's bleeding.'

'Oh, God. Blood on Sally June's shoe. That's all I need.'

'You seem pretty miserable.'

'I am. To add to it, this pin's gotten loose and my strap shows.' She wriggled, trying to reach her back.

'Come here, I'll fix it for you.'

They stood before the mirror. Jennie saw a stocky woman with graying hair cut like a man's, and a large, egg-shaped face with drooping cheeks. She wore a plain black dress of expensive silk.

'There. The pin's fixed. What're you going to do about your feet?'

'Relieve them a little and then suffer through the rest of the night, I guess. There's nothing else I can do.'

'Are you the girl who's visiting Peter?'

'Yes, how did you guess?'

'The accent. Everyone else is from around here. Besides, I heard you were coming. And the dress I remembered from Sally June's party. I thought it was a nambypamby dress even on her.'

Jennie burst out laughing. The words were so apt, and she liked this woman's bluntness, the bright, shrewd eyes that redeemed the homely face.

'It was nice of them to lend it to me, though. I really have no right to complain.'

'That's true, you haven't. By the way, I'm Aunt Lee Mendes, the one who gave Cindy a colt for her birthday. I suppose you heard about that.' She chuckled.

'Well, yes, it was mentioned.'

'I'm sure it was. They all love me in their way, my family, but they feel I'm an odd one, and I daresay I am. However, the colt's a beauty. If your feet weren't killing you and it wasn't so dark, I'd take you out to the stables now and show him to you. To tell you the truth, at the last minute I hated to part with him. I'm crazy about animals. Are you?'

'I would be if I had any room for them. Where I live, there's not even decent space for a dog.'

'A fancy apartment in New York, I suppose?'

'No. A row house in Baltimore.' Jennie looked squarely at Aunt Lee. And from her mouth came words that she hadn't intended to speak, that were perhaps entirely out of place. For some reason, nevertheless, once she had spoken them, she felt good. 'My family's poor.'

The woman nodded. 'Then I suppose you've never been at a party like this before.'

'Frankly, no.'

'Feel out of place, do you?'

'A little.' She added quickly, 'At college we all get together a lot, and I'm really very friendly –' She stopped, wondering why she was spilling out such personal revelations.

'I see you are. And very determined. Peter isn't, though. You've probably noticed.'

They certainly were right about this woman's oddness. Yet maybe one only thought she was odd because most people covered up all the time, and she simply said what she was thinking. It puzzled Jennie.

'No, Peter isn't,' Aunt Lee repeated, 'but he's the salt of the earth.'

'That's what he said about you.'

'I'm pleased he did. We're very fond of each other. I remember all our summers at the farm, where he'd spend weeks at a time. I taught him things, real things, taught him to ride a horse, to drive a tractor, to plant and harvest and love the earth. Yes, he's a good boy. Too good for his own good, I sometimes think. Too – obliging. That's the word. Obliging.'

Jennie had begun to feel restless. She didn't want to discuss Peter with this strange woman. Wincing, she put on the shoes and said, 'I'd better be getting back.'

'Yes, you'd better. I'm staying here a little longer. The din from all those talking heads gives me a headache.'

Peter came over to her. 'Where've you been?' he asked. 'I've been looking for you.'

'I had to take off my shoes. I met your famous Aunt Lee.'

'What did you think of her?'

'Well, she's certainly different. But I liked her, in a way. Do you mind if we don't dance anymore? I really can't.'

'Oh, I'm sorry. Your poor feet.'

They sat down at a small lace-covered table near the French doors that opened onto the terrace. Music floated in. A waiter brought drinks.

'It's not such a bad night, after all,' Peter said.

'You said you couldn't stand formal dances.'

'I can't. But one has to make adjustments, do what's expected. . . . Poor baby, you're unhappy about the dress,' he said softly.

'I didn't tell you I was.'

'There are lots of things about you that you don't have to tell me.'

Immediately she was contrite. 'I'm sorry. I shouldn't spoil things. The dress really isn't that important.'

He took her hand under the table. 'You've been uncomfortable with my family. They're not easy to know. They can seem distant. But when you get to know them, you'll see. You'll feel easy with them. I'm sure you will.'

He was right. Like a child, she had been fretting inwardly, but nevertheless it had showed.

'We'll have tomorrow to ourselves,' he said. 'They're all going to a play after dinner, but I told Mother to return our tickets because we already saw the play and it was awful.'

'What play?'

'I don't know. I never heard of it.'

They laughed, and Jennie's spirits rose as fast as they had fallen.

It was like an evening in full summer. Birds swooped down across the lawn and up again to the topmost branches, catching gnats in midair, calling and twittering, darting and sailing until the fall of night. At last they were still.

'How beautiful it is,' Jennie murmured. From the dim house a few lamps glimmered in the downstairs rooms, left on until the family should return. Only the maids' rooms on the third floor were bright. Unlit, the pool lay black as silk, puddled with silver wherever a moonbeam fell. And the two who had been silently gazing into the silver recognized the moment, stood up, and, still without speaking, entered the poolhouse together and closed the door.

She was to look back upon this visit with mixed memories. Love in the poolhouse had been a different experience from love in a motel on a highway with the sound of trucks shifting gears at the intersection. To rise from each other's arms and walk out into the still, sweet night . . . But then there was Mrs Mendes's farewell to remember.

'So nice to have had you with us,' she had said, but her lips had closed on the words with faint dismissal. Or was that just more of Jennie's nervous nonsense? Well, whatever it was, it was a learning experience, she told herself, amused at the schoolteacherish phrase. Now they were both back to their own world on the campus, to work and friends and weekend love. She was seventeen, and life was good.

3

One afternoon while working on her term paper for Sociology 101, she happened to glance up from the desk to the calendar. The date jumped up off the page; something crossed her mind. Afterward she could not have said why it should have done so at just that moment, but it did. She looked again at the date, counted back, frowned, and counted again. Her periods often were irregular, so lateness never worried her. Besides, Peter had been very careful, he said. Nevertheless, her heart made a rapid leap before it subsided into a steady hammering.

I'll wait a week, she thought. It's nothing.

She did not mention it to Peter, and she waited more than a week, trying to put it out of her mind. It had always been her way of coping with problems, to admonish herself: Pull yourself together; use your head, not your emotions. Calm, calm. Things have a way of straightening out if you just keep calm.

But one day toward the end of the second week, on her way to buy a pair of sneakers, she passed a doctor's office and on the spur of the moment walked in.

The doctor was a middle-aged, tired-looking man who, with kind consideration, did not look into her face as she spoke. Nor did he ask any personal questions, for which she was grateful. If he had probed, she would have begun to cry in spite of her determination, and probably he understood that. She left a urine specimen, and he promised to call her with the results of the rabbit test.

She paid the woman at the reception desk; then, out on the street, she suddenly began to shake and tremble as reality, as actual possibilities, swept over her. The businesslike exchange of money and the impersonal mask of the receptionist's face had somehow made things seem official. Having no heart to go shopping for sneakers, she went back to study, reading words without knowing what they meant. That night she slept fitfully, bothered by dreams, in one of which a pitiable rabbit came to her with tears in its eyes.

A few days later the telephone brought news of the positive result.

'Would you like to make an appointment now to see the doctor? It's important to start prenatal care at the very beginning, even though you seem to be a healthy young woman.'

'Well, not just now. I'll call back.'

Carefully she replaced the receiver and sat for a while in a sort of trance. Through the open window came the familiar sounds of life, which was continuing quite without regard to what was happening to Jennie Rakowsky. A voice called, 'Bobbee-e-e-e.' Somebody dropped a pile of books with a thunderous slam on the stairs outside the door and swore. From the floor above came the tremolo of a harmonica.

She sprang up. Peter would be in the library this afternoon. At once she felt lighter. The weight of fear shifted within her. What was she thinking of? She wasn't alone, for heaven's sake! Peter would know what to do. He'd think of something.

He was at his usual table, with elbows propped and chin in hands, concentrating over a bulky book. She had a glimpse of a diagram embedded in a rectangle of thick text before he looked up in surprise and closed the book.

She smiled. 'Hi. You almost through?'

'I can be. What's wrong?'

'Does something have to be wrong for me to stop by?' She was satisfied that her voice had no tremor.

'You don't fool me.'

His concern almost broke her resolve. She steadied herself. Be brave and controlled. 'Why? Do I look funny or something?' Light. Keep it light. It's not a disaster.

'It's your eyes. Something's happened.' He stood up to gather his books and papers. 'Come on outside.'

They went out into a bright late afternoon. Friends stopped them; they stood under the thick trees along the walk, unable to break away. More people came and walked along, talking of unimportant things, and Jennie's heart began its hammering again. She sensed that Peter was trying to get away from the group, but they were accompanied across the street. Two girls from Jennie's hall passed; they had taken off their sweaters and tied them around their waists; they were eagerly talking; she had been like them only a little while ago.

When finally they were alone, they circled back and sat down on some steps. He put his hand under her chin and turned her face up to his.

'So? Tell me.'

Fear flooded back, even under his steady gaze. 'You can't guess?'

'I don't think I can.'

'I went to the doctor a few days ago.' She met his eyes. 'Now you can guess.'

'Oh. Oh.'

She sighed. 'Yes. Peter, what are we going to do?' This time her brave voice ended in a kind of wail, and tears sprang, blurring the trees, the grass, and the bricks.

He looked down at his hands, turning them palms up. And she, following his gaze, saw what an intimate thing a hand is. She knew his so well: the long fingers, the narrow white rims on the oval nails, the fine reddish hair on the wrist.

And she waited. A breeze abruptly shook the leaves, sending a shiver of cold down her back. He looked up from his hands.

'It may not even be true.'

'It's true.'

Her own hands had suddenly come together in a piteous gesture and lay twisted in her lap. Peter reached over and separated them, taking one between his own hands.

'Well, then, we'll just have to do something about it, won't we, if that's so?'

And he smiled. The smile went straight to her heart.

'Like what?' she asked.

'Give me time to think.'

Neither of them spoke for a while. The wind came up more strongly, and Jennie clasped her cold arms. She wondered what he might be thinking of. Then he looked at his watch.

'It's six already. Come on, let's go to our spaghetti place. We can think better on a full stomach.'

There was no one they knew in the restaurant, and they got a booth in the rear where they would be unseen.

'I'm not hungry,' she said, the familiar menu in hand.

'You have to eat.'

A ridiculous expression came into her head: *Eating for two*. She felt like gagging. 'I can't, I really can't.'

'Just some soup. I'll have the same. I'm not hungry, either.'

For a few minutes they sat again without speaking. Jennie managed a few mouthfuls and laid down the spoon.

'God, Jennie, I'm sorry. I feel like a clumsy, ignorant fool. I thought I was being so careful. I was being careful. Dammit, I don't understand.'

'Nothing's a hundred percent.' It hurt her to see him like this. Only yesterday he had been so carefree, had bought a new guitar and some music. 'It's my fault too,' she acknowledged. 'I mean, I should have kept track. I was careless; I am careless. It's pretty far gone already.'

He looked up quickly. 'Too far to do anything about it?'

'You mean an abortion?'

'Well, yes. Of course, I would find the best place where it would be safe. My God, I wouldn't let anything happen to you! You must know that.'

She sighed again. All afternoon such deep sighs had been rising, as if her lungs needed to be filled. 'I couldn't . . . I don't want . . . Regardless of the time, I couldn't, anyway.'

Very gently he asked, 'Why not? Why couldn't you?'

'I'm not sure.' Pop's Orthodoxy? Rooted, after all, in her agnostic head and in spite of her indifference to it?

'So if you're not sure, that means you could. Think about it. It's done all the time.'

'I know.'

A girl in high school had had an abortion during senior year. Everybody knew it. She'd gone on to graduate with the class, had gone on with her life as if nothing had changed. And yet Jennie shuddered. Involuntarily her hands went to her hard, flat stomach.

She had no feeling for what was growing in her, no vision of its possibilities. It was an interloper, feared and unwelcome, and yet she couldn't kill it.

Peter saw her gesture. 'There's nothing much there, Jennie. An inch or two – maybe less.'

But it's life, clinging and fastened. To rip it out and

throw it away, a bloody mess . . . Her thoughts trailed off and she raised her eyes to Peter's, which were questioning and troubled.

'You have to believe me, Peter. It's all right for some – I don't judge anybody else – but I just know I can't.'

Silence again, while he spooned the soup. Then he raised his head, struck the table lightly with his fist, and made a firm, cheerful mouth.

'What the hell! What's the fuss about? Then we'll be married. That's that!'

A tremendous joy made a huge lump in her throat and almost choked her. A second later it receded in doubt.

'Peter, I wouldn't want to be married to a man who "had to" marry me and would resent me afterward.' At the same time she knew that she was hoping for and counting on a denial.

'Jennie, darling, how could you even have a thought like that, when we're the way we are? It's true this is all the wrong time for it, but we were going to get married eventually, so we'll have to find a way to manage it now. Come on, don't be afraid. I'm here with you.' He summoned the waiter. 'Bring us dinner, after all. We're hungrier than we thought we were.'

And while Jennie listened, letting the words pour comfort like a warm shower, he kept on talking. 'Forgive me for what I'm going to say. It sounds like crap, I know, but the fact is – oh, hell, you saw, so why be coy about it? My parents are well off, really well off. Money doesn't mean a thing. I never thought I'd give a damn about that. You know me well enough to know that actually I've sort of been in a mild rebellion against their style of life and some of their ideas, but in a pinch like this' – he grinned – 'in a pinch like this it comes in handy.'

His confident grin gave wonderful relief. Quickly, calmly, he had accepted her position and adjusted to it.

She, who was given not to calmness but to mercurial changes and large gestures, felt the strength in his quiet posture.

'They'll see us through, no doubt of it. Oh, it won't be the most pleasant thing to have to explain, but once all the stiff lectures are over, they'll come through. Listen, we're not the first guys this has happened to, and we won't be the last. Buck up, Jennie, and eat the spaghetti.'

A vision took shape in her head, a vision so clear that she could see it in color. There'd bc a small apartment, two rooms – maybe even one – off campus; they could go to classes and take turns with the baby. They'd go on to graduate school; she'd pay them back herself once she was a lawyer, pay them back with her own earnings, not Peter's, because she'd want to show them who she was and earn their respect. Yes, she would earn their respect in spite of it all. And when they saw how happy she made their son, they would come to love her.

'I'll get a part-time job in the labs or someplace, work nights and weekends so we won't have to depend on my parents for everything,' Peter said.

Visions, then, were already taking shape in his head too. He added, 'You'll be going home to tell your parents this weekend, while I fly home.' It was partly a statement and partly a question.

Jennie shook her head. 'I'll probably go home, but I'm not sure I can tell them before we're married.'

How could one hurt them, remembering their past? She had read all the books about children of the Holocaust survivors and heard about the groups that met to advise and learn from one another, although she had never gone to one. It was true, you really did have a different feeling about your parents when you saw pictures of the European terror and knew that the father and mother who sat across the table from you every night talking about household bills and homework had been through all that. They weren't like other people's parents. How could you put their strength again to the test, the strength that surely must be so fragile?

'You're really not going to tell them?' Peter asked, raising his eyebrows.

'Maybe I will. I'm not sure. They're very loving.' And she said simply, 'You would have to know them to understand.'

He asked no more. 'Well, I'll talk to my folks. I know they seemed formidable to you.' He gave a small, rueful laugh. 'My mother's favorite saying is "Shape up," and frankly, it's an expression that makes me sick, it's so military. But two things they both respect are frankness and courage. So I'll be frank and they'll be fair. I have to hand it to them – they're absolutely fair, Jennie, they really are.' He reached across the table and kissed her fingers. 'There isn't a thing in the world to worry about.'

He looked so earnest. She hoped they wouldn't put him through too much at home before they got over their first anger.

'Trust me, Jennie.'

'I trust you. I always will.'

'How's Peter?' Mom asked.

'He flew home this weekend.'

'So that's why we have the pleasure of your company?' Mom laughed. 'Sit down. I just came in from the store. Have a cup of tea before I start dinner.'

Beyond the kitchen the dining room was visible, with two plates set and the candlesticks in place, ready for the blessing. On Friday night they ate in the dining room, just the two of them, observing the ritual exactly as if they were surrounded by children and relatives, as Jennie knew they longed to be. She sat down across from her mother at the kitchen table.

'I got beautiful geraniums this year, double pink ones, something new. Look,' Mom said.

On the porch railing stood a row of geraniums in pots. A few feet beyond them stood Mrs Danieli's pots, but her geraniums were the common red. Mom followed Jennie's gaze.

'No comparison, is there?' she asked.

'No, Mom.' The question touched her. Almost anything these last few days since the scene in the restaurant with Peter could have brought her to foolish tears: a Dylan Thomas poem read in English class, or an old wife helping her old husband onto the train in Philadelphia. Now it was the geraniums, the meager flowers stretching toward the sun. She felt a swelling in her throat. Foolish. Mom expected conversation. Unlike Pop, she needed to fill every silence. Besides, there was something Jennie wanted to know.

'So how's everybody on the block? The Danielis? The Dieters?'

'Oh, the Danielis are fine, happy about the baby. Not like the Dieters down the street,' Mom said darkly.

Jennie wanted to talk about the Dieters. Gloria Dieter had 'gotten in trouble' last year and was back home with her unwanted baby.

'Are they treating her any better than they did?'

Mom shrugged. 'I don't know. People hardly ever see them. They hide in the house. Gloria puts the carriage on the porch and runs inside.'

With a shaking voice Jennie spoke softly. 'It's not as if she'd robbed a bank or killed somebody.'

And she waited for an answer. . . .

'True, true. But these are crazy times. I don't know.' Mom took up the folded newspaper. 'Look at the stuff you read! It makes you sick. What has the Vietnam war got to do with the way these kids behave, I ask you? It's a bad war, but what has free sex got to do with it, I ask you? A disgrace. Look, look at this!' It was an article about a well-known activist who was pregnant. 'Look at her! Not married, having a baby, and proud of it! Proud of it, mind you. A college girl with all that education, but when you come down to it, behind all the fancy talk, what is she?'

Jennie was silent.

'Oh, but I pity the parents! You work with all your heart to make a good life for your children, and this is what you get for it?' Mom shook her head, commiserating with the unknown parents. Then, sighing deeply, she allowed her face to brighten. 'Thank God your father and I don't have such worries about you. You're a good girl, Jennie, and always have been. Do you know, you've never given us one minute's trouble since you were born, God bless you?'

Jennie said, very low, 'But things can happen to what you call "good girls" too. What should a mother do – I mean, I'm just being curious – what would you do, for instance, if I came home like that girl and told you I was –' Her own little cracked laugh brought her to a stop.

'My God, I can't even think of such a thing, so how can I answer? A girl like you, to wreck her own life?'

If I could tell you, put my head on your shoulder and tell you, what a relief it would be –

'You'd throw me out, I guess. Out the door.' And she forced a laugh, a convincing one this time, meaning, Of course, all this is ridiculous.

'Throw you out the door? Who throws a daughter out the door? But I'd rather die myself, I'll tell you that.' Mom took off her glasses, revealing the soft, remote expression that came upon her plain face whenever she spoke of her murdered parents, of her wedding day, or of the day when Jennie was born. 'It would mean that everything we ever taught you went past your ears. Deaf ears, it would mean; wasted words. All the years, the way we live, thrown out like garbage. Oh, come on, what kind of sad, crazy talk is this? Have a dish of ice cream with me. I've got a sudden yen for coffee chip.'

So it's quite clear what I can expect, Jennie thought. The ice cream slid down her throat, giving no pleasure. She had a recollection of herself at the Mendeses' table eating ice cream; there, too, there had been a feeling of detachment from the others in the room. Here, though, the reason was hardly the same. She could almost feel how it was to stand in Masha-Marlene's shoes, to be of her generation, with her past and her memories in her head. One had to understand.

On Monday, back at school waiting for Peter's return, she had reassuring thoughts. When we're married, even though the baby will be arriving early, it will be different. Mom and Pop will be happy for me. What parents wouldn't be pleased to see their daughter married to someone like Peter? It will be fine, then, when we're properly married.

He was not there for Monday's classes, nor for Tuesday's. Was that a good sign or a bad one? A good sign. Naturally there would be arrangements to make.

Late Wednesday afternoon the telephone rang at the end of the hall, and Jennie was summoned.

'I'm back,' Peter said.

Her heart sprang high. 'And what happened?'

'I'll tell you when I see you.' His voice was flat, without answering joy.

Her heart sank. It was an organ that might as well have gone floating around her body for all the stability it had; sometimes it even went down into her feet.

'I've rented a car. I'll pick you up in ten minutes.'

'Rented a car! Where are we going?'

'Just to have a place to talk. There's never any private place around here where some jerk won't interrupt.'

'That's silly –' she began.

'Ten minutes.' He hung up.

A drenching rain blew in the wind. She got her raincoat and was waiting at the door when Peter drove up. She got into the car and saw his solemn face. When he moved to kiss her, she turned her lips so that his met her cheek.

She knew, she knew.

'Give me the bad news,' she said.

'It isn't necessarily bad news. Why do you say that?'

'Because I can tell. Don't play with me, Peter. Give me the whole story straight out.'

He started the car. 'Let me find a quiet street to park on, and we can talk.'

On a side street, in front of a row of quiet homes, he stopped the car. In the now torrential rain, the street was deserted. When the motor was shut off, there was no sound except the rain clattering on the car roof, spattering the windows. It was a desolate sound.

'Well, Peter?'

'They don't want us to get married now.' He looked not at her but straight ahead through the windshield.

Her mouth went dry. 'No? What do they want, then?'

'They think, they say, we're too young.'

'That's true. We are.' She spoke steadily. 'But what about ... shall we call it our little complication? Or isn't that important?'

He turned to her now. In the gray half-light she could see a pleading expression. 'Jennie, don't be sarcastic. Please, I've had a hell of a time.'

She was instantly tender, responding to his need. 'I'm sorry. But what about it? What are we to do?'

'They think you should ... get rid of it. I explained

how you feel about that, but you know – you know, it does make sense, Jennie. I've thought it over. They convinced me. It really does make sense.'

'*They* convinced you,' she repeated. '*They* think it makes sense. While I am the one at the center of it all. What do they, or you, have to do with my body, with *me*?'

'Jennie, darling, listen. You can't imagine what it was like. Such anger. It took me two days to get us all to stop ranting and to talk. My mother was in tears. I never saw her like that except when her own mother died.' And he repeated, 'You can't imagine.'

'Oh, yes, I can imagine, but what difference does it make? They're telling me what to do with my own body.' She began to cry. 'Peter, I told you I can't bring myself to do that. I don't want a baby, I don't love it, but I told you – and I'm telling you again – I can't kill it.'

'But think! In a few years we'll be married and have as many babies as you like. You want to finish college and go to law school, don't you? Where's the money to come from if we get married now?'

'You said they were rich and they'd help. You said so.'

'Well, I thought so. But I can't squeeze something out of them that they won't give, can I?' For a second he put his head down on the rim of the steering wheel. 'Oh, Christ!' he groaned. He turned back to her. 'My father's willing to give whatever you need to take care of it. And more. Anything you want, he said. Take a trip to Europe. Rome. Paris. Buy things. Rest yourself and get over it. As much as you want, he'll give you.'

Then Jennie was shaken by a rage such as she had never known. It was a killing rage; she could have killed. And she pounded the dashboard.

'What does he think I am? A slut to be paid off? Europe? Do you know what you're saying? He offers me a vacation

... what do I want with a vacation when I'm asking for love, for help, to be accepted –'

'Jennie! You have love! I love you, you know I do. How can you talk like this?'

'How can *you*, unless they've convinced you too? Am I a slut to you too?'

'Don't use that word. It's nasty. It stinks.'

'Don't tell me what words to use! I'll use whatever words I want. I'll tell you right now what happened there. I can hear it and I can see it as clearly as if I'd been hiding behind the door. Your mother, that icicle ... You think I don't know what she wants? A girl like that snippy kid – what was her name? Annie Ruth or Ruth Annie or something? "We've been friends for generations, you know. And isn't it just lovely that the young people are engaged? A secret romance – we never guessed." Yes, it would be a different story if I were Miss Old Family instead of Miss Nobody. There'd be no talk of abortion, just a quick wedding under the trees in your garden. No, pardon me, in Miss Old Family's garden. I'm sure they'd have one. And the baby would be a seven-month, such a darling –' Her voice had risen in outrage.

'God, Jennie, don't! It's not like that at all!'

'Of course it is! Any idiot can see it. I knew it the moment I walked in the door. And you – you let yourself be brainwashed. You, the big, brave man who was going to take care of me. "Don't worry, darling, I'll take care of everything."'

Peter turned the ignition key, and the windshield wipers began to clack.

'There's no sense going on like this if you're only going to scream at me, Jennie. We have a problem, and screaming won't help.'

Her nerves snapped. 'Shut those damn wipers off, will you? I can't hear myself think.'

She sat for a moment, bringing herself under control. Then she remembered something.

'Did you by any chance see your Aunt Lee?'

'Yes, I went to her.'

'Ah! And she said?'

'I'll tell you. She said we should get married. She liked you. She said she'd lend us some money.'

'She did?' Jennie's eyes filled. 'Why, that's absolutely wonderful of her!'

'Well, she's like that. Romantic under the crust. Funny for a Lesbian, when you think about it.'

'That's a cruel thing to say.'

'I didn't mean it to be cruel. It's just the way it strikes me.'

'Will she lend us enough to get by?'

'Jennie . . . I can't take anything from her, no matter how little or how much. My parents would be furious. They were furious when I told them.'

'Why? If they don't want to help, I should think they'd be glad to have somebody else do it for them.'

'It's a long story. She has a tendency to interfere. I shouldn't even have said anything about it.'

'To them or to me?'

He sighed. 'To either, I guess.'

But he had told her, had been honest enough to tell her, and she softened.

'Oh, Peter, what are we going to do?'

The windshield wipers echoed, *To do, to do, to do*. He turned the key again and the wipers stopped.

'What are we going to do?' she repeated.

'I don't know.' He was staring out at the rain.

Gloom seeped into the car. Her swift, furious outburst had left her tired. If I could just go to sleep, she thought, just sleep and wake up with all of this gone away. And she, too, stared out onto the black, wet street. The walls of the houses that faced one another on either side made a tunnel out of the street, a long, dark tunnel with no light at the end.

Peter spoke into the silence. 'If you would have the abortion, it would solve everything.'

She had that picture again, the red picture, the color of blood, the sharp, steely flash, the destruction. She gasped.

'Is it that you're afraid?' he asked, gently now.

'Afraid of pain? You know it's not that.'

A few years ago she'd had a compound fracture of the arm and had borne the pain bravely, they told her. She knew she had. Besides, giving birth was hardly painless.

'What, then? Can you really tell me?'

'I have told you as best I can.'

'It's done all the time. Quite safely. Even though it's illegal. There are safe places. Competent doctors.'

Wearily she repeated, 'Maybe it's the way I was brought up. I can't do it. My parents are Orthodox –'

Now Peter interrupted. It was his turn to be angry. 'Your parents! You can't even talk to them about it! You're afraid to talk to them. At least I was able to talk to mine.'

'I've told you that too.'

Mom in the kitchen, scooping the ice cream: 'Everything we taught you, all thrown out like garbage.'

Jennie's anger rose again. 'You don't want to understand. I can't talk about it to my parents. Why don't we get married, Peter? We could manage somehow. Your father would have to help. He couldn't let us starve. My parents would do something, too, some little something –'

'My father would tell me to quit college and go to work.'

'He wouldn't!'

'Wouldn't he? You don't know. He has principles.'

'Principles! How can they possibly justify themselves?'

'I'll tell you. They'll say that if a man is old enough to father a child, he's old enough to support it.'

'That's what they did say, isn't it? And you believed them.'

'You have to admit it makes sense.'

'Sense, yes, but no heart. There's no heart. Cold, cold moneybags,' she said, clenching her teeth. 'Yes, if my father didn't own a delicatessen ... You think I didn't see your mother's face when I told her? A face like a shark.'

'Jennie, that's far enough. Leave my mother out, please.'

Loyalty, after all this. Loyalty to his mother. She felt choked.

'How can I leave her out when she's in control of my life?'

'No, we were in control of our own lives, Jennie.'

'How can you talk like that? What have they done, how did they brainwash you? Well, maybe they've managed to make you feel like dirt, but I don't feel like dirt, I can tell you. I don't, I won't, and they can't make me. Neither can you.'

'This is a stupid conversation.' He started the engine. 'You're all wrought up, and we're getting no place fast.'

'Stupid is right. Take me back to the dorm.'

She wanted to hit him. Was this Peter? Where were the strength and the smiling confidence? She had relied on him, but the soft, appealing opal eyes with which she had fallen in love were, perhaps, too soft. 'Too obliging,' the old lady had said. He was only a scared boy.... And she was lost.

Neither spoke until they drew up before the dorm. Then he laid his hand on her shoulder.

'Jennie, take it easy. We're both beside ourselves. That's why we're quarreling. I'm going to phone my father tonight and talk to him again.'

She pulled away and opened the door. 'Good luck,' she said bitterly.

'Don't be bitter. We'll work out something. Please. Believe in me.'

She mustered a small smile. 'Okay, I'll try.'

'I'll call you after I've talked to him tonight, okay?'

'No, wait till the morning. I'm exhausted. I want to sleep and not have to think about anything for a few hours.'

'All right. First thing tomorrow, then. And, Jennie, remember that we love each other.'

Maybe I'm being unfair, after all, she thought as she trudged upstairs. It's awful for him too. She was so tired, just so tired.

All the next week she cried silently at night and woke heavy-headed, forcing herself to go to class and study. It was like waiting for a train or a plane so long delayed that one begins to think it may not be coming at all. Peter was in the same condition. Every day he consulted his father, who needed to consult with others.

'His lawyer, probably,' Peter said. 'He never moves a step without lawyers.'

Every day he met Jennie briefly, always in a public place where they were never able to touch each other. Neither of them was in the mood for it, anyway. But the mute appeal in each one's face was reflected in the other's.

'Are you feeling all right?' he kept inquiring.

She was perfectly well. There was no hint of any change in her body. She would probably go close to the end of term without showing.

By the second week Peter had news. His father had arranged for a place in Nebraska, a respectable, church-run home for unwed mothers. It sounded like something out of the nineteenth century; Jennie hadn't known that such places still existed. But apparently they did, and a girl would be anonymous there, cared for until she gave birth, at which time, if she wished, the baby would be given up for adoption.

'How does that sound?' Peter asked.

They were in a car again, parked this time outside of the zoo. A woman, passing by, was trying to comfort a squalling baby in a carriage while a toddler pulled at her skirt. This image fled across Jennie's eyes and printed itself in her head after the woman had turned the corner and gone from sight. The image was soft and blurred, all curves in the flicker of light under new leaves. The mother, her long hair drooping like a loosened scarf, bent over the infant; the child's round, strong head butted against the mother's red skirt; it was an image of unity.

And she knew that this was one of the rare random pictures that she would keep, as she had kept the face of the most beautiful woman she had ever seen, while riding on a streetcar at least five years before. Or the morning when, through the silence of a street thick-muffled in snow, there had come the sudden clamor of church bells, and she had stood until the last vibration ceased.

Peter asked again, 'How does that sound?'

She could barely open her lips, so great was the tiredness that lay on her.

'I'm thinking.'

The same thoughts ran over the same track. The little flat could be furnished so cheaply; the bedroom things could even be brought from her room at home; they'd need, then, only a table and two chairs for meals; a desk and lamps for studying; the baby furniture; and some yellow paint, a sunshine color for the corner where the baby would sleep; it would take so little....

But he didn't want to. I suppose I could force him, she thought. It's been done often enough, God knows. Yet to live like that, begrudged ... To bring up a child like that ... Surely the child would come to feel it.

'Have you thought?' He took her hand. 'Your hand's so cold. Poor Jennie. Oh, poor Jennie.'

She began to cry. All this time she had been able to keep her tears for the privacy of her bed, but now suddenly they came in a gush, an explosion of tears.

He put her head on his shoulder. 'Darling, darling,' he whispered, kissing her hair. 'I'm so sorry. What a stupid bastard I am to put you through all this. Jennie, we'll have babies, I keep telling you. You'll be a lawyer and we'll have a home. We'll have everything we want. It'll be better for the baby, darling, don't you see that? To be in a wonderful family – so many couples can't have children and want them so much, older couples, ready to take proper care of a child. We just aren't ready yet, don't you see that?'

He held her close, repeating himself as if to reinforce what he had already told her a dozen times or more.

A wonderful family, she thought. Ready to take proper care. That's not like killing, is it? That's life. Giving life. It seemed now that she could feel the life moving in the pit of her body, although that was, of course, absurd, since it would be months before she would feel anything. Yet it was *there*.

After a long while her weeping subsided with a long, deep, final sigh.

'I suppose it will have to do. Yes. Adoption,' she murmured.

'We'll handle it this way,' Peter said at once. 'You're due around the first of November, you say. You can go out there whenever you think best. I don't know what excuse you'll make at home or how to explain that you won't be coming back here for the start of the semester, but you'll think of something.'

'Yes, I'll think of something,' she said wanly.

'Maybe you could say you're taking a special course out there or have some sort of scholarship in French or something. I don't know. I don't suppose – I mean, would your parents know about special courses or anything like that?'

'You know they wouldn't.'

'Then you could get away with it?'

'Yes. Yes.'

'And, Jennie – you'll be back here for the second half of the year. We'll be together again.'

So they spoke. And so, out of necessity, there was a mending. Amid the rush of final examinations, at brief intervals they clung to each other, reassuring themselves that all was as it had been, all was well. Then came separation: Peter home to Georgia and Jennie home to Baltimore. He was to come back before the start of the new semester to see her off to Nebraska.

By late summer when Jennie's time for departure came, she had gained a little weight, which pleased her mother.

'See how beautiful you look with a little weight on? Now don't start to diet again, will you?' And she said, 'I hope you're doing the right thing, making this transfer. I don't know anything about college credits, but I do know about men. I mean, when you've got a boyfriend like Peter, it does seem crazy to leave him. I know it's only for a few months, but still,' she said, while pressing Jennie's miniskirt, which was already too tight at the waist.

Pop looked up from the newspaper. 'Jennie will have ten boyfriends in love with her before she's married, don't worry.'

In Pop's eyes she was a miracle of beauty and brains. She was perfection.

And she said gently, 'Yes, Pop, Mom, don't worry about me. I'm fine.'

Her mother looked up. Hairline creases bunched on her forehead between her eyebrows.

'I worry. Who can help worrying about a child? You'll

find out when you have one.' She looked old. 'I love you, Daughter.'

There was such a sore, hard lump in Jennie's throat that she had to turn away and bend over the suitcase.

'I love you, too, Mom. I love you both.'

Peter and Jennie met in Philadelphia the day before the plane was to leave. He rented another car, and they drove out in late afternoon beyond City Line Avenue, onto the highway, and to the motel where they had first made love. In a dismal fast-food restaurant across the road, they ate a rather silent supper. He held a hamburger between shaking hands, then put it down half-eaten, as if he were unable to swallow.

'You all right, Jennie?'

'I'm fine. Just fine.'

'Maybe I'd better give you the tickets and all the papers now, before I drop them or something. Here, put them in your bag. Everything's there, the bankbook and the cash. There should be plenty. The place – the home – has been all paid for, so you don't need to lay out a thing. This is just for you.'

She glanced at the bankbook. Five thousand dollars had been deposited.

'This is ridiculous,' she said. 'It's much more than I'll need. I want a couple of maternity skirts and that's it. I can wear my own blouses without fastening the bottom button.'

He was staring at the wall behind her. She had embarrassed him. Maternity clothes were too intimate for him, who knew every part of her body.

How awfully young he is! she thought, feeling tall and taut, mature and proud.

'There's more if you need it,' he said, ignoring her

objection. 'That's one thing about my father. He's generous, and always has been.'

Generous. Without a visit, a letter, even a telephone call in acknowledgment of the situation, or of her very existence as a human being.

'You have the address at home, of course. You're to get in touch if you need anything. Anything at all.'

'I told you, I won't need anything.'

'You never know. I wish you would take more, but you said it was insulting.'

'And so it would be.' She sat up straighter. 'Will you get me another glass of milk? I haven't had my quota today.'

He flushed. 'Of course.'

So the prenatal diet was an embarrassment to him too. Strange. Well, not strange when you think about it, she realized as her hand clasped the tumbler. She, after all, was the one who had to feed this – this *person*. Just then the person moved within her, rippling, stretching its arms or legs, making itself more comfortable. She smiled.

He caught the smile. 'What is it?'

'It moved.'

'Oh. I didn't know.'

'Yes, they move. It's what's called "feeling life."'

He bent his head, feeling miserable.

'You don't show anything yet,' he observed after a minute.

'I'm carrying small, the doctor said.'

'Is that good?'

'Yes, it's good.'

'I'm glad.'

'I need some dessert.'

'Of course.'

'Just fruit. A baked apple, if they have one.'

He sat there watching her eat the apple. She was thinking that she would remember this moment, this hour, the way the chill seeped into the room with the sound of thunder and approaching storm, the way the light speckled the dirt on the windows as the daylight faded. . . . A man stood up and got a bun from under a glass dome on the counter. Philadelphia sticky buns, they were called. He put his feet up on the heavy salesman's case next to his chair. She heard his sigh. He looked a little like Pop.

'It's going to storm in a minute,' Peter said. 'We'd better make a run for the room before lightning strikes.'

There stood the bed, wide enough for three, with a hideous pea-green spread on it. The television faced the bed. Its huge blank eye stared into the dingy room. It hadn't seemed dingy like this the first time. Yet it must have been.

But all we saw then, all we felt, Jennie thought, was the burning and the haste. It didn't matter where we were. He unbuttoned my dress, my red wool, bought new for the occasion. He took off my shoes and unhooked my bra in that order. I remember everything, how the clothes fell and how I stood there feeling proud because of the look on his face. I remember everything.

'Shall I turn on the TV? Anything you want to see?' he asked now.

'Not especially. Just if you want to.'

'Well, it's too early to go to sleep.'

'I'll take a hot shower. I'm suddenly freezing.'

'Summer's just about over, I guess.'

It was strange that such simple, declarative sentences were all it seemed either of them could summon to express the feeling that should have been boiling in them.

They'd lost what they had. At least *she'd* lost it. Where had it gone, the love? Frozen. Did that mean it would thaw again?

Huddled on the bed in her bathrobe, Jenny watched a play on public television. It was one of those fine English productions with marvelous actors and exquisite scenery, all lanes, fields, old stone houses with portraits, fires under great carved mantels, and big black retrievers stretched out in front of the fires. Secure and solid. Did people ever feel lost and lonely in such places?

Half of her mind watched it, and half of it watched Peter. The bright light of the television screen gleamed in the darkened room and glinted on his face. She thought again, He's so young. Too young to have faced his family down. I'm older inside than he is. Why? Is a woman always the older one? So many questions without answers! What difference does it make? It is the way it is. We are what we are. He's under his family's thumb. But then, so am I, although for other reasons. It's 1969, and people like us are doing things that were scarcely heard of ten years ago. Maybe those people who do whatever they want to do without fear, without shame, all come from what they call 'liberal' families who've trained them that way. I don't know. At any rate, there are more like us than like them. They're only the ones who get written about.

The play was over.

'Beautiful,' Peter said. 'The English know how to do it, don't they?' And he said, 'Someday we'll go to England. You'll love it all, the Cotswolds, the Lake District, the moors.'

In bed, he put his arms around her, and she knew he was waiting for a response. She laid her head against his chest. A few cold tears ran down over her temples and stopped. Not only grief, but also desire, had ended within her, and only a numbness remained. Stress did that. Pregnant women, she had read, felt desire as much as ever. In normal circumstances they would. Looking forward together, being together, staying together.

She was shivering again. He stroked her hair. 'Jennie,

Jennie, it will be fine. You'll come back and everything will be the same.'

He had already said that so many times! And she had believed, had wanted to believe. Now, suddenly, she knew it would never be the same. She couldn't have said how she knew that everything was all over and finished. Did he really believe they would see England or anything else together? She supposed that he did because he wanted to believe it.

But when something is dying, one shouldn't prolong the pain. Fear wounded what we had. Now let it die in peace.

He held her. They held each other. And after a while they fell asleep.

In the morning he took her to the plane. Going down the ramp after the final embrace, she turned to look. His lips moved to say: *I'll write*. His hand went up with a little wave, meant to encourage and cheer.

She knew she would never see him again.

The house, once a rich man's fine Georgian home, was spacious, with spreading wings. Jennie's room was one of the best, a single room overlooking a sea of autumn trees, oaks and maples, red and gold. One window faced a side driveway so that she was able to watch the arrival and departure of the girls – and some of them were really girls, no older than fourteen – who like herself had come here to hide. She noted the Lincolns, Cadillacs, and Mercedeses, the well-dressed parents, the expensive luggage. This place must cost a fortune. But then, Peter's parents were generous, weren't they?

On the first night she was so overcome with loneliness that she had to pull her hand back from the telephone. She had begun to dial the number at home. In her mind's ear she heard herself crying, 'Mom! Pop! Help me, I want to tell you the truth.' And thought then of Pop's blood pressure, his kidneys, money, the rent at the store, how they would manage if he became too sick to work.... And thought, I must get through this alone.

But strong resolve did not suffice. She woke that first day to find herself encompassed by a thick, gray, muffling cloud that muted the sunlight. She wanted only to stay in bed with the covers pulled over her head, and had to force herself to get up. Where was the courage that, up until now, had stiffened her? She was cold with non-specific, nameless fears. The future was void. After the child was born, who would Jennie be? What kind of a person, with what purpose?

The chilly web of gloom still clinging, she went through the expected motions. It was a good place and people were kind. No one asked questions. Some of the young women, waiting, wanted to chat with her about themselves, while others kept their silence. As she looked around in the dining room Jennie thought, Everyone here has essentially the same story, and still it is different each time. Variations on a theme.

Peter wrote to her. The letters were filled with assurances and admonitions to take care of herself; they were marked with Xs; they might as well have said nothing. She answered with banalities: 'The place is nice, the food is good, I am well.' And these words also added up to nothing. When the fourth or fifth letter came, it seemed too much of an effort to answer it.

During the second week she was sent to a counselor. Mrs Burt was a purposeful young woman with an array of diplomas behind her desk. After the first visit, which was taken up with practical concerns – the doctor, the birth, and the proposed adoption – Jennie ventured to confess.

'Is it terrible of me not to answer his letters? It seems

so useless.' And she said, 'I don't understand what's happened. Where has love gone? I wanted to spend the rest of my life with him. I would have died for him. And now . . .' She put her face in her hands.

'It's all right to cry,' said Mrs Burt.

But Jennie's eyes were dry. 'I don't cry anymore. I've done all that. This is worse. I feel as if nothing matters at all. I've even stopped thinking about the baby, and I'd been so careful to eat well and make it healthy. Now I don't feel hungry, and I don't even try to eat.'

'Maybe nothing else matters to you just now, but *you* matter.' The voice was both gentle and positive. '*You* are really all you have, do you know that, Jennie? The *me* – that's all anyone of us has. Because if that falls apart, then there's nothing left for us to give to anybody else. Now, if you don't want to write or talk to anyone, the decision is yours, and you're entitled to it without guilt.'

Jennie looked up. Maybe if Mom had been like this, she could have told her the truth. But then, this little American lady surely hadn't had Mom's wounds, hadn't lost her parents in the gas ovens or fled across the Pyrenees with strangers. So leave Mom out.

She said only, 'Thank you.'

'You're a mass of guilt about everything, Jennie – about why you're here in the first place. And about your parents, your interrupted education, the whole bit. And anger – you're seething with it, though you don't want to admit it. But recognize that you've a right to be angry! It's why you're depressed.'

'You can tell I'm depressed?'

'Of course, my dear. I've surely seen enough depression in this place. Depression is anger turned inward. Did you know that, Jennie?'

'I didn't.'

'Well, it is. Now, if yours doesn't lift very soon, we'll get some help for you. But I have a hunch it will. You're tough. You'll make it.'

And in time it did lift. One morning when Jennie awoke, the cloud was gone. Whether it would return was open to question, but for now it was gone. She raised the window and looked out with pleasure at early winter, at snow-covered hemlock and spruce, at juncos fluttering on the bird feeder. She felt an appetite for breakfast and for a walk in the cold, brisk air. Many of the girls at the home, including Jennie, avoided the shopping center because they feared being stared at by people who would guess where they came from. This morning she didn't mind.

'This is a time to be used, not wasted,' Mrs Burt had advised. 'Why don't you get some books and read ahead on the subjects you'll be taking when you go back to school in February?'

So she made her first withdrawal from the fund that the Mendeses had put in a local bank. With it she went to browse in a bookstore and came back to put Sandburg's *Lincoln* and Tennessee Williams's plays, along with a fat new novel, on her dresser, there to be gazed at and cherished because they didn't have to be returned to a library. Then she sat down with a box, not a bar, of chocolates and began to read.

Peter wrote again with the news that he was transferring to Emory University in Atlanta in February. He didn't understand why she hadn't written in so long. She must please let him know whether anything was wrong.

Transferred. To keep him away from her, from further contamination. So his family could keep an eye on him. She tried to imagine their conversations. At the shining table in the dining room? No, Spencer, the servant, would be there, and they wouldn't talk in front of him. Perhaps in front of the fireplace, under the ancestor's portrait. Or in the room with the flowered carpet, talking sense into their son. Poor boy. She felt contempt for them all.

Could he really believe, as he had said, that they would be back together someday and go on after this as though nothing had happened to change them? Yes, maybe he really could believe; it was much more comforting that way.

Now Jennie's time drew nearer. As she thought less and less about the baby's father, she began to think more about the baby and about all the babies in this house who were waiting to be born and given away. All was accident! From their very conception to the moment they were turned over to strangers, whose pasts they would inherit and whose benefits would shape them, all was chance. But then, didn't chance also govern those who were not given away?

One morning she was summoned to Mrs Burt and greeted by a smile of unusual pleasure.

'We have a couple who want to take your baby, Jennie. We think they're wonderful people, really perfect. Do you want to hear about them?'

Jennie folded her arms on her little, pointed belly, which looked like the narrow end of a watermelon. Something moved under her palms, thumped lightly, and rippled away. A warning, a reminder, a plea?

Mrs Burt must have read her silent lips, crying, *No, I can't . . . can't part from you. God, tell me how I can*, for her look was keen.

'Are you sure you want to talk about this right now? We don't have to if you don't feel like it.'

But you have to feel like it, don't you? There can't be any going back. Back where? Oh, you don't want to do it, Jennie, but you know it's best; you've gone over it a thousand times.

She raised her head, straightened her slumped

shoulders, and spoke clearly. 'Please go ahead. Tell me.'

'He's a doctor. She's a librarian and plans to retire for a few years until the child is of school age. They're not yet thirty, but they've been married for seven years without a pregnancy. They have a loving relationship. They travel and ski and hike in the mountains.' Mrs Burt paused.

'Go on,' said Jennie. A librarian. There will be books in the house.

'We try to match the child to the home, as you know, with the same intellectual background and physical appearance if we can. These people both have your dark hair. Hers is curly like yours. They're of medium height and healthy, of course. They're both Jewish. Do you want to hear more?'

'Please.'

'They live in the Far West. The home is very fine, not a rich one, but the child will want for nothing. There's a large yard, a good school, and a warm extended family of grandparents, aunts, uncles, and cousins. We've checked everything most carefully.'

'I suppose they wanted to know about me and about ... the father.'

'Of course. And they're very eager to have your child.'

Jennie shook her head. Strange. They'll take him ... her ... away, and our nine months together will vanish as if they had never been.

'You'll have plenty of time to change your mind after the baby is born, if you wish.'

'No. This is the way it has to be. You know that.'

'Nothing *has* to be. But I think we both seem to have agreed that this is a good solution all around.'

'I think –' Jennie swallowed. Unexpectedly a lump had come into her throat. 'I think – tell the doctor I don't want to see the baby at all.'

Mrs Burt's eyes were very kind. She spoke softly. 'That's probably best. In these circumstances we often advise it.'

'Yes. So you'll be sure to tell the doctor?'

'Yes, Jennie, I'll tell him.'

Several times at the shopping center, Jennie found herself looking intently into carriages and stopping to make comments to young mothers, in order to have a chance to look at the infants. She stood staring down into the pink or red face of an eight-pound human being, either wriggling or asleep under its covers. And always her feelings fluctuated between resolve, so painfully achieved, and that so terrible sorrow at having to part with what was still as tightly attached as her arms and legs.

One day on her way to the bookstore she passed a shop and went in to buy a yellow bunting with a carriage cover to match.

'For a friend of mine,' she said, and was struck in the instant by this shocking denial of her own situation. 'I want her to have it before the baby comes. Yellow will do no matter what she has, won't it? And I'd like that cap, too, the embroidered one.'

The saleswoman looked at Jennie's old coat, which now barely closed in front. 'That one's expensive. It's hand-embroidered.'

'That's all right.'

A bitter thought crossed her mind. The most expensive one – why not? – for the Mendeses' grandchild. She stifled the thought. Nasty, Jennie, and not worthy of you.

In her room that night she examined her face in the mirror for a long time. Would there be anything of her in the child's face? It might be round like hers, or square like her mother's; opal-eyed like Peter's; or – God forbid – long and sharp like his mother's.

After a while she got up and began to write a note.

Dear Child,
I'm hoping that the parents who bring you up will give you this when you grow old enough to understand it. The mother who will give you birth and the –

She'd started to write *man* but instead changed it to *boy*.

– who fathered you are good people but foolish, as I hope you won't be. We were too young to fit you into our lives. Maybe we were selfish, too, wanting to go on with our plans undisturbed. Some people wanted me to do away with you – to abort you – but I couldn't do that. You were already growing, and I had to let you grow to fulfillment. I had to let you have your own life. I hope with all my heart that it will be a wonderful one. I will give you away only to wonderful people who want you, and who will do more for you than I can. I hope you will understand that I am doing this out of love for you, although it may not seem much like love. But it is, believe me, my daughter or my son. It is.

Then, without signing the note, she laid it on the embroidered bonnet, closed the box, and retied the taffeta bow.

They took her in the middle of the night. The birth was quick. Shortly before dawn, after no more than four hours of a pain that grew sharper and sharper, so that the last ones were agonizing and inhuman, so that she bit her lips and pulled with desperate, sweating hands at the side of the bed, she felt one last awful lunge. Then abruptly there was relief and ease. Lying there in that merciful first relief, she heard a cry like a lament, and then high over her head, it seemed, a distant voice saying, 'It's a girl, a fine girl, Jennie. Seven pounds, three ounces.'

Raising herself on one elbow and tired now, so very tired, she saw a vague, dizzy blur: A nurse or a doctor, someone in white, was carrying something wrapped in a blanket and walking away with it.

'Has she got everything she's supposed to have?' Jennie whispered.

'Everything she's supposed to have. Ten fingers, ten toes, and good lungs. You heard her cry.'

'Nothing wrong?'

'Nothing at all. She's perfect. You've done a good job, Jennie.'

She went home. She withdrew the Mendeses' money from the bank, over four thousand dollars, having spent only five hundred. For a moment she had thought of returning the balance with a courteous, cold letter to express her independence and contempt, and then she thought better of it. Be practical! Mom had taught her that, and some of the teaching had rubbed off. The money would go part of the way toward law school. Next summer and every summer she would go to work and put every possible penny away. Then, with whatever little Pop might be able to give her, she would somehow get through. She had to get through. This she wanted now – more than anything in the world.

Because it was the cheapest way to go, she took the bus back home. Now, in November, she rode for two days through continuous cold, traveling through the back streets of run-down cities and out again onto the highway. The tires sang in the wetness; past bare, twiggy trees, roadside litter, and rusty junkyards.

Suddenly, in a vacant lot beside a ramshackle dwelling, she had a glimpse of two horses nodding over a fence. And one threw up his wonderful bronze satin head to snort and began to run, with the other following, and the two went racing with pure joy around that derelict, bare lot.

I'll remember that, she thought. It's one of the odd, small things that stick in one's mind. Perhaps it's an omen.

At home things were as they had always been. Her story was well rehearsed and was accepted.

'It's good to have you closer to home again,' Pop said.

'Not that we see you all that much, but it's nice to know you're only a couple of hours away,' Mom amended.

Pop remarked that Jennie had lost weight, and Mom said that was too bad, but what can you do with these girls? They all want to be thin as a board.

'Our college daughter, God bless her. Only one thing bothers me. You broke off with Peter, didn't you? You found somebody else?'

'Yes to the first and no to the second. I've plenty of time, Mom. Don't rush me.' Jennie gave them a smile. It was supposed to say: See how young and carefree I am?

'Who's rushing? I was only being nosy.'

'Well, I just don't like him anymore. If he ever telephones, tell him I'm out. Tell him I went to Mexico or Afghanistan.'

Peter didn't telephone, but he wrote again, asking why she hadn't answered his last letter. She read that letter again. What was the matter? he asked. Had she cast him out? He was concerned about her health. He loved her. And he was sorry about not returning to Penn, although he hoped he could manage to come north during Christmas week. But he made no mention of any future beyond that.

So much for the golden months and the golden promises! Childish and strengthless it must all have been, to have ended this way. And in her bed she pressed her face into the hard mattress, forcing the tears back into her head because she didn't dare show wept-out eyes in the morning.

Very, very slowly, as the agonies began to lighten, she felt a dull anger creeping to replace them. He had never even asked about the baby, only about her *health*, as though she had merely gone through sickness or surgery. No, the Mendeses didn't want to hear about the baby, that was clear. And they had brainwashed their son, crushed him into subjection. Poor, weak Peter. And poor baby...

But the baby wasn't poor, she reminded herself. She was cared for and loved, sheltered somewhere in the unknown West. Jennie glanced at the globe that had stood on the desk in her room since grammar school days. The West was vast. San Diego had palm trees and ocean. Mountains and snow encircled Salt Lake City. Portland? They called it the Rose City. It would be nice to think of the child growing up in a place with such a pretty name.

One day, piece by piece, she tore all Peter's letters into shreds, gave away everything he had ever given her, and sat down at her desk. Writing a final letter to him, she surprised herself by being able to dismiss him without recrimination. She said nothing about the child; since he had apparently been afraid to ask, he didn't deserve to know.

With the letter sealed and stamped, she felt proud, decisive, and mature. The past was past. The way now was forward. There was no Peter and there was no baby. It never happened.

It happened.

What can I do? I'm about to be married and my life is organized; it has direction. Why must this happen *now*? Why must it happen at all? Please. Oh, God, please don't let this happen ...

Then she put her face in her hands and sobbed aloud.

After a while she got up, pulled on a pair of slacks and a jacket, and went out onto the street. The wind was blowing icy cold from the East River, or maybe all the way across from the Hudson. She drew the jacket closer and began to walk, then to run. She had no idea where she was going, but she had to move. When you're exhausted, Jennie, you may go home.

The streets were quiet. Occasionally a car went by with a swish of tires and a flare of light, two menacing lights approaching and two sparks of red glare receding as it sped away. Lights were few in the apartment houses, dark fortresses in which sleepers lay stacked thirty stories high. It was long past the middle of the night.

Only the great hospital, a dark bulk under the moving, cloudy sky, was awake. From a distance of two blocks, as she ran, the sight of lighted windows scattered up and down the building's height and breadth distracted her from her terror. Always, coming home at night, should she pass that way, she would feel a sharp awareness of what might be happening behind any one of those windows.

Now, approaching the emergency entrance, she was halted in her run. Police cars, ambulances, and a cluster of onlookers – from where assembled at this hour? – blocked the sidewalk. A few feet from where she stood, a stretcher was lifted; there was a small commotion of white coats; there were the lights of another ambulance whining to a stop; then another stretcher, and she had a glimpse of long black hair and a frightful, bloody mask where a face ought to be.

Jennie's breath went hot in her throat, and the salty taste of blood was in her mouth as she looked away, and then, against her will, looked back.

'Move on,' a policeman ordered, dispersing the group on the sidewalk.

Among them, a woman wept with her hand over her eyes. A man walked away, damning the legal system.

'He was out on parole. Ten days out, broke into the house and slit their throats. Raped her first. The husband's dead, they said –'

Wanting to hear no more, Jennie resumed her run. The bloody face . . . She sped out into the middle of the street, away from doorways and alleys, running as if she were being pursued.

When she had raced up the stairs and locked her door, she was exhausted. But the terror at the hospital had put things back into proportion. The macabre night scene, the cries, the bloody face . . . This other trouble, this phone call, was nothing in comparison.

Reason reasserted itself. Victoria Jill Miller had lived nineteen years without her and could surely go on living without her. She would be better off not knowing Jennie. She might think she wanted to see her natural mother, but that would only lead to an emotional crisis in the end. These adoption committees were a lot of busybodies. What could a committee understand about that long-ago agony and despair? It was no business of theirs, anyway. What right had they to come now, to encourage this intrusion?

I have so much to do, Jennie thought, tense with the pressure. This case is so terribly important. Jay feels responsible for me, he's told them all how competent I am, and now I have to prove myself. It won't be easy. The builders are a big outfit, Jay says. They'll fight hard. I have to prepare so thoroughly, I can't waste a minute. I have to get started tomorrow morning. Call experts, water engineers, make traffic studies, roads, access, assessments. Get moving. Can't let anything else clog my mind. Can't.

Her thoughts were on a seesaw: Now that I've refused to see the girl, she'll think better of it and let it drop. They'll probably not call again. And if they should, I'll just repeat my position until they get discouraged. But surely they won't call again.

Will they?

4

Two weeks later Jennie went back upstairs for the meeting of the planning board. Although she felt sufficiently prepared by now, having put all other business aside, she clung to Jay.

'I wish you could go. Are you sure you can't?'

'Sure. I've got to be in court all week. But you'll do fine without me. Dad's got the group together for supper before the meeting, so you can be introduced to everybody and have time to talk over any new angles. You'll charm them, Jennie girl.'

'Charm isn't exactly what they need. They're looking for results.'

'Do as well as you did in the Long Island case and you'll give them results. Come on! You'll knock them dead.'

The New York Times reported temperatures of five to ten degrees above zero upstate. Her warmest coat was two years old but still good-looking, although the edges of the cuffs were slightly worn. She stood at the closet door, holding a sleeve, arguing with herself, and then, abruptly thrusting the coat away, went out to buy a new one. She was feeling something she seldom felt: a need for indulgence. So she set off toward Fifth Avenue, where it took very little time to find an extravagantly beautiful russet woolen coat lined with fur, and a skirt to match. With them went a cream-colored cashmere sweater and, for a change, a cream-colored blouse of heavy silk. On the way home she made a long detour to an ice-cream shop, one of the fern-hung copies of a turn-of-the-century ice-cream parlor that were so popular again, and bought her second extravagance, an enormous tower of chocolate and whipped cream, a sweet, sweet comfort.

If anybody ever needed comfort, she told herself, I'm the one. For two weeks she had been walking around with her thoughts still on a seesaw. Will they phone again? Won't they? And she called to mind those terror-filled minutes before examination papers are handed out: Will I make it? Won't I? She finished the chocolate sundae and went home to pack.

Shirley, watching, gave approval. 'That's a stunning outfit. Now put on the pearls.'

'Pearls? I'm going to a business meeting in a country town.'

'So take them off for the meeting. But they look perfect with both the blouse and the sweater. Don't you think it would be nice to show your mother-in-law –'

'She's not my mother-in-law.'

'Don't quibble. She will be in another couple of months, and it would be nice to show her how much you appreciate her present.'

'Okay, maybe I will.'

Yet Jennie knew she wouldn't. Why not? Because something was there, the knowledge of being under false pretenses, and a sense of not being deserving of the pearls. That was why.

Jay's father met her at the railroad station and drove her the rest of the way. A glossy, white film spread over the fields and laid long, drooping fingers on the hilltops.

'Snow's early this year,' the old man remarked. 'Quite a sudden change from when you were here.' And glancing down at Jennie, 'You look very lovely today.'

'Thank you.' Demurely she accepted the compliment. It hadn't been conventional flattery; there had been approval in it.

False pretenses. I am not what I appear to be. An outsider is what I am. It was the same in Georgia nineteen years ago.

For nineteen years she had wiped away all memories of Peter, expunged them as with an ink eradicator. Only once, when a stranger had left open on a library table a directory of American scholars, driven by a momentary curiosity, not caring at all, not giving a damn as she had put it to herself, she had looked under *M*, and there she had found him, Peter Algernon Mendes, with a list of his degrees and writings. He had made a name in archaeology as he had wanted to do and was now – or had been, three or four years ago – teaching in Chicago. So each of us, she had reflected then, and did again now, each of us has gotten what we set out to get, with nothing kept of that year's starry infatuation – or had it perhaps and truly been love? If we could have stayed together then, might we still be together now? And then this girl, this Victoria Jill – queer name – would be living with us instead of searching all over the country.

'Enid's got a good crowd coming,' Arthur Wolfe was saying. 'The committee's grown so, it's surprised even me – how this thing has gotten people all fired up. There's been so much publicity since you were last here, it's amazing. Both sides have plastered the town with posters. Of course, the newspapers are in the fight too. There's a chain that has half a dozen papers throughout the county, and it's liberal, all for keeping the land in wilderness, but the local paper wants the development. There's a lot of nastiness coming into it all, I'm sorry to say. It seems it's all people talk about – more than Russia and disarmament, or the election.'

Evening had fallen when they arrived. Cars were lined up in the driveway and parked far down the road. Light streamed out of every window of the house, so that it stood snug and bright among the dark, tossing trees.

Safe haven, a house like this – if you belonged here, Jennie thought.

The pleasant buzz of conversation was audible even before Enid opened the door, crying out in welcome, 'Why, here you are, Jennie! Everybody's dying to meet you. Come in.'

Forty or fifty people moved through the rooms. Probably, Jennie thought, they were the cream of the town: two doctors, the consolidated school's principal, some teachers, the owner of the variety store, a nurseryman, a Christmas-tree farmer, and some dairy farmers. Altogether, an assortment of people who were decently united on one thing: the importance of preserving some part of the natural earth for the future.

Jennie was given hot buttered rum, led around and introduced, and taken to the dining room, where a fire snapped and a long buffet table had been set.

'No lawyers, you noticed,' Jay's father remarked as they filled their plates with turkey, corn pudding, and salad. 'As I told you, they're steering clear of our side. No money in it.'

Jennie smiled. 'So you've had to come far afield, all the way to New York, to get me.'

'Yes, and we're glad we did. Jay says you've been working overtime on this, rounding up expert witnesses.'

'It wasn't too difficult. Fortunately the same engineers who did the studies on my Long Island case have been prompt and cooperative. They'll be here tonight.'

The old man's admiration was plain in his face. 'I'm going to compliment my son. He always did know how to judge people. Come, I'd like you to spend a few minutes with our best friend on the town council. I introduced you when you came in, remember? George Cromwell, over there with the woman in the plaid skirt? He's a dentist. He's got the energy I used to have.'

Cromwell was dressed, like everyone else, in country fashion – woolens, sweaters, and heavy shoes. His thick white hair contrasted with a plump, unlined face, young for his age.

'I think you two ought to get together and talk strategy,' said Arthur Wolfe. 'Why don't you take your plates out to the sun parlor? I'll see that you're not interrupted.'

'May I call you Jennie? I'm George to you,' Cromwell began.

'Of course.'

'I understand congratulations are in order. They tell me it's not official, not till you get your ring, but I'm an old friend, so they've let me in on the secret. You know, they're wonderful people, the Wolfes. They don't seem like summer people. Not that we have many summer people up here – we're too far away to attract them. They fitted right into the town, have been so generous to the police and the volunteer fire department. Why, Arthur was a volunteer himself when he was younger.'

Jennie glanced at her watch, and George caught her glance.

'Well, down to business,' he said. 'Is there anything you want to ask me?'

'Just about some of the people I might need to persuade especially.'

'Well, there's the mayor, of course. We'd certainly like to have him on our side. He controls most of the rest of them.'

Jennie nodded. 'Because he controls the goodies, appoints the police chief, et cetera.'

'So you're familiar with all that. But you ought to know

that our mayor – well, I'm not very fond of him, I can tell you. I never liked him. Chuck Anderson's his name, owns a couple of gas stations here and over at the lake. Looks like his name. I don't know why the name Chuck always suggests somebody beefy and tough. But I could be all wrong. Gosh, your name suggests a little brown wren, and you are definitely no wren, young lady.'

Jennie controlled her impatience. 'Tell me who's on the planning board.'

'You've met them all here tonight. The planning board is a mix – some of them top-notch and some of them Chuck's people. He never bothered too much about the planning board, though, because they serve without pay. Let's see, there's a librarian, Albert Buzard; then there's Jack Fuller, who owns the biggest dairy farm, five miles north of town. They'll be on our side.'

'What about the rest of them?'

'Well, frankly, it depends on whether you can sway them, fire them up. I understand you've done that before. They'll be surprised to see a woman, though. We've never had a woman lawyer in town.'

Oh, my, Jennie thought, stifling amusement.

'The council can override the planning board, you know. So even if you win out tonight, you'll still have the council to reckon with. They'll all be there tonight too.'

Arthur Wolfe opened the door and peered in. 'Time to start. There's an overflow crowd, I hear, so they've had to move the meeting to the school auditorium.'

'Wow!' George shook his head. 'It's a pretty big school building, too, a consolidated school. You've got your work cut out for you, Jennie.'

The parking lot was almost filled, and a large crowd in boots and woolen caps was already streaming up the steps of a typical redbrick, white-trimmed, small-town American school.

Arthur Wolfe chuckled. 'Will you look at that!' Just in front, a battered old car splashed with muddy snow was plastered with signs: I DON'T GIVE A DAMN ABOUT DUCKS; VOTE FOR PEOPLE, TO HELL WITH RACCOONS; KISS MY AX.

Enid was worried. 'It's getting so nasty. I was told that the developers have brought people to this meeting who don't even live in the township.'

'Nasty, it's true. But you can see the other side too. It's hard to explain to a man who sees the possibility of a few years' worth of jobs that we have to think of the larger community and of future generations. Put yourself in his shoes if you can,' Arthur Wolfe said.

Jennie sighed. 'I can. I work every day with people who don't have enough of anything. There could be conflict in my mind, too, over this issue, except that I've told myself, and I really know, that we're right in the long run. But as you say, that's hard to explain to people who need things right now.'

And Arthur, helping the two women as they slid across the icy pavement, repeated Cromwell's friendly warning: 'You've got your work cut out for you, Jennie.'

With the aid of a large map and pointer at the front of the auditorium, the proposal was outlined for all to understand: five hundred attached condominiums, seventy-five single-family structures, dam, lake, golf course, tennis courts, swimming pools, and ski run.

The board members sat in a row, slightly elevated, on the platform from which the principal, flanked by the Stars and Stripes on one side and the school flag on the other, ordinarily conducted school assemblies. They wore the same air of authority. Occasionally Jennie intercepted a glance from one of them; male and middle-aged, they were probably thinking that she ought to be at home right now preparing the next day's lunch boxes for her children.

The meeting was now about to enter its third hour. After the customary give-and-take among experts; technical reports from environmental engineers, consulting engineers, surveyors, and sundry planners; after keen, persistent questioning by Jennie and by the attorney for Barker Development – the audience, some of whom had had to stand, was restive. People wanted to be heard. They wanted action.

'We have a procedure now,' said the chairman, 'that we have to follow. I believe we have some letters to be read into the record. If you will, Mr McVee.'

'Just one. We have a letter from David and Rebecca Pyle, dated September fourth.'

Dear Sir,

We write to tell you of our concern about the proposed development in the Green Marsh. Our adjacent farm lies lower than the northern end of the property in question, and it is our fear that the water supply, on which our dairy herd depends, will be curtailed and contaminated if the marsh is drained and the lake enlarged. We now have a clear, pristine lake, and it must not be destroyed to become instead a breeder of disease.

If the developer really believes that this will not be the case, then we think he should be made to guarantee in writing that the development will bring no harm, and be prepared to meet the cost of any damages if it should.

We rely on this board to make the right decision and to protect our interests.

Sincerely,
David and Rebecca Pyle

A letter with a legal tone, Jennie said to herself. They've already had advice.

A question came from the dais. 'Do you have any comment about that, Mr Schultz?'

The attorney for Barker, quick on his feet, was standing before the question had been half spoken. He was a young man, about Jennie's age, wearing skillfully chosen country clothes, slightly worn but not too much so, with a sweater visible under his jacket. His manner was engaging.

'As to written guarantees, Mr Chairman?'

'Yes, if you care to.'

Mr Schultz smiled, raising his eyebrows in mild surprise. 'Well, sir, as we all know, that's unheard-of. We stand on our record, which should be sufficient. Barker Development has built condominiums in Pennsylvania, New Jersey, throughout New England, and in Florida. The quality of their work is what has built their reputation.'

Jennie responded. 'May I speak, Mr Chairman? This is not an answer to the very reasonable request in this letter. We have a serious problem here, one that I have certainly tried to bring out this evening. We need to know specifically about things like backup flooding, water elevation, and so forth and so on, if they build as they have outlined. I have noted that Mr Schultz has not brought a water expert to testify.'

'Mr Chairman, Mr Bailey spoke at some length. He is a qualified engineer.'

Jennie persisted. 'But not a water specialist.'

Schultz gave a slight shrug, as if to say, Why quibble? 'Specialist enough, I think it's reasonable to say. We had no idea we would meet up with . . . may I call them rather finicky objections? We expected to be welcomed with enthusiasm, and I believe we shall be, because we are going to improve this town, and most of its citizens understand that.'

Jennie, still facing the chairman, shook her head. 'But there are some citizens who do not see things that way. They're not unsophisticated people who can have the wool pulled over their eyes. There have been other doubts and objections besides the one we just heard: letters to the newspapers –'

A harsh voice interrupted, loudly enough to startle the whole assembly. 'They don't speak for me, and neither do you!'

All heads turned. In the third row a man stood boldly, as if he had just thrown a fastball and was waiting to see who would catch it. About forty-five years old, he had a strong, rather good-looking face with thick black hair and several days' growth of dark beard. He wore a motorcycle thug's black leather jacket; opened, it revealed a soiled shirt and a powerful chest.

The astonished chairman reprimanded him. 'Address the chair please, and no one else.'

'Fine. I'll tell you just what I think. They and their preservation committee! And a bunch of foreigners come up here from New York. They don't want anybody to make a dollar, do they? Sure, they've got all they want, so who cares? Who gives a damn!'

Voices broke out all over the hall.

'Foreigners? Since when is New York City a foreign country?'

'Quiet here!'

'He knows what he's talking about!'

'Damn right, he does!'

'Should be thrown out, the fool!'

'Good boy, Bruce!'

'Oh, shut up!'

'Quiet here! Have some respect!'

'You're out of order, Mr Fisher. Please moderate your language or sit down.'

The gavel was pounded fiercely. Order was restored and questions were resumed. Someone asked about recreation facilities, to which Mr Schultz replied that there was to be a clubhouse, a baseball field, and water sports on the enlarged lake.

'All for the use of the purchasers?' inquired Jennie.

'Well, yes, it will be a club community. A clubhouse with the usual features.'

'But at present,' she said softly, 'the land is available to everyone, to all citizens, for recreation. Your development will take it away from them, and that should be noted, I think.'

The harsh voice rang out again. Fisher stood up and scoffed. 'For everyone! For a handful of nature nuts, that's who. Bunch of Communists from the city come up here and talk about nature. Wouldn't know an owl from a polecat if they fell over one. Communists, that's all. Against progress, against private property. People want to invest. They've a right to invest their money. The country was built by people like this Barker outfit.'

Young Mr Schultz put on a benign expression in acknowledgment of the praise. Crazier and crazier, Jennie thought.

The chairman raised his voice. 'I'm telling you again, Mr Fisher, sit down.'

Fisher ignored him. 'You're nothing but a hired gun, Miss Beluski, or whatever your name is. I can't pronounce it. I'm not a rich man like the folks who hired you.'

There were cries of 'Shame!' and also some applause.

'Out of order,' shouted the chairman, his mild face now flushed, his expression baffled.

'I represent a group of concerned citizens, and I'm no more a hired gun than Mr Schultz is.' Taking care to observe protocol, Jennie replied not to Fisher but to the chair.

'A hired gun!' repeated Fisher in defiance.

The chairman rose from his seat. 'Mr Fisher! We shall have you removed from this hall if you don't sit down and keep quiet.'

Fisher sat down. Out of the corner of her eye Jennie watched him. What she saw was concentrated hatred. But why? That voice ... He looked about seven feet tall. And the black leather jacket seemed a symbol of violence. She controlled a shiver. Silly ... He was only a common tough, some sort of mental case. It was all in a day's work.

'It's late,' the chairman said. 'There's time for a brief summation if either of the attorneys wishes to make one. After that this board will study the matter and will report by the end of the month. Mr Schultz?'

Schultz spoke briefly. 'Actually I have nothing to add. Barker Development rests on its reputation and its willingness to invest substantial sums in this town, thus showing confidence in the town's future as it enters – as we all make ready to enter – a new century. We hope that no overemphasis on conservation will be an obstacle to the welfare of human beings. It is a sentimental, elitist attitude, revealing a preference for wildlife – for deer or migrating birds – over human beings. I thank the board for its courtesy,' he said agreeably, 'and leave with confidence that you will vote on the side of progress.'

Jennie had intended to be brief and factual. But the easy smugness of her opponent, coming after the hostile disruption, shook her intensely, and when she stood to speak, her voice quivered.

'Mr Chairman, this is an historic moment for your town. I do believe that everybody here will have reason to remember how you decide the question that has been brought before you this evening.

'I'm well aware of the conflicting thoughts some of you must have. You want jobs, and these people are offering to create them. But I remind you that the jobs will be short-lived. They don't really solve your problems. These builders will flock in and be gone in a couple of years.

'I'm aware, too, that if the Green Marsh is destroyed, it won't be the end of the world. But it will be the end of a part of your particular, familiar world.'

The auditorium was quite still. People were listening. The members of the board were leaning forward, watching Jennie.

'Even if it should be true – and I don't believe it – that this project wouldn't affect the water table, there are too many other things to be reckoned with. Think! All that gorgeous land and the creatures who have lived on it for thousands of years would be gone forever. All the space and the peace that have served you and your children . . .' She felt impassioned, which surprised her. She saw herself as she'd stood with Jay that morning at the top of the rise overlooking the marsh, the lake, the dripping trees; the immensity of foggy green had stretched as far as one could see, to the northern line where the silent hills began.

Her mind wandered. She had been so free that morning, as if she'd had wings. There'd been no weight, no looming threat of disaster, no hovering cloud. Now the cloud closed in again, the weight clamped down on her throat, and she faltered. And then in panic remembered where she was. They were waiting. . . .

Mercifully her mind picked up the thread of her thoughts, and she was able to go on.

'It is not fair to vote all that away, to give it away in exchange for short-lived dollars. Let us at least give the state a chance to incorporate this land within the wild and scenic system, so that others, years from now, may walk there and fish and swim and watch the birds and the changing seasons. I ask you, gentlemen, I plead with you to deny this application.'

For several seconds after Jennie stopped speaking, there was a marked, unusual stillness, without a cough, a rustling of paper, or shuffling of shoes. Every face in the row on the dais was turned to her, and she had a flashing thought: Why, they all look surprised!

The chairman said as he rose, 'Thank you very much. Thank you all. The meeting is now adjourned.'

Slowly Jennie made her way through the crowd as it pressed toward the exit. As they moved forward, some people offered congratulations. 'I teach sixth grade, and I'm trying to give my pupils some understanding of what you said.' And, 'You spoke to the point,' and, 'I couldn't agree more.' But other faces were stony, staring at her with disapproval as they passed, and deliberately turned away.

Far ahead, at the foot of the short flight of steps that led to the outer lobby, she saw the Wolfes waiting for her. Suddenly she was weary, unsure of her accomplishment. It was just then, as she started down the steps, that she was roughly shoved in the small of the back. She staggered, tripped, and was saved from falling only by stumbling against, and being caught by, the man in front of her. Shocked and furious, she cried out, and turning, she found her face only inches away from the laughing mouth – wet, red lips; decayed brown teeth – of the man in the black leather jacket.

'Why, you . . .' she began. 'What do you think you're doing?'

Still laughing, he gave her a jab in the side with his elbow as he slipped through an opening in the throng and ran out the front door.

Jennie's heart was still pounding when she reached the Wolfes. They were flushed with excitement, and for some reason unexplainable even to herself, she hid her distress.

'Jennie! You were marvelous!' Enid cried. 'You really were. Wait till we tell Jay!'

It had begun to snow. Sticky, wet flakes fell slowly through the still, windless air and must have been falling during the hours when they had been indoors, for the icy pavement was hidden now under soft fluff, as was the car. Jennie and Enid got in while Arthur scraped the windows.

'I really think you moved the board people. I kept watching their faces. Some of them I'm sure of,' Enid said. 'The chairman, certainly.'

'He was probably on my side, anyway, before I said a word,' Jennie reminded her.

'Well, all right, but there are others who were on the fence before. I know. Mr Sands kept nodding at some things you said.'

Arthur started the car, and they joined the slow line leading out of the parking lot.

'Yes, you gave them something to think about,' he agreed. 'You did well, coming up against Schultz. Talk of smooth! He knows his business and knows how to persuade.'

Through the veil of snow Jennie thought she recognized the battered car with the signs, and her enemy driving it. The huge head; the huge, round shoulders ... but perhaps not ...

'Who was the man in the windbreaker who made all the noise?' she asked.

Arthur Wolfe sighed. 'A bad sort. Name's Bruce Fisher. He's a cousin of our mayor. He lives in a shack on a couple of acres just this side of the Green Marsh. The way I figure – and it's pretty obvious, since his land gives level access to the lake on that end, where otherwise the road would have to go up a steep grade – he's had a good offer and he doesn't want anything to get in the way of it.'

Anything or anybody, Jennie thought. He actually tried to trip me on the stairs! But that's crazy! Of course it is. Yet don't people shove people in front of subway trains? So why not this?

'He's been in trouble with the law half a dozen times,' Arthur continued. 'Served a few years in jail too. I think Chuck got the sentence reduced. Funny, they're not close – outwardly, anyway. Chuck wouldn't exactly invite Bruce to a dinner party, and yet they stick together. Once he aimed a shotgun at some kids who took a shortcut across his land on the way to the lake. Chuck got that squashed. He lived with a woman until he beat her up one time too often, so now he lives alone. Or, I should say, lives with a pair of pitbulls he's trained to kill. In short, he's not a nice guy.'

'Was I too emotional in my summing up?' Jennie asked now, needing to change the subject. 'I'm sort of hearing myself all over again. Was I?'

'Goodness, no,' Enid said. 'It was just right.'

'But don't be too encouraged,' Arthur reminded her. 'Even if you should win over the planning board, the town council has the final vote. They'll be the tough ones. Don't underestimate our mayor. Chuck loves money.'

'Most people do,' Jennie said.

'Yes, but I have the feeling he loves it more than most of us do. He's not above selling his vote, nor are some of his cronies I could name but won't.'

Jennie thought aloud. 'The Barker people have a good reputation. I wonder whether they'd risk it to bribe a small-town mayor. They've got much bigger projects than this one.'

'It wouldn't have to be a bribe. Just a big offer to the mayor's cousin, as I said. Ten times what the land's worth, for instance. A perfectly legitimate offer.'

'I should have figured that one out myself.'

Arthur stopped the car at the front door of the house, where the potted evergreens in their wooden tubs formed two white pyramids.

'I'll put the car away, and maybe you'll make us some hot buttered rum, Enid? It's the right kind of night for it.'

'Yes,' he said as they sat in the kitchen, warming their hands around pewter mugs. 'Yes, you might want to go on and make a name for yourself in this field of law, Jennie. You've got the feeling for it, and goodness knows these are tense issues, and we're going to see more and more litigation over them as the planet gets more crowded.' He reflected, 'It's not easy to pit immediate gains against the long-range view. Most people don't want to imagine what the world may be like after they're not in it anymore.'

'Don't keep her up, Arthur,' Enid said. 'Her eyes are closing. Go on up to bed, Jennie.'

But her eyes were not quite ready to close. Lying in bed in the plain, snug room with its one dormer window and sloped ceiling, she listened to the last noises of the night, the dog being let out to bark at whatever he might have seen or heard in the profound country quiet, then the dog being let back in, the door thudding, and finally the footsteps on the stairs. Family sounds, routine and comforting. This was the first time Jennie had been with Jay's parents without his presence. And unlike the gift of pearls, unlike any formal words, the simple fact of being there not as a guest but as a family member who sat with them in the kitchen and slept under their roof meant full acceptance.

And just as suddenly, in the lovely warmth of this awareness, the hovering cloud of fear descended again, falling over her to chill and cling.

She's in New York.... She wants to see you....

5

Whenever the phone had rung at home in the evening, Jennie had run to it in hopes that it would be Jay calling, and it usually was. But these days it was different, because she knew it was foolish to go on hoping that there wouldn't be another call from Mr Riley.

That night, however, it was Jay.

'Just got off the phone with Dad. Then he put George Cromwell on. They're all delighted with the way you handled things. They're delighted and I'm proud.'

'I'm so glad, Jay.'

'Now listen, I've decided that tomorrow's the day. We're going for the ring. I want you to meet me downstairs in front of my office at three. And I won't take no for an answer. We can walk over to Cartier's.'

When he had hung up, she sat for a moment at the telephone, assessing her own feelings. Cartier's. A ring, to make official the bond that was so strong and tight between them. She ought to be feeling unadulterated bliss. She was the luckiest of women! It was wrong and absurd to let fear, to let anything, spoil –

The telephone rang again.

A woman said, 'Miss Rakowsky?'

A woman this time, yet Jennie knew before another word was spoken. She knew.

'My name is Emma Dunn. Mr Riley talked to you a while ago. He's turned the case over to me.'

The case. I'm a case in a social worker's file.

'There's no case,' Jennie said.

'Well, we needn't call it that. But there is a problem, although there shouldn't be. Have you thought about it any more?'

Act sure of yourself. Don't let her feel that you're wavering or intimidated.

'Yes, I have. I gave Mr Riley my answer, and I haven't changed my mind.'

'We were hoping so much that you would change it after you'd had time to think it over.'

'I thought I made myself very clear.' Jennie spoke sternly. 'This ... this matter was settled years ago. It was supposed to be a confidential arrangement, and a permanent one. That's how I want it to stay.'

'She's such a delightful girl. If you could see her –'

'Look, do you know what you're doing? You're opening an old wound, and it's cruel of you. Don't you realize that?' She ought to hang up. Just slam down the receiver on this intruding stranger. And yet it would do no good. They'd only keep calling. Maybe she'd even find them at her door one night when she came home. Maybe Jay would be with her. Jennie shuddered. Now her voice was shaking.

'I was eighteen years old. I was all alone. His family didn't want me. I wasn't good enough. And he was a helpless baby, no good to me at all. My parents, poor souls ... Listen to me, I had to fight my way through my trouble then without any real help from anybody! And I'll fight now if I have to. So will you please just leave me alone? Will you just do that?'

The voice became conciliatory. 'Nobody wants to fight,

Miss Rakowsky. Quite the contrary. Your daughter wants to come to you with love. She feels that need.'

'Mr Riley said she didn't need anything. I have no money, anyway, you know,' Jennie said, and felt instant regret. It had sounded so coarse, and she hadn't meant it to.

'Money is not what Jill wants.'

She didn't want to know; she wanted only to be rid of the whole business, yet something compelled her to ask, 'Isn't she happy with her family?'

'Oh, it's nothing like that at all. In fact, the family is quite understanding about her wish to see her parents.'

'Understanding! What about my wishes, my needs? This was a closed chapter in my life –' Jennie's voice caught in her throat.

The woman must have heard the catch, because she responded sympathetically. 'Why don't you come to our office to talk? Telephone talks aren't any good. Face-to-face, we'll understand each other. Come in for counseling. We want to help you.'

'I don't want help!' Now Jennie was openly weeping. 'I haven't asked for any, have I? I'm getting along fine the way I am – or was getting along, until you opened this Pandora's box that was meant, according to law, to stay shut.'

'The law is changing. People want to know where they came from. They have a right to know –'

'I have rights too! This is my private life you're talking about. I don't want to hear about the laws changing. I'm a lawyer, and I understand –'

'We know you're a lawyer, Miss Rakowsky. So surely you, of all people, know that the law often changes with the mores, with the times.'

Jennie was exhausted. It was too much of an effort to hold the telephone.

'Look, I don't want to talk anymore. I've said it all. I just want you to go away. I'm going to hang up. I just want you to leave me alone.'

'I'm afraid that isn't possible,' the mild voice replied.

Jennie hung up. Her tears were not tears of sorrow but of anger and fear. Even while they were falling, cold and slippery as glycerin, she knew that. Behind shut lids, between eye and brain, dark anger and bitter resentment were taking shape, billowing like smoke, coal-black and furnace-red, swirling in the image of a rising genie. How dare they track her down like detectives, as if she had committed a crime?

And yet . . . Poor girl. Perhaps she's desperate. No, she isn't, she's at Barnard, and they said she's fine. Except that she thinks she needs me. How could she possibly be desperate, though? No, it's me. I'm the one who's desperate.

The room, with only one lamp lit in the corner, was dim. The armchairs took on the shapes of seated men, a tribunal sitting in judgment upon Jennie. The tall curtains were men standing, frowning, waiting to seize and take her away. Then the light, as it struck the round copper pot that held the fern, printed a jeering face upon its bulging surface, and as Jennie moved, changing the angle of vision, the face moved, too, and opened an ugly, mournful mouth to weep.

Am I to go crazy here in this room?

'Looking for her parents,' the woman had said. Yes, she had said that, hadn't she? Could they then possibly have found Peter too? She searched her memory. Had she given his name to those people at the home? But of course there was a record; his father had paid the bill, so there had to be a record.

Well, if the agency had traced him to the Mendeses – tall people beside tall columns in the blossoming Georgia afternoon – she'll get no welcome, that's for sure. God knows, Peter may have six children by now. God knows. You'd do well to stay away from those folks, Victoria Jill.

And now came an ache. It caught her like a stitch in the side after a breathless run uphill. It hurt so sharply that for an instant she could not breathe for the pain. Victoria Jill. 'They call her Jill.' I wonder whom she looks like? She must be a little bit like me – a little bit, at least.

Dry-eyed now, Jennie put her head down on the desk beside the telephone. If only there were someone to talk to! But there was no one, not even Shirley, her neighbor, who would only give quick comfort and end by telling her not to take everything so seriously. Long minutes passed before she could raise her head and go to bed.

There was a cold wind on the avenue, and Jennie went into the lobby to wait for Jay. The filigreed bronze entrance of a brokerage office faced the identical entrance to a bank on the opposite wall. Farther from the street, close to the elevators, was a florist's shop, its windows filled with pastel, out-of-season blooms, bringing an incongruous gaiety to the serious environment of business and finance. But then, maybe it wasn't incongruous at all. People walked briskly in this neighborhood and looked pleased with life; they were just the people who would celebrate life with flowers. She chided herself: Don't be bitter. People may look carefree, but that doesn't mean they are, any more than you. Anyone seeing you in this coat – for a visit to Cartier's she had thought it proper to wear the new coat, along with Enid's pearls – would think you hadn't a care, either. Nobody rides free, Jennie.

Nothing escaped Jay. He hurried over, kissed her, and drew back with a little frown of concern.

'You look so tired! Done in. What's wrong?'

'I didn't sleep well, that's all.'

'Anything bothering you?'

'No, it just happens sometimes.'

They walked west toward St Patrick's Cathedral. Across Fifth Avenue stood a succession of airline offices. Even at this distance one could see the splashed color of the posters in their windows. Jay, glancing in their direction, said, 'I've been thinking – those two weeks at Caneel Bay won't be long enough for a honeymoon. Next summer, when school's out, my parents can take the children up to the country and you and I will have a month in Europe. We'll get a car and drive around with the top down. We'll stay at châteaux, drink wine, and eat foie gras. That'll be our real honeymoon.' He tightened his hold on her arm as they crossed the side street. 'However, I must say I'm looking forward to the two weeks all the same.'

She didn't answer. Traffic lights turned red at the intersection; brake lights were red; bloody red blinked everywhere. She wasn't prepared for a vacation in the West Indies. The Isles of June, some explorer had once called them, and she had been looking at pictures of palms and beach grapes, unmarked sand on crescent beaches, gulls and pelicans, sails and parasols. But with things grown shadowy and uncertain, she didn't feel like simply packing up and departing for pleasure, leaving behind a looming, unsolved threat that would have to be faced when she got home. It would be less risky to hang on at her desk in the office and be here to cope with trouble when it came, as assuredly as it would. Yes, yes, it would.

'Here we are,' said Jay.

Even the outside of Cartier's was a jewel, a Renaissance palace of cut stone. Walking in ahead of Jay, Jennie felt that people must know this was her first time inside.

He went straight to the rear, where a rather elegant gentleman, who had been seated at a desk, stood up.

'Mr Wolfe? Good to see you again. I've put some very nice rings aside for you, I think.'

Jay made an introduction, adding, 'Whenever I see you, it's a happy occasion.'

'Yes, your father's golden wedding present to your mother was the last. About a year ago, wasn't it? Well, now, since you didn't specify anything, I've got some pear-shaped, some marquise, and some emerald-cut stones to show you.'

On a velvet tray, half a dozen brilliant diamonds shimmered under the chandelier's light. All was sparkle and velvet. The exquisite shop was a velvet box, hushed and hidden from the roar of the city.

There was a minute of silence, during which Jennie was supposed to be considering the rings. Instead she was thinking again, with hands joined and sweating in her lap. If only I had told him at the start! But now, going into the third year, when he thinks he knows me ... I've told him all about my family, my childhood, what I want out of life. I've opened myself, I've told him everything. Everything except ... And he has opened himself to me. I know, because of the most secret, intimate things he has disclosed, that he has hidden nothing; if he had wanted to hide, he could have hidden them too. He has been honest with me....

Jay looked curiously at her, thinking perhaps that she was overawed and unsure of what was expected of her.

'Look carefully, Jen,' he said. 'I want you to fall in love with one of them before you say yes.'

'They're all so beautiful. I just don't know.'

'You have long fingers,' the salesman observed. 'You would wear an emerald-cut well. Not every woman can.'

Jay held up one of the rings. 'Blue-white?'

The man nodded. 'Very, very fine, Mr Wolfe.'

Jay knew about diamonds. He must have bought them

for his first wife, Phyllis. A girl with no secret past. A wife for a man like him.

'Try this one on, Jennie.'

She reprimanded herself: Show some excitement, for heaven's sake.

'Oh, it's gorgeous, Jay. Yes, gorgeous.'

The ring slid easily onto her finger.

'Hold your hand up to the light,' said the salesman.

Every color of the rainbow met there, and yet the fire on her hand was white, as sunlight glittering on sky reflected in blue water turns all to white, to silver and white.

'Well, what do you think?' asked Jay.

It was so obviously expensive! If it were less so, maybc she would feel less like cringing.

'Don't you think ... something smaller would be better?' she asked.

'Why? You're thinking it's ostentatious?'

'I wasn't. No.'

'You were. I know you. But you know me too. I wouldn't want you to wear anything ostentatious. This size is right for you. Now try the other shapes.'

She submitted, holding her hand out to one ring after the other. What a pity not to be thrilled at a moment like this!

Now Jay, perceiving her shyness, took charge. 'The pear-shaped one is less becoming,' he said, and the salesman agreed.

The two men considered. A yellow diamond was brought out and rejected, as was a round one. Her choice narrowed down to a marquise, the original emerald-cut, and a second emerald-cut. The salesman kept taking them off and putting them on. The two pairs of eyes questioned Jennie.

'I'm confused,' she murmured.

'Do you want to leave it to me?' asked Jay.

She mustered an easy smile. 'You pick it. You're the one who's going to be looking at it across the table.'

So the first emerald-cut ring was chosen. Then a wedding band of diamond baguettes, narrow enough to be worn on the same finger, was put away to be sized, after which Jay wrote a check, which Jennie didn't see, and they went out to the street.

'Painless, after all, wasn't it, Jennie? Arc you happy, darling?'

'You know I am.'

'You were so quiet.'

'I was embarrassed. My fingers are ink-stained. Didn't you notice?'

'So what? Sign of honest labor, that's all.' He laughed. 'I didn't tell you, I'm not going home tonight. The kids are staying with Phyllis's parents. It's their grandfather's birthday. So you'll be having an overnight guest. Hope you don't mind.'

She felt a quick rise of desire. There were never enough nights when they could be together. She didn't answer, just looked up at him, and the look spoke enough.

'My Jennie,' he said.

They walked quickly downtown, then east. The cold increased as dusk fell, with a damp prediction of snow in the air and a wind that took one's breath, making speech difficult. Jay spoke first. 'The usual place?'

'Why not?'

'The usual place' meant a restaurant two blocks from her apartment. Small and plain, it served superb Italian food. Lutèce, La Côte Basque, and others like them were for weekends after a day of leisure – or relative leisure, to be more exact, since Jay always had some weekend work.

'Everybody loves Italian food,' he observed, unfolding his napkin.

Years ago in Philadelphia there had been another 'little Italian place,' a cheap one with red-checked tablecloths. All day these startling images, so long forgotten, had come flickering back.

This table had a fresh white cloth and a handful of carnations in a glass container. And she urged herself silently, It's 1988. I'm in New York. Here. Now.

Facing the table hung a garish picture in thick, oily blues, ultramarine and cobalt, framed with hideous gilt.

'Awful, isn't it? It doesn't half do justice to the Bay of Naples. We'll go there, too, Jen.'

'Oh, I want to.'

'We ought to be hearing soon from the planning board about your case,' he said.

The cloud clung, gray and damp. She wanted to dispel it; she wanted comforting, the way a troubled child, wanting to be comforted, pretends to have a pain. So because she was unable to tell him of the real pain, she found a secondary one.

'I had such a nasty experience, Jay, really nasty.' And she told him about the man who had shoved her on the stairs.

'My God!' Jay cried. 'Did you tell my father?'

'I didn't want to. I don't know why, I just didn't want to.'

'You should have.'

'What could he have done about it? Nothing. I couldn't prove it, could I?'

'Well, true enough. But the next time you come before the town council, I'm going to be there. Not that I expect any open attack or anything,' he said quickly. 'The man's a low-life, a sneak. A psychopathic personality.'

'Your father's guess is that he's had a big offer for his land, which he'll split with the mayor.'

'It makes sense. There's no telling how many others on the council are in on the deal too. Those few acres, because of where they lie, are worth plenty. You know, Jen, in a way I'm almost sorry I got you into this fight. You take your work so much to heart! I'm afraid you'll be awfully upset if you lose.'

'You're thinking I will, aren't you?'

'There's a chance. The mayor only needs five votes on the council to win. So I just don't want you to be too encouraged, that's all.'

'So much skullduggery in such a little town!'

'You've no idea. City people, when they're fed up, like to imagine a life that could be more innocent and decent if they moved out of the city, but let me tell you' – Jay grinned – 'Chuck Anderson was elected as a man with a clean record. Chuck the Challenger, Honest Chuck. There'd be no more graft in road repair, no kick-backs on building permits – the usual stuff. Then, six or seven years back, an ugly business was dragged out into the light, something about Bruce Fisher – your friend – who'd been involved in a gang rape out near the lake. A rotten thing; the girl was fourteen. Well, it's a tangled story, and I don't remember all the details, but what does stand out in my mind is that Chuck had known all along about Fisher being involved in it and had at the time lied to protect him. So with the next election coming up, what does he do but come out in public with a full admission and apology? A heartfelt, teary repentance, beating his breast: "I did wrong, I should have told you all long ago, I can only ask your forgiveness." Et cetera. And so everyone admires his courage and they reelect him.'

'Well,' Jennie said. 'it did take courage. He didn't have to admit it, did he?'

'Yes, but you see, when a person has waited that long to come out with a truth, you wonder what else he hasn't admitted about himself and what's going to come out next. I can't feel the same ever again about anyone who does that, no matter what else is good about him. I simply lose my trust.'

Jennie was silent. Pasta and veal lay on her plate in a heap that suddenly was repulsive.

'And you see,' Jay said, 'he's straying from the straight and narrow again right now, isn't he, in spite of the past few years of good government? We all really know he is, even if we can't prove it. At least not yet.'

Jennie took a forkful of meat. It was like rubber in her mouth, although she knew it had been well prepared. Jay was eating his with obvious enjoyment.

'Yes,' he resumed thoughtfully, 'it's sometimes too late to make a clean breast of things.'

'Too late?' echoed Jennie.

'Too late for anyone to have confidence.'

'Yes.' She nodded.

'You're not eating,' he remonstrated. 'Don't you feel well, honey?'

'It's just that I'm tired. I told you.'

'Maybe I shouldn't stay tonight.'

'Oh, please! I want you to. I'm not *that* tired!'

Flash your bright eyes, show him that you want him, because you do want him so terribly, though at this moment, not with desire but for reassurance.

Jay, Jay, don't leave me. I can't lose you.

'Has my mother called you about next week?' he asked.

'No. What about it?'

'Well, she will. They're coming in next week, or maybe the week after, and she thought you might like to do some Saturday-afternoon shopping with her and the girls. She's been buying Sue's and Emily's things ever since they lost their mother, and she thought you'd like to start taking over the job.'

'Of course. Of course I would.'

'Family obligations descending on you already.' He smiled, teasing.

'I don't mind obligations.'

The words sounded flat to her ears, unlike the thoughts that now ran in a frenzy around and around in her head: If only he didn't have a family, parents, children, and heaven knew what other relatives, to sit in judgment of her! If only they weren't who they were, if only Jay were a nobody with no home, no job, no name, no ties, and they could go to some faraway place where no one could find them and start fresh in a whole new life without a past!

Fantasy, absurd fantasy. And she remembered the night, so short a time ago, when she had put his little girls to bed and been so filled with thankfulness and confidence and love.

They walked back through the wind again, now risen to a blast, so that they had to push against it, running with heads down. Back in the apartment, they rubbed icy hands together.

'Hot showers next,' Jay said.

'Hot coffee first or afterward?'

'Neither. Just a shower and bed. We'll be warm enough in bed.'

Together they stood under the prickle and sting of rushing water, soaped and brushed each other's backs, then, in the steaming little box that was Jennie's bathroom, toweled each other dry.

He held his palms against her breasts, curving his fingers.

'Look, they fit exactly.'

And the familiar softness ran, dissolving like some

sweet, thick liquid in her throat, and her knees unlocked so that her legs could hardly hold her straight. There was such force in him, but not like the force in other men, which could sometimes be frightening, so that one had to hold back or meet it with one's own strength, to defend oneself both physically and emotionally against domination. With Jay, there was only giving, total giving, so gentle was his power.

Yet at the same time she knew her own power over him too. He needed her. She felt the miracle of his need, saw it in his eyes, widened now with anticipation and a kind of joyful mischief.

He picked her up, carried her to the bed, and turned the lamp off. And the night closed over them.

In the morning she made an early breakfast: freshly squeezed orange juice, pancakes, and coffee.

'I hate rushing in the morning,' she informed him. 'I always like to get up an hour earlier and take my time.'

'That's funny, I do too. Jennie, isn't it marvelous that we keep on finding new things about ourselves that are just alike!'

'Don't think I eat pancakes every morning, though. This is only in honor of last night, I want you to know.'

'They're good. You make a helluva pancake.'

A narrow band of sunshine fell over the little table. In another half hour the sun would have moved around the corner of the building and the kitchenette would require electric light, but at this moment its glow was a celebration, and she loved it, loved the fragrance of roasted coffee, the flaming gloxinia on the windowsill, the black-and-yellow striped tie against Jay's white shirt-front, the quiet closeness of being just two together instead of encircled by children or relatives or strangers in a restaurant.

'Well, the date's coming closer,' Jay said, 'and I've even bought a new suit.'

'Me too. Very bridelike. You'll be surprised.'

'Let me guess. Pink?'

'I'm not telling. But you'll like it. Shirley helped me pick it out.'

'Oops!' Jay made a funny face.

'Don't worry, she knows what's what, and then I only have to tone it down a little.'

'Jennie, darling, whatever you wear will be –'

The telephone rang. She went to the living room and picked it up.

'Good morning,' said Emma Dunn. 'I'm sorry to call you this early, but I tried the last few nights and you were out.'

In those few seconds Jennie's palms went slippery with sweat.

'I can't talk to you. I'm on my way to work,' she said, keeping her tone calm.

'I understand. I'll take just a moment. Tell me when you can come in to see me. At your convenience. You name the time.'

'Quite impossible. I'll have to hang up now.'

'This isn't going to go away, Miss Rakowsky. Jill isn't going to go away, I have to warn you. So you'd do better to face –'

Jennie hung up, wiped her hands on a handkerchief, and composed her hot, stinging face.

'Trouble?' asked Jay.

'No, why?'

'You look bothered.'

'Well, I am. This client ... poor thing, she has such a sad life, it's awful.'

He said kindly, 'You can't mix emotions with law. They'll grind you down if you do. Maybe you should have an unlisted number at home. Although, come to think of it, you won't be at this number much longer.'

He stood up and reached for his briefcase. A fit of trembling seized her when he bent down to kiss her. Tears, in spite of all the resolve, lay in her eyes, not falling.

Jay looked astonished. 'What is it? You're crying!'

'No, no. I . . . it's just . . . I'm thinking about us, and it just got to me. I felt . . . I'm so happy.'

'Good grief! Women!' He laughed, mocking his own stereotypical male reaction. 'Can a man ever understand them? Hey, I'd better run, and you too. I'll call you this afternoon.'

Jill won't go away. Persistent, isn't she? Tenacious. Like you, Jennie? she asked herself.

She washed the few dishes, dabbed on eye shadow and lipstick, and, still shaken, went to work. It was a relief to know that the whole day was to be spent in the office rather than in court. Like an animal in its den, she thought, I take shelter in my small space, with its desk, books, two chairs, window high above the street, and closed door. The typist answers the telephone and will say I'm not here if I instruct her to. I haven't done that yet; I'm not entirely beaten down yet.

Jill won't go away.

Today, of all days, clients came in with children and babies. Poor women, rootless in the indifferent city, they had no place to leave them.

'This is my Ramon. He was two last week. Say hello to the lady.'

Ramon stared out of ink-black eyes, then ducked, hiding his dirty nose in his mother's skirt.

'He's a big boy for two,' Jennie said, having no idea how big two-year-olds are supposed to be.

'Yes, and strong. This is Celia. She's eight months.'

The baby, held in the bend of the woman's elbow, was

extraordinarily beautiful, with delicate features that bore no resemblance either to her mother's or her brother's. She gave Jennie a jubilant smile and reached a pink hand out to her, as if in recognition of some shared, joyful secret. Jennie took the hand, and the small fingers clung to it.

'She's lovely,' Jennie said.

The woman nodded. 'They're my diamonds, my jewels, these two.'

The words rang in Jennie's memory of ancient history, taken for two semesters at college: Roman Cornelia displayed her children: *These are my jewels.*

And this woman, too, was tired and dispossessed. She looked curious now, wondering perhaps why Jennie was still holding the baby's hand. Jennie dropped the hand.

'Well, now, let's see what we can work out for you, Mrs Fernandez.'

Late that afternoon, when Jay made his regular telephone call, he had news.

'Good or bad?'

'Both. The good is that the planning board turned down Barker's proposition. And the credit goes to you.'

Pleased, Jennie nevertheless had to examine things candidly. 'They were a good group to start with. As I told your parents, they had probably had their minds pretty much made up before I opened my mouth.'

'That's only partly true. Some of them were impressed with what you said when they met you beforehand at the house, and some only changed their minds when they heard you at the meeting. They thought you really bested the other side. The vote was close, with two dissents.'

'What's the bad news?'

'It's not so much bad as merely disagreeable. My father and a couple of others on the preservation committee have been getting a series of scurrilous, anonymous letters, mailed from ten or fifteen miles out of town. Dad read one to me over the phone. It was pretty disgusting.'

'Threats?' She thought of the vicious shove at the top of the stairs.

'In a way, but not precisely. Cleverly done, just not enough to pin down legally. But very abusive, all the same. You were mentioned, too, in some of them.'

'I'm that important? I'm flattered.'

'Apparently they feel you are. Obviously whoever's behind all this is worried about the town council's vote next month, and they're afraid you might persuade them. George Cromwell – who's on the council, you remember – says that Barker has sent in rafts of papers, more of those detailed water reports you spoke about, from a specialist this time, as well as a lot of other things. They're really worried, he says.'

'But they couldn't be the people behind those letters, could they?'

'They *could*, but somehow I don't think they are. It seems too crude for them to do. And yet, who knows? That's some rough gang in the town. Fisher's a prime example, as you found out. And our mayor might well be using him for his own purposes. Don't forget there's big money at stake. Big money. Anyway, I don't want you walking around town alone when you have to return. I'm going to stay with you.' Jay changed the subject. 'How about a movie tonight? There's a great one right around the corner from your place.'

Ordinarily, Jennie thought when she had hung up, this business of the Green Marsh wouldn't be so disturbing. She would have called it a tempest in a teapot, a bunch of disgruntled locals writing nasty letters – that was all. But she was so tense these days, and it wasn't like her.

A glass of milk might help soothe her. When she took the carton out of the refrigerator, she dropped it, and a white river slid across the floor. On her knees, wiping it up, she thought, A feather's touch will snap these nerves of mine.

And this news of Jay's was more than a feather's touch, on top of everything else. For even though there had been no further calls from Emma Dunn, the expectation of another one was ever-present, so that every ring of the telephone sounded alarm.

This anxious, expectant waiting was like a fear of falling. Once, a long time ago, she had seen a movie in which a train, having become detached from its engine, began to hurtle down from an alpine pass. Rattling and clacking down the track, slamming around curves, it sped and quickened as it descended, while the passengers, helpless, frozen, incredulous in their seats, too horrified even to scream, stared out at flying pines, angled cliffs, snowfields, tilted arcs of sky, and whirling mountains; stared down to where, thousands of feet below, doom waited. It was strange that she had no memory of how the movie ended, only of the awful helplessness.

Saturday: a difficult, disjointed day whose events had no logical relationship to one another.

In the morning there had been the trying on of the wedding outfit, which Jennie had ordered at Saks. It was only her second experience with what Shirley called 'courtier' clothes, the winter coat having been her first. Facing the mirror in the fitting room, she almost did not know herself.

Ruby velvet brought a pink cast to her face, which glowed against her bright black hair. Pleated ecru lace framed her neck and circled her wrists. The skirt lay smoothly on her narrow hips and swayed at the hem.

'It couldn't be better,' the saleswoman said with satisfaction.

No, it couldn't.

'I would suggest black sandals, very thin straps, almost no shoe at all except for heels. Very high ones, unless your man isn't . . .' The woman hesitated.

Jennie smiled. 'He's very tall.'

'Well, then. And a tiny black bag. Velvet, preferably. Or a very fine suede would do nicely.'

'You've been such a help,' Jennie said. 'I want to thank you.'

'Oh, you're easy to work with. It's been a pleasure. So many women don't know what they want.'

What I want. A clear mind. And she stared back at the mirror. You there in red velvet, dressed for your wedding, you're an impostor, you know that, don't you? You have misrepresented yourself, concealed the truth about yourself, you of all people, you who've sworn to uphold the law. You've lied, to put it plainly. Impostor!

Under a brilliant sky in motion, with a winter breeze shaking the flags all up and down Fifth Avenue, and the air just cold enough to be charged with energy, she walked toward Bergdorf Goodman, where the girls were to buy dresses for birthday parties and dancing school. Enid would have to show her how to care for these children. All of a sudden the responsibility she was to undertake loomed very large.

They were waiting for her on the ground floor: the imposing woman dressed quietly in gray with two small girls beside her. Sue and Emily stood on tiptoe to be kissed.

'Hi, Jennie.'

'Oh,' said Enid, 'is that what they call you?'

'Why, yes,' Jennie said, surprised. 'What else?'

'Aunt Jennie, I should have thought.'

'Well, either way I don't mind.'

Why did the trivial comment start up such a troubling train of thought? In the elevator; upstairs in the children's department, where they'd bought dresses in navy-blue taffeta, in white lawn and flowered challis; later, as they crossed the street and entered the Palm Court for lunch – Jennie saw darting images, like sparks, of Atlanta again, and then the same chilly reaction: *Outsider! You don't belong*. Why? For there was really no resemblance between those people and these, between that woman and this. These people had welcomed her! Yet there was something. . . . They had standards, rigid standards. Their liberalism was for the less fortunate, people from whom less was expected 'because they haven't had our advantages.'

And sitting now over chicken salad, while the little girls' big eyes were already fixed on the desserts, Jennie was aware once more of that quality of elegant, superior assurance that had been her very first impression of the Wolfes, most particularly of Enid.

No, decent as they were, they would be shocked; they would find it hard to forgive her for starting her life with their son in deceit, with a lie.

The conversation around the little table was light and pleasant. Enid made only brief mention of the Green Marsh affair, just to say that it had grown even more ugly than expected and that it seemed to be the only thing anybody talked about in town. Otherwise the talk was dominated by the children, whose day it was intended to be.

After lunch they crossed the avenue to FAO Schwarz, where Emily and Sue chose a birthday present for Donny, a life-size toy raccoon, an accurate replica complete with tail rings.

'Girls, I should say you've had a wonderful day,' said

Enid. 'And I should say it was time to take you home. You must have plans for the rest of the afternoon, Jennie. With your tight schedule you don't have time to spare, I'm sure.'

'That's true. I can always find plenty to do.'

'Well, then, we'll be leaving you here.' Enid kissed Jennie's cheek. 'Say good-bye to your Aunt Jennie, girls.'

The response was obedient. 'Good-bye, Aunt Jennie.'

Jennie watched them walk toward a taxi and thought, They have aunts, but I'm not one of them. Funny, Enid got her way. I don't mind. What difference does it make whether they call me 'aunt' or not?

I said I always had plenty to do, and I have, but I don't feel like doing it. I just feel like sitting down and doing nothing.

She crossed back over the avenue and sat down on a bench, warmed enough by the full sun to be comfortable. And drawing her coat about her, her hands thrust into the pockets, she sat for a while thinking of nothing special, just watching the traffic pass, halt, and start up again.

She couldn't have said how, or from what buried cells in her convoluted brain an impulse came, but suddenly it was there – uninvited by any conscious process; not even welcome; startling; perhaps even somewhat crazy. After only the smallest hesitation she got up and began to walk westward toward the subway. Never before having been where she was going, she had to ask for directions. At 116th Street and Broadway, she left the subway and climbed to the street. Barnard was only a short walk away. Surely no one would see any reason to question a young woman who sat on one of the campus benches, ostensibly waiting for somebody.

Nevertheless, having sat down, she felt the absurdity of being there. All right, it's foolish, foolish curiosity. I wouldn't know her if she were to stand in front of me.

How could I? Maybe she's that one in the Norwegian ski cap, walking slowly while she reads. Maybe she's one of that group, gossiping by the door. Yet perhaps I would know her through some resemblance – not to her father, God forbid. If I did see her and was sure that it was she, the curiosity would be satisfied and I'd just walk away. Isn't she the one person in the world I don't want to know?

For an hour Jennie waited. Nothing happened. There were neither hints nor clues. Girls, graceful, clumsy, sloppy, chic, dull or vivid, occasionally beautiful and occasionally ugly, passed before her. One thing they possessed in common: youth. You could only wonder what each was going to do with the years that lay ahead, or what the years would do to each, for the world in the eighties, and woman's place in it, were more complex and difficult than ever. And Jennie's chest filled with pity and nostalgia, sorrowful and tender.

As the sky went gray, the short winter afternoon turned colder. It had been a mistake to come, an aberration, and it was a good thing she hadn't recognized the girl. She ought to have known better. And shivering, she stood up and walked back to the subway. There would just be time to shower and dress before going out to dinner with Jay.

How sad it was now to feel unnatural in his presence! Bitterly she remembered how, such a little while ago, she had watched the clock's hands creep and had counted the minutes until he should ring the doorbell.

That afternoon he telephoned. 'Jennie, I've got to beg off. I've got a fever, a rotten cold coming on. I'm home in bed.'

'Oh, darling, I'm sorry. I wish I could take care of you.'

'Well, you'll have that privilege soon. I hear you had fun with Sue and Emily. They really love you, Jennie. I'm so glad.'

'I am too.'

'Jennie?'

'Yes, dear?'

'I want one of our own, yours and mine. Is that okay with you?'

'I've dreamed of it so much, Jay, with a cleft in its chin, and your eyes . . .'

'But, darling, if it should turn out that you couldn't have any, it wouldn't matter, you know that too. We'd be together and that's everything. . . . What'll you do with the evening now that I've stood you up?'

'Oh, read. I've brought some files home from the office. And go to sleep early.'

'Good. Build yourself up for Caneel. Have you got your new racket yet?'

'Next week. I've been putting everything together. Don't worry.'

'I won't. Hey, I'm sneezing my head off. I'm going to hang up.'

Actually she had not been putting everything together but had been postponing her lists and errands. These last weeks, during which she ought to have been making ready, had been too stressful to think of lists and errands. But time was growing short and tonight would be a good night to start.

With pencil and paper she began to check off. Bathing suits. Three, the good blue from last year, plus two new ones. Beach robes – to wear at lunch, Jay said. A beach bag, that flowered one she'd seen in a window; it would go with everything. A white cardigan in case of a cool night. A new folding umbrella. The old one was a wreck. Shoes for the traveling suit, navy-blue. Shoes for –

The doorbell rang. That was strange. She never had unexpected visitors. People always called first.

Cautiously she approached the door and looked

through the peephole. The hall was very dim, so that she could barely distinguish the figure that stood, miniaturized and distorted, in the tiny, round glass: a woman with full, shoulder-length hair. Jennie strained and blinked.

'Yes? Who is it?'

There was a second's pause before the voice, nervous and young, replied.

'Jill. It's Jill. Will you let me in?'

'Oh, no,' Jennie whispered. Her spine froze.

Yet, like those helpless people on the mountain train, she had known what was to come.

6

Home was more than two thousand miles away from the astonishing city that rumbled beyond the dormitory. Gladly and bravely, Jill had left it for this place; yet there were unexpected moments when, coming upon her own face in the mirror beside the bed, the memory of home flared so vividly that she could hear again the voices calling in the yard behind the house, or smell the dinner's meat broiling on the kitchen grill, or feel on her bare feet the slippery coolness of the floor in the upstairs hall. Curiously the room that Jill remembered best was not so much her own small, rose-colored bedroom – in which stuffed animals and, later, books stood on the shelves, where at bedtime the single window framed the rising stars – but rather the large room at the end of the hall where her parents slept.

There in a top drawer was kept the bedtime box of chocolates from which, after her bath and before her teeth were brushed, the treat was given. There before the bay window stood two soft, wide chairs. The one on the left was Dad's; on Sundays, if he didn't have to see any patients in the hospital, he sat and read, scattering the paper around his feet. The opposite chair was the 'story chair,' wide enough for Jill and Mom to sit together while Mom read aloud.

At the foot of the enormous bed, whenever there was

a new baby in the family, stood the bassinet. Refurbished each time with fresh ribbons and netting, it remained until the baby was old enough to be comfortable in a regular crib in a room of its own.

'Very tiny babies like tiny spaces,' Mom explained, 'because they've just come out of a tiny, warm place, you see.'

That must have been the second time, when Lucille was born. Jill was four, and she remembered how her mother had grown fat and suddenly been thin again as soon as Lucille came out of her tummy. When Jerry had been born, Jill had been a baby herself, not even two years old, so she didn't remember him. But Lucille's arrival was clear in her mind.

A tiny, warm place. That was puzzling because the baby looked too big to have been inside anybody.

'Was I inside of you too?' Jill asked.

'No,' her mother said. 'You were inside another lady's tummy.'

Well, that was all right. It wasn't important. For a long time she thought no more about it, although it was odd that later, when she did begin to think about it, that scene could revive itself and be so sharply drawn: Lucille wrapped tight in a flannel cocoon, Jill at the head of the bassinet, and her mother dressed in something long, with black shapes on white.

Years later she asked, 'Mom, did you ever have a bath-robe or a housecoat that was black-and-white, plaid or flowered, maybe?'

'Why, yes. I had a Japanese kimono that Dad bought on our trip to Japan before we had you. It was beautiful, black peonies on white silk. I wore it till it fell apart. What makes you ask?'

'I don't know. It just suddenly came into my mind.'

But that was much later. Her childhood was crowded,

the days were full, and the neighborhood was filled with children. Relatives came and went in the afternoons. She supposed, when she was older and learned about sibling rivalry and jealousy, that the reason she hadn't suffered them as much as she might have was that there were so many laps for a little girl to sit on, so many arms to hug her. If her parents were momentarily too busy with a younger child to play a game with Jill or take her somewhere, there were always Aunt Fay, two sets of grandparents, and three sets of cousins.

People smiled at her and praised her red hair. When she started school, every morning Mom tied it back with ribbons to match her sweaters and skirts. Once, as she left the living room where Mom was having coffee with a friend, she heard the friend say, 'Such a lovely child, Irene. And what luck she brought you! To think you had three of your own after you adopted her!'

'Yes,' Mom said, 'she brought us luck.'

But weren't there 'four of your own'? If you were adopted, were you not really Dad's and Mom's 'own'? By then, of course, Jill knew the meaning of the word *adopted*. And that night when Mom came to tuck her into bed, Jill drew her down on the bed.

'Stay here,' she said.

Mom took her hand. 'Is it a story you want, Jill? A short one then, a chapter in *Winnie-the-Pooh*, because this is a school night.'

'No.' The question she wanted to ask seemed babyish for a girl in third grade, a girl in the advanced reading group.

'What, then?'

Jill, clinging to the hand, shook her head.

'Please. If anything's troubling you, you'll feel better if you tell me.'

The question burst out of her mouth. 'Do I belong to you? Like Jerry and Lucille and the baby?'

'Oh,' Mom said. 'Oh.' She pulled Jill from under the blanket and rocked her. 'What makes you ask that? Did anybody say . . . ?' And without waiting for an answer, she rushed on. 'Belong to us! You are our dearest, beautiful, big girl, our very own. . . . Why, everybody loves you, Grandma and Grandpa, and Aunt Fay . . . and Dad and I most of all. Why, of course you belong to us. Why, whom else would you belong to?'

She pressed her cheek into Mom's neck and whispered, 'I thought maybe to the lady who grew me.'

'Oh,' Mom said very softly. And she waited such a long time before answering that Jill drew back to look into her face. It was very serious, the way it had been when they had that talk about taking things out of the medicine chest.

'No, darling. You don't belong to her anymore.'

'What was her name?'

'I don't know, Jill.'

'Was she nice?'

'She was very nice, I'm sure, because she had you.'

'But why did she give me to you?'

'Well . . . well, it's a little hard to explain. You see, sometimes things happen to people, like not having any money, for instance, not having a nice house with room for a little girl. So you see, since she loved you and wanted you to have all that, and since we wanted a little girl very, very much, so . . . well, that's how it happened. Do you understand?'

Jill supposed it made sense enough. 'But is there any more?'

'Any more to tell? Oh, yes! We were so happy, Dad and I. We ran out right away and bought the bassinet. You were the first baby to sleep in it. You were one day old when we brought you home, younger than Jerry or Lucille or Sharon. Remember how small Sharon was a year ago? Well, you were even smaller.'

'And I had red hair.'

Mom laughed. 'Not right away. You were bald, like all my babies.'

All my babies. Mom's voice had a warm, good feeling, a sleepy feeling. After a while Mom laid her back down in the bed and drew the blanket up. She pulled the blinds down, kissed Jill's cheek, came back to kiss her again, and closed the door.

My babies. We wanted a little girl so much. Then it was a good thing to be adopted. It meant that you were really wanted. People wouldn't go to such trouble to get you, buying houses and high chairs and carriages and all that stuff, if they didn't want you.

No one in the neighborhood ever asked Jill about being adopted, because most people knew it, anyway; but she wouldn't have minded if they had asked. It could, in a way, be a distinction, like bringing home an excellent report card, or knowing how to get the dinners ready that whole week after Mom had broken a bone in her foot. Being adopted was only another aspect of her *self*, like having freckles on her arm or being sure on skis – all things taken for granted and therefore seldom thought about.

One day the sixth-grade teacher gave an assignment. They had been talking in class about how America was made up of people who had come from many different places, bringing their differing customs and experiences. Now they were to find out all they could about their own ancestors and draw a family tree.

'See how far back you can go,' the teacher said.

One boy in the class had an Indian great-grandfather and was very proud of being a 'Native American.' Another boy knew his great-great-grandmother, who was ninety-seven and could tell about coming to New Mexico when it was still a wilderness.

'It's really fun,' the teacher said. 'In learning about your ancestors, you'll be surprised what you learn about yourselves. So ask plenty of questions!'

After supper that evening, Jill walked over to her grandparents' house. Mom's parents had both died a few years before, but Dad's were healthy and lively; they were immediately interested in Jill's project.

'You would have enjoyed my father,' Grandpa said. 'He was a great dancer. When he was an old man, he could still do the peasant dances he'd learned when he grew up in Hungary. You should have seen him! He had a strong heart and a lot of good humor.'

Gran wrote down the names of her parents and even remembered the maiden names of her grandmothers. She added anecdotes. Jill saw that Grandpa and Gran were both enjoying themselves. Reluctant to let her go, they made her sit down at the table for lemonade and cake. A sudden stream of sea-green light from the spring evening outside fell on the table across from Jill, lay on the man's graying head, touched the woman's manicured nails, and traveled up to her tanned, plump, animated face. It was at this moment that Jill had a profound sensation of separateness.

All of this has nothing to do with me, she thought. It is not my history.

At the proper time, careful not to hurt their feelings by making an abrupt departure, she thanked them and walked home. Boys from the high school were playing baseball in the field. At the corner house, the father was tending his carefully irrigated lawn; it would be dead and brown by June, no matter what he did. From the house opposite Jill's, piano music tinkled. Everything was cheerfully familiar, yet she felt distant from it, faintly sad.

At home they were all on the back patio. From the front hall she could see their dark heads clustered, bent over something on a table – a newspaper or a map. She went quickly upstairs to her room and stood before the full-length mirror to study herself. Her face was long and narrow, not like any of theirs. Already she was taller than Mom. Jerry and Sharon looked like Mom, while Lucille looked like Dad's father. She brought her hair forward over her shoulders. Bronze glinted in the copper ends; the sun had laid gold streaks from temple to crown. Who had given her this hair? Or these teeth that were being straightened, when everyone else in the house had even teeth?

On her desk lay a sample family tree. She sat down and began to draw a copy, filling in the spaces: Mother, Irene Miller; Father, Jonas Miller. She put the pen aside, and sat gazing out at the blank sky. Night fell abruptly, as if a shade had been lowered. There were noises downstairs as the cat was called in and doors were shut. The brother and the sisters came up arguing over first use of the shower. Because Jill's room was dark, no one came looking for her, and she sat alone, not exactly close to tears but very still inside, troubled by the strange new sadness.

Her light flashed on. 'Jill!' Mom cried. 'We wondered what took you so long. Dad called Gran just now and she said you'd left an hour ago. You scared us.' From over Jill's shoulder she looked at the blank paper. 'Tell me, what's wrong?'

Jill swiveled on the chair. 'This. I can't do it.' And now her eyes grew wet. 'If I put down all I know, it'll be a lie.'

'I don't think that's the kind of lie, if you want to call it one, that matters. Just write down everything you know about our family. You're part of it.' Staunchly Mom added, 'Write it as if you were Jerry or Lucille or Sharon. Or the baby.'

Jill whispered. 'But I'm not any of them. I'm me.'

Mom closed the door. 'Sit in a comfortable chair,' she commanded. 'We need to talk, you and I.'

Now that the moment for some sort of revelation was apparently here, Jill was afraid. It was like opening a box received from strange hands; you didn't know what might jump out, a bomb or snakes.

Trembling, she asked, 'What about?'

'About what's obviously on your mind. I promise I'll tell you as much as I know.'

'What did she look like?' Jill whispered.

'I was told,' Mom said evenly, 'that she had dark, curly hair like mine. They try to make a close match. So maybe she was much like me.'

'I see. And my father?'

'They never told us.'

'I wish I knew their names.'

'That can't be, darling.'

'I suppose they weren't married.'

'No.'

'It's all right, Mom. I'm twelve. I know about things like that. She got pregnant and he wouldn't marry her.'

'I don't know whether it happened as you're putting it, that he wouldn't. Maybe he couldn't. They were both so young, not halfway through college. It must have been very perplexing, very hard for each of them.'

'They should have thought of that before they ... did things,' Jill said, feeling unexpected anger.

'People don't always think, Jill.'

'You always say – a girl, especially – you tell me it's wrong to let boys do things.'

'I know I do. And yes, it is wrong. But still, when people do wrong things, we try to understand them and forgive, don't we?'

An image formed itself: In tall grass a girl lay looking

up into the eyes of the boy who bent over her. The image was alluring and at the same time repellent; at the movies one waited to see what would come next, and yet one didn't know whether one wanted to see it. And if the boy and the girl were one's father and mother . . .

Mom was watching Jill. The corners of her mouth turned up into a fraction of a smile, but her eyes were anxious. It was the expression she wore when a child hurt himself and had to be comforted, an expression grown familiar over the years, as were the parallel creases on her forehead, or the small gold studs that she wore every day in her ears.

'Don't we, Jill?' she repeated, and continued, 'You shouldn't blame her. She didn't do anything bad. She made a mistake, that's all.'

'May I come in?' Dad knocked. 'Or is this a private conversation?'

'No, come in. Jill and I are having a talk about her birth.'

'Oh, are you?' Dad sat down and frowned a little, as though he were prepared to listen hard.

'I think Jill's bothered because her birth mother wasn't married,' Mom said. 'I think she feels that makes her different from other children, from her friends. Am I right, Jill?'

Dad took his glasses off and put them back on. Somehow the gesture made him seem serious and wise. It's the way he must look when he talks to patients in his office, Jill thought.

'Listen, Ladybug,' he said. 'I'm going to say a very selfish thing. If that poor young girl hadn't had so much trouble, we'd never have had you. And you're one of the best things that ever happened to your mother and me. Don't you know that? Don't you?'

She nodded.

'And I think – I hope – we've been best for you.'

'I know.' Close to crying, now that they were giving her all their earnest attention, she forced herself not to. 'But what I need to know is . . . Oh, you've told me she had no way to care for me, and I guess I understand that, but still, how could she have done it? Could you give Mark away?'

The parents glanced at each other. They were thinking, probably, of Mark in his crib right now. He slept with a teddy bear on either side, which made three heads on his pillow. When you went to see him asleep, you smelled talcum powder.

It was Mom who spoke first. 'Yes. If we had no home and couldn't give him what he needs, we love him so much that we would.'

'Think of how she must have loved you to do what she did,' Dad said. 'Think of that. And then try not to think of it anymore, if you can. You have a whole, good, wonderful life ahead, with so much to do.' He laid his hand on Jill's knee; the hand made firm pressure, as if he *owned* her, and that felt good. She wanted them to *own* her. When she put her hand over Dad's, the lump of tears melted away out of her throat.

'Anything else you want to say, Ladybug?'

'Well, I have to finish the family tree.'

'Let's see.' Dad examined the paper. 'You have two choices. You can tell the teacher why you don't want to do it, or –'

Mom interrupted. 'I can write a note of explanation instead.'

'Yes. Or you can fill in the spaces with the information you have. Either way will be all right.'

They were both standing over her, smiling, but their raised eyebrows were questioning. She felt that she was expected to smile in return, and actually now, seeing them there so united and solid together, she began to feel more like doing so.

'It's late,' Mom said. 'So finish your homework.' Her no-nonsense voice was comforting too. 'Skip the shower tonight, for once. You need your sleep more.'

Alone again, Jill took up the pen. Two choices, there were. She thought hard and in less than a minute had made one. One path led nowhere, just trailed off into darkness, as in those closed canyons that they sometimes saw when hiking in the Jerez Mountains. The other was a straight road to be traveled on a clear day.

So she took up the pen and started to fill in the spaces. Father: Jonas Miller, born 1940, in Phoenix. Mother: Irene Stone, born 1942, in Albuquerque. Grandfather: Otto J. Miller, born 1915 . . .

To say that as she grew toward, and finally into, adolescence, Jill was afflicted by heavy doubts about her birth would be untrue. She was too active, too successful, and too secure within her family for that. Yet it would be equally untrue to say that she never doubted again.

In certain circumstances the subject was jolted abruptly back into her consciousness, there to lie and trouble her until with effort she was able to argue it away. As she grew older it became more difficult to argue it away.

On a weekend camping trip with friends near Taos, the sun deceived her on a windy day, burning hot enough through the clouds to raise painful blisters.

'People with your complexion have to be wary of the sun,' the strange doctor admonished kindly. 'If you've got brothers and sisters, tell them to guard against skin cancer. It's the price red-haired families pay for their beauty.'

Her hair was such a marker! Sometimes she almost wished she didn't have it. For if her hair had been brown like the rest of the family's, would she have thought so much about herself? Now, whenever she saw a tall, red-headed woman in her thirties, she thought: Could she be the one? Briefly her heart would thump and then subside as she remembered what Mom had told her about dark, curly hair. Was it the father, then?

The bad thing was that such questioning made her feel not only that vague, recurring, quiet sadness but guilt besides. Why was she not able to accept her good life as it was?

In the summer before her senior year in high school, Gran, who had taught French, took Jill and Lucille to France. It was adventure and delight; the three were to speak no English if they could help it, even to one another. They traveled on local trains and buses to villages off the tourist track. They walked on country roads and ate basket lunches in the shade of the plane trees. Gran was young enough to keep up with the girls' pace, while the girls were old enough to care about the museums and cathedrals that Gran knew so well.

They spent the last few days in luxury, resting at the sea at Eze-sur-Mer. The hotel was filled with Germans, British, and Americans. One evening after Lucille and Gran had gone up to their rooms, Jill became acquainted with a girl of her own age who had, like herself, been observing in the center of the garden an enormous, room-size cage, filled with exotic, tropical birds. They ordered ice cream and sat talking on the terrace.

The girl, Harriet, was friendly and blunt. 'Are you here with your family?'

'My grandmother and my sister.'

'Oh, is she your sister? You don't look at all like her, do you?'

Jill could not have said why she replied as she did. 'I'm adopted,' she said.

'Really? So am I.'

For a moment neither girl spoke. Then Jill said, 'You're the only person I've ever met who's like me.'

'You've probably met plenty but didn't know it. People don't talk about it. I know I don't.'

'That's true. I never said it till now.'

'I think it's really nobody's business, is it?'

'That's true, too, but I don't believe that's the reason.'

'No? Then what is?'

'I think it's because we – I, at least – don't want to think about it.'

Harriet drew her chair closer, and Jill understood that this stranger was feeling the same emotion that had just swept her: a sense of close understanding never felt before with anyone else.

'I said I don't want to, but I do think about it,' Jill said.

'I don't. Not anymore.'

'You don't want to know who your mother was, at least?' Jill asked softly.

'I know who she was – is. I've seen her.'

Jill was aghast. 'How did that happen? Tell me,' she begged.

'I was born in Connecticut. It's one of only four states that don't keep sealed records.'

'Is Nebraska one of them?'

'No. And let me tell you, when records are sealed, they're sealed. You'll get nowhere, so best forget it.'

'I can't forget it. The older I get, the more I seem to need –' Jill's voice cracked and she stopped.

The other girl waited for a considerable time, until Jill was ready to speak again.

'Tell me. What was it like when you saw her?'

Harriet looked away at the squawking birds and the sea beyond the rocks. 'She was drunk,' she said. She looked down squarely at Jill. 'I've never told anyone except my father and mother, but I'll tell you because I'll never see you again and because ... well, I see you need to know. So this is it. She was awful. She was tragic and terrible. She's married – he looked as if he liked his liquor too. They had two boys, my half brothers. They were fighting when I got there. The house was filthy. I don't know where my original father is, and I doubt that she knows, either. She clung to me and cried and begged me to come back again. Yet in a way I don't think she really wanted me to. I think she was ashamed. We had nothing to say to each other.' Harriet paused. 'It was another world.'

The brutal images darkened Jill's spirit. 'Have you ever seen her again?' she asked.

'That happened three years ago, and I've gone once every year since, during Christmas vacations. I live in Washington, and I'm glad I'm no nearer. We write to each other, although there's not much to write about. They're – she's – kind, and I feel – I don't exactly know what I feel about her, except that I'm awfully sorry for her and awfully glad I have the parents I have. As I said, it was another world.'

'I suppose you wish you'd never found her.'

'No, to tell the truth, I don't. It's much better this way. I don't have to worry and dream anymore. Now I know.'

Gran was reading in the next room when Jill went upstairs. 'I saw you from the windows, so I knew you were all right. You had a long talk with that girl. Is she nice?'

'Very. She's adopted. We were talking about it.'

Gran was silent.

'She met her mother. Her birth mother.'

Gran looked over the top of her reading glasses at Jill; the look was long and touched with pity.

'I don't think that's a good thing at all, Jill,' she said.

Now Jill was the silent one. And her grandmother asked, 'Was it a good experience for her, did she say?'

Jill was not going to betray a confidence, so she answered only, 'I don't know.'

'It could destroy another family, you know. What if the woman was married now and hadn't told her husband about the child? What about any other children she might have? Or her own parents, for that matter? The damage could be fearful.'

'One could be very careful about all that.'

When Gran took her glasses off, Jill saw that her eyes were very troubled.

'You could be – if it's you we're talking about, and I assume it is – you could be totally rejected. We don't want you to be hurt that way, Jill.'

'I think I'd like to take that chance,' Jill said, very low.

Gran sighed. 'There's something more. Have you thought how you might hurt your parents?'

'I would ask them first. I would explain how I love them and that this has nothing to do with my love for them.' Jill crossed the room and put her hand on her grandmother's shoulder. 'Are you annoyed with me, Gran?'

'No. But I'm unhappy because you are. Will you think this over more carefully, Jill? Think further and then, if you must, talk to your father and mother about it when we get home.'

So she thought some more but still held back from bringing up the subject when she got home. Arguing with herself, she could see conflicting possibilities. Suppose the woman who had given birth to her turned out to be a tragic disappointment like Harriet's drunken mother? On the other hand, the girl had said, in spite of it all, she was relieved at last to know. . . . And then, of course, that first mother might well be the loveliest woman on earth, kind, wise, beautiful. . . . Somewhere she breathed and lived – oh, she was too young to have died! – but where?

On a dim, rainy, Saturday afternoon, Jill and Mom, alone in the house, were cooking together, baking bread and pies for the next day's dinner with guests. It was a pleasant custom. Mom had taken a course with a pastry chef and was now teaching her daughters.

But today Mom, humming while she peeled apples, was distracted and unlike herself. Wondering, Jill glanced at her from across the floured board and caught a glance in return.

'You've had something on your mind for a while, haven't you?' Mom asked.

Jill evaded the question. 'I don't know what you mean.'

'Gran told us about your talk when you were away. We waited for you to say something, but you didn't. I suppose we should have spoken first. I suppose we hoped you'd forget, but I see you haven't.'

'I've tried,' Jill murmured.

Her mother went to the stove, moved a pot that needed no moving, and came back.

'There's something Dad and I intended to give you when you were eighteen. But last night we decided to let you have it now. I'll go upstairs and get it.'

In a moment she returned and handed Jill a letter, saying, 'Let's sit on the sofa in the den.'

The handwriting was feminine but firm. Curious and apprehensive because of Mom's solemnity, Jill began to read. There was only a single sheet, and she scanned it in moments.

Dear Child,

I'm hoping that the parents who bring you up will give you this when you grow old enough to understand it. The mother who will give you birth and the boy who fathered you are good people but foolish, as I hope you won't be. We were too young to fit you into our lives. Maybe we were selfish, too, wanting to go on with our plans undisturbed. Some people wanted me to do away with you – to abort you – but I couldn't do that. You were already growing, and I had to let you grow to fulfillment. I had to let you have your own life. I hope with all my heart that it will be a wonderful one. I will give you away only to wonderful people who want you, and who will do more for you than I can. I hope you will understand that I am doing this out of love for you, although it may not seem much like love. But it is, believe me, my daughter or my son. It is.

'Oh, my God!' Jill cried. 'Oh, my God.' She put her hands over her face and rocked and cried.

'I know, I know,' Mom whispered, and, taking hold, laid Jill's head on her shoulder. So they sat close, holding each other.

After a long time Jill sat up, wiping her eyes. 'I've gotten your shoulder all wet.'

'It's nothing, nothing. Are you all right?'

'It's a beautiful letter. . . . I can't believe I'm holding it in my hand. Such a beautiful letter.'

'Yes, I cried, too, when I first read it.'

'If only she'd signed her name!'

'Darling, you're missing the point. That's the last thing she would have done. She wanted confidentiality above all things. She was scared. She felt threatened.'

For a while Jill considered, imagining herself in a situation like that, but she wasn't able to make it ring true.

'Maybe,' she said, 'since so much time has passed, she's changed her mind and wishes she could see me.'

'It's possible. But even so, I don't know what either she or you could do about it. That's the law.'

'I think it's wrong, and I'm not the only one who thinks so. I've read that there are lots of people and active organizations who are trying to change it. Don't you agree they should?'

'I'm not sure I do. There's much to be said about keeping a child secure in one family, with one loyalty and no conflicts.'

'A child, yes,' Jill countered. She was beginning to feel a renewed impulse toward action. 'But not an adult. Mom – in a few more months I'll be eighteen.'

'I know that.' The mother's voice was touched with sadness.

And Jill, at once aware of the sadness, put her arms around her. 'Mom, you'll always be my mother. You've done everything for me, you've been –'

'Oh, when I think of what we went through to get you!' Now the sadness merged into laughter. 'References and investigations, a thousand questions. We were so afraid we wouldn't be as perfect as the agency seemed to think we ought to be. And when finally we came to get you, that raw November day, it was sleeting and we had you wrapped like an Eskimo . . .'

So they sat and talked all the rest of the afternoon, while the rain splashed from the eaves and sluiced the windows and the dinner went uncooked.

It was decided: Dad would go to Nebraska with Jill and find out what they could.

'It looks the same,' he said as they drove up in the car they had rented at the airport. 'I wonder whether Mrs Burt is still here.'

Down the long corridor between the mansion's library and solarium, Jill followed him. She thought, My mother walked here. Right here.

'You all right, Ladybug?' Dad asked.

'Fine. I'm fine.'

Dad went into the office. 'I want to pave the way, show

my credentials as a doctor – it might carry a little weight, who knows? And make clear that you've come with your parents' blessing.'

Jill sat down in the anteroom, a beige, neat place with comfortable chairs and magazines. It was the waiting room of a doctor or lawyer in any prosperous community. Hearts beat faster in these waiting rooms, she thought.

After a long time Dad came out to her. He whispered, 'Mrs Burt retired two years ago. This one's not the most lovable person in the world, but come on in, anyway, and do your best.'

The young woman behind the desk was attractive, but she didn't smile when Jill was introduced. She was a businesslike type.

'Your father has told me what you want,' she began, addressing Jill. 'Surely you must know you can't have it.'

'I suppose I hoped,' Jill murmured.

'The records are sealed. The original birth certificate, not the new one issued after your adoption became legal, is in the hands of the state, in the Bureau of Vital Statistics. And sealed,' she repeated. It was as if she were slamming the door.

Nevertheless Jill persevered. 'But your records here? I thought – oh, I want so much to know, only to know!' And realizing that she had clasped her hands in supplication, she unclasped them and continued in a reasonable tone, 'I hoped you would understand and help me.'

'But you knew better, Doctor,' the woman said to Jill's father. Her manner was respectful, yet it contained a reprimand.

'Yes, I knew. But there is here a psychological need that can't just be ignored.'

'It is curiosity, Doctor.'

'I differ with you. It is more than that.'

'If we were to satisfy all these requests, then the

promises that were made to the original mothers would be worthless, wouldn't they?'

During this exchange Jill's eyes rested on the desk. A Lucite nameplate stood facing away from her. She had a quick knack of reading either backward or upside down: Amanda Karch, it read. Behind it lay a large legal-size file. Clearly it must be the agency's private record of her birth. She felt a surge of ferocious anger. Here lay the truth only a few feet away, and this woman, knowing the truth and seeing as she must Jill's awful need for it, refused it. By what right? This insignificant bureaucrat, this self-important –

And suppressing her anger, she asked quietly, 'Are there ever any circumstances in which records are unsealed?'

'Very rarely. You have to convince the courts that you have good cause; for example, a serious illness that is difficult to diagnose and which might be genetic, or a severe illness of a psychiatric nature that might be a threat to sanity. Rare situations.'

'I see.'

'None applies to you.'

Jill did not answer. Her eyes returned to the file and stayed there.

'I would advise you to dismiss this from your mind. You have, so your father told me, no other problems. Then you're a lucky young woman, aren't you?'

'Yes,' Jill said.

Dad took her hand as he spoke. 'Needless to say, Miss . . .'

'Karch.'

'Miss Karch. Needless to say, we are terribly disappointed.'

The woman half rose, dismissing them. 'I understand, Dr Miller. But I can only tell you again, for your own good, put this out of your mind. Don't let this useless question become a neurotic obsession. Don't disrupt your lives.'

'Thank you very much,' Dad said.

They were driving back to the airport when Dad suddenly drew over to the side of the road.

'What do you think, Jill? Shall we go home? Have you got any other ideas?'

Miserable in her defeat, she answered with a question. 'What idea could I have?'

'Taking it to court.'

'You heard what she said about that.'

'Cold fish,' Dad muttered. 'Though I suppose she must know what she's talking about.'

'It would cost so much to get lawyers, Dad.'

'Don't worry about that.' He started the car. 'As soon as we get home, I'll make some inquiries. Now let's have a bite to eat. Dinner on the plane won't amount to much.'

It was late evening when the plane began its descent over New Mexico. The mesas threw dark blue shadows over the brick-red earth. To those who knew nothing about this land, the cliffs were no more than immense walls of rock. But to those who knew it well, they were the home of an ancient people. Down there the mesquite grew, the piñon pine shook in the wind, and the river ran. Jill stretched and craned to see whether she could identify any familiar places.

'Remember the time we started on a Sunday and Jerry forgot the water bottles?' Dad asked. 'Which reminds me, I think we're going to win the battle for the farmers over those water rights. It's a hell of a thing, diverting water from farms to supply a resort hotel for dudes.'

Jill understood his attempt to take her mind off her problem. It saddened her to see her father look so troubled, and she said quickly, 'Dad, you don't have to humor me. I've lost today, but I'm not down-and-out, and I'm not giving up.'

A month or so later Dad reported the results of his investigation. There was indeed no chance at all of winning in court. Attorneys here at home, as in Nebraska, were positive about it. The court required good cause, and Jill had no good cause.

She took the news stoically. By that time she had been admitted to Barnard College in New York and had her game plan in place. Once there, she would seek out one of the adoptee organizations about which she had read. Others in her situation had been successful, so there was hope for her.

With some bitterness she remembered the warnings of that chilly woman at the home for unwed mothers. She had called Jill's search an obsession. Well, it was as good a word as any, she supposed.

So she packed her new clothes with many differing emotions: sorrow at leaving home, excitement about her new life in New York, pride in her achievement – and the obsession.

The organization's office was in a wing of a simple, private home in a small town not far from the city. There were two little rooms, in each a desk and a row of green metal filing cabinets.

'We're a small group,' said Emma Dunn. 'I'm a retired social worker, and this has become my full-time project. I'm adopted myself, you see. Mr Riley is the sole other staff member and the rest are volunteers, a few of them teachers, psychologists, a couple of lawyers, and the others just plain good people. Now sit down and tell me about yourself.'

When Jill's brief story was finished, she nodded. 'It's

the usual beginning. Do you have your birth certificate? I mean, it goes without saying, the certificate that was given out after you were adopted.'

'It's at home.'

'We'll need it, unless you know the names of the hospital and the doctor.'

'I do, but he wouldn't tell anything, I'm sure.'

'You said your father's a doctor. Could he get in touch with this doctor? Sometimes doctors do things for each other.'

Foolish, Jill thought. It wouldn't work. But she conceded that it would be worth a try.

When she phoned home that night, Dad agreed to try, as she had known he would. A few days later he called back. His voice had a downbeat.

'It didn't work, Jill. He's an old man, still in practice, and very sympathetic. But he can't break the law. He made that clear, and I understood. I was even a little embarrassed about having asked him to.'

'Thank you, Dad. Thank you, anyway.'

'Is everything else all right, Jill? Working hard? Having fun?'

'Yes to both. New York's wonderful. I've made friends and I love it, but I'm thinking of Christmas vacation and coming home too.'

'So are we, dear. We miss you terribly.'

'Christmas vacation' put a thought in her head. How would it be to take a detour on the way home with a stopover in Nebraska? Suppose she were to see the doctor herself? Maybe a nurse or secretary could be approached. The thought turned into a resolution and stayed with her through the term.

Accordingly, on a day of bitter cold, with snow high on the western plains, she found herself sitting before still another desk opposite a white-haired, partially deaf old man. The lighted windows from the building across the narrow street enlivened the dark afternoon. When he had finished, very kindly and clearly repeating to Jill what he had already told her father, the doctor remarked, 'You're looking at the hospital where you were born.'

Quite dispirited by now, Jill only nodded.

'I only wish I could help you, young lady. I really wish it. But if I were to speak those words to you, they would haunt me. I've never stepped outside of the law, and I'm too old to start now.'

'Words? What words?'

'Your record. When your father called and gave me the date of your birth, I went back to my dusty files. I only delivered one baby that day, a girl.'

Jill's eyes filled. So close, so close again . . . right there on the desk.

The old man coughed and bent down to open a drawer. 'Darn those pills. I never know where they are.'

And Jill leaned forward. On a typed sheet she had time to recognize only one name upside down: Peter . . . Alger something . . . Mendes. She drew back just as the old man's head came up.

'I'm really sorry I can't help you, my dear.'

She had to get out of the office fast, to write down the name. Her heart was hammering. Had she imagined a twinkle in the doctor's eye? He'd given her a bit of a chance without breaking the law. Whoever this Mendes was, it was a clue, at least. Perhaps he was a relative or a friend of her mother's. Or perhaps he was her own father?

At home late that night, trembling, she told her parents.

'Peter Alger,' Mom said.

'Not Alger. There were more letters.'

Mom reflected. 'What else could it be but Algernon?'

'It's an odd name,' Dad said. 'Why does it ring a bell in my head?'

'You've heard it?' Jill cried.

'It seems to me I've seen it. Seems to me that I read it in some periodical. Maybe he's a doctor who wrote something in one of the medical journals. Well, I'll have one of the girls in the office go through the medical directory on Monday. There are lists of all the physicians in the United States, you know.'

'No, not a doctor,' Dad reported on Monday evening. 'Still, that name bothers me. It's the Algernon that sticks in my mind. Maybe I'm imagining the whole thing, yet I seem to see it on a page and see myself reading in the office, the way I do when I eat my sandwich for lunch. Doesn't seem to be too long ago, either.'

'Well, what do you generally read, then, besides medical journals?' asked Mom.

'A lot of things. All the magazines for the waiting room, *National Geographic*, *The Smithsonian*, besides all the popular stuff. And then my special-interest pamphlets and brochures, Bureau of Indian Affairs, the Sierra Club – whatever's lying around.'

'You'll never find it,' Jill said.

'Don't say that. The more I think about it, the more sure I am that I saw that name within the past year. And we generally keep things on the shelves for a year or so. They fill up the space and look nice.'

It's a wild-goose chase, Jill thought. And yet one never knows.

The winter passed, the summer came and went, and the sophomore year began. She had gone back to Emma Dunn and given her the name for whatever use the committee might be able to make of it. And then one evening Dad telephoned.

'You're not going to believe this! I've found Mendes. It was in an article on Indian archaeology that came today. He's a professor of archaeology in Chicago. Wait, here it is. Write this down. . . . What are you going to do, write to him?'

'I think I'll telephone right now,' Jill said. 'I wouldn't be able to sleep tonight if I didn't.'

'Okay, good girl! Call us back. Let us know what happens.'

How to begin? 'Hello, my name is Jill Miller. I read about you, and are you a relative of mine'? No, that was stupid. He wouldn't know Jill Miller from a hole in the wall. Just tell him the truth.

She was weak in the knees, but she obtained the number from Information and dialed it. A brisk voice answered. When she had given her name and identified herself as a student at Barnard, she began:

'I have a strange request. I was adopted at birth, and I'm looking for my parents. Somehow, by accident, I came across your name, and I wondered whether you know anything about . . . about who I am.'

There was a pause before a reply came. 'Where was it that you found my name? In what state?'

'In Nebraska. That's where I was born, in a home for unwed mothers. But I'm speaking from New York now. Are you perhaps a relative of my mother's?'

'Tell me' – and now the man's voice was no longer brisk – 'tell me how old you are.'

'Nineteen.'

There was a long, long pause. Jill thought he had left the telephone.

'Mr Mendes? Are you still there?'

'Oh, God, yes, I'm here.'

'Mr Mendes? Do you know my mother?'

'I knew her.'

She thought the man might be crying, and she was suddenly afraid. There was a beating, a wild throb in her head. Her voice came in a whisper.

'Her name? What was her name?'

And the man's voice trembled back. 'Janine. She was called Jennie . . .'

Jennie. Dark curly hair. That's all I know. But this man, at the other end of the wire, knows the rest.

She gripped the phone. 'You do understand that you have to tell me everything, don't you? It's not right to let people suffer –'

'She was Jennie Rakowsky. We were at college together. She's a year younger than I, and we –' He stopped.

Jill had to lean against the wall. 'Then you – you must be – are you?'

'Yes. Oh, yes! My God, I don't believe this. Out of nowhere. I want to see you. Can I see you? When can I?'

'Oh, you can . . . you can. But where is my mother?'

'I don't know. I haven't seen her since, nor heard.'

Jill wept. 'It's so terrible! And still . . . I looked so long. I tried. How can I find her?'

'I'll give you the address where she lived in Baltimore. And my address. I want to see you. Jill, what do you look like?'

'I'm tall; I have red hair. Long red hair.'

'I have red hair. Jill, give me your address and your telephone number. Let me call you back, this is an expensive call.'

'It doesn't matter.'

'How did you find me?'

'I'll write and tell you. My father saw your name. He reads about Indians, we live in New Mexico –'

'Out of nowhere. My God, out of nowhere you came.'

She hardly slept. She called home with her astonishing news and on Saturday took the train to Baltimore, where she went to the address that Peter Mendes had given. It was a row house on a poor street. A black woman answered the door. No, she had never heard the name. The people behind her, they were named Danieli, they had been here for years, and maybe they knew. Oh, yes, they remembered the Rakowskys, but they had moved away years ago, after the father died. Jennie Rakowsky had been a sweet girl, pretty, and so smart. No, they had no idea where to look for her.

On Sunday she telephoned Peter Mendes to report.

'I thought of something yesterday, Jill.' He was excited. 'I phoned you but you had already left. It's this. Jennie always wanted to be a lawyer. There's a national directory of lawyers. I was stupid not to have thought of it before. It's Sunday, so I can't search, but tomorrow I will, and I'll let you know.'

Again she hardly slept. 'Sweet, pretty, and so smart,' they'd said. He was tall and had red hair. Even over the telephone you could tell he was sensitive and good. Peter and Jennie. Jennie and Peter. All day she walked around with the awareness of their existence overlying every thought.

Late in the afternoon, Peter telephoned. 'Jill, imagine, she's in New York! She's an attorney; she got her wish. I have the address for you.'

Jennie in New York. And all last year we were both here and didn't know it. When I tell Dad and Mom – I've got to tell them tonight.

'Jill, I think you should go easy. She wanted, insisted, on secrecy. You mustn't call her the way you called me. It's too much of a shock.'

'I wouldn't have done it to you the way I did if I had known who you were.'

'It didn't harm me. But it might harm her. She may have a family, probably does. Be careful, that's all I'm saying.'

'I will be. Oh, I will be! I've been working with an adoption organization, and I'll ask them what to do.'

'Good idea. And I'll keep in touch with you. I can't wait

to see you. Send me a picture in the meantime, and I'll send one to you. Jill, is this real? I keep asking myself . . .'

Emma Dunn brought Mr Riley to hear Jill's story, which she poured out in a rush, her words tumbling and falling, her face flushed and her hands waving in emphasis. She saw that they were both moved.

'I have to see them! I'm going to Chicago to see Peter, but first Jennie. Imagine! So close. I could probably walk to where she is.'

'Well, don't do that, Jill. Let us do it for you. We've seen too many of these meetings end in great pain. That's not to say that this one will,' Emma Dunn said quickly. 'Let's do it right so that it won't end that way.'

But the suspense and the joy were overwhelming. Things had gone so well after the long year of failed attempts that now Jill felt free to assume there would be no more obstacles. So it was that her light, exultant heart fell all the more heavily when Mr Riley called to tell her that Jennie Rakowsky wanted only to be left alone.

'She says what was done nineteen years ago can't be undone now.'

'She said that?' Jill asked.

'Yes, but it doesn't mean she won't change her mind. Let's give her some time to think it over.'

'Is it because she has other children, do you think?'

'I don't know. We'll find out.'

'How will you?'

'We have ways. I'll let you know. And, Jill, I wasn't surprised, so don't you be. It happens all the time, as I warned you.'

When she told them at home, Dad said the same thing, and Mom added, 'We were afraid this might happen. I hope it all works out for you, but, Jill, if it doesn't, you have to accept it. You can't let it crush you. Be satisfied with Peter in Chicago.'

When Peter called, he gave comfort. 'It will all straighten out,' he said cheerfully. 'Just be patient.' She saw him at the other end of the wire, youthful, perhaps too cheerful in the face of her distress, not fatherly like Dad, but still so welcoming. And she was grateful.

Days went by, and a week, then more weeks. The next time it was Emma Dunn who called to say that she had made another unsuccessful try to talk to Jennie.

'Don't give up. It's only two times, Jill. I'll call again. She has neither husband nor children. I have a feeling she'll finally say yes.'

Now, though, Jill was beset with a sense of urgency. It was as if she had done all but half a mile of a marathon; the goal was there, but her legs were so tired and her breath was so short; yet she must make that great, final push; she mustn't lose now. Never mind all the cautionary advice. Never mind her parents or Peter, or the Rileys and the Dunns. Just go for it.

So one night after dinner she went to her room, showered, and changed her clothes, to present herself at her best. She called a taxi. I will be calm, she told herself, and in the telling, she believed she felt her heart slow down. She entered a house and climbed some stairs and rang a bell.

A woman's voice answered: 'Who is it?'

'It's Jill,' she said. 'Will you let me in?'

7

With arms and legs gone rubbery, bracing herself with her left hand on the wall, Jennie unlatched the door. Light from the living room's lamps fanned out upon a tall young girl. Hair, Jennie saw first. Masses of splendid, undulating, russet, shining hair. Copper. Red. Red hair.

She slumped against the wall. Stared. Put her hand flat on her chest where her heart knocked, and knocked, and might suddenly stop altogether.

'I'm sorry,' the girl said softly. 'I'm sorry. . . . Are you going to faint?'

Jennie straightened up. For a fraction of an instant, outside of herself, she saw herself having a dream, a nightmare from which she would awaken in gratitude for daylight and reality. And then in the next instant, wrenched back into herself, she saw that this *was* reality: that the girl was alive and real and poised to come through the doorway. She moved aside, her rubbery legs hardly holding her up.

'Come in,' she whispered.

They stood in the center of the room facing each other, six or seven feet apart. There was no feeling in Jennie, suddenly no feeling except a frightful awareness that she was numb. Shreds of thought blew like leaves across vacant ground: What am I supposed to do, to feel? I'm numb, I'm not able to do or feel, don't you see? And, anyway, this may be a mistake. Yes, of course it's a mistake. Yes.

But then there's the hair. How many people have hair like that? Now look into her face. Look into the stranger's face.

'You're thinking you're not sure who I am. But I'm in the right place. I'm Jill. Victoria Jill. They've told you about me.'

'Yes,' Jennie said, her voice making no sound, so that she had to repeat, 'Yes, they have.'

They were still standing apart, at almost half the distance of the little room.

'You need to sit down,' the girl said. 'You're shaking.'

They moved to the chairs that flanked the sofa. Now they were only four feet apart.

She stares at me, Jennie thought. Her gaze moves from my stocking feet to my face and stops there. She wants to meet my eyes, but I have seen a glisten start in hers, and I cannot cope with, I am not ready for, tears, and I have to turn away.

Still, we have not touched each other, not even grazed hands. If this were a movie, we would be hugging and crying, but I am still empty. She looks away toward the window, which is black except for a slender oblong of light where a curtain across the street has fallen open. She looks toward the light. Her white silk shirt is low at the neck, so that I see the muscles of her throat contract as she swallows hard. Her face is narrow, thin, and lightly, delicately freckled over the nose, which is small but beaky, not like mine, nor like his. Her eyes are dark with heavy lashes, and the whites are so clear as to be almost blue. Piece by piece, still only half believing, I pick her apart.

The girl turned suddenly around. 'This is terrible for you. I'm sorry.'

And Jennie, the strong one, who so proudly coped with crises, was unable to answer.

'Do you need anything? Water? Brandy?'

'No. Thank you, no. I'll be all right.'

'You're sure?'

'I'm all right. Really.'

Jennie listened to the silence, and to the clamor of her thoughts. A fire engine shrieked alarm in the street below; when it went, the silence was deeper. Without sound she was speaking to herself: My head has begun to hurt; hammers smash it from forehead to nape. I put my hand to my forehead, as if a hand could halt pain. I have just realized that if Jay weren't sick, he would have been here a minute ago when the doorbell rang and would be here with us now. The scene is absolutely unimaginable.... And I look again at the girl – daughter – in my chair. Now she is concerned, as if afraid I may be sick, and she won't know what to do with me. She doesn't understand – how could she? – that she is a bomb tossed into the middle of my life.

The girl spoke. 'Aren't you going to say anything? You're not just going to sit there looking at me, are you?'

The faint rebuke was tempered by a small, coaxing, rather rueful smile, along with an anxious puckering of the forehead, or what could be seen of the forehead under the bangs.

Jennie's answer slipped out of itself. 'Do you mind my looking?'

'No, of course not.' Jill leaned toward her with chin in hand. 'Well, what do you think of me?'

Jennie's eyes stung, stretched wide to let no tears form. She answered, 'You're pretty....'

'You're pretty too.... Oh, do you have a feeling that this can't be happening? Can you believe we were in this same city all last year and didn't know it? I had no idea. I always thought you must be someplace in the Midwest, since I was born in Nebraska.'

How calmly she speaks! Such poise! One would think we were a pair of acquaintances who, after many years, had just met somewhere by accident. She must be quivering inside just as I am, but she is handling her tremors and this astounding situation so much better than I am. My hands are still shaking while hers lie still on the arms of the chair.

'I was born and grew up in Baltimore.'

Be prepared now for hundreds of questions. Answers are what she came for. Her mind, going back and back, must be a tangle of questions.

And now Jennie began to feel the girl's pain along with her own. Imagine what it must be not to know who made you! All my life I shall remember Pop: his mustache; his kind, hairy hands; his voice, so gravelly even when he laughed. And Mom, round, cheerful, warning, talking, eternally talking.

'We live in Albuquerque.'

'I knew you were somewhere in the West. I wondered where.'

'It's beautiful, but New York is marvelous for me. I've been to the opera and the Museum of Modern Art, everywhere. It's marvelous.'

The poise was waning. Not quite ready yet for knife-sharp truth, she wants to touch neutral things first, to chatter, to come very gradually to the heart of the matter. For me, too, Jennie thought, it is the only possible way.

'So college gave you your chance to see New York.'

'I'd been here once before. My grandmother took me to Europe for my high-school graduation present, and we stayed here for a few days.'

'That was a wonderful present.' How banal, how ordinary my remark, while my heart still races!

'I know. This was my other present, this bag. She bought it for me in Paris.'

A large Vuitton bag stood on the floor at the girl's feet. 'I know it's nice, but I didn't really want it.'

Paris. Vuitton. The girl – she must stop saying, even mentally, 'the girl' – wore a good bracelet watch and tiny diamond studs in her ears, things that Jennie had never had for herself and never could have given.

But some comment was expected. 'It's a good size. You can even carry a couple of books in it.'

'Oh, I use it, even on campus sometimes. We have a nice campus for a college in the city. You should see it. Have you ever?'

'No,' Jennie said. I was there this afternoon, hoping to see you. Hoping not to see you.

'Well, you should sometime.'

We circle, spiraling idiotically through trivia, coming fearfully closer and closer to the center where the knife lies.

Jill opened her mouth and closed it, then opened it again. 'Just a while before I graduated from high school, that's when Mother gave me your letter.'

'My letter?'

'The one you wrote before I was born, that was in the box of baby clothes.'

'That one. Oh, yes.'

Actually she had forgotten. It was true, then, that you could really block out anything you wanted to, anything that hurt too much to be remembered.

'We were alone in the house one afternoon. She sat with me and waited while I read it. We both cried.'

'I can't remember what I wrote.'

'Do you want me to tell you? I know it by heart.'

Jennie put up her hand. 'Oh, no! Please, no.'

I will not let myself be torn to pieces. Now that she has

told me this much, I will have to keep seeing them, her and the woman who is her mother. . . . On a porch, she said. Bare mountains. Red mesas. Is Albuquerque on a mesa? Wind chimes tinkle. Cactus grows on the lawn. There's a swing on the porch, with the two of them in it, and the woman's arms around the girl's shoulders; I see she has a thoughtful face, the face of an intellectual, with a gray streak in her dark hair. I don't know why I see her like that.

'That was the day I first knew I absolutely had to find you,' Jill said.

'Not before then?'

'Not really. But once the idea came, it stayed with me all the time. I knew I had to know where I came from.'

'And your . . . parents?'

'Whether they minded? Not at all. They understood.' Jill paused. 'My red hair . . . I looked so conspicuous among the others in my family. If you know what I mean.'

That glorious hair. Poor soul, wondering where it came from.

'You have your father's hair,' Jennie said. And she, too, paused. 'It ran in that family. Maybe you look a little like them. . . . I didn't know them well.' Then she blurted out, 'It's painful for me to talk about them.'

'You don't need to. Just tell me about yourself.'

'Tell about myself?' Jennie repeated, feeling a bitterness. 'A lifetime in an evening?'

'There'll be other evenings, Jennie. Do you mind if I call you that? I wouldn't feel right calling two people Mother.'

'I don't mind.'

To tell the truth, it seems absurd to call me Mother. I haven't been a mother. And 'other evenings,' she says. It's only to be expected. Once having taken the first step, others must follow; one doesn't just stop in place. So the road extends, with no imaginable end, except possibly a stone wall for me. She waits now for my history. Her ankles are crossed, the posture seemingly demure, yet already I know that this girl – Jill – is not demure. But then, neither am I.

'You came from Baltimore, you said.'

'My parents were poor Jews from Europe, survivors of the death camps. We had very little, but it was a good home. My father's dead, my mother lives in Florida, I have no brothers or sisters –' She choked and stopped.

Crazy, this is, we two here, having this conversation, all of it surreal like Dali's melting clocks and dream vistas, distant houses, lost time. And I, reluctant, as if on a doctor's couch, awakening blurred memories, long ago put away to sleep.

'Excuse me,' Jennie said, wiping tears. 'I don't usually cry.'

'Why don't you? There's nothing wrong with crying.'

'Once I start, I'm afraid I won't be able to stop.'

She's strong, this girl, sensible, in charge. She leads tonight, and I follow. I'm not used to that.

Jennie made a lump out of the wet handkerchief and straightened herself again in the chair, saying almost timidly, 'I'm not sure how to go on.'

The response was a quiet one but prompt. 'I suppose – I wish – you could tell me why you haven't wanted to see me, why you've resisted for all these weeks. I didn't want to force you by coming here like this, but there wasn't any other way.'

'It was –' Jennie said, stumbling. 'I mean, it's impossible to face, to be reminded –'

She backs me into a corner. In a courtroom I can thrust and parry; I haven't been trapped there yet. But this girl is not going to let me go. And now she's in my mind to stay, so that I'll never forget her. I'll see her face forever and hear her voice. She speaks well, good diction is so important, young people all seem to slur these days, they speak so badly. . . . And she sits with grace, tall in the chair. She'd fit into Peter's family. . . . And isn't *that* ironic? Oh, the pain in my head won't stop.

At that moment Jill said, 'I wanted so much to fit into your life, to be a part of it.'

Jennie gasped. 'How can that be? It's so late. Too late for us. You don't – I mean, we don't fit into each other's lives.'

'No, you were right the first time. You could fit into mine. You just don't want me in yours. You said so to the people who called you.'

'I didn't say it like that.'

How cruel, how stupid of them to have told her that way! And yet I did say it, didn't I? I said they should leave me alone. Look at her. . . . Her skin is like milk, and the blue veins at the temples, where the hair falls away, are so thin, her lifeblood flows in them. . . . Now she's grieving, she's hurt. . . . I was right from the beginning. It was better for neither of us to know the other, ever.

And Jennie spoke very softly. 'I only meant, it's hard – yes, I said impossible – to have any relationship after nineteen years. That's all I meant.'

'We could try. We can try right now to communicate.' Jill looked at her watch. 'It's only nine. You could tell me a lot in the next hour or two. If you wanted to,' she finished.

Jennie sighed. 'I'll do better. I'll sketch a family tree and send it to you. I'll write some anecdotes, all that I know about my side. As to the other – his – I can't tell you much. I knew nothing except the very little he told me, that they were Southerners – you might call them Jewish aristocrats, I suppose. I don't know any more.'

'It doesn't matter. I've already talked with Peter, and he's told me.'

Jennie stared. 'You . . . you *what*?'

Jill stared back. 'I found him, the same as I found you. We've had long conversations by telephone these last few weeks. He's in Chicago, and he's asked me to fly out there next weekend. *He* was so excited when I called him! *He* wanted to get in touch with me that same day.'

Dumbfounded, Jennie could only let the words pour over her like ice water.

'We have a lot in common.' The girl's voice, rising, held triumph. 'He's an archaeologist. You didn't know that, did you? He's a professor. And I went on a dig once in Israel, so we had a lot to talk about. He sounds like a wonderful person. I can't wait to see him.'

After shock, thoughts flowed, and Jennie began to see more clearly the young person who sat opposite. An extraordinarily determined young person, she was, and clever, too, keeping back the business about Peter until she had heard first what Jennie had to tell her.

And she said carefully, 'I'm glad for you, Jill. And for him, too, if this is what you want. I hope good comes of it.'

'Why shouldn't good come of it?'

'I don't know, exactly, because I don't know anything about him. I only know that a life can have many complications –'

'Like your life?' Jill's eyes, demanding, met Jennie's and held.

This time Jennie's held too. 'Yes. Like mine.'

'But you won't tell me what yours are.'

'No. My complications are my own.'

The momentary, following silence threatened Jennie, and she opened her lips to break it. But Jill spoke first.

'He wants to see you.'

Jennie started. 'Who? Peter? Wants to see me?'

'Yes, he says now that I've made the move, it would be a good thing for us all. He's coming to New York during the semester break.'

'Oh, no! Oh, no! You're not going to do this to me, either of you.'

'I don't know how you're going to prevent it. He wants to, he told me so.'

'I won't have it, do you hear?' Jennie cried out furiously. 'I simply won't have this outrage!'

Netted and caught. Peter again, summoned back from the dead. In the next room the clothes for a honeymoon are spread on the bed. The impostor's honeymoon ... Jay ... oh, my dear, my dear, am I going to lose you? Oh, I'm determined not to, and yet I know I will. I see the writing on the wall. I see it.

'What are you people trying to do to me?' she screamed.

Jill picked the Vuitton bag from the floor and stood up. Her eyes were filled with tears, but she spoke coldly.

'You're not at all what I hoped for. I never thought you would be like this.'

Jennie stood too. 'What did you think I would be like?'

'I don't know, but not like this.'

Tense, taut, trembling, the two confronted each other.

'Yes,' Jill said bitterly, 'I do know. I thought at least – at least you would kiss me.'

And Jennie wept. Grief burst open in her throat. 'Oh,' she said incoherently, 'you come here like this ... so that I can't even believe what I'm seeing ... nineteen years. I open the door. And now he too ... I can't think straight. ... Of course I'll kiss you.'

Jill drew back. 'No. Not that way. Not if I have to ask for it.'

The tears ran over and, unwiped, slid down her cheeks. She opened the door and ran out into the hall.

'Wait!' Jennie called. 'You mustn't go like that! Oh, please –'

But the girl was gone. Her quick steps clattered on the stairs; the outer door thumped shut and echoed through the house. For a long minute Jennie stood hearing the echo, then turned back into the apartment and sat down with her hands over her face.

The first immediate sense of unreality returned. This couldn't have happened. Yet the girl's lipstick was there on the floor as proof of her presence. It had rolled out of her purse most probably, when at the start of tears she had reached for a tissue. Jennie picked it up: Marcella Borghese, Rimini Rose Frost. She let it lie on her palm. It grew warm, lying there so long, while she thought of the girl's smile, her angry, beautiful eyes, and her tears.

'I read the letter that came with the baby clothes . . .'

A child looking for her mother. Poor child.

But she has a mother, has always had a good one. Why me, now?

You know why. Don't ask.

Poor child.

But they will ruin everything, she and Peter. Peter coming back from the dead.

How can I ever keep the two of them separate from Jay? How dare he, how dare the two of them do this to me?

After a long time Jennie got up, turned the lamp off, and took a Valium from the medicine cabinet. Only once in her life, under stress of root-canal surgery and an infection, had she taken a tranquilizer. Tonight, though, she would have swallowed anything that could dull the confusion and despair.

In the morning her mind felt clearer. 'The important thing always,' she reminded herself aloud as she sat in the little kitchen having coffee, 'is to keep one's head.'

But Jill had gone crying, and gone like that across the city in the dark. Surely amends must be made! I don't remember exactly what I said, Jennie thought. I only know I was beside myself. Something had to be done, though. A sensible, quiet talk. We could go someplace for lunch and I could explain things better. We'd both be less emotional a second time, I think.

She was reaching for the telephone book when the telephone rang.

'Good morning,' Jay said. Amazing man, he was one of those people who are cheerful and vigorous when they wake up. 'A miracle! My fever's gone, I feel fine, and how would you like to have a Sunday jog in the park? The kids are with the grandparents all day.'

She thought quickly. 'Oh, darling, I thought you were sick and I made other plans.'

'Oh, hell, what other plans?'

'I . . . there's some friend of my mother's in town from Miami. I have to take her to a museum or something. We're supposed to have lunch.'

'Well, I could put up with that. I'll take you both to lunch.'

'She's an old lady, Jay, you'd hate it.'

'What makes you think I hate old ladies? Listen, you'll be an old lady someday, and I don't expect to hate you.'

'Honestly, it would be awful for you. As a matter of fact, there are two of them, and one of them has a husband. They're nice, but they're really very boring people.'

'You meet plenty of boring people when you practice law. I'm used to them.'

'Yes, but why should you suffer on a Sunday? Besides, you had a fever last night and you're supposed to stay indoors for a day afterward at least.'

'I'm actually being rejected,' he complained in mock sorrow.

'Yes, for today you are. Go on back and relax with the paper. I'll call you later.'

She hung up. Lies and subterfuge already. I hate myself for it. That's what comes of lies. They beget more lies.

Nevertheless she dialed the Barnard number. Now, waiting for Jill to come to the phone, she had a recollection of dormitory smells – sweet talcum powder and the sharp odor of cleaning fluid – of dormitory noises, rock music, ringing phones, and high heels rapping; she saw Jill hurrying down the corridor, the hair lifting from her shoulders as she ran, anticipating a call from some young man, or perhaps from home.

'Jill,' she said, 'this is Jennie.'

'Yes?' The tone was cool.

Say it boldly. 'I was concerned about last night, about whether you got back all right.'

'I got back all right.'

'I'm sorry that my being upset was so hard on you. I thought maybe you and I could have a talk and clarify things a little. Would you do that?'

'Well . . .' Now the tone was cautious. 'When?'

'Today. Lunch, I thought. Around one o'clock.' She decided quickly; best to make it downtown on the West Side, someplace where none of Jay's friends, most of whom lived on the Upper East Side, would be apt to go strolling on a Sunday. 'The Hilton on Sixth Avenue at Fifty-third Street. It's nice there, they don't rush you. Shall I meet you at the registration desk?'

'I'll be there.'

'And, Jill . . . it'll be easier for us both this time.'

'I hope so.' A hesitation. 'I'm glad you called, Jennie.'

We'll talk things over calmly and work them out, Jennie said to herself. She's old enough, and surely she's smart enough to understand that people have differing circumstances, that you have to make allowances for one another.

Jennie's spirits were still sanguine as she waited in the lobby of the great hotel. She had always been a people watcher, and today her observations of the passing scene were especially sharp.

Here was a handsome, petulant woman with a tired husband, there a middle-aged man pushing a young girl in a wheelchair, here a young couple with shining faces and cheap new honeymoon luggage, there two businessmen arguing, and an embarrassed mother struggling with a kicking child. Ebb and flow, and survive.

She saw Jill before the girl saw her. She hadn't realized last night how tall Jill was. The height, like the hair, came from him. She had good carriage, a long, free stride in her pleated plaid skirt and camel-hair jacket. For a moment the men with the attaché cases stopped arguing and turned to look after her.

Something leapt in Jennie. 'Surprised by joy.' Who had written that? I'm surprised by joy. This person coming toward me now belongs to me! She put out her arms, and this time Jill came into them.

They stood then, laughing a little and crying a little, until Jennie spoke. A surge of energy and hope came running through her, and she grasped Jill's hands.

'Didn't I say it would be better today? I knew it would! Come on, let's eat, let's talk!'

But in the dining room they suddenly became silent.

'It's funny, I don't know how to start,' Jill said. 'That's what you said yesterday, isn't it?'

'Just let it come as it wants.'

'It's not coming.'

'All right, I've an idea. Tell me about your first time in New York.'

'Well, we stayed at the Plaza. I'd read all the Eloise books when I was a child, so I wanted to see it. We ate in the Oak Room, where Eloise must have had dinner some nights. And once we went out to a French restaurant – Lutèce, I think – and had duck with orange sauce and two desserts.'

She seems younger than she did last night, Jennie thought. I mustn't stare like this, she told herself, and buttered a roll instead.

'I love everything French. Of course, I'm glad I'm American, but if I couldn't be American, I'd want to be French. My grandmother taught French before she retired.'

'Did she? My mother speaks French – not very well. She lived in France before the Nazis came, but she's forgotten a lot. If you don't use it, you know . . .'

'I'd like you to tell me more about her.'

'Well, I will. But it's a long story.'

Mom would be stunned by all this; then she would weep.

'We had the best time together in France,' Jill resumed. 'The best. She knew just where to go.'

'She sounds like fun.'

'We always had fun in our family. Would you like to see some family pictures? I've brought an envelope full.' Jill leaned across the table. 'Here's one with all of us, taken last summer on Dad's birthday.'

Eight or ten people stood and sat on some steps below a door with flowering shrubs on either side. In a corner of the foreground was the edge of a barbecue kettle. An American family scene, Grant Wood, but contemporary. Jennie startled herself with a touch of jealousy and stifled it at once.

'All those children . . .' she began.

'Isn't it amazing? Mom had four of her own with no

trouble at all after they got me. But I understand that often happens. This is Jerry next to me, he's a year and a half younger. This is Lucille, she's fifteen, this is Sharon, she's twelve, and here's Mark, the baby. He's seven.'

'And this is your mother?'

'No, that's Aunt Fay. This is Mom here in front of Dad.'

Here they were, this very average-looking man and woman in T-shirts and shorts, smiling for the camera and squinting into the light. These were the parents who had held and cherished the hand that now brushed Jennie's as they passed the pictures back and forth.

Some comment had to be made. 'They look young.'

Jill considered. 'Yes, younger than they are. And they act young. They're happy people.... You know, I feel sorry for people with messed-up families! Half the people I meet seem to come from homes where nobody laughs. Or where they hate each other, you know?'

'I know.'

'Were you ever married, Jennie?' The tone and the look were childishly blunt; in an older person they would be thought of as rude.

'No,' Jennie said, feeling discomfort, which she covered with enthusiasm. 'Have you got more pictures?'

'Well, let's see. Here's one. We go skiing a lot. We only have to drive an hour.'

Behind the group and around it lay mountains, folded and ridged like newspapers that someone had crumpled and flung to the ground, dark and dry, the color of cinders next to the snow.

'Once I imagined you were in California,' Jennie said. 'I kept seeing the Pacific.'

'New Mexico's just as beautiful, in a different way. Our sky's so large, so blue all day, and the sunset's rose-colored, so bright that it burns.'

Jennie smiled. 'You speak like a poet.'

'I write poetry. Very bad, I'm sure.'

This girl, like most people, was multifaceted, a cluster of contradictions. The previous night she had been, among other things, cool and controlling. Today she was ever so charmingly naïve.

'You really ought to see New Mexico. Do you ski?'

Jennie shook her head. 'It's an expensive sport.'

'Oh. Have you got problems? Are you poor?'

The question amused Jennie. 'Some people might call me poor.' The top-floor walk-up, the simple furnishings. 'I'm satisfied with what I have, so I don't feel poor.'

'You must be happy with your work, then.'

'I am. I'm a defender of women – poor women, mostly. And now I seem to be taking on another interest, too, something I didn't know I cared about that much.' She was aware that pride had crept into her tone, born of a surprising impulse to show who she was and what she had achieved. 'I'm in the middle of a tremendously important fight right now.'

'I'd like to hear about it,' Jill said, laying down her fork.

So Jennie, divulging neither name nor location, related the story of the Green Marsh. The story grew vivid in the telling; this was the first time she had spoken of the issue to anyone not involved in it, and as she talked, she could feel the strength of her own convictions coming through.

'There's a movement something like that at home,' Jill said when Jennie had finished, 'to save the Jerez Mountains from developers. Dad's active in it. He's on every conservation committee you can think of. We've each got our thing. Mine's Indians, their social structure, ancient and modern.' She regarded Jennie over the rim of the coffee cup. 'Peter's done work on the southwestern Indians too. That's an odd coincidence, don't you think?' And when no comment came, she asked, 'Do you mind that I even mention him at all?'

Jennie's reply was quiet. 'Jill, I do mind some. I don't want to think about him. Please understand that.'

'If you hated him so, why didn't you have an abortion?'

'Oh, my God, the questions you ask! It wasn't a matter of hatred. I didn't hate him then, and I don't now.' She put out her hand and laid it over the girl's free hand. 'I never even considered an abortion.' She could have said, 'They wanted me to,' but she refrained. 'Never.'

Jill looked over Jennie's head across the room. Jennie thought, I'm learning her ways already. She looks beyond you, or down at the floor as she did last night, when she is considering her next words.

The next words came. 'I'm surprised you never married. Didn't you ever want to be?'

An honest answer was expected. But Jennie could only be halfway honest about this.

'Once.'

'To my father?'

'It didn't work out.'

'How awful for you!'

'For the moment, yes, it was.'

'Only for the moment? But didn't you love him?'

'If you can call it love. I thought it was, anyway.'

Jill, not answering that, looked down again. And Jennie, relieved for the moment of face-to-face contact, examined her once more. How much might she already know of love? Men would find her appealing; to be sure, she didn't have classic beauty, the symmetry that once had been essential in our culture, but standards had changed. That hair alone was enough, then the assurance, the intelligence – 'A delightful girl,' Mr Riley had said, or maybe it had been Emma Dunn.

'So whether or not it was love, you had me.'

Jennie said steadily, 'Yes, I went away by myself and had you. I was alone. My parents never knew.'

'Why didn't they?'

'It would have hurt them too much. It's hard to explain. You would have to know them to understand why.'

'I can't imagine having a baby at my age.'

'I was younger than you are now.'

'How frightened you must have been. No, I can't imagine it,' Jill murmured in a tender voice.

'I couldn't imagine it, either.'

That cloud again, that heavy gray blanket, oppressed Jennie. A dull sadness fell into the iridescent room. People were pleasantly chattering away; so many were in family groups of all ages. Festive and at ease with one another . . .

Jill cried out, 'How brave you were!'

'Where there's no choice, one had better be.'

'How terribly hard for you to give your baby away!'

'If I had known you or even held you, it would have been impossible, and I knew that. So I never once looked at you when you were born.'

'Did you think about me often afterward?'

Where am I finding the strength for this torture? Jennie asked herself.

'I tried not to. But sometimes I imagined where you lived and what your name might be.'

'It's a silly name, isn't it? A silly combination. Victoria is for Mother's sister, who died. Jill is the name they call me by.'

Jill smiled, showing teeth of the immaculate evenness that is usually the work of an orthodontist. Yes, she had had the best care.

'I couldn't allow myself to think about you. It was done, finished. You were in good hands, and I had to go on. You can see that, can't you?' And Jennie heard the plea in her own question.

'You picked yourself up and went to law school. You made something out of your life. Yes, I can see.'

It was a simple observation to which Jennie could think of no reply, so she made none. The even dialogue – statement given, statement returned – seemed to have reached a stopping place.

Jill spoke next. 'But after all, you haven't told me very much about yourself, have you?'

'I don't know what else there is to tell you. I've given the facts. There aren't very many.'

Abruptly a new expression passed across Jill's face: a puzzlement in the eyes; a tightening, almost a severity, about the mouth. Subtly but unmistakably, another *atmosphere* had come between the two women. But it was understandable, wasn't it? With such floods of feeling, two sets of experiences, two lives so wide apart in age, in place ... and everything ...

Cheerfully, to dispel this atmosphere, Jennie suggested dessert. A waiter came, fussed with the plates, and recommended pastries from the cart.

'I really don't want one,' Jill said. 'I only took it to make the lunch last longer.'

The admission touched Jennie. 'We'll find a place to sit and talk some more in one of the lounges. No need to hurry,' she coaxed brightly.

'I thought perhaps you might be in a hurry. Then why don't we go to your place?'

Jennie shrank. They had been an hour and a half over this lunch, and still she hadn't made the point she'd intended to make. Jill must understand there could be no more visits to the apartment. She must. What if, for instance, Jay were to take it into his head to drop in this very afternoon? Or any other time?

'Jill, I have to tell you, I'm sorry, but we can't go to my place.'

The clear eyes opened wide, alert on the instant, probing as they had done last night.

'Why not?'

What trust can you have in a person who hides her true self for years, and then suddenly decides to reveal herself? Jennie thought. You can only wonder what else is hidden. . . .

Her nervous hands, palms upturned, made a small protest.

'It's terribly difficult to say this, to explain. But there are things – deep personal things, reasons –' Helpless before that probing gaze, she stopped.

Jill waited, saying nothing, which forced her to begin again.

'You see . . . I tried to say it yesterday, but I did it very badly, I know, and gave you the wrong idea, that I didn't care about you. But the way things are with me . . . There are reasons.' The nervous hands were in her lap now, clasping each other. 'What I'm trying to say is, you mustn't get in touch with me. You mustn't ever come to my house or even telephone. You have to promise me that. I'll be the one to get in touch with you.'

'I don't understand,' Jill said. Her cheeks were flushed.

The aura that had begun to warm them when they embraced in the lobby and talked across the table, the intimate sadness, the tenderness, the animation, all now vanished under the new atmosphere.

'I don't like it, Jennie. First you give and next you take back. Why?'

'I know it's hard to understand. If you could just trust me –'

'You don't seem to trust me!'

'How can you say that? I do trust you. Of course I do.'

'No, you're hiding something.'

How stern she was! And a fighter too. She'd fight for principles and stand up for rights, her own and others'. In the space of an instant, Jennie saw who Jill was.

Jill's eyes were wet and shining. 'Is it me?' she persisted. 'Are you ashamed of me?'

The word *ashamed*, containing as it did an element of partial truth (not ashamed of you as a person but of your emerging from my denial of the truth), along with this attack, yes, this furious attack from someone whom Jennie had never harmed, for whom God alone knew she had done the very best she could, made anger rise again. And she knew that she was angry at herself for having to inflict this hurt, for causing these tears.

She had to defend herself. 'Shame has nothing to do with it, believe me, Jill. Can't you try to accept what I offer? I want my independent life.' Need pushed her; she spoke rapidly, urgently. 'You have yours. Peter has his. I never bothered him for anything. Isn't it fair for me to have my independent life?'

Now Jill's tears ran hard. She spoke through them scornfully. 'Independent life! Am I stopping you by sitting in your living room?'

'Of course you don't mean to, but all the same, it would be –'

Jill interrupted her. 'This lunch was a deception. You came here to tell me in the nicest possible way to stay out of your way. That's all you came for.' And she pushed her chair back as if to rise.

'Sit down, Jill. Sit down. Let's be reasonable. I beg you. Eat your dessert.'

'Jennie . . . I'm not a baby to be pacified with sweets.'

'You're not being fair to me! I said I'd call you, didn't I? Whenever I can, I will. I only said you shouldn't be the one to –'

'I won't call you, don't worry. You needn't have any fears about me. But I'll tell you something. I can't answer for Peter. He was pretty well shocked by what you said to the search committee. He'll be more shocked next week when I tell him about today.'

Jill rose abruptly, upsetting her chair. A waiter rushed to retrieve it, heads turned toward the small commotion, and Jennie reached for Jill's arm.

'Don't go like this,' she pleaded, keeping her voice low. 'Don't run away again. Let me pay the check and we'll sit someplace and talk.'

Jill gathered bag, gloves, and scarf. 'There's nothing to talk about unless you tell me we can behave normally to each other. That I can ring your phone like anybody else and . . . can you tell me that?'

The waiter stood holding the check, and a woman at the next table was staring in open curiosity. Appalled and shaken, Jennie sought new words, a fresh approach.

'Can you?' Jill repeated.

'No, not exactly. But listen, hear me out –'

'I've heard you, and I don't want to hear any more. Thank you for lunch.'

Jennie watched her go. Without strength to follow and aware that it would be of no use, anyway, to do so, she sat gazing at Jill's plate, on which the ice cream was already melting over the pie. Strawberry, it was. A pink puddle. So that's the end of my daughter, come and gone in the space of a day. Raging eyes, a retreating back, and a puddle of ice cream in a dish.

The waiter coughed, a reminder of his presence. She took the check, paid, and went out to the street. Taxis stood at the curb before the hotel's entrance, but she had no wish to get home so soon, there to sit bewildered and alone. So she turned north instead and began to walk.

In the park, brown with winter, the twiggy treetops, still wet after rain, were washed with a metallic sheen. The cold sky raced. Sunday afternoon was a bleak time, no matter what the weather, unless you were with someone you loved.

Yet she was in no condition just now to be with Jay. She was in no condition to be with herself, either. And, giving up, with no place to go but home, she hurried eastward. Nearing home, she began to run down the last street, up the stairs and into the apartment, where she bolted the door and sat down, out of breath with effort and weariness.

Voices rang: Jill's, Jay's, Mr Riley's, her own father's, her own mother's, and Jay's mother's making a plaintive clamor, each for his own reason. Jennie, Jennie, what's happening to you?

When she turned the television on, the voices were stilled, only to be replaced by that of an enthusiastic young woman chuckling with delight over a new detergent. She switched the television off and lay down on the sofa.

I'm tired. So tired. Sick at heart, as they say. I thought we could iron things out, that I could find some compromise. I really believed I could, and look what happened! Such a quick temper the girl has! She hardly gave me a chance. Still, from her point of view, I suppose my secrecy is baffling, like a door slammed in her face. But I was willing to go partway, and I said so, didn't I? I had in my mind that I would call her sometimes; I really would. I couldn't just go on for the rest of my life as though I'd never seen her. How could I?

And yet my offer would be no real relationship at all, would it? She knew that. And it wouldn't work, anyway. No, married to Jay, in his house, with his children, I would be a juggler with a dozen balls in the air; eventually I'd be bound to miss one, and then they all would tumble. . . .

She fell into an exhausted doze and was awakened, in a room grown dark, by the ring of the telephone.

'Hello,' Jay said. 'How was your day?'

'My day?' she repeated, and then remembered her mother's friends, the museum and lunch. 'Oh, not too bad. A little too long. I was asleep just now.'

'Well, I had a miserable Sunday. Being alone in this apartment is like being alone in a stadium. It echoes. I couldn't stand it. I took the dog for such a long walk that he's knocked out.'

'I'm sorry I abandoned you. I won't do it again.'

'Don't forget tomorrow night.'

A client of Jay's was the sponsor of a modern-dance recital which, being a lover of ballet, Jennie did not especially enjoy. But feeling the need to keep up her courage, she made herself sound bright.

'Of course not. I'm looking forward to it.'

She slept restlessly, waking often to hear traffic dwindle as the night deepened and to hear it start again as black turned to gray, to white, and finally to a row of yellow bars between the slats of the venetian blinds.

There was just so much that makeup could do. Trouble left its wretched mark even on a young face, even after the most careful application of eye shadow, eyeliner, lipstick, and blush. Tie on a red-and-white scarf, walk briskly, and smile; it made little difference because the mark was there.

Dinah, the typist, inquired whether Jennie felt all right. Her first client advised her to take it easy because there was a lot of flu going around. By mid-afternoon she was starting to wonder whether she really might be ill. Her eyes wandered, unseeing, over the records on the desk, and then out toward the building across the street where lights were coming on as the afternoon darkened. For an instant she saw a picture of Jill, also at a desk, and also, perhaps, unable to focus her thoughts. Then she was almost overwhelmed by pity, until returning anger surged. Unfair, unfair to be held this way, 'between a rock and a hard place,' as Mom used to say.

Dinah appeared at the door to inform Jennie that a Dr Cromwell wanted to see her.

Cromwell. What on earth could he be wanting? Jennie's mind was a million miles away from the Green Marsh.

The old man wore, along with a polka-dotted bow tie, the affable expression that she remembered. Natty and spruce, he looked exactly like what he was, a small-town gentleman visiting the big city.

'Gosh,' he said, 'I was expecting to see one of those offices with a mile of corridors, carpets, and oil paintings. I was in one of those places one time, made me feel small. Even New York dentists' places are –' Aware of his unintentional disparagement, he corrected himself. 'This is nice, though. Comfortable place to work in. Well, how are you? Busy getting ready for the wedding?'

'Oh, it will be very quiet,' she said.

'Even so, I hate to come to you with another problem. It's about a phone call.' His bland face took on a timid, worried expression. 'First we had all those anonymous letters, but you know about those.'

Jennie nodded. 'Anonymous, but no secret that Bruce Fisher probably wrote them.'

'Probably. No secret that he's half crazy, either.'

The more recent events in Jennie's life had pushed some others to the back of her mind, but now they leapt up in full, vivid force: the vicious thrust on the stairs and the cunning grin as the man fled past.

'But what I want to tell you is – Oh, I don't know whether he had anything to do with it, maybe not, but you never know. Why, I remember that case, it was twelve or fifteen years back, more likely fifteen, when he and a crowd of –'

Jennie, concealing impatience, said kindly, 'You were going to tell me about a telephone call.'

'Yes, of course. Well, I've had two, actually. They may not mean anything, but then again they may. And Arthur Wolfe says I must talk to you about them. He can be a worrier, Arthur can. Still, in the circumstances –'

'Who called you? Do you think it was Fisher?'

'It didn't sound like Fisher at all. I'd know his voice. Besides, this man gave his name. John Jones.'

Jennie made a wry face. 'John Jones!'

'Yes, it sounds phony, doesn't it? But he was very polite, even friendly. He said he was interested in the Barker proposition –'

'What does that mean, "interested in it"? Is he a partner, or what?'

'Well, he wasn't clear about that. I got the impression he just worked for them or something.'

'What did he want with you?'

'Well, he knew I was on the town council, and he realized I had the town's interest at heart, and he thought it would be a good idea for us to get together and talk. He thought we'd find out we weren't so far apart, after all.'

'And what did you say?'

'Well, I said I didn't think we could, but that if he had anything new to say, it should come up at the town council's next meeting.'

Jennie gave approval. 'Just the right answer, George.'

'But he said no, that most ideas were developed in executive discussions beforehand. He said he'd heard about me and had a lot of respect for the intelligent work I'd been doing on the council, and he'd been wanting to meet me. I can't figure out how he knew so much about me.' The old man blushed.

'Why? What else did he know about you?' she asked,

feeling as though she were leading a child through cross-examination.

'Well, it really surprised me that he knew about Martha's cancer. My wife, Martha, you know. It's been in remission for three years, but now they say she needs another operation. As a matter of fact, she's with me in the city. We're seeing somebody new at Sloan-Kettering tomorrow.'

And Jennie, observing the old, wrinkled throat above the natty bow tie, the old throat that she hadn't noticed before, felt soft pity.

'I wonder how he knew. Surely you don't have friends in common.'

'Oh, no. He comes from New York.'

Unless he's made inquiries in town, she thought, and asked, 'Exactly what did he say about your wife?'

'Just that he'd heard about her illness and that I must have a lot on my mind. That I must have big expenses.'

'Oh?'

'Of course, they are awfully big. That's the God's truth. Not that I wouldn't spend my last cent for Martha. Still, I'm only a small-town dentist. . . . Say, are you thinking this could have something to do with a bribe? Are you? Because Arthur Wolfe said –'

'Do you think so?' Jennie queried. Poor old man. Poor child.

'Well, I did wonder. And Arthur Wolfe –'

'Don't wonder anymore. Of course that's what he's leading up to.'

'Oh, my,' George said. He reflected a moment. 'I suppose he's trying everybody on the council, one at a time.'

'No, George. That's not the way it's done. And certainly not in this case. I'll tell you why not. The way it is now on the council, the vote stands four to four. You've got the mayor and three cronies on one side. The mayor says he hasn't decided yet, but we all know he has. And on the other side, you've got four who probably aren't going to budge, two summer people who probably don't want a development near their rural retreats; Henry Pope the lawyer, who's got a rich wife; and the Presbyterian minister. So that leaves you. Speaking plainly, you're the only one they think they can easily buy off, and you cast the ninth vote, the deciding vote.'

'You've got it all figured out.' Cromwell gave a long, tired sigh.

'It's my job to figure it out.'

Neither said anything for a moment until Cromwell exclaimed, 'So all I have to do is refuse to see him! Then what am I worried about? Nothing!'

'I wouldn't say that. I said there were four who probably wouldn't budge. Probably. Okay, the minister won't be bought, but while I don't think the others would be, either, still ... they might be. Henry Pope, for instance. The Wolfes tell me his law practice isn't all that great. Who knows what he might do if the offer were big enough?'

Cromwell looked dismayed. 'Oh, I don't believe Henry would ever –'

Jennie interrupted. 'You don't believe, but you don't know, either, do you? So if this Jones person fails with you and then tries Pope or someone else, he could get his fifth vote, couldn't he?'

'I suppose so. What are you getting at?'

'What I'm getting at is that he mustn't fail with you. We have to get the bribe offer on record.'

'How do we do that?'

'I'm not exactly sure. I want to think about it.'

'Now, you mean?'

'Stay awhile. I want to look something up.'

Row on row of brown-bound volumes stood on shelves

across the room. Searching, Jennie found what she wanted and set it on the desk with a thump. She read, took some notes, and called Dinah.

'Bring me the file on the Fillipo case, will you, please?'

One of her clients had been released from a wretched affair with a drug dealer when he had been sentenced to prison. There was something in the record, she recalled, although the case had been finished at least four years earlier, about the defendant's having been trapped by a taped conversation.

George watched her nervously while she turned pages; his foot, which was in her line of vision whenever she raised her eyes for a moment, kept tapping the floor in rapid rhythm.

At last she put the papers aside. 'Would you consider wearing a wire, George? Go to lunch with Jones and tape him?'

George started. His answer came with a quaver. 'That's – I mean, that's awfully dangerous, isn't it? If he should find out –'

'There's always a chance. I can't tell you otherwise,' Jennie replied seriously. 'But it's also highly unlikely. Very. This sort of thing is done all the time in crime investigations, you know.'

'How's it done?' The foot was tapping harder now.

'I honestly don't know the exact mechanisms. We'll find out when we see the district attorney.'

There was a long wait, during which the old man seemed to be searching Jennie's face. She met his eyes frankly.

'All right. I trust you, Jennie. I'll do it. If I didn't trust you, I wouldn't do it.'

She was touched. 'Thank you for the trust, George.'

He hesitated. 'It's a matter of principle,' he said. 'Being a good citizen. I suppose that sounds corny these days.'

'Not to me, it doesn't.'

'Well, then, let's go. What's my next step?'

'Just this. When he calls again, which he will, you'll set up an appointment. Meanwhile I'll see the district attorney. If he okays this, then you'll go to be wired, and that's it. That's the whole thing.'

She saw that George, in spite of his apprehension, was beginning to expand with pride.

'Wired,' he repeated. 'It's like something in the movies.'

'Like the movies and like life.'

George looked at his watch and stood up. 'Gosh, I've got to get Martha at four, in ten minutes.'

Jennie rose, too, and held out her hand. 'Don't worry too much if you can help it,' she said kindly.

'I'll try not to. It's just having too many problems at one time, that's the hard part.'

'Yes,' she said to herself when the door had closed behind the old man. 'I know. Well do I know. Too many problems at one time.'

'I have a strong hunch that it's our good mayor who put "Jones" on to George Cromwell,' Jay said. 'Obviously somebody with a motive told him about George's problem.'

After the dance recital they had stopped at a delicatessen for corned-beef sandwiches and coffee. The privacy of a back booth, high-walled, was a relief after the recital, which had given Jennie more of a headache than she had already. The pounding music, the jerky, piston thrust of the dancers, all angular jutting knees and elbows, were supposed, she knew, to represent the fragmentation of modern life. But she herself was too fragmented to care.

'Yes,' Jay said, 'the more I think of it, the surer I am. It's Honest Chuck the mayor who's behind this.'

'There's so much I'll never understand. A firm like

Barker – would it make so much difference if they lost this one job when they've made, and are making, millions elsewhere?'

'So much difference? Seven or eight million difference, I'd estimate. But there's more to it than money alone, Jennie. It's a question of not wanting to lose. It's a power game. They don't want to be beaten by a handful of jackass nature lovers, which is how they see people like us. These people hang tough.'

'I suppose that's why they are where they are, isn't it?'

'That's why a lot of very gentle, decent people are where they are, too, because their ancestors hung tough.'

Sadness, like a chill, swept over Jennie. For a moment she seemed to see the world as on a map, a maze of intersecting paths, an elaborate board game in which all the players were competing to cut one another off, so that no matter what anyone wanted to accomplish, even the most simple thing, which was just to be let alone, was not possible without fighting for it.

Jay continued thoughtfully. 'There's another angle we could take, you know, through the Environmental Protection Agency. Half the tract is wetlands.'

Called back to the subject, she agreed. 'It's another approach.'

'But it all takes time. Meanwhile we've got to stop them in their tracks. Or rather, old George will have to stop them. I'm surprised he's willing to go ahead with it.'

'He's scared to death, poor guy. But he feels committed. He said it's a matter of principle. He's such a fine old guy.

'When are you going to see the DA?'

'I'll call tomorrow and hope to see him in the afternoon.'

'You ought to have my dad along, don't you think?'

'Of course. George can go later. He's going to stay here for a day or two while Martha has tests at the hospital.'

Jay shoved the plate away. 'I'm not as hungry as I thought I was.'

'You're tired,' Jennie said tenderly.

'To tell you the truth, I am. A bad thing happened today. One of our young men sort of fell apart in my office. His wife walked out on him yesterday, and he had to go to somebody to cry, I suppose, and he picked me.'

'What made her leave?'

'He says she told him she just got tired of being married, wanted an open marriage, all that stuff. But who knows? I wasn't there, I didn't live with them. But I'll tell you, his tears got to me.' Jay reached across the table and grasped both her hands. 'Oh, Jennie, what a blessed thing it is to believe in someone absolutely and completely, to know another human being as well as you know yourself! I want to be married to you so badly, I can't wait.'

What wouldn't Shirley give, she and all the others, for a man who would say this!

'You don't answer me,' he said. Two small lines appeared between his eyebrows.

'Do I have to? Darling, you shouldn't even need an answer. You ought to know.'

'I do, I do. Shall we go back to your place?'

She felt a flood of longing, and of sorrow also, because the longing for him was now diluted, and because his familiar hands, the nails with half-moons, and the cleft in his chin, and the single dark wave that kept falling over the temple were all not perfectly her own anymore. She had such queer feelings sometimes, as though they were about to disappear while she was looking at them.

And Jill, young Jill, was the sole reason for these queer feelings. When her eyes filled yesterday, the tears made a path down her cheeks and rolled inside her collar. Will I dream about her tears tonight? Will I ever see her again? Can I bear never seeing her again? But I don't think she wants to see me – not on my terms, anyway. And I can't see her on hers. How can I?

Jay was waiting. 'But you said you were so tired,' she told him.

'All right, then. No love tonight.'

They went out to the street. Under a lamp he tilted her face up to his. 'So sweet you are. I don't mind tonight. I can wait. In a few more weeks I'll never have to wait again, will I?'

8

It was Arthur Wolfe's authority and name that had impressed young Martin, the district attorney, with the importance of their story. There had, after all, been no actual offer, in so many words, of a bribe, Jennie reflected. And Martin had remarked as much at the beginning.

'Not yet,' Arthur had told him. 'But there will be one, make no mistake. I know what I'm talking about. I've seen our mayor and his friends in action here. I've been active in township affairs for a good many years, you know.'

The young man had nodded. 'And county affairs, Mr Wolfe.' He had smiled. 'I'm remembering that article a while back where they called you "the watchdog."'

Arthur had laughed. 'And now we have two dogs,' he had said, indicating Jennie, who had added somewhat grimly that the way things looked, they'd be needing a pack before they were finished.

Now Martin was questioning her. Wary and keen, he kept his eyes on hers as his questions and her answers flowed.

'So you really believe there's a relationship between the man who shouted at the meeting and shoved you on the stairs and the one who telephoned Cromwell?'

'Yes, I do. To begin with, there's his reputation. And you have only to look at him to feel the anger in him. But there have to be others too. A person or persons in Barker

Development, making connections. I know it's all still vague, hard to tell where the connections begin or where they may end. But there are connections, I'm positive.'

She looked out of the window, where a worn-out, dark green shade, stopped at the halfway mark, revealed through the lower part of the pane a network of thin black branches and a complex webbing of twigs. A web without beginning or end. The waning wintry light was ominous, and she understood the primary cause of her dark mood.

Martin got up and switched on a fluorescent light that hung above the massive desk so that it could glare upon the stained blotter, scarred chairs, heaped papers, green metal file cabinets, and tan walls. No brightness could cheer this government-issue room. Nevertheless Martin's tone was brisk.

'And you think this man Cromwell can handle it?'

Arthur looked uncertain. 'He's not a quick thinker, by any means, my old friend. But he's brave, he's willing to try, and we have no other choice.'

'You people really care,' Martin said rather gently.

'Somebody has to,' Jennie answered.

Martin tipped back in his chair. He made a steeple with his fingertips and reflected.

'Can he switch lunch places? What I mean is, at a lunch wagon on a country road there's no way any man I send could make himself invisible. There mightn't be more than two cars in the parking lot. Can't Cromwell find a busier place in the center of town?'

Arthur shook his head. 'The arrangement's already made. George can't ask to change it without arousing suspicion.'

'Well, then he'll have to chance it all on his own. Without protection.'

'Are you thinking he'll need any?' Arthur was troubled.

'Hardly likely. Our being there is more moral support

than anything else. So he'll just have to do without it.'

'George will manage,' Jennie said. She had a momentary picture of the old man's proud stance and his proud words: 'It's a matter of principle. Being a good citizen.'

Martin stood up. 'I want you to meet Jerry Brian. I put him on the case when you called.' He pressed a button in his desk, and a moment later another young man, almost a double of Martin himself, entered the room.

Martin made introductions, explaining, 'Jerry's the man who'll get Cromwell ready.'

Arthur was interested in the mechanics of the procedure.

'Simple,' Brian explained. 'There's a microphone under your shirt, a recorder, some wires not much thicker than a hair, and that's it. Simple.'

'Jerry will prepare your man early that morning. Have him here and ready by nine at the latest,' Martin directed.

'Tell him there's nothing to worry about,' Brian added. 'Nothing to worry about.'

The two of them are the same type, a reassuring one, Jennie thought. It's the height, the physical strength, and the calmness. In a strange way, although they were so different from him, they reminded her of Jay....

Outside in the parking lot, Arthur gave a sigh of relief. 'Well, step number one is finished. I was afraid they might think we were making a mountain out of a molehill.'

'No, Martin understood. I think he was impressed that we're doing all this when there's nothing in it for us.'

'Just the shape of the country's future. That's all that's in it for us.'

'Of course. Nothing personal, is what I meant.'

White hills loomed over the town. The afternoon was still, with the moist feel of snow in the air. Arthur paused.

'Listen to the silence. I love this north country. I hope you'll come to love it too.'

Jennie just smiled.

'I believe you're learning to, the way you're fighting to save it.' They got into the car. 'But you do look tired, Jennie. Are you working too hard?'

'Work has a way of piling up. I guess I've been doing too much.'

'Well, try to level off if you can. Take time to smell the roses.'

The cliché, which ordinarily in someone else's mouth could have been irritating, now rang with kindness. It was – the word leapt into Jennie's mind – *fatherly*. And a cold-water chill ran through her. He was fatherly to her, and she was lying to him.

'At least,' the old man continued, 'you'll have a break over Thanksgiving weekend, with nothing to do but sleep and eat. Enid's getting in enough food for an army.'

It was, fortunately, not more than a ten-mile ride to the station where she was to take the train back to the city. All the way Arthur kept talking, so that she had to respond appropriately to his remarks about Barker Development, the mayor, and George – or to his comments about Jay and Jay's children – while through it all her internal voice was crying: Jill ... what about Jill ... ? I'm so afraid ... afraid.

9

It was five degrees above zero when Jennie and Jay and the children arrived in the country for the long Thanksgiving weekend, but the air was dry, the sun dazzled the icicles that hung like stalactites from the eaves, and one didn't feel how cold it was. Indoors, the house was pleasantly crowded, for Jay's brother and his grown children had arrived, along with various aunts, uncles, and cousins. Every fire was lit; every room had an arrangement of gold and bronze chrysanthemums; every little table bore a dish of grapes or nuts, of popcorn or chocolate or ginger cookies. Jennie was surrounded and bathed in the warmth of talk and the fragrances of wood smoke, food, and flowers. This was her first real introduction to the extended family, and she understood their natural curiosity. She had taken great pains to look good, and saw, as a result, their frank approval of her new white knit on which Enid's pearls gleamed so softly.

Mom, after learning of Enid's gift, had sent a pair of pearl bracelets from Florida. Playing with the bracelets at her cuff, she thought of Mom. A woman needs another woman to confide in. . . . At this moment Mom was probably boasting a little about her daughter to a circle of widows in the courtyard of the apartment house. Dusty palmettoes, heat and clatter . . . At this moment, too, in

Chicago, Jill and Peter were meeting. Where? How? Jennie's head spun.

'Well, thank goodness George got through safely yesterday.' Arthur Wolfe spoke into her right ear. 'You've heard from him, of course.'

'Only that it was definitely an offer of payment, which we expected. He didn't read the tape on the phone, so Jay and I will go over to his place and listen, if you'll excuse us.'

'Poor fellow. I admit it was a case of better him than me. It took a bit of courage to sit all wired up in a diner. I'd be thinking the wire might fall down around my ankles, or that something else might go wrong.'

'It took more than a bit of courage,' Jennie replied, and thought again of Bruce Fisher, who might or might not have had anything to do with the business. More likely might. It was a shivery thought.

George Cromwell's office was in a wing of a simple frame house, on a street of similar houses a few blocks from the center of town. The house, which needed paint, was obviously not the home of an affluent man. This impression was fortified by the interior. In the sitting room, into which George led them, the upholstery was shabby, the old oak pieces dark and dowdy. The house and its furnishings had passed intact from Martha's grandmother on George's wedding day, along with Martha, who was now resting upstairs.

George placed his little machine on the table and held up a tape with an expression both proud and a little sheepish.

'You won't believe your ears. It's all here.'

'What does he look like, this John Jones?' Jay asked.

George grinned. 'He gave me his right name. Said you couldn't be too careful on the phone. His name's Harry Corrin. Fellow about forty-five, but then – it's hard to tell.

Enormous yellow, crooked teeth. Bad bite. Being a dentist, that's what I always notice first, the teeth.'

Jennie saw a twitch of amusement on Jay's lips. 'I suppose he was very friendly, George?'

'Oh, friendly, yes. But here, let me start the tape. I'll give you the second one, where he really gets down to business. The first time we just talked about the town and the kind of buildings the Barkers put up, and how I really ought to see some of them and then maybe I'd understand better that they didn't come here to ruin the town. That sort of thing. It took up the whole tape. Sort of getting acquainted, you might say.'

'Did you give any opinions?' Jennie wanted to know.

'Oh, just enough to let him think I was interested. I wanted to lure him along.' The tape whirred. 'Ah. Here it comes.'

Interspersed among the background sounds of passing voices, the screech of chairs on a bare floor, the clink of dishes, and the occasional ping of a cash register came the two voices: George's elderly quaver; the other one young and with a coaxing quality.

'So, do you see things a little differently than you did before we talked yesterday, George? If you don't mind my calling you George?'

'Not at all, Harry.'

'Well, do you get my meaning? That we're not going to mess up your town?'

'Well, in a way I do, although I'm not certain. I'd have to do a lot more thinking.'

'Sure. Sure. You're a very intelligent man. Shrewd too. You like to make dead certain before you give your opinion.'

A silence followed, during which one could imagine George nodding rather gravely and the other man observing him, during which dishes rattled again and somewhere outside an engine backfired.

Then Harry's voice resumed, lower this time, more sympathetic. 'You've got a lot to think about these days, anyway. I know. I mean, your wife's being so sick. It must cost you a bundle.'

'Yep. Big bills.' One heard George's sigh.

'I hear it's terrible what hospitals and doctors charge these days. Can eat up a man's life's savings.'

'True,' George said. 'Very true.'

'And more, I hear. Some people even have to go in debt.'

'I hope I won't have to do that. But it may happen yet, who knows?'

'Is it that bad, George? That's terrible. A man your age stands on his feet all his life filling teeth, and now he's come to where he has to borrow to keep his head above water.' Silence again. 'Yes,' said Harry mournfully, 'I get a laugh when I hear somebody say "Money isn't everything," when I know – and you must know it, too, right now – that it sure as hell is. What a difference it would make to your peace of mind if you had a nice little bundle put away!' The voice went low, so that Jay and Jennie had to strain to hear it. 'Say, if you had fifty thousand in the bank, in cash in a safe-deposit box, you could sleep nights. Right, George?'

'Well, fifty would help. But as you say, the bills are something to see.'

'All right, seventy-five. If you had that, you'd sleep even better, wouldn't you?'

'Hah! And where the dickens could I ever hope to find that kind of money?'

'Hey, George! There are ways, you know it. And when you have friends, nothing's impossible. Listen, George, I like you. You're smart and you're a man of your word, I can tell. And I'm a man of my word too. Good faith, that's what it's all about in this life. Right, George?'

'Sure. Always.'

'Okay. So one hand washes the other, as they say. I snap my fingers, and in my hands I can have seventy-five thousand green whenever I want it, just like that. Whenever.'

'Whenever what?'

'Whenever Barker gets the go-ahead to build. Simple as that.'

'You don't mean –'

'I mean.'

Silence followed. One imagined George pretending to be absorbing the fact. Presently he said, 'Oh. And the seventy-five – would it be for me only?'

'The way we figure it, you're the one, aren't you? Your vote does the trick.'

Once more there was a silence, into which Harry broke rather anxiously. 'It's even possible – don't hold me to it – but I have an idea that it could even be raised to a hundred.'

'A hundred! I'd be in the money!'

'Yep. All green. Nice and tidy in the safe-deposit box. How about it, George? You like that all right?'

'Oh, boy, I guess I do.'

'You'd better believe you do. Listen. I'm going back to the city tonight to get the go-ahead on the numbers. I'll be back here Sunday.'

'Same time, same place?'

'Right. And listen, I'm pretty sure it'll be okay for you to count on twenty-five now and the rest when it passes. If it doesn't pass, you return the twenty-five.' There was the sound of chairs being scraped back, and then Harry's voice, friendly and upbeat. 'But it'll pass. Okay, George? It's up to you.'

'Sure. Okay. Sounds good to me.'

'See you.'

George switched the tape off, exclaiming as if he had just thought of it, 'Didn't he take a chance, though, being seen with me?'

'Not really,' Jennie said. 'Neither a chance for him nor for you. Nobody around here knows him.'

'Ah, yes, of course. I see.'

'You'll need to set aside some time so we can give the tape to the district attorney,' Jennie said.

'Do I have to go along?'

'Of course you do. You're the star witness.'

'Ah, yes, I see. I suppose he'll be bringing the twenty-five thousand tomorrow. What do I do with it?'

'Nothing except hold on to it.'

George sighed, and Jennie said gently, 'Buck up, George. Everything's working out just right, and you've nothing to fear. We're starting back to the city at about four tomorrow, so will you give us a call right after your meeting?'

Jennie kissed the old man's cheek. 'George, you've been perfect. Just perfect.'

Sunday was a mild day. In the direct sunshine icicles began to shed slow drops, and the tip of a breeze blew powder from the surface of the snow. In the morning the children went sledding, after which Jay and Jennie took them to the drugstore in the village to buy candy bars for the long drive home.

While Jay went into the store, she waited in the car, stifling as always the same tormenting thoughts. Suddenly she had one of those odd, almost uncanny sensations that come with an awareness of being watched. Turning then, she looked directly into an unforgettable face. Bruce Fisher was leaning against a lamppost a few doors down from where the car had stopped. For an instant only, they made eye contact, but even after Jennie looked away, the feeling persisted that he was still staring at her. When Jay came out of the store, she told him.

'Don't look now, but Fisher's standing over there.'

'I know. I saw him when I went in.'

'He makes me shiver.'

'Understandably. Still, we mustn't let ourselves be paranoid about him. After all, he does have a right to stand on the street in his own town.'

Yet afterward they were to wonder. . . .

The rest of the morning followed a quiet Sunday pattern: the newspapers and a long game of Monopoly, which included everyone except Donny, who watched cartoons on the VCR. Then came midday dinner, followed by Donny's nap and packing their suitcases.

It was almost four o'clock. Jay was just saying 'If George doesn't call, we'll reach him tomorrow' when the telephone rang.

'You take it, Jennie, it's your case.'

George's booming voice came over the wire with such intensity that Jay and his parents looked up in surprise.

'George! You're all out of breath!'

'Oh, I've had a terrible time! Terrible! It's no wonder I'm out of breath. You won't believe what happened. Harry came in, I was sitting in the booth waiting, having a cup of coffee, and the minute he walked in the door I saw he was mad, but mad as you can't imagine. You never saw such a face, it was black. I swear the blood was black, it was so dark and –'

Jennie interrupted. 'Please. Just tell me what happened.'

'Well, people have been watching my house! They must have been! He knew you and Jay were there yesterday. Who could have told him? Oh, you can't believe . . . He called me every kind of filthy name. I don't mind that, but he was in such a rage! He said I had double-crossed him and I was dead wrong if I thought I could get away with it; nobody ever did that to him and got away with it.' George was almost sobbing. 'And then he reached across the table – there was nobody in the place except the counterman, and he'd gone back into the kitchen – and he grabbed me by my necktie and said he'd bash my face in. And then – I hate to tell you this – but I lost my head and I told him to go on and try to do it, just try, because I have everything on tape and he was in big, big trouble and he'd better know he was.'

'You didn't! You couldn't have!'

George said mournfully, contritely, 'Yes, I did.'

Jennie turned from the phone. 'They had an argument, and George told him about the tape.'

Arthur, in disgust, threw up his hands.

'I'm awfully sorry,' George was saying. 'Awfully sorry. I know it was careless of me, I know –'

'Careless!' Jennie cried. 'Is that what you call it?'

'Oh, I'm so sorry. I just lost my head when he grabbed me, just lost my head.'

She sighed. 'What happened then?'

'He threatened me.'

'Tell me how. Specifically.'

'Well, not specifically. Just . . . just threatened, I don't know. Said I'd pay for it unless I handed over the tape. The one from before and the one I had on me. And I told him I didn't have one on, and that the other was in safe hands where he couldn't get it. Of course, it's home, hidden in my house.'

'Of course,' Jennie said.

Safe hands. It wouldn't be hard for anyone to figure out who else besides George might have it.

'I hope you people won't be too furious with me.'

She sighed again. 'Being furious won't help. Where are you now, home?'

'No, I'm at a pay phone on the highway. I just left the diner.'

'Well, go on home and rest. You've had a bad time.'

'Yes, I'll be on my way. I left Martha alone.'

Jennie hung up. 'Well, here we are.'

'Naturally I always knew,' Arthur said, 'that George had, shall we say, limitations? But of all the simpletons!'

Jay considered the situation. 'Wait a moment. This really may not be the very worst scenario. Now that they know they've been taped, the prudent thing would be for them to disappear from the scene, withdraw their offer, and hope against hope that the tapes won't be submitted to the authorities. Or' – and here Jay looked very sober – 'or else, if anyone should decide to get hold of the tape, it could be a bad scenario, an extremely bad scenario.'

All were silent while obvious, rather nasty, possibilities were considered. After a moment Jay looked at his watch.

'Well, it's Sunday and there's nothing we can do now, so I suggest we just start back home.'

Enid laid her hand on her son's arm. 'You will be careful? I'm thinking of some awful person storming into your office or into Jennie's. Whatever would you do?'

'We'd manage.'

'You would, I guess, but what if they think Jennie's got the tapes?'

'Jennie's tough.' Jay grinned. 'You don't know her yet. She'll keep her eyes open.'

'Well, I hope. Do take care of yourselves.'

By tacit agreement nothing more was said on the subject during the ride. The children opened bags of M&M's and counted red cars on the road. On the way out of town they passed the lane that led from the highway to the Green Marsh. And Jennie, recognizing the turnoff, had a poignant recall of the morning, not six weeks past, when she had stood there with Jay and life had seemed so bright, so hopeful and easy. And only a few hours later the telephone had rung.

Her mind went back now to Peter and Jill. Right this minute, very likely, Jill was flying back to New York after seeing Peter.

'What's wrong?' Jay asked.

'Nothing. Why?'

'I thought I saw out of the corner of my eye that you were frowning.'

She made light of the remark. 'Hey! You're supposed to keep your eyes on the road. Yes, I guess maybe I was frowning, thinking about George and the whole business. We're getting more than we bargained for.'

'Talk about it tomorrow. Let's have music for now. Want the tail end of the Philharmonic?'

'Fine.'

The Eroica swept into the car. And Jay's hand, for a minute or two, covered Jennie's, which lay on the seat. The pressure, the possessive gesture, the living warmth of that hand, the majestic music – all caught at her heart.

Oh, my God, please. Please . . . Jennie begged silently.

She closed her eyes, and he, thinking she wanted to sleep, withdrew his hand. Indeed, the music and the hum of the engine would soon put her to sleep if she allowed them to. She knew she was one of those rare people who, instead of being sleepless when they are beset, are overwhelmed by sleep. It's only a form of escape, she thought, remembering her course in elementary psychology. Laying her head back on the seat, she allowed the escape.

Traffic was light on this winter Sunday, and they reached the apartment sooner than expected. Jennie went upstairs to expedite the children's going to bed. Jay took charge of Donnie, and Jennie, as usual, supervised the girls.

While they brushed their teeth she drew the curtains, pulled the blue-sprigged coverlets off the beds, hung up their country pants and jackets, and put out their school clothes for the morning, plaid kilts and red sweaters. Racks of clothing hung in the twin closets: down coats for weekdays, velvet-collared English coats for parties, yellow straw hats with daisies and ribbon streamers for the coming spring. On impulse she picked up a hat; the streamers dropped long, these innocent ribbons worn in places to which little girls went all dressed up – to the circus, maybe, or to visit relatives on holidays. And she wondered whether Jill had ever worn a hat with ribbons when she was eight years old.

Squeals of hilarity came now from the bathroom. Emily, who had recently discovered what she thought of as dirty jokes, was regaling her sister with them from the superiority of two more years. In another mood Jennie would have been amused by their mirth. But in this mood she could only question: Had Jill worn a bow in her hair when she was eight? Or six? And had she worn plaid kilts and told wicked jokes and stolen candy to hide under her pillow and been quick at checkers or Monopoly?

The ribbon was still in her hand when the girls came back to the bedroom. Sue looked surprised.

'I was admiring the hat,' Jennie explained.

And again guilt chilled her. It was as if even her thoughts had had no right to intrude on this place. And with only a part of her mind, she finished the bedtime ritual: the hair combing, the brief story, and the goodnight kisses.

She had just turned out the light and gone into the hall when Jay summoned her.

'Did you hear the telephone ring?'

'No, why?'

'Come in here.' She followed him into the living room. 'Sit down and prepare for a shock.' Jay was pacing, excited and at the same time grim. 'That was my father on the phone. You're not going to believe this. George Cromwell's dead.'

'My God!'

'His car turned over on the back road going home.'

Jennie shuddered. 'Killed outright?'

'Yes, they're positive. No pain, thank God.' Jay was still pacing up and down the room. 'The police suspect foul play. He had not been speeding. He was hardly the type for it, anyway. There were car tracks only inches behind his, but unfortunately they can't be identified. There were snow flurries, which started right after we left, Dad said, and everything's blurred. The way it looks, he was deliberately cut off at an elbow bend and forced off the road. There's an outcropping of rocks at that point, and he smashed into them.' Jay clenched his fists. 'They killed him. Or caused his death. It's the same thing.'

'Do you suppose he was followed from the diner or from the pay phone where he was talking to me?'

'I'm almost positive, Jennie.' Jay hesitated. 'It's so rotten, I hate to tell you, but whoever did it – They found his pockets turned inside out. But nothing was taken, and his wallet was intact.'

'So they were looking for a tape.'

'Yes, but of course he had none on him this time.'

'It's – it's unreal. Only a couple of hours ago I was talking to him.'

'My dad's just broken up. George and he were friends for almost fifty years.'

'Old George . . . I'm so sorry we ever got him into this business! Such a good soul! An innocent. Never really grew up.'

'Honey, he wanted to be in it. And how could we have expected a thing like this?'

'Now I'm thinking about Martha. To walk into a dying woman with news like that! The world's such a rotten place, sometimes I can't stand it, Jay.'

He came over to sit next to her and put his arms around her.

'I don't suppose,' he said, 'it'll ever be different. I almost have to believe that evil is inborn. Original sin, or something like that. To be so greedy that you kill. If they're the ones who did it,' he added after a moment. 'We can't be sure.'

'That's the lawyer in you speaking. The rest of you is sure, isn't it? You sounded as if it were.'

'I guess it is. Yes. It is.'

There was for a little while nothing more to be said. The room was so still that Jennie could clearly hear the hurried ticking of Jay's wristwatch. Suddenly her eyes filled with tears and her choked cry broke the hush. Jay's arm tightened and his free hand grasped hers. She felt small, shrunken with shame because he was surely thinking how soft she was, how compassionate, to cry so for George. And she was crying for George, truly, but for so much more: for Jill; for herself; for lives that should, if only one were decent and kind, be lived so easily, so simply under the sun – and were not.

Presently Jay said, 'First thing in the morning, I don't have to tell you, Dad and you will have to get in touch with the DA and tell him what you know about the lunch. Unfortunately there's hardly a clue, except that the man had big teeth. There are an awful lot of people with big teeth,' he finished wryly.

Jennie closed her eyes. 'The mind doesn't take it in. All this hatred because of a piece of land. I keep seeing the cattails around the pond. And wasn't there an enormous weeping willow at the bottom of the hill, or do I imagine it?'

'No, it's there. A very old one, which is unusual. They seldom get that old.'

'They want it all so badly, those people.'

'Many, many dollars, Jennie.'

Both fell so still again that the silence tingled in the room. This sheltered space – where long draperies spilled over onto Persian rugs and lamps held pearl-pink lights aloft on crystal arms – was a safe cocoon ten floors above Park Avenue, a million miles away from a lonely road where no one watched while a man crashed headlong into death.

Jay said gravely, 'Keep your door locked.'

'Who doesn't do that in New York?' she answered in a light tone to reassure him. Nevertheless, she understood his meaning.

'If they think you have the tape, it's the same as if you actually had it.'

'They can't very well run me off the road here in the city.'

'You're right, but still I worry. You know me, I'm a worrier. I don't like where you live. There's no security. I'll feel satisfied when you're living behind these doors with me. And you won't wear your ring when you go to court, will you? Or in your office?'

'Of course not.'

He could not know how uncomfortable, quite apart from any fear of being robbed of it, that ring made her feel. Over this past weekend, when naturally she had had to wear it, to stretch forth her hand so that it might be seen and admired, she had had such a queer feeling, as though she were wearing something that was not hers. She had not shown it to any of her friends but kept it hidden in a box of cereal on the kitchen shelf.

'Well,' Jay said, 'I'll call downstairs to the doorman and have them get a taxi for you.'

They parted somberly. The old man's death had laid a heavy hand upon them.

10

For Jennie there were now two heavy hands, one on each shoulder bearing her down, but the weightier hand belonged to Jill. If only they could have made some agreement! For those few moments when they had had their arms around each other, she had been moved beyond words. This resilient, hard young body, this thick, sweet-smelling hair, had come from her, from Jennie Rakowsky. But the girl was hot-tempered and unreasonable, she thought again with sharp resentment. She at least could have tried, couldn't she? She didn't even listen or try to see that I must have some reason on my side.

She felt helpless. And there was so much else to be done this morning: neglected mail, telephone calls to clients. And, immediately urgent, a call to the district attorney.

'I've already talked to Mr Wolfe,' Martin said. 'Understandably, he was pretty upset, and I didn't get much information from him. Anyway, you're the last person who talked to Cromwell. What can you give me?'

'No leads, I'm afraid. George was practically incoherent. To tell the truth, I was pretty upset myself, too, and –'

'Of course. Just take your time. You'll be surprised how much you'll recall.'

So speaks the surgeon before the operation, with calm encouragement. Jennie took a deep breath as she tried to retrieve disjointed scraps of that fateful conversation.

'I do remember the name. Harry Corrin. Naturally he wasn't John Jones. I suppose he isn't really Harry Corrin, either. I think George said he was in his forties. He had huge yellow teeth. George noticed teeth.' Foolishly, hysterically, Jennie giggled. Then, recovering quickly, she went on. 'It was an angry scene. Furious, George said. It seems that somebody saw me and Jay – Arthur Wolfe's son, Jay – going to George's house. So he, this Corrin, figured that George was double-crossing him, and he threatened to, I think, "bash his face in." And then George lost his head and told him he had something on tape, and he, Corrin, was in trouble.'

'Good Lord,' Martin said.

'It's so, so awful! I'm sure he's the man, aren't you?'

'We're never sure of anything until we're sure. Incidentally, who's got that tape? You?'

'No, no. It's got to be in George's house.'

'Okay, we'll let it lie till after the funeral. It's safe there, and we can't bother the poor woman today.'

'When is the funeral?'

'Day after tomorrow.'

'What time, do you know?'

'Afternoon. But it's private, in case you were planning to come up.'

'Of course I was.'

'Well, it's strictly private because of Mrs Cromwell's illness. If the weather's bad, she won't even get to the cemetery.'

'Awful,' Jennie said again.

It was a relief, though, not having to go. Funerals always made one think too much, but this one would be harrowing. She could see it and smell it: sweet, musky flowers blowing on the heavy coffin; sleet whitening the turned earth next to the grave.

She came back to the present. 'If I can help, Mr Martin, you have my number.'

'Fine. I'll keep you informed as we go along.'

When she had hung up, she sat for a few minutes, looked with unfocused eyes at nothing, and was acutely aware of feeling weak. At the same time she was seeing herself as her clients would be seeing her today, and the contrast was strange indeed. For them, Miss R. was the problem solver, capable and sharp-witted, the modern professional whose Oxford-gray skirts stood for serious purpose, whose apricot silk shirt and silver earrings stood for womanly warmth, and whose large, paper-laden desk, textbooks, and computer were her impressive tools. All morning people came and went, bringing their questions, puzzles, complaints, and tears. All morning she listened, took notes, and gave answers, while in the back of her mind her own hard questions ran their rounds.

She thought about Jill's weekend in Chicago with Peter. It was infuriating to think of them together. Where had he been when Jill was born? He had no right, no damn right to play the father now! 'He wants to see me,' Jill had said so proudly. 'He's not like you.' It was absurd. No, worse, it was obscene.

Peter had had nothing to do with the girl, nothing at all beyond those few minutes of sexual delight on a spring evening in a garden, while she, Jennie, had grown a human being, fed her with her own blood, felt the birth pain and the pain of relinquishment. He hadn't even asked about the baby then! And now he welcomed her. Now he claimed her!

Oh, but when Jill walked with him, wherever they had walked in Chicago, strangers must have seen, without pausing to think, that here was a father and his daughter! That height and that hair alone were unmistakable bonds. There was no sense trying to deny it. What a shock of recognition must he have felt at first sight of that splendid girl! And Jennie trembled with outrage at the unfairness of it.

Meanwhile, in the midst of this turmoil, and with another part of her mind, she was still thinking about yesterday's tragedy. Jay would be keeping in touch with developments through his father. She looked at the desk clock. It was time for Jay's call, which always came toward the end of the afternoon. So when the telephone rang, she picked it up without waiting for Dinah to answer first.

'Hello, Jennie? This is Peter.'

She almost dropped the receiver. She could have ripped it from the wall. Damn phone, I hate it! Like a snake, it whips out of the innocent grass as you stroll down the hill.

'Is that you, Jennie?' The voice lifted, youthful and jaunty.

'It's Jennie, all right.'

'Of course you're shocked to hear from me.'

'Not really. Jill said you threatened to call.'

'Oh! She couldn't really have said "threatened," could she?' The question was touched ever so lightly with humor.

'To me it was a threat.'

Peter ignored that and went on. 'She's so lovely, Jennie. Just so lovely. This weekend, the whole thing – I can't believe it's real.'

'It's real enough.' She heard her own voice, its dry tone, the dismissal of it. Remarkably, a cold calm had settled over her.

Why am I even listening to this person? I ought to hang up. So damn mannerly I am.

'A lot of water's gone over the dam.'

'Nineteen years. What do you expect?'

'Well, I certainly didn't expect what's happened.'

'Nor did I, I assure you.'

'You sound so angry, Jennie.'

'Should I be throbbing with joy?'

'There really could be some joy in all this, you know.'

'Hooray for you if you've found some.'

'I'd like to help you find some. That's why I've come here.'

'Come where?'

'To New York. I flew in with Jill last night. She had to go back to her classes, but I'm rather a free agent, so I decided to take a little time off to see whether I can get you and Jill together.'

'You've turned out to be an altruist, haven't you?'

'Jennie, hate me. Go on. You've every right. But don't take it out on the girl. She's so unhappy that you don't want to know her.'

'That's not true!' The cool, calm surface cracked. 'I never said I didn't. I tried to explain, but she didn't give me a proper chance, just stood up and ran out in a temper.'

'I can imagine. She's impulsive, or just plain young. Don't you remember being young?'

'All too well!'

There was a moment's pause before Peter spoke again. 'Jill said you looked wonderful.'

'That's nice. That should make me very happy, I'm sure.'

'Jennie, please. Give her a chance.'

'I thought I gave her a chance.'

'You did, and it didn't work. Okay. But will you try once more? Really, you should.'

This man, resurrected out of a buried nightmare, has the nerve to tell me what I should do! she thought angrily.

'I'm staying at the Waldorf.'

The Waldorf. Yes, only the best. Staying with his wife, maybe? God only knows.

'... dinner tonight,' he was saying. 'The three of us. I'd like to make peace between the two of you.'

It wasn't in her, after all, to ignore sincerity. And she replied quietly, 'I've thought about this – I've thought of very little else these past weeks. It would have been so much better if she'd never found us. Found me, anyway. I don't know about you.'

'As for me, I have to say I'm glad she did. I never dreamed it would happen, but now that it has, I'm glad. I've had my share of shame over the years, Jennie. I don't think there are words enough in the language to express my sorrow over what I did.'

Against her will, she was moved. The phrase *over the years* made a falling cadence, an echo remote, nostalgic, sorrowful, and lost. She saw him standing at the airport gate with arm upraised in farewell, a bewildered, anxious, frightened, useless boy.

'So, will you?' he pleaded. 'Tonight at seven? It's not for my sake. I have no right to expect anything from you. It's for her. She tried so hard to find us and looked so long.'

'I don't want to,' Jennie said very low, but thought, And yet, in another way, I do.

'I didn't hear you.'

'I don't want to,' she repeated, and cried out suddenly. 'There's too much pain here! Too much pain!'

'I know.'

'You don't know. You didn't give birth to her.'

'Mine's a different kind of hurt. It concerns you; what I did, and didn't do, to you.'

'Peter, this talk serves no purpose. You're tearing open a wound that healed a long time ago. Don't do it, please.'

'All right, I won't. But will you come tonight, however hard it is? Please?'

How could she refuse? 'I suppose I'll have to.'

'I'll wait for you in the lobby on the Park Avenue side.

Will I know you? I mean, you haven't dyed your hair or anything?'

'I look the same.'

'At seven, then.'

'At seven.'

She looked up to face a blur of rain on the greasy window glass. Vague impulses stirred and mingled: reluctance and a trembling dread, along with an unfamiliar sense of fatefulness. As rational and practical as Jennie was, she scorned the idea that anything could be 'ordained.' Yet it seemed as though this happening today were inevitable, as if everything in the past had been treacherously, secretly moving toward it.

Now, although it was not easy to admit, she felt a touch of curiosity to know whether or how in nineteen years Peter had changed. And there was something more: Really, she wanted him to see how well she had survived, how successful she was, and how desirable still. It embarrassed her to have such a foolish wish, but there it was.

She was to meet Jay for dinner tonight. Now, what excuse to give? Biting her lips, she frowned and thought, then thought some more. He wouldn't be pleased with any reason, that was sure. And Mom always said she wasn't a good liar, that anyone could see through her excuses. But she had to find something plausible. Finally she concluded: a client. That would do. A poor woman who works late and has to be seen in the evening. That was something he would understand and condone.

She picked up the telephone. Lie upon lie, the edifice was building higher.

11

He came striding from the bank of elevators down through the carpeted, gilded splendor of the lobby. Tourists clustered, bearing cameras; women in glittering formal dress on their way to grand events moved past; but the tall man with the red-crowned head stood out in the diverse crowd. For an instant he stood scanning the scene; then, finding Jennie, he came swiftly toward her with both hands outstretched.

'Hello, Jennie.'

'Hello, Peter.'

They shook hands. The gesture was curiously formal. She wasn't sure what she had expected him to do – or expected herself to do, for that matter.

'Gosh, Jennie, you're right,' he said. 'You really are just the same.'

'And so are you.'

The bright opal eyes still smiled. The voice still had the old ring that could bring enthusiasm to the most simple remark.

Then simultaneously they remembered Jill, who, standing slightly in back of Peter, was regarding them both with open curiosity. Peter put his arm around Jill, pulling her close.

'This is an historic moment, and it calls for champagne. I don't know what the drinking age is in New York, but whatever it is, you're going to have champagne tonight, Jill.'

Jill didn't answer. Perhaps she didn't want to acknowledge Jennie, or perhaps she was only waiting for Jennie to speak first.

'Hello, Jill,' Jennie said. 'We meet again, don't we?' Conciliatory, pleading.

'Hello.' The tone was flat.

'Well,' Peter said, obviously choosing to ignore the awkwardness, 'it's past time, and we've a table waiting.'

Jennie fell deliberately behind and followed them. They shine together, she was thinking. They have the same walk, with long, springing, almost loping steps. Without knowing it, Jill was a Mendes. Suddenly Jennie felt too small, despised herself for the feeling, and did not understand it.

At Peacock Alley they turned left, entered the restaurant, and were led to a table on which stood an arrangement of pink roses. Peter had made a celebration. Another pink rose lay across Jennie's plate and Jill's. Beside each of the two plates was a little blue Tiffany box tied with white ribbon.

'Open them,' he commanded. His face sparkled when two identical silver bangle bracelets emerged from their tissue-paper nests. 'They did me a special favor with the engraving, a rush job.'

Jennie's bore, in a swirl of old-fashioned script, the words 'From Jill to Jennie with love' and the date. Obviously Jill's must say the reverse. What a childish gesture, in spite of being kind and well meant! As if this conjunction of three human beings who, in their various ways, were suffering through these moments, were a festival!

'I want you to remember this day,' Peter told them.

As if it were a day one could forget.

Jill spoke first. 'It's lovely. It goes with my necklace.'

She had taken off her beaver jacket, revealing a silver chain worn over a gray wool dress.

Jennie followed. 'Yes, lovely. Thank you, Peter.'

'Let's order, shall we? Then we can talk. We've a lot to talk about.' He kept smiling. He was working hard to stimulate them. 'How about shrimp for an appetizer? Or else soup? It always goes well on a cold night. I got the hot-soup habit from living in Chicago. That wind off Lake Michigan took some getting used to after living in Georgia most of my life, let me tell you. I think I'll try the lobster bisque myself. But take your time, you two, no hurry.' He went through the menu. 'Veal. Swordfish. Let's see, filet mignon sounds good, doesn't it? Can't make up my mind.'

Jennie urged silently, Do stop trying so hard, will you? It's foolish, it's crazy, being here like this. If all the elegant people in this room could know who we are, they'd have something else to talk about. 'Fantastic,' they'd say.... Why did I come here? Oh, I know very well why I came....

But it wasn't going to work, because Jill obviously intended to ignore her. She, too, probably had been coaxed to this meeting against her will. Nevertheless she was eating heartily, while carrying on a dialogue with Peter. It seemed almost as if they were in league against Jennie. No, that was absurd; Peter wasn't a man to be in league with anyone or against anyone. That much she remembered. He simply wasn't aware of Jennie's exclusion, or of the charged atmosphere.

When the champagne was poured, Peter raised his glass. 'To health and happiness and peace among us.'

Jennie's swallow, on a churning stomach, sickened her. When she put down the goblet, he looked anxious.

'Don't you like it? It's Dom Pérignon.'

'It's excellent, but I'm usually a Perrier woman.'

'I remember when you were a ginger-ale woman.'

She could have corrected him: I wasn't a woman. I was a girl, a child who turned into a woman too soon. But the reminder would have been brutal and would have served no purpose, anyway.

The dialogue, like a volleyball, passed over her bent head while she tried to eat.

'There's no landscape like it,' Jill was saying. 'All those miles of yellow and cedar and piñon. And the sweet air. Nothing like that anywhere, either.'

'And quivering aspen along the river,' added Peter, and said to Jennie, 'Jill says you talked about New Mexico together. She knows a lot about the Anasazi, the Ancient Ones, probably more than I do. I only spent a couple of weeks two summers ago, mostly studying the kivas. Religious meeting places, council houses. Below ground. Very interesting. But you probably know about them.'

'No, not a thing,' Jennie said, refusing to help him.

For a moment he looked pleading and hurt, then, once more mustering cheer, he returned to the land of mesquite and staghorn cactus.

As for me, I'm done with pleading, Jennie thought. I can't even as much as catch Jill's glance, although I know that when she thinks I can't see her, she is examining me slyly. Perhaps she's trying to imagine the primal scene – don't we all at some time or other? At least they say we do. Yes, it was a warm, silent evening, the gravel on the driveway smelled of dust, and we had to hurry before they all came home. That's how it was. That's how you come to be sitting at the Waldorf Astoria, Jill, in your fine dress and your dignity, with your poor heart pounding, as it must be.

'I feel sort of melancholy when I've wasted a day,' Jill was saying, 'because it can't be retrieved. There's one less day to live. It's not that I need to have accomplished anything much. It's more that I need to have been aware and really alive.'

'I know exactly what you mean.' Peter was eager again. 'I'm the same way myself. I suppose we'll be finding more and more ways in which we're alike.'

Jennie laid the fork on the plate. The food simply would not go down. This Situation – years ago she had capitalized it in her mind, and did so now – was intolerable. Like an octopus, Jennie's anger reached out now, stretching its tentacles toward the two across the table, and then sucked back into itself, disgusted. How quickly she had changed! In a few short weeks her cherished confidence in herself had vanished. And they just went on talking, those two, their glib words pouring, unhampered by whatever inner turmoil they might be undergoing. Yet they were in control.

She reached into her purse for her lipstick, which she did not need. In the little mirror her wounded eyes were darkly circled.

'Jennie, you've not said a word. Come talk to us,' Peter urged.

It was as if he were delicately reprimanding a sulky or a bashful child. What could he be thinking of? Surely he must see that Jill wasn't speaking to her.

'It's pretty obvious why I'm not talking,' she replied.

Peter put down his fork. 'All right. All right. Time to get down to brass tacks, I see. You two have to get together, you know you do. You have to reach some understanding.'

'Nobody *has* to do anything,' Jennie said. 'This is a false situation to begin with.'

'I don't see anything false in a girl's wanting to know her parents.'

'Maybe not. If it worked out smoothly for everyone, it

would be wonderful. But this hasn't worked smoothly, and you can't force it to, Peter. Nor can I.'

'But it happens that I'm certain you can, Jennie. Why don't you want to accept our daughter completely, with no secrecy? What are you hiding from?'

The words *our daughter* and *hiding* enraged her. 'You may not question me!' she cried. 'You just may not, do you hear? Who do you think you are, you of all people, to question me?'

Hurt and reproachful, Peter said, 'Well, if you're going to be so hostile –' when Jill interrupted.

'The first time I see the two of you together – the first time, mind you, a thing I dreamed about – you fight! It's unbelievable! You actually *fight*! I used to imagine –' She stopped. 'I'm all choked up. Oh, why didn't you marry each other and keep me? Keep your own child? Why? Oh, I don't even know what I'm saying. But look at this mess you've made! Look at it!'

Jennie turned to Peter. His flush was as painful as newly grown skin after a burn. Under lowered lids his eyes glistened. She saw that he was stricken, unable to reply, and in a flash she understood his memories: the windshield wipers clicking in the rain on the dark street and his own words, 'Jennie, Jennie, don't worry, I'll take care of everything.' In that second, pity for him, and for them all, obliterated anger.

Jill's tears spilled and she moved aside in the chair, showing to Jennie only her profile, humiliated as a woman is by public tears. The silence that fell upon the flower-decked table and its pathetic gaiety was accentuated by a burst of laughter that rose somewhere above the moderate buzzing in the room. Dismayed by Jill's pain, neither Jennie nor Peter could meet each other's glance.

Presently Jill dabbed at her eyes and took a sip of water.

Jennie waited with resignation. Peter's flush had still not died down, but he began to speak cautiously, as if addressing the air.

'This is too much for us all. I should have known it would be. It was stupid of me to expect it to go smoothly.' No one refuted him. His fingers made nervous taps on the tablecloth, as if he were considering something. Then, abandoning the empty air, he addressed Jennie. 'A restaurant is no place to talk our hearts out,' he continued. 'I know you and Jill broke up at your lunch because she wanted to go back to your apartment and you wouldn't. I thought that was such a strange issue! Maybe, if you'd make it clearer, it would help us.'

Jill answered, this time including Jennie in her remarks by giving her an intense, almost a challenging look. 'It wasn't only that. It wasn't especially that I wanted to *be* there, only that I wanted to know why I *couldn't* be there. Why I must never get in touch with you but wait for you to call me. You've built a wall. It felt like – it feels like – the Berlin Wall.'

Yes, Jennie thought. And I, like a Berliner, am trapped behind it. Caught. Locked in. And once more, moderately, with obstinate patience, she tried to present herself as a person with rights.

'Sometimes I think that privacy's becoming a lost privilege. Why shouldn't it be enough to say that I have my own reasons?'

'In the circumstances it's not nearly enough,' Jill said sternly. 'You wouldn't say it was exactly a loving welcome that you're giving me, would you? I know the committee people – Mr Riley and Emma Dunn – told me it wouldn't be easy. They said I should be patient and – and I think I have been, but I never expected anything like this.'

For an instant Jennie dropped her forehead into her hands, which were cold on her aching eyeballs.

'Ah, you won't see. . . . Is it impossible for you to take me as I am?'

Very softly Peter asked, 'Let me ask you something frankly, Jennie. Are you perhaps married? With children? Is that it?'

She raised her head. 'No. No to both.'

'Then you're free, like me.'

The room was hot, and although not crowded, it still gave Jennie the sense of too many people crowding in. She felt dizzy; perhaps in her agitated state the half glass of wine was doing it.

'Then you're entirely free,' Peter said again, this time in a rising tone, a question.

Jennie was sick. It must have shown in her face, because Peter broke off to stare at her. I can't take any more of this, she thought. They're people who can't be trusted. I never could tell them the truth. They would harry and harass me until Jay found out.

They will do it, anyway.

Overcome, she now had to flee from them, had to get out, to shut a door behind her. She stood up, seizing the suit jacket that hung on the back of her chair.

'I can't stay,' she said brusquely. 'I can't. Don't you see I'm sick?' And repeating, 'Sorry, sorry, I can't stay,' she left, almost running, racing through startled strollers in the vast lobbies, just as her daughter had run from her that other day.

On Park Avenue there was snow in the air. Low clouds above the skyscrapers were stained rust-brown where the city flung up its lights. I'd like to get on a plane and fly beyond those clouds, she whispered to herself; I'd mount and soar and fly to any place at all. Instead she got into the first taxi that drew to the curb, opened the windows to inhale the sharp wind, gave the driver a bill, and, without waiting for change, raced up the stairs to her refuge.

The bedroom was untypically neglected. She had dressed in such haste, in order not to be late, that her workday clothes were not put away and now lay where they had been dropped: a skirt on a chair, a blouse on another chair, shoes in the center of the floor along with the overturned contents of her briefcase, which had fallen off the bed. Scattered papers trailed on the bed and the floor. She scuffed through them without picking them up, pulled off the bedspread, flung her outer clothes away, and, in bra and petticoat, threw herself down on the bed.

The room was a prison, yet there was no place else to go. She turned and turned on the mattress. Demons, winged and black, plucked and clawed: the old, simple man lay dead on the frozen road among dark trees; Peter and Jill nagged and probed and wouldn't let her go; Enid Wolfe appraised her with level, steady, analytical gaze. . . . The demon wings, bat wings, fluttered, and the hands were alligator claws.

She leapt from the bed. If nothing else could drive them off, maybe whiskey could. It wouldn't take much to get the ginger-ale woman drunk. She had never in all her life been drunk.

Filling a fruit-juice glass, as if she had a July thirst, with the Chivas Regal that was kept on the shelf for Jay, she swallowed it and shuddered. Awful stuff! Burning rubber! It singed her mouth, ran to her head, and flamed its way down to her feet. It was like being struck by lightning, or hit by a truck.

Barely able to walk, she clung to the walls all the way back to the bedroom, where she managed to turn off the phone and the lamp before falling again across the bed.

Something was ringing. It sounded far away, as if some

pests on the street were making merriment with a damn-fool bell.

'Oh, God Almighty, will you stop that?' she mumbled. Her lips felt thick, her mouth dry, and it was too much trouble to open it.

Suddenly she understood that the ring was close; it was in the apartment, her own doorbell.

'I'm sick of this,' she said aloud. The room swayed when she sat up and spun as she stumbled toward the light that burned in the little foyer.

'Who are you? What the devil do you want?' she cried, pulling so hard at the door that it slammed against the wall.

'Peter. It's Peter.'

She blinked, not sure she understood. 'Wha-what are you doing here? Peter? You?'

He stepped in, closed the door, and locked it.

'You scared the hell out of me! I didn't know what was happening to you. But I had to pay the bill before I could rush after you.' He was out of breath. 'And you'd just disappeared! So I put Jill in a taxi, had to scrounge around for a taxi for myself, and – and here I am. How are you? Are you all right?'

'So . . . you see how I am. Fine. I'm just fine. Just.'

He came nearer, to stare at her in astonishment.

'Jennie, for God's sake, you're drunk!'

'I don't know. Maybe.' She began to laugh. 'I can't stand up. I guess I'll have to sit on the floor.'

'No, no.' He caught her just as her legs gave way; her bones were melting. 'Come on. You're going to bed.'

'I was *in* bed. Damn you for getting me up! Now I'll have to cry again.'

He shook his head. 'What have you been drinking?'

'I don't know. Lemonade. Mouthwash.' She giggled and

wept. 'Oh, I'm sad, so sad. You can't know how sad I am. Nobody knows.'

He was holding her. Strong hands under her arms held her upright. He spoke gently, 'I'm sorry, Jennie. But let's get you to bed. You're not used to drinking, are you? Still the ginger-ale girl, are you?' Half-carried, half-pushed, she was being led toward the bed.

'Ginger-ale girl. Sure. That's me. All the time.'

'This crazy bed . . . Papers and pocketbooks and shoes all mixed up in it . . . How can you lie in a bed like this?'

'None of your business. Mind your own business. Keep out of my pocketbook.'

'I'm not in your pocketbook. Look, I'm putting everything on the chair. Look.'

But propped up against the headboard, she was looking directly at the mirror over the dresser. Her eyes wavered over a watery shape, gaped at puffed cheeks and smudged mascara, at a transparent half-slip and at one round breast that had escaped from the lace brassiere.

'I'm a mess. Oh, Lord. Oh, Lord, I'm a mess.'

'You won't be a mess in the morning, after you've slept.' He pulled the blanket over her naked breast. 'Seriously, Jennie, I have to tell you, you shouldn't open the door without knowing who's there. Don't you know that? Don't you know what could happen?'

'I don't care. I don't care, don't care, don't care, don't –'

'All right, that's enough. Here, let me straighten the pillows. Now lie back and sleep. I'm going to go stretch out on your sofa.'

'No you're not! You can't stay here. Get out!'

'I am definitely not going to leave you in this condition. In the morning you'll feel a whole lot better, you won't believe me when I tell you about this, and you'll even laugh at yourself. Then we'll talk about things, and after that I'll get out.'

'I don't want to talk about things with you. I want you to leave me alone, you hear me? Go away. Stay away.'

'I'm going away, as far as the other room for now. Okay, I'm turning your light off.'

'Leave it! I have to get up, go to the office. I'm a working woman.'

'Jennie, it's Monday night, a quarter to ten, and you're going to sleep this off the rest of the night.'

Darkness dropped down again. It was warm, warm darkness, like tropical air. You don't know anything about tropical air, Jennie. You don't know anything, don't want to know anything. Peter's here, and isn't that funny? I'm laughing, it's so funny. I'm crying. Oh, let me sleep, all of you, everybody. Get out of my life.

She woke. Again she had no idea how long she had been sleeping, but this time, although terrible knives and hammers were savaging her head, consciousness was a little clearer. She knew what had happened and what was happening. Peter was on the couch in the next room, and beyond him, someone was at the door ringing and pounding.

She sat up. The light went on in the living room. Stocking feet slid over the bare floor where the rug stopped, moving cautiously over the creaking board toward the door. She had a subtle awareness of relief at not being alone. Those men . . . looking for the tapes . . . Nonsense . . . not nonsense.

Peter called out, 'What do you want?'

'Take that chain off the door and let me in or I'll have the police here in three minutes,' Jay shouted.

Jennie's heart stopped.

'Who the hell are you? I can have the police here in three minutes myself.'

'What have you done to Jennie? Damn you, take that chain off, I said!'

'Damn yourself! I haven't done anything to Jennie. She's asleep in bed.'

And Jennie was whimpering into the dark: Take hold of yourself. The moment's come, it's here, not even in the way you feared, but worse, so much worse. She turned on the lamp. Her brassiere had come loose and fallen off; the half-slip was wrinkled over her thighs. In her dizzy haste she looked for a robe and couldn't find one; throwing on the suit jacket that lay on the chair and holding the skirt in front of her, she ran to the living room.

Peter, in undershirt and trousers with belt unbuckled for comfort, was still at the front door, through which, in the gap where the chain had been loosened, there appeared the frantic face of Jay.

Jennie's voice was broken. 'It's all right, Peter. Open the door.'

Jay entered. He stared first at Jennie, who was holding the skirt like a screen, then at the disheveled man and back at Jennie.

'Who is this? Jesus Christ, what's happening? Has he hurt you?'

'No, no. He's a friend. It's all right.'

'All right? A friend?'

'Yes, I mean, it was unexpected, he just came. I didn't know he was coming, and so –'

A wave of vertigo unsteadied her, and with knees buckling, she crouched against the wall. Jay pulled her up. Holding her by the shoulders, he examined her intently.

'You've been drinking, or someone's given you something.' He whirled around at Peter. 'What's going on? Who the hell are you? What have you done to her?'

Bewildered, with his customary flush mounting, Peter

fumbled. 'Peter Mendes is the name. And it's true, I'm just a friend, Jennie's friend from Chicago.'

In her weakness, hysteria took hold of Jennie. Peter looked so funny, with his hair all mussed and no shoes; while Jay stood in his dark suit, white shirt, and foulard tie. She made a sound like a giggle, terror and tears in a giggle.

Jay shook her gently. 'Jennie, for God's sake, talk to me! I've been wild with worry all evening. There was no answer on the phone. I called your office and a woman in the next office said you hadn't been there since half past five. With muggers on the streets and what's happened to George –' He stopped, looking puzzled. 'You knew we had to talk tonight, and you broke the date. It's the second time you broke one –' He stopped again. 'I'm thinking, I'm thinking I've gone crazy here. I think I'm not seeing what I'm seeing. You're naked!'

Through the open door, the bed loomed like a sultan's pleasure couch; tumbled in quilts, with both pillows crushed, it dominated the cramped little room. The three pairs of eyes, as if directed by the same thought, now focused on that bed.

Jay's face was as bleached as the other man's was reddened.

'You,' he said queerly, 'is it you I'm seeing, Jennie?'

'Please, just let me tell you –'

'Yes, tell me why you lied to me about having a client. Tell me what's happening here in the middle of the night.' His voice was rough, close to tears. He panted and trembled. 'On the other hand, maybe you shouldn't bother to tell me.'

She ran to him and, raising her arms to plead, forgot the skirt, which fell to the floor. When she bent to pick it up, the jacket parted, revealing her breasts. Jay pushed her arms away and turned from her.

The most tragic situation could be partly ridiculous. Wasn't that strange? And stranger still that in this most awful despair a person can stand apart and see herself, beaten and ridiculous.

'Jay, hear me.' Her words tumbled askew from her mouth, and she began to weep. When her hands flew to her face, the skirt dropped again, revealing her in the transparent petticoat.

'Is this you?' Jay repeated thickly, as if he had been stunned.

'You have to excuse her,' Peter said. 'She never drank before. She was upset. She's not herself, not the real Jennie.'

Jay looked at him. 'And I take it you know who the real Jennie is?'

'I knew her a long time ago. We had some things to talk about.'

'Ah, yes. So you did. I see you did. Plenty to talk about.'

With arms straight at his side, like a soldier at rigid attention, Jay stood. Only his hands moved, clenching into fists, loosening and clenching again.

'If someone told me my father had set fire to our house or my mother had robbed a bank, would I have believed it?' He spoke to himself, as if he were alone. 'Oh, my God, when white is black and black is white, then anything can happen. Anything at all.'

'Jay . . .' She wanted to speak, but horror grasped her throat and no words came. She was aware that she wasn't functioning as one ought to function, and yet her mind seemed to be working right; the contradiction was bizarre.

Jay moved to the door, which was still open to the public hall, and looked back across the room. Jennie had a swift perception: He had the expression of one who is leaving his home for the last time, printing it on his memory, or – could it be so? – of one who, with contempt, is casting away all that he had ever known of a place. There was a stillness without speech, a very brief stillness, only enough for the chiming brass carriage clock on the desk to strike the half-hour and then to encompass the tinkling vibration it left in the air. In the brevity of those few moments an image, not even a thought, rather a shred or a fragment, flashed in Jennie's mind and dissolved: the coach, the white horses, the glass slipper, and all the brightness dissolved.

'I'll never believe in anything or anyone again,' Jay said.

And he walked away. The door swung on its weight behind him and clicked shut.

Jennie stood with her back and the palms of her hands flattened against the wall. Peter went to the bedroom closet, came back with a robe, and put it over her. In silence she begged, Don't ask me anything. Please, no questions.

And he did not. As if he had understood, he took one of her hands and held it between his to warm it, saying only, 'You're cold.'

'I can't,' she began, meaning, 'I can't talk.'

That, too, he understood. 'You needn't talk. I'm not going to ask you anything. But you have to go back to bed while I make some tea.'

The tea was hot and milky. He held the cup and wiped the spill that came from her dry, quivering lips.

'The hot milk will put you to sleep,' he whispered.

When she had drunk, she lay back on the pillow. The lamp in the corner, distant and dim, threw a rosette on the ceiling. He stroked her forehead; firm fingers moved in rhythm. And she let herself sink and sink. Die . . .

When she woke in the morning, Peter was sitting in a straight chair near the bed. It occurred to her that he might have been sitting there all night.

'I've made breakfast,' he said. 'First, though, go shower and do your hair.'

But now she was completely clear, and everything that had been foggy the night before sprang out like a headline in the *Times*. Jay's face had been blurred, doubly blurred, by his anguish and her own. Yet she was distinctly seeing his eyes; they must have registered in her subconscious. Now they were fixed upon her in a fierce glare of pain. Once, while still a young girl living in the row house, she had seen a man in the yard at the end of the street whipping a dog and had never forgotten the poor dog's eyes. . . .

She turned her face into the pillow and cried, excruciating sobs that shook her body. So people weep when someone dies. I remember Mama when Papa died. I thought the crying would kill her too.

After a while, when the sobbing ceased, Peter came back to the room. He waited, not speaking, only shaking his head a little, smiling a little as one pities and gently reproaches a child: *Ah, don't cry*. . . .

'There was nothing,' she said. 'We did nothing.'

'No, but it certainly looked as though we had done something.'

'We were going to be married.'

'Who is he?'

'A lawyer.'

'You don't trust me?'

'No.'

He smiled again and shrugged.

'Are you angry because I won't tell you his name?'

'It doesn't matter.'

'You've been very nice to me, Peter.'

'Of course. Wouldn't you have done the same?'

'I suppose so.'

'You would. You of all people would.' He had sat down

on the straight chair in the corner and now gave her a straight, piteous look of appeal. 'I'm feeling horribly guilty. I don't know your story, but it's not hard to figure it out – some of it, anyway – and I see that my being here has made terrible trouble for you again.' When she didn't answer, his forehead wrinkled. 'It's the second time I've come into your life. What can I say? Can I do anything at all?'

'Nothing. What is there to do?' It took too much strength to talk, but he looked so wretched that she had to say something more. 'You didn't do this on purpose. You meant well, staying here with me.'

'You scared the life out of me when you left the table like that. Jill was scared too. You looked – well, frantic. Yes, frantic. That's why I had to come.'

'I've been frantic for quite a while.'

'Because of him? You didn't want him to find out about Jill?'

A leftover sob caught in her throat. 'That wasn't – that wasn't thinkable.'

He asked no more, and for a minute or two neither spoke. She felt unkempt, unclean, and miserable because of it. Making a great effort, she forced herself to sit up and asked him to leave the room. Modestly wrapping herself in her Turkish bathrobe, she went to the shower.

Under the lulling patter of warm water, she stood, mechanically soaping herself. In a kind of lethargy she stood too long, wasting water, taking refuge in the curtain of gentle heat. Then she got out, brushed her teeth and flossed them, and brushed her hair; its dark waves fell into place. But the face in the mirror was devastated, with red eyes sunken to half their normal size under fattened, glossy lids. Ugly. It didn't matter. Nothing did. One tidied one's hair and flossed one's teeth. What sense did it make? What difference, if one's teeth should rot?

'You look better,' Peter said.

'I look like hell. Look at me.' Perversely she wanted him to acknowledge the devastation.

'Well,' he said, changing the subject, 'how about having coffee in bed?'

'Bed? I have to go to work, Peter. It's eight o'clock.'

'You're in no condition for work today, and you know it, Jennie. Go on back to bed for now. You can get up later.'

He had made toast and a boiled egg, which she didn't touch. It had been days since she had had any appetite, anyway. For a while he watched her sipping the coffee, hugging the cup between her palms, and then said, 'I'll call your office for you, unless you want to do it, and say you're sick.'

'You can do it. Just ask for Dinah.' All energy, all ambition had seeped away, yet she had to show fortitude in the face of devastation. 'Say I'll definitely be in tomorrow.'

'I'm not sure you will be. You're entitled to time off.'

'I'm not "entitled" to anything.'

'Why are you so hard on yourself? You've had a shock. You were in a state of shock, as if there'd been a death.'

That was a strange way to describe it, yet it did feel like a death. I'm not certain I know how to go on from here, she thought. It makes no sense, that everything can end this way. All over in two or three minutes.

'He said something when he was standing at the door,' she began. 'I can't seem to remember exactly what it was. Can you?'

As Peter looked puzzled, she prompted, 'Last night when he was leaving. I'll call him Joe because that's not his name. I'm trying to think. Was it something about not believing?'

'Oh. Do you really want to know? Do you have to go back over it?'

'Yes, I want to know.'

'He said, "I will never believe in anything or anybody again."'

The words, even secondhand, had an elegiac ring, a terrible finality. For a time she listened to them inside her head, then asked Peter whether he thought 'Joe' could have meant them.

'Never is a long time, Jennie.'

'You're right. It was a stupid question.'

So then, sometime or other, there would be another woman. And shutting her eyes, she let herself imagine in every fleshly detail the women to whom he would turn in bed and open his arms. What words would he speak? The words they had said to each other in their special language?

Oh, they can fill a thousand pages with pop psychology, and write off jealousy as something immature and degrading, but it's true nevertheless that jealousy is torture, and people kill because of it, and kill themselves too. It's loss, final loss, and worse.

So now you know, Jennie, you know as if you were in Jay's skin, how he felt when he saw you here last night.

The doorbell rang so abruptly that Peter started.

'It's Shirley from across the hall. She generally rings to ask whether I want to walk to work with her.'

'Okay. I'll say you've got the flu.'

When he returned, he looked amused. 'If you ever saw amazement on a face! Her eyebrows went up to her hairline.'

Jennie said bitterly, 'I can imagine. You don't look at all like the man she's used to seeing here in the mornings.'

'She wanted to come in, but I said I was taking care of you, that I'm an old friend and a doctor too.'

'Thank you. I didn't want her to see me like this.' It was odd that she wasn't ashamed to have Peter see her. 'Shirley's a good soul, but she talks too much. She knows everything about everybody.'

'You must have other friends. I think you should talk to a friend today.'

'I don't want anyone.'

He countered gently, 'But you need some help until you can straighten things out.'

'They may never be "straightened out," don't you see? I'll probably have to manage by myself, so I might as well get used to doing it now.'

They were brave, commonsense words; still, Jennie only half believed them. Surely Jay would come back and want some explanation. . . . Then she reminded herself: Even so, the question of Jill would still be there, and she would only be back where she had been in the first place.

'Excuse me. May I ask you why you say "never"?'

'It's a long story.'

'Maybe you can make it shorter.'

'Well, I lied to him. And he has never lied to me. Oh, you don't understand! You would have to know him, and everything that's gone before.'

Peter looked doubtful but asked no more. And Jennie, stepping outside of herself for an instant as was her habit, saw herself sitting up in bed facing this longtime stranger who was subtly beginning to become familiar again. A faint red stubble had grown on his cheeks overnight; she could remember the time he had talked about growing a beard. She could remember . . .

And she made a comparison: He wasn't much younger than Jay, although he looked much younger, lighter somehow, as if life were easier for him. Maybe it had been. She realized that she knew nothing about him except that he was a professor. For a second she had a vision of him in a professional pose, perched on a desk with one leg swinging; he would wear polished loafers and a cashmere pullover in an argyle pattern. She wasn't sure whether he would smoke a pipe and decided that he probably wouldn't; it would be too much of a cliché. The girls would be arch with him. The boys would respect his height and powerful frame. But she really knew nothing about him.

'Are you married?' she asked.

'Me? What made you ask?'

'I don't know. Just wondered.'

'Not married.'

'I read about you once. It was in a directory of American scholars. I was glad to know you were a success. That you'd arrived where you wanted to be.'

'You were glad?' He was surprised. 'After everything that happened between us, you could be glad for me?'

'The one thing has nothing to do with the other,' she said simply.

He shook his head. 'What makes you so kind? But then, you always were.'

She smiled slightly. Indeed she had been kind to him. And she said, 'It's not just that. I admire a good mind that hasn't been allowed to go to waste.'

'Well, I'm certainly no Schliemann in the ruins of Troy, but I have written about some interesting discoveries in our southwestern deserts, and I do like teaching, so all in all, I'm fairly satisfied with my life. But tell me about yourself, about the law business.'

He was almost jocular, and she saw that this was an awkward effort to divert her thoughts and change her mood. But everything went abruptly queer and bleak again. The winter light, thin and blue as skimmed milk, was unkind to the little room that could be so cozy at night: the chest of drawers was scarred; the white curtains were yellowed and flimsy. Failure dwelled here.

Since she had not replied, Peter spoke once more, this time more seriously. 'I don't like to leave you alone this way. I wish I didn't have to go.'

'Back to Chicago now?'

'No, I've planned on a week here in the city. I'm to meet a few people in the Archaeology Department at Columbia. There's a conference this afternoon and a couple of dinners. Then next week I'll have to fly back to Atlanta.'

She made no comment.

'It's my parents' fortieth anniversary. A milestone.'

Still she was silent.

'I know you don't want to hear about them.'

She could have countered with a question: Since you know it, why talk about them? But that wasn't her way, so she answered only, 'It really doesn't matter to me at all, you know.'

He flushed. 'Well, I only wanted to say that I have to go to Atlanta. Otherwise I'd stay and try to help out. Help Jill and you. . . . Oh, you know what I'm trying to say, Jennie. Mostly help you, although I don't know how.'

'I don't, either. So you'll do just as well by going to the celebration in Atlanta,' she said coolly enough.

He seemed to have a need to pursue the subject. 'It'll be only a small celebration. The family's shrunk. A lot of the relatives have died off since you – I mean, there won't be so many of us there. Sally June has no children –'

Jennie could see them all at the dark-grained, candle-lit table, each of them seated behind a neat pool of white linen. In winter the view from the tall windows would be subdued: dark evergreens and sere lawns. The sister has no children, so they have no grandchildren. That would be a hurt, especially for people like them, with all their pride in lineage and continuity.

And she couldn't resist a question. 'Have they never asked, never mentioned...?'

'No.' She saw that he was unable to meet her eyes. Yet he added, 'I often wonder whether they think about it or ever mention it between themselves.'

'Are you going to tell them, now that you know?'

'I'm not sure. I can't think what's best. Can you?'

'Me? I can't think at all,' Jennie said with bitterness.

They were both silent until Peter said, 'I hate to leave you here alone with trouble like this, but I have to.'

'Of course you do. Please go. Don't be late because of me.'

'I'll telephone you. Or maybe I'll stop by again.'

'You don't need to.'

'I know I don't, but I will. There's a pitcher of water on the table. Lock the door when I leave.'

Another wave of despair swept over her when he had gone. It was as if all the radiance of life, the hope, the sunlight, and all the wild, sweet joy had been swept away. And never, never had she been so tired.

She prayed for sleep. For a long time it would not come. But after a while the separate noises of horns and engines began to merge into a single monotonous, oceanic roar, and sleep was ready to engulf her. Even while she knew she was making only a temporary escape, the escape was blessed.

Off and on, Jennie slept through the day and the night. On the second morning her physical strength had returned enough for her to get up quickly, dress, eat a little something, and take stock. Another day away from the office would not bring disaster, she decided. Hope, which she doubted even as she felt it rise, encouraged her nevertheless. Perhaps it would be wise to wait at home. Jay might come. . . . He would telephone the office, learn that she was sick, and then –

She was considering this when the doorbell rang. She went to answer it.

Shirley's glance swept over Jennie. 'All better, are you?'

'Pretty much. A twenty-four-hour bug, I guess. Or just a touch of flu or something.'

'Good. Lucky for you your friend was here. He said you almost fainted.'

'It hit me hard.'

'Tough. Well, I'm taking the afternoon off. I'll probably come home early, so if there's anything you want, you'll know where to find me.'

'Thanks so much, Shirley. But I'm all right. I really am.'

When Shirley left, Jennie poured a second cup of coffee and sat down again. Things in the tiny kitchen had been put back in the wrong places. The black-lacquer tray was on the top shelf instead of the bottom. It looked better on the top shelf next to the black-lacquer jar of Chinese tea. Peter had done that; he noticed such things. He was meticulous and perfection was important to him; he was, after all, the son of the house with the tall white pillars. The house where Jennie had been unwanted. And she had borne a grandchild for them! Her head dropped into her hands, and although she had been shivering a few minutes ago, she was overcome with the heat of her pounding blood.

Yet Peter had just been so good to her! And Shirley too. They'd wanted to help, and she must be grateful. She was. But the only one who could really help was Jay.

And the morning drifted past.

Early in the afternoon she became shockingly aware that, lost within herself, she had given no thought to George Cromwell. Under the frozen earth, the guileless, kind old man lay in his new grave. Guilt brought a hot flush to her cheeks. She must at least send some flowers to his widow and drive up to see her soon. In her despair she had almost forgotten that other woman, and she frowned now, weighing that woman's pain against her own. But they were too different to be weighed; they were at the opposite ends of life.

I'll go now about the flowers, she thought. It'll only take a few minutes, and if Jay comes and finds I'm not here, he will wait.

He will not come.

When she opened the door to the street, she saw with dismay that Peter was approaching the house. This was too much!

She had no need of him, and no wish for any heart-to-heart talks about themselves or Jill.

'So you're going out!' he exclaimed. 'Well, you look better than you did yesterday, anyway. How are you feeling?'

'I'm fine, as you see.'

He peered down at her. 'I don't know about "fine." But certainly improved. Going anywhere special?'

'Only to the florist on the avenue.'

'Mind if I walk with you?'

'No.' And she told him, 'I know I said I'm fine, but I'm very tired. So please excuse me if I don't say much.'

He made no answer. Few people were out on this raw afternoon, so that the nervous, rapid clack of Jennie's heels was loud, and Peter's silence, in consequence, was heavier and mournful. She felt oppressed by a strange sensation of distance, as if she had been away for a long time. At a drugstore on the avenue, next to the florist, she stopped as if to collect herself, and stood watching a boy arrange a little pyramid of perfume bottles, Nuit de Noël,

Calèche, Shalimar – all the lilting names. Shalimar was sweet, like roses, sugar, and vanilla. Sweet candy, Jay always said, kissing her neck. And turning from the window, she was so blinded by her tears that she would have bumped into a man going past if Peter had not caught her arm.

In the flower shop she gave her order for roses to be telegraphed to Martha Cromwell, and went out again into a day grown blustery and heartless.

Peter broke the silence. 'May I ask you just one thing? I won't burden you, Jennie, but have you talked to him?'

'No.'

He winced. 'Oh, God, it's my fault.'

'It would have ended, anyway, in the circumstances.'

'Jill, you mean. It's because of her, you're saying.'

'Oh, Peter, I'm not saying anything. For God's sake, don't make me think anymore! I want to be empty forever.'

'Funny, that's what Jill said about herself yesterday.'

'You've seen her again?'

'Yes, I had to be at Columbia, I told you. So we had lunch. I told her about you, told her everything. Do you mind that I did?'

'If I do, it's too late, isn't it? But no, I guess I don't mind.'

'She cried, Jennie. She thinks she treated you harshly. She wouldn't have been so insistent if she'd known how things were with you.'

'She didn't mean to be harsh. Tell her I understand that. I don't want her to feel guilty because of me.'

'It would be better if you would tell her all that yourself, Jennie.'

Jennie threw up her hands. 'Don't you know we'd only go over the same ground? It wouldn't come to anything.'

'You can't be sure of that. Isn't it worth trying?'

Apologies, explanations, and probably more tears, she thought, and repeated, 'It wouldn't come to anything.'

'I'm not trying to force anything on you. But she is so young. Her childhood was yesterday. Please think about it.'

Jennie sighed. 'All right. I'm thinking, and this is what I think.'

'Think about it some more, please.'

His voice was soothing. He was coaxing her, and she knew it. And he was probably right. No, he was surely right. Jill's childhood . . . what do I know about it? But I know how it hurts not to be understood. As Jay to me, so I to Jill. All related, intertwined like a knot.

But I can't unravel it now. I can't.

And lowering her head against the wind, she hurried homeward. Halfway there, she stopped and held out her hand.

'Peter, I want to say goodbye here.'

'You don't want me to go back to the house? That's okay, Jennie. It makes sense. But will you do one thing? Will you really think about talking to Jill?'

'I'll do my best, Peter.'

She was turning the key in the lock when Shirley's door opened.

'Hey, where've you been, anyway? I thought you'd never get back.'

'What do you mean? I wasn't out more than half an hour. Forty-five minutes, maybe.'

'Jay was here.'

Jennie's heart shook. 'And? Did you talk to him?'

'He rang my bell when you didn't answer. I told him I'd seen you go down the street – I was just coming home then – with your friend, that doctor from Chicago.'

'You told him that?'

'Of course. Shouldn't I have?'

How amazing that one's heart can faint while one's voice stays steady!

'What did he say?'

'Nothing. Just thanked me and left. He's such a gentleman! Oh, I did tell him you were feeling better this morning, and that your doctor friend must have said it was all right to go out for a while.'

With a hopeless gaze Jennie's eyes rested on her friend. Sophistication could be a surface quality, a flair for dress and a collection of worldly mannerisms; beneath all these, Shirley was only a good-hearted, thoughtless, garrulous child. Her chattering tongue, unknowing, had just now put the final seal on Jennie's fate. With this second event, the return of her 'Chicago friend,' there was no way at all Jay could trust her again.

'I think I'll lie down awhile,' she said faintly.

'You shouldn't have been out in this weather. You look positively white. I don't care what anybody says, it doesn't make sense to risk pneumonia –'

But Jennie had already gone in and closed the door.

Now she was numb. She sank onto a hard chair in the hall and stared at the floor. The little rug was marked in squares, four from side to side, seven up and down. Seven fours are twenty-eight. . . . Time bent, and her wandering mind began to spin, so that Peter, the young one and the present one, began to spin, merged with Jay, so that light merged with dark and fear overlaid them all. What should she do next with her life? What *could* she do next? And abruptly, as on a cold morning after long postponements one suddenly jumps out of bed, she went to the telephone and dialed Jay's office number.

The secretary's familiar voice was ever so slightly unsure, or embarrassed, or cool; whichever it was, Jennie knew at once that the response was untrue. No, Mr Wolfe had not come in. As a matter of fact, he probably was not coming in at all today. No, she really didn't know when he would be back or where he was. This from the friendly gray-haired woman who had always had a few words for Jennie and had even been promised an invitation to the wedding!

It was three o'clock. Three was a reminder: The children had come from school. Of course, she thought, this is what I must do. Emily and Sue will tell me if he's at home. Her hand was poised above the telephone. If he was there, what would she say? How to begin? Oh, my dear, my dearest, hear me. Hear what? Yet her fingers dialed the number.

'Is this you, Sue?'

'No, it's Emily.'

'How are you, darling? This is Jennie.'

'I know,' the child said.

'Tell me, is Daddy there?'

'I don't know.'

'Darling, what do you mean, you "don't know"?'

The child murmured unintelligibly.

'I can't hear you, Emily. What did you say?'

'I said Nanny doesn't want me to talk on the telephone now.'

'Does Nanny know you're talking to me?'

'I think so. Yes.'

So Jennie knew well what had happened. Never, never would Jay have told his children anything ugly about her; certainly he never would tell them to be rude to her. He must simply have told Nanny that he didn't want to speak to her, and Nanny had said something about it to the children.

And she saw Jay in the library, where he most often used the telephone. It stood on the desk, next to the statue of Lincoln on the chair in the memorial. The wing chair was dark green leather with brass nail heads. He might even be sitting there now, alone with his disillusionment.

She saw Emily answering the telephone in the hall. Emily always liked to run to the phone, which made Nanny angry. The woman was so rigid, and Jennie had been thinking how, after they were married, very tactfully she would convince Jay to find someone else.

'I've missed you, darling,' she said now.

'I've missed you, too, but Nanny says I'm not to talk anymore.'

'Good-bye, Emily,' Jennie answered quietly, replacing the receiver.

Suddenly she heard herself wail; a most terrible cry it was, an outburst of anguish and despair. When a knife cuts or a child dies, such cries are heard. She clamped her hand over her mouth to choke her sobs, which shook her body so that she was bent over in pain.

After a while, a long, long while, the sobs died away into a deep, exhausted sigh. She stood up. She reached into the cupboard and drew from the cereal box the Cartier's box with the ring. Then she went to the bedroom and took the velvet box with the pearls from under a pile of sweaters. The ring had never belonged on her finger. Its cold diamond eye was aloof. The pearls, opulent as silk, slid through her hands; let them go back to be worn on the kind of neck to which they were accustomed. In the kitchen she packed both boxes into a small carton, wrapped it with heavy twine, and sealed it with heavy tape. All the time her teeth were clenched; she became aware of that when she had to telephone the post office for the ZIP code.

Writing, with a hand that had to be steadied, the name J. Wolfe, she thought, This is the last time I shall need to write his name.

At the post office it took all of her money, all she had had in the secret emergency cache at home, to pay for insurance on the package. It seemed to her as she handed it over to the man at the counter that this must be the feeling one had after surgery, pain and relief that it was over.

The way now lay ahead, she thought resolutely. Yet there came a flicker of doubt, a question: When have I said that before? And the answer came: You said that after your daughter was born. Don't you remember?

Maybe I ought to move, she thought on the way home. This neighborhood, although it isn't his, is too full of him. That store where we watched the angora kittens and almost bought one, our Italian dinners, the record shop where we stocked up on compact discs – Shall I remember every time I walk past?

The day was darkening toward night, and the wind was cutting. Discarded papers scooted along the dirty gutters of the iron-gray city. I must take hold of myself, she said silently. A mood like this mustn't be allowed to last. It was too easy to slide into depression. She remembered those grim weeks before Jill's birth, when she had sat staring out of a window into afternoons like this one, dirty, windy, and frozen.

At the front door of her building she passed a man hurrying down the steps. She thought his glance lasted a few seconds too long, as though he was taking notice of her. She thought perhaps she knew him and then thought he was the man with whom, earlier in the day, she had collided at the drugstore window. Yes, surely it was he. Nonsense. In her present state of mind she was apt to imagine anything. But maybe it *was* he. The tape, she thought. Oh, surely not!

Back upstairs, she found that she had left her door unlocked. 'Nerves,' she said aloud and sternly. 'You never did that before. You're just not thinking.' She began to shiver. The temperature must have dropped very low. No, it wasn't that. It was nerves again. She scolded herself.

'Make some hot tea and eat. You've not had a mouthful since breakfast.'

Warming her hands around the cup, she sat staring out at the cold sky. Thin clouds scudded over the pale, sinking sun. The kitchen clock's loud tick emphasized the silence and the emptiness. When she had drunk the tea, she stood up and began to walk up and down the living room. Her mind traveled through the day just past. There was something – wasn't there something? – she was supposed to think about.

Yes. She was supposed to think about Jill. 'She's so young,' Peter had said. 'Her childhood was only yesterday.'

That's true. And now she grieves because of me. Why should she grieve so young? Time enough for that later when she's older. Plenty of time ... There's no longer any reason why she can't come here now. No reason at all.

Very subtly Jennie began to feel that an exchange was in the making: a lover, a husband lost and a daughter found. Plans erased and substituted by some gigantic finger in the sky, as if one's own will didn't count for anything. Well, it hasn't counted, has it, Jennie? All the hope wasted, and all the energy gone down the drain! One has an image of another person, like mine of Jay, but how true is it? For that matter, can one's image of one's own self be true?

After a while a decision made itself. She went to the telephone and called Peter's hotel.

'I've been thinking, as you asked me to,' she told him. 'Tell Jill to feel better and to come for supper – you call it dinner – tomorrow.'

'Oh!' Peter said. 'Not at your place?'

'Yes, here, not in a restaurant. The three of us, at six.'

'Jennie, is it all over, then – with him?'

Firmly, quietly, she answered. 'It is, and I don't want to talk about it.'

'I feel for you, Jennie. I feel for you; believe that I do. But I can't help feeling a little gladness too. For Jill. And she'll be so happy when I tell her.' He was genuinely, almost tearfully grateful. Jennie imagined the smile that opened upward to his eyes and crinkled there. 'God bless you, Jennie. I had a hunch we could count on you in the end.'

She put the receiver down on the desk, where a heap of files from the office lay neglected.

You'd better see to them, she said to herself. Go back to work. Get used to the way things are. You have no other choice.

But the ache lay like a stone.

12

Through Peter's efforts the little supper, which had begun so warily, turned lively in the end. He added a bottle of wine to Jennie's simple menu of salad, chicken, and fruit. He flourished a tight bouquet in a lace paper collar. The expansive gesture, so typical of him, made her feel slightly irritable; he acted and always had, she remembered, as if flowers were a cure for every mood, quick cheer and a kind of balm. Nevertheless they did grace the plain table.

Jill brought one of those expensive cakes made of nuts and bitter chocolate that came from European bakeries on the Upper East Side. In contrast to Peter's jovial manner, she seemed chastened, with the anxious look of someone bringing a little gift to a house of mourning, offering it with a half-apologetic murmur. Peter must have drawn a portrait of disaster, of Jennie in collapse.

It was he at first who led the conversation, carefully steering it away from the personal. He apparently had decided that food was a safe topic, and began to entertain them with anecdotes about a clambake in Maine, snake meat in Hong Kong, and Sacher torte at the Hotel Sacher in Vienna. The last, he said, was overrated.

'Much too dry, I thought.'

Jill had spoken very little, so little that Jennie had begun to think, in spite of what Peter had reported, that she was still filled with resentment. Or perhaps only with apprehension? Now, suddenly, she spoke.

'Mine's not dry at all. I have a better recipe for it. And, anyway, I always take a cake out of the oven five or six minutes before you're supposed to.'

Somehow this fashionable young woman with her short black skirt, high black boots, and long scarlet fingernails didn't fit the picture of one who always took cakes out of the oven.

'Then you can cook?' Jennie inquired curiously.

This time Jill looked straight back. 'I'm a good cook. Mom and I take courses together.'

'I think that's wonderful. It wouldn't hurt me to do something like that. I'm not much good in the kitchen,' Jennie said, thinking, She *unfolds*. It's like turning new pages in a book, a whole shelf of books.

The reply was polite, conventional, a guest-to-hostess reply. 'But you can't be in the courtroom and the kitchen at the same time, after all.'

And Jennie, understanding that the implied compliment was a peace offering, smiled. 'No excuse. I could find time if I tried hard enough.'

Peter, seeing that the conversation was beginning to warm up for flight, and obviously wanting to keep it flying, added eagerly, 'I see all those files on the desk there. You haven't told me anything about your practice. Is it general law or do you specialize?'

'Jennie's an advocate for women, didn't you know? Poor women, battered women, working women,' Jill said quickly.

It seemed to Jennie that there was admiration in Jill's tone, and this excited her, and remembering suddenly Jill's remarks at their ill-fated lunch about conservation in New Mexico, she responded as quickly. 'That's certainly most of what I do, but I've also done some environmental work. In fact, I'm in the middle of a hot fight right now.'

Then fear came, a pang of alarm; if she was in the middle of it, she ought to be attending to it. Four days had passed since George's death. Assuredly Martin had secured the tape by now and perhaps even had gotten hold of some clues to the death. Why had she not heard from him? She thought in dismay that she should be talking to Arthur Wolfe or with whoever had taken George's place, and yet how, in the circumstances, could she?

And she said in a bleak voice, the words escaping involuntarily, 'George was buried yesterday.'

Puzzled, Peter inquired who George was.

'No, I haven't lost my wits,' she said. 'I was only thinking aloud.'

Now it was natural for her to explain about George. So it was that, without divulging names of either people or places, Jennie began to tell the story of the Green Marsh.

The other two were fascinated. And to Jennie's ears it seemed that a fervor had crept into her telling, as if she had been recounting or pleading the case of a child or woman who had been treated without justice or care. Wordlessly Jill and Peter finished the meal, helped to clear the little table, and took their coffee into the living room with Jennie talking all the while.

'I'm very torn. I'm seeing this work of conserving nature as important, as important as my work with women's rights. If we don't stop devouring our lakes and hills for profit, there won't be any rights left for women – or for men, either – will there? Oh, if I were rich, I'd just buy land and buy land and give it away to the state to keep! That place is so beautiful, it makes your heart ache to think of what they want to do with it.'

'I know what you mean,' Jill said indignantly. 'The papers at home are always filled with the same kind of news, a lot of angry litigation over zoning and water rights. And what do you think of them cutting redwoods in California? Trees that have been growing for a thousand years! It makes my blood boil.'

Peter made a gesture of discovery, as if a new idea had surprised him. 'I'm sitting here thinking: Wouldn't it be great if we could meet out West some summer, up in the California redwood country, or even down in Santa Fe, maybe, and rent a jeep to go exploring?' He glanced at the other two. 'Maybe it's impossible . . . I don't know. I just thought . . .' he finished somewhat wistfully.

And Jennie thought, You're moving much too fast. It was typical of Peter, but the motive was praiseworthy, and it was wonderful that they were all really able to talk to one another by now, instead of at one another.

This was no surface chatter, it had substance; and Jennie began to feel her muscles shedding tension. Her shoulders relaxed, and she leaned back on the couch. Jill's hand lay near hers; the narrow, pretty fingers and bright nails were somehow touching in their contrast to the girl's sober words.

'And can you believe somebody actually wants to build a shopping mall on a Civil War battlefield? They're messing up the Arizona desert, there'll be nothing left. . . . Listen, Jennie, you've got to stay in this fight. You've got to.' Jill's eyes flashed boldly.

Something stirred in Jennie, a quickening of pride and self-respect. The events of the past few days, her behavior, her failure – all had diminished her; it had been so painful to be inadequate and small, rejected, in contrast to these two. Now she had spoken to them with authority, and they had listened.

'I surely want to stay in the fight,' she replied, then had to add, 'Though it may not be possible to stay in this particular one. But there'll be others.'

'Why not this one?' Peter asked.

'There are reasons too complicated to go into.'

'Just answer this much: Would there be any danger in it for you if you did go on with it?'

'Oh, I don't think so.'

'It's so awful, what happened to that man in the car. Do be careful,' Jill warned.

The girl really likes me, Jennie thought. There's a note in her voice that isn't fake. She means it.

'I'll be careful.' She smiled at Jill, thinking, A few days ago I wanted to die. Now I don't. Mom lost everyone during the Hitler years, yet she lived, didn't she?

Jill smiled back. Peter had a peaceful, satisfied expression. For just a second it occurred to Jennie that the three of them looked like a family settled back for a quiet evening at home after a good dinner.

Such queer twists and turns! She'd felt so much righteous rage, and now she was thinking how kind Peter was, how warm Jill was.

Jill looked at her watch. 'I've a history quiz tomorrow and I'm behind in the reading. I really should do some work tonight.'

Jennie stood at once. 'Of course. Peter, you'll get a taxi for her.'

'I'll do better than that. I'll ride back with her.' He put his hands on Jennie's shoulders, turning her toward himself. 'I want you to know this was wonderful tonight. Wonderful.' He shook a little with emotion. 'We'll never forget it, any of us.'

'No,' Jill said. She hesitated a moment before saying quietly, 'I'm sorry you've had so much trouble, Jennie. And I know it's because of me.'

It was a piteous appeal. The proud young face seemed to recede into what it must have been in the childhood Jennie had not known, wistful and moody, with darkly circled eyes and mobile lips ready on the instant to quiver into anger, grief, or laughter. Who among her ancestors had bequeathed this volatile nature?

'Oh,' replied Jennie, purposely vague, 'causes go way back. There's never any one cause.'

'But I've ruined everything for you. I know I have. I told Peter so.'

'I've had my part in the ruination too,' he added glumly.

There was no possible answer except assent, yet nothing was to be gained by adding blame. All were at fault, each in his or her own way. So Jennie made a small gesture of dismissal and, needing to say something, said only, 'Let's look ahead if we can, not back.'

Jill spoke. 'I wish I didn't have to leave when there's still so much more to be said.'

'Maybe you two can get together some afternoon soon,' suggested Peter.

Jill said quickly, 'I could do it tomorrow. My last class is at one.' She was eager. She wanted to cement the new relationship in a hurry. 'We could go anywhere. The museum, the Metropolitan. We could look around a while and have tea.'

Jennie had planned to go back to the office. She had hidden at home, licking her wounds, long enough. Dinah had been calling with messages. She ought, furthermore, to be checking with the district attorney. It puzzled her that she had heard nothing about the case.

But in the face of Jill's appeal, what difference could one more day make?

'All right. We'll meet at the front steps, just inside the door if the weather's bad.'

She heard them walk downstairs, and on impulse ran to the window to see them emerge from the building and walk away to the avenue. And again there came that odd sense: We are linked, joined, we belong. The feeling darted, pricked a little hole in her head, and fled. Yet she still watched, craning her neck until they were out of sight.

The dark blue night sky raced above the city; wind-blown clouds billowed, hiding the stars. Mesmerized by the moving sky, she reflected, We should look up more often. It chastens and puts things in proportion. At least while you're looking at it, she thought wryly, and was about to pull the blinds down when something caught her attention. A man was standing in the light of the streetlamp, peering up at the house. Was it absurd to imagine that he was watching her window? Of course it was. He had only paused to turn up his coat collar. Then he went, walking toward the river.

My God, my nerves again. They're shot, Jennie thought, whether I want to admit it or not.

She wanted to keep her mind on Jill, but it kept wandering. They looked at an Egyptian statuette, four thousand years old; man and wife stood together, she with her arm around his waist and he with his arm around her shoulder. Timeless, endless human love! And a terrible resentment flared in Jennie, driving the blood into her cheeks and throbbing in her temples, so that she had to force herself to speak normally.

'Well, have we had enough? I could use a chair and some tea.'

'You're tired? Have I made you walk too much?' The girl was anxious; this was genuine concern, just as on that first night when she had thought Jennie was about to faint.

'No, no, of course not. I'm not an invalid.' Then, as if she had sounded impatient, Jennie added quickly, 'You're such a kind person, Jill.'

'And so are you.'

'I try to be,' Jennie said seriously.

'Well, you are. I know that, now that I understand more. I truly do, and I want you to know that I do,' Jill replied with equal seriousness.

Jennie ordered tea and sat for a while gazing over the surrounding tables and heads. If there were a window, Jill would be looking out of it, Jennie thought. I am really learning her ways; she likes long necklaces to play with; today she's wearing two strands of burnt-orange enameled beads, probably Burmese or Indian, smooth to fiddle with and click together.

All at once Jill said, startling Jennie, 'I'm glad you like Peter again.'

'What makes you say I do?'

'You're not angry at him anymore, and you were terribly angry when he first called you.'

'There's a big difference between just not being angry and actually liking someone.'

'But you do like him, I could tell last night.'

'It was just that we were having such a nice time.'

'More than nice. It was beautiful. Didn't you think it was beautiful?' Jill insisted.

The girl's ardor disturbed Jennie. Slowly she stirred her milky tea and considered a moderate reply.

Finally she said, 'It's good that we did it.'

'But wasn't it astounding? I mean, think about it! We were like a family. We *were* a family.'

When last evening the same thought had sped through Jennie's mind, she had dismissed it as an exaggeration. Now the thought alarmed her.

'You already have a family, Jill,' she said firmly, as if to sound a warning.

'I know that I've been very lucky. I had a wonderful childhood, and I still feel all the warmth of it. I didn't have to become an adult overnight the way you did, and I'm very, very thankful for that.'

'And I,' Jennie said, 'am very, very thankful to your parents for giving you that wonderful childhood.'

Now she hesitated between her native instinct to express herself, letting the waters flow, and her learned control, protecting her privacy, damming the waters.

And she said, frowning a little, feeling a tension in her forehead, 'I want to say things that I've made myself forget. I worried so! I wondered whether you were still alive. Perhaps some childhood disease ... or an accident? And I thought, What would become of you if *they* died? It could happen. Your birthday was such a bad day for me. I never looked at the calendar when November came.' She glanced at Jill, who turned her eyes away as one turns from the sight of pain.

'Jennie – don't. There was never anything like that.'

'You're told you will forget, once the child has been given away,' Jennie murmured. 'But it's not true. You don't.'

'That's what Peter says. You don't forget.'

Peter. What had *he* to forget, for heaven's sake? But of course he had plenty, and of course, being the person he was, he must have lived through sadly troubled hours. I'm in such a strange mood today, Jennie thought. I seem to feel a kind of pity for the world, even for all these chatting strangers, sitting here at lunch in this beautiful place. How can anyone know what any one of them has endured or will have to endure?

Yes, Peter.

'I've been thinking –' Jill began, and stopped. 'You won't be angry if I tell you something?'

Jennie had to smile. 'I won't be angry.'

'All right, then. What I've been thinking is, is there maybe a chance that you and Peter could ever – I mean, you both got along so happily last night. Not right away, of course. But maybe sometime?'

'Jill, don't fantasize. Please.'

'Oh, but is it really fantasizing? I don't think so! I have a feeling that Peter would –'

Jennie interrupted. 'Why? What has he said?'

'He hasn't actually said anything. I just have a feeling.' Jill laughed, moving her hands so that her scarlet nails sparkled. 'Full circle. It would be so tidy! I'm a very tidy person. Compulsive, almost.'

'I'm not,' Jennie said rather dryly, looking down at her own unvarnished nails.

There was a silence until Jill spoke, flushing as brightly as Peter could. 'Oh, I've said the wrong thing! I only meant, now that the man you were going to marry –' She stopped. 'Oh, worse and worse! I've really put my foot in my mouth, haven't I? People always tell me I should think before I open it. I'm awfully sorry, Jennie.'

She seemed for the moment so extremely young and so contrite that Jennie could say only, 'It's okay. Really, okay. Just a difference of opinion.'

Jill said more happily, 'Well, that's what makes horse racing, as Grandpa always says.'

'Yes, my mother always says it too.'

'Shall I ever see your mother?'

Oh, Mom had so wanted a grandchild! She never would have moved away to Florida if there had been one.

'I don't know, Jill. I don't know whether it would be the best thing for her if I were to tell her about you now. I'd have to think hard about it.'

Jill nodded. 'I understand. I do understand a lot better than I did last week, you know.'

Jennie touched Jill's hand. 'You've told me, and I'm thankful for that. How about a piece of cake to wash down another cup of tea?'

'My weight. I've got to watch it.'

'Oh, have a piece. You don't do this every day. Besides, you're skinny.'

'Men like skinny girls.'

'Not all men.'

'My boyfriends do.'

'Did I hear plural or singular?'

'Plural. I did have a special one all last year, but I decided it was dumb to be tied down to one person, especially when I wasn't in love with him. He was very smart, a physics major, and nice-looking, but that's not reason enough to give all my time to him. Don't you agree?'

'I definitely agree.'

'Someday,' Jill said earnestly, 'I want to love somebody so much that I can't imagine living without him. And I want to be loved like that in return. Is that too romantic, too unrealistic for the 1980s, do you think?'

'No.' Jennie spoke very softly. 'I should say it's the only way.'

'So in the meantime I've been selective. Right now I've got three who like me a lot. One's a musician and gets tickets for everything, even when they're sold out. We go to the opera on Saturday afternoons. I learned to like it in Santa Fe. You've heard about our opera there, I'm sure.'

Eating cake, drinking tea, Jill rattled on about men, friends, grades, and books.

'Then there's this group I go with. There're about eight of us and we're open to everything, rock and disco – I love to dance – and now a few of us are wading through Proust in French for our seminar. It's a challenge, let me tell you.'

All this energetic cheer was, Jennie knew, partly for her benefit, to create an optimistic atmosphere, but also it was because Jill was feeling comfortable with her. And Jennie, listening not so much to words as to tone and mood, said to herself again, How young she is! How innocent and wise, how trusting and wary, how very dear! No real wounds yet except for the one I gave, and I think that's healing. I'm healing it for her now – thanks to Peter, who made me do it. Maybe she'll get through her years with no wound more terrible than this. I hope so. Some people do.

When they parted, they kissed each other.

'I wish for you,' Jill murmured, 'whatever you wish for yourself.'

What I wish for myself, Jennie thought as she walked away. At this point and after everything that's happened, I just don't know. I'm only drifting.

'In bed already?' Peter asked when she answered the phone.

'Yes, I want to get up very early and get down to the office.'

'Are you sure you're ready to go back into the rat race?'

'As ready as I'll ever be.'

'You haven't heard anything? Do you mind my asking?'

She dodged purposely. 'Heard what?'

'You know. From . . . him.'

'It's over, Peter,' she said somewhat sharply. 'I've already told you that.'

'God, what a shame! I don't understand people.'

'Peter, I don't want to talk about it.'

'Okay, okay. I just want you to know you have me.'

She didn't answer.

'You're not alone in the world.'

The phone clicked.

'Jennie? Are you there?'

'I'm here.'

The phone clicked again.

'That noise. I thought you'd hung up on me.'

'You know I wouldn't do that.'

'I was thinking. You know I mentioned something about next summer. Do you think you'd like that? Just a week or so out on the Indian reservation, you and Jill and I?'

In spite of herself, she was touched. And she answered softly, 'Peter, I can't think that far ahead.'

'All right. Another time, then. I really called just to find out how it went today.'

'Oh, it was good! We saw some wonderful things. She wanted to see some eighteenth-century portraits for her art history class, and then we went to the Egyptian wing. She's very well read, very bright.'

'She's a treasure, Jennie. We produced a treasure, you and I. Sometimes when I think of her I have to chuckle, she's so much like you.'

'Like me? Why, she's a carbon copy of you.'

'She looks like me, but I mean her attitudes, that high indignation over injustice. And a temper. What a temper!'

'You think I have a temper?'

'Can you ask? You've got a fierce one! And stubborn! Once you've made your mind up – when you made it up to get rid of me before Jill was born.' He fell silent and then said sadly, 'I've worn a hair shirt ever since. Believe me, Jennie.'

'Don't, don't,' she whispered. 'This is no time to talk about it.'

'I suppose it isn't. Well, take it easy, will you? Don't overwork yourself tomorrow.'

When she hung up, she thrust aside the document she had been reviewing. From somewhere in the old building came the sound of music, someone's record player turned on too loud. But it was pleasing, a piano concerto, melodious and nostalgic. Wine and roses, she thought, and put her head back, closing her eyes. The bed was soft and the quilt so beautifully warm, making sleep seem possible this time...

Peter, in a white summer suit, danced under paper lanterns. She was troubled because she knew so little about him. They really had spoken only of Jill. Now Jay came, his dark, mournful face framed in a doorway. Then someone who was neither Jay nor Peter, but both of them, was standing over her in a painful light. And she was terribly sad because she didn't know who it was.

Waking, she saw that the lamp was glaring into her eyes. Now, switching it off, she was wide-awake again. For a long time she would have to lie staring into darkness.

13

The peach-colored silk blouse rustled, her mother's pearl bracelets clicked on her wrist, and her feet slid into the black lizard pumps that she had been saving for 'afterward.' Since there was to be no afterward, she might as well wear them now, might as well put her best foot forward. But she was jelly inside.

On her way to the bus she analyzed herself. You're dreading the return to the old life, the one you liked because it was so stimulating, so full of color while you were living it. But now you dread going back, because now you know it was empty jingle and jangle, for all the important talk, the plays and galleries and bright young men. The bus lurched. With every stop and start, it carried her farther downtown and farther back in time. She stared straight ahead. Desolation chilled her and she hugged her coat closer.

A woman got on and sat beside her. Moving to make room on the seat, Jennie was repelled. The woman had a hostile face; hard and jutting, it looked as if it had been cut out with a can opener. Jennie moved nearer to the window and pulled her coat tighter.

Suddenly the woman spoke. 'Excuse me, but I do admire your shoes. I wish I could wear shoes like those, but I have such trouble with my feet.' She smiled and the eyes that had seemed so harsh shone mildly.

'Thank you,' Jennie said, adding, since it seemed only right to say something friendly, 'They're very comfortable.' And as intensely as the quick aversion had come, Jennie felt a rush of gratitude toward the stranger. To think that one could be comforted, that one could find human warmth in a trivial remark about a pair of shoes! And she arrived at her office oddly quieted.

'The flu really knocked you out, didn't it?' Dinah observed. 'You've lost weight.'

'A little, I guess. I didn't expect you in on Saturday.'

'I'll stay half a day. I've postponed all but the most important appointments so you can get your strength back.' She followed Jennie to the inner office. 'Look at these. They came a few minutes ago.'

On Jennie's desk in a tall, thin vase stood a spray of ruby-red roses, their heavy perfume sweetening the stale air. For a second she thought they might be from Jay. Stupid! She touched a lush, curved petal. There was no need to read the card, but she read it anyway, surprised that she could still remember the unusual script, partly cursive and partly printed.

'Good luck on your first day back. Love, Peter,' it said. And then, squeezed below, came an afterthought. 'And Jill.'

Peter and his flowers! She fingered them thoughtfully.

'A dozen. I counted. Aren't they gorgeous?' Dinah was impressed and curious. And as Jennie didn't answer at once, she added, 'There's a pile of mail. I've sorted it and put the important stuff on your desk. There was a special-delivery certified letter that I opened. I thought you'd want me to.'

'Of course. What is it?'

'From those people up in the country. The land case.'

It was a short, typewritten note on Arthur Wolfe's letterhead, written in his capacity as the new head of the

Preservation Committee. She was informed that 'other arrangements' had been made for legal counsel and was requested to send the bill for her services. And that was all.

She stood still, holding in her hand what was in essence a repudiation of her total self. A flush of shame prickled down her back, as if her body were burning. She had been stripped. How could they have done this to her? All her work, so dearly wrought, had gone for nothing. And yet, given the circumstances, how could they have done otherwise? And, anyway, would she want to continue working with Arthur Wolfe? No, it would be impossible, and Arthur Wolfe had seen that it was.

Yet her heart broke.

'Write an answer, Dinah,' she directed. 'Say I acknowledge receipt of the letter and that I am not sending a bill for services. What I did, I did because I believed in it, and I never expected to be paid in the first place. Say that. And do it now, please, Dinah. I want it to go in the mail this afternoon.'

She kept standing there holding Arthur's letter. Then suddenly something occurred to her that should have occurred before. She had every right not to be excluded from knowledge of events that she herself had set in motion! She had every right to know at least what was happening to Martha Cromwell. What if that man or those men had gone to the house looking for George's tape? It would only be logical to try there, where the sick old woman was now alone, wouldn't it? Cold fear shocked Jennie's veins at the picture: the frame house hidden behind gloomy hemlocks at the end of the street, its front door darkened by overgrown vines on the porch. A man could slip in and slip out again, unseen and unheard. . . . She had to know.

Without another thought she picked up the telephone and dialed.

'This is Jennie Rakowsky. I'm a friend of Martha's, and I'm calling to ask about her,' she said.

A young woman's voice sounded against a background of buzzing talk. 'Oh, I know who you are! You're the lawyer who spoke so beautifully at the meeting that time.'

The words brought a little glow to Jennie, a glow that she needed just then, and she thanked the woman.

'How is Martha? I hear so many voices, and I'm glad she's not alone in the house. I was afraid she might be.'

'Alone? Goodness, no. The neighbors are taking turns to be with her. There are never fewer than two of us with her, day or night. Right now the place is jam-packed, and we intend to stay.'

'Oh, that's wonderful! I was so worried.'

'You can speak to her yourself. She's in bed, of course, poor soul, but there's a phone upstairs.'

'I'm doing fine,' Martha told Jennie weakly. 'I'm holding up better than I ever thought I could.'

'You're like George. You've got guts. Tell me, Martha, has anybody been looking for the tape? Have you got it safely hidden till the case comes up?'

Martha sighed, began to speak, then sighed again. 'Jennie, I don't know how to begin to tell you. This business has been a fiasco from the start.'

'What do you mean?'

'Well, on the day of the funeral my niece came to tidy up the bedroom. George had put the tape, disguised in a paper grocery bag, under the bed. I didn't think about it – naturally I wasn't thinking very well that day – and she threw the bag out in the trash. It's incinerated, Jennie. Gone.'

Jennie felt a surge of crazy laughter. A grocery bag under the bed! How typical of George!

'I'm so sorry, Jennie. The chief weapon's gone now, isn't it?'

'I'm afraid so. Well, the Preservation Committee is back where it started, that's all.'

'I hear you're not the lawyer anymore. What happened?'

'It's a long story. Too long.'

'Without you they're going to lose.'

'Oh, you give me too much credit. I have no influence on the board. They'll vote the way they want to vote.'

'No, there's a couple of swing votes that can go either way, easily as not. And you're a spellbinder, Jennie.'

'Well, thank you for the kind words, but I'm out of it now. Take care, Martha. I'll keep in touch.'

Out of my hands, she thought. So Barker Development will win, the land will be destroyed, and Martha and I and the rest of us will be safe. A mixed bag, after all the effort, the fuss and fury. Talk about irony!

Her work had piled up to the sky in less than a week. Papers and appointments filled the morning. As always, almost every woman who came in either brought a child along, had left one with a neighbor, or was ripely pregnant with one. So many of these women had no dependable, permanent man, having either been deserted by one or having never had one. Hard lives, these were, and still Jennie could not help but think, with some bitterness, that they had a certain freedom, too; there was no secrecy about the way they lived, and no explanations were needed.

All morning they came and went. She had lunch at her desk, a bad sandwich, mostly mayonnaise, and a soft drink, there being no time to go out for anything better. The telephone rang. The mail came and another pile accumulated. By one o'clock when Dinah left, Jennie was working away.

'You must be awfully tired,' Dinah said with concern. 'Why don't you go home?'

'I'm fine. I'll just stay on another hour or so.'

She wanted to be tired. It would be such comfort to go home exhausted, there to eat some simple cheese and fruit, go to sleep and not think about Arthur Wolfe – or anybody.

Someone was knocking at the outer door. Her first impulse was to ignore it and let whoever it was go away. The knocking became insistent. It occurred to her that it might be the terrorized girl who had come in a few days ago with blue-green bruises all over her neck and arms. Her lover may have come back in another temper. She got up and opened the door.

A well-dressed man of early middle age, wearing a gray overcoat, stood before her.

'My name's Robinson. I know it's late, but I saw the light. May I come in?'

He was already in, following Jennie into her room, where the debris of the busy day, papers finished and papers not finished, littered every surface.

He laid his attaché case – pin seal and brass buckles – on the floor beside a chair, removed a small sheaf of Jennie's papers from the chair, and handed them to her.

'Mind if I sit down?'

She took her papers from his hand, thinking, He's cool, mighty cool. Who is he?

'You've got a nice place here,' he said, looking around at the mess. 'And the flowers. I raise roses myself. It's a hobby of mine.'

'What can I do for you?' Jennie asked, wary now.

'Somebody's got to think a whole lot of you to send those. They cost, those long stems. They cost a bundle.'

Who was he? The hairs on Jennie's forearms rose. An

animal besieged in its den recognizes danger. But where is safety? Where can one hide?

'I asked you,' she said, keeping a level tone, 'what I can do for you. What is your business?'

'Well, this and that.' When he smiled, his gums, which were knobby, white, and slick, were revealed above extraordinary, oversize, yellowed teeth.

'Big teeth,' George had said. 'The biggest teeth you ever saw.'

But the name hadn't been Robinson, she was sure, although at the onset of panic, alone here with everyone gone home from next door and silence in the outer hall, she couldn't think of the name. It made no difference, anyway. She tried to steady her thoughts.

'Yes, this and that,' the man said. Manicured fingers played with the hand-tailored cuff on the other arm.

'"This and that" tells me nothing. Do you have a legal problem? I'm a lawyer.'

'Well, I know that, don't I? And also that you've had experience with adoption law. I know that too.'

Startled, Jennie looked into a pair of narrow black eyes, the eyes of a rodent watching from a hidden corner.

'Adoption?' she said. 'Not particularly.'

'No? I heard you had.'

'Not at all.'

'Oh, come, I know better. You're surprised.' He smiled again, and the teeth glistened. 'People hear things. Crossed wires. There are ways.'

The click on the phone, the man on the steps and under the streetlight. The day she forgot to lock the door...

It all came clear. They had stopped at nothing in their search for that tape. They couldn't go to George's house because of the crowd; moreover, hadn't George led them to believe that 'someone else' had it? Logically that someone would be Arthur Wolfe or Jay or herself. All this flashed through her mind in a few seconds under the scrutiny of those cold, basilisk eyes.

A short pain shot through her chest. One could have a heart attack; even as young as she was, it was possible. Still, she kept silence.

'Yes, yes. There are certain people, a certain person, who would be interested to know what it is that you know about adoptions. Even one that happened a long time ago.'

How strange, Jennie was thinking. The twisted strands come together. Peter and Jill and the Green Marsh meet and twist together at Jay's feet. Or they would, if Jay's feet were still standing where they stood before.

'You'd just as soon he wouldn't know, I'm sure. No more good life, no more riding around the country in his cute two-seater Mercedes.'

This was the man, then. The car belonged to the Wolfes and was kept in the country. She'd been out in it with Jay.

'What do you want?' she asked, forcing herself to speak.

'You know what I want.'

'If I knew, I wouldn't ask,' she retorted, astonished that she was not only able to talk but also to show a bit of defiance.

'Look, we've each got something on the other. So if you're smart, you won't play games with me. I want the tape.' And when she didn't answer at once, he leaned forward in the chair as if he were about to leap out of it. 'And don't say "What tape?" This isn't the time to play dumb.' At the same time his voice was low and controlled.

Her palms were wet with the sweat of terror. 'I haven't got any tape.' The black eyes looked at her now without expression. And she said, 'That's the truth. I never had any.'

He swiveled around in the chair and looked toward the window. Across the street the office building had gone mostly dark, except that here and there lights were being turned back on as the cleaning crews began their rounds. She tried to remember what time they started work here on this floor but couldn't remember, couldn't think of anything except fear. She should have had more sense than to stay alone in a deserted building.

'Too bad about the old man, wasn't it?' he said, still with his back to her.

'What old man?' she said, parrying.

He whipped about, leapt from the chair, and stood over her so that she drew back, instinctively protecting her face from a blow.

'Jennie, Jennie, you're wasting my time.' He was smiling at his effect upon her. 'I'd just as soon not knock your teeth out. Now, you're a smart gal, a lawyer, so you don't need me to draw pictures for you. Here it is, final offer: Hand over the tapes and I keep my mouth shut about the kid and the other guy. What could be sweeter?'

'As to the kid,' Jennie said, 'you can tell the world, for all it matters. And as to the tapes, I tell you I know nothing about them. I haven't anything to do with the entire affair anymore.'

'What the hell do you mean by that?'

'What I said. I'm not the lawyer. I've been fired.'

'I don't believe you.'

'If you'll let me get up from this chair, I'll find the letter.'

She was beginning to think again. The animal in its lair fights for its life.

'I'm not stopping you,' he said, and showed his feral grin.

'You're standing too close to me. I want to protect my teeth.'

He laughed slightly and stepped back. 'You've got nerve. I like that in a woman.'

With shaking hands she rummaged through the stacks of papers on the desk while he stood waiting, so close to her that she could hear his breathing. In a desperate hurry she whipped around and overturned the stacks.

'I guess you haven't got it. I guess you've been feeding me a lot of bull.'

'You guess wrong. It's here. It has to be.' Unless I threw it out. Did I? If I did, God help me.

'I thought he was going to smash my teeth in,' George had said. But he had done worse than that.

'I don't know. Give me a minute.'

'I'm not going to stand here all night, you know.'

She could hear the silence in the stone corridor beyond the door. Silence roars, one says. Like the sound of waves when you hold a shell to your ear. Like the rush of blood to the head.

She bent down. The wastebasket hadn't been emptied yet. That's where it would be. Oh, it had to be!

He grabbed her arm, the strong fingers pinching painfully. 'Hey! What do you think you're doing?'

She tipped the overflowing basket onto the floor, knelt down, and feverishly separated scraps, crumpled advertisements, torn envelopes, the morning paper. Please, please, let me find it....

'Here it is!' The letter had been partially ripped across the top but was clearly legible. She held it up to him.

'You see, I told you. I've been fired.'

He studied the letter first, then studied Jennie, who had risen and sat down again because her knees were buckling.

'So,' he said, 'so you don't really give a damn what happens now, do you?'

She thought, He will go to the Wolfes next. But there is nothing I can do about that, and nothing that they can't cope with better than I can.

'No,' she said, 'that's right. I don't give a damn.'

'And you don't give a damn, either, whether he finds out about your kid.'

He was standing so close now that his knees brushed hers. 'So you're playing the field again.'

'I don't know what you're talking about.'

'Sure you do. The kid's father.' He seemed amused. 'Old home week, hey?'

Her teeth began to chatter. She'd read about chattering teeth but had never experienced them. It was strange, the way they rattled and wouldn't be still.

He reached out and touched her breast. 'You're a good-looking woman.'

Her hands flew to her breasts. He pulled them away.

She looked up at him, trying sternness and reason. 'Why do you want to do this? It's not worth the trouble you'll have.'

'I'll give you six guesses why. You thought you'd outsmart me, didn't you? Putting a wire on the old fool.' He had a tight hold on her hands. 'I wonder how you'd look with a broken nose. Or maybe a few cuts on your pretty face?'

'I'll scream –'

'Go on, scream. Who'll hear you?'

His fist, on which there gleamed a gold ring, solid and domed like a rock, flashed toward her face. Quickly she dodged and fell, striking her head on the edge of the desk. Pain shot through her stomach; vomit rose in her throat. He bent down, seized the front of her shirt, and raised her. The tearing silk screeched. His huge, slick teeth loomed, his face was distorted with fury, his tobacco breath was hot, the fist came up again. . . .

Then from the far end of the corridor sounded the noisy clash of the elevator door and a babble of voices, a clatter of heavy shoes and clinking pails. 'The cleaning crew! They're coming in!' she cried out, sobbing.

In an instant he was up on his feet. 'Shit!' Grabbing his attaché case and overcoat, he was out the door before Jennie was up off the floor.

Faint and swaying, she held on to the back of a chair. She was still standing there, pulling the ripped blouse together, when the door opened and a boy came in, trundling the paraphernalia of pails, mops, rags, and brooms. He stopped and stared at her.

'That man!' she gasped. 'Look in the hall! Has he gone?'

The boy shook his head. 'No English.'

She wanted to thank him over and over, to get down on her knees before him. He would have thought she was crazy. Perhaps he thought so, anyway.

Trembling, hoping her knees would hold her up, she put on her jacket; gathered her coat, bag, and gloves; and then, afraid to go downstairs, sat down again. What if he was waiting for her on the sidewalk? But no, she must try to think logically; of course he wouldn't be out on the street where she could cry for help. But would he try again at home?

The telephone was at her hand, but she was shaking so badly that she couldn't hold it. She said aloud again: 'I have to think. Call the police? To look somewhere for a man in a dark overcoat among the thousands of men in dark overcoats on the streets of New York? Absurd! Call Martin upstate?' Her face ached, she was weak, she needed someone to tell her what to do. How alone she was without Jay! Then sudden terror struck her. What if that – that *creature* were to go to Jay's house? The stupid, snobbish nanny would admit him simply because he wore an expensive coat and looked like a gentleman, wouldn't she? She and the children might be there alone. Or even if Jay were there by himself and the creature had a knife – Now Jennie's quivering hands behaved as she dialed the number. This was only a call of warning, for nothing else, for no plea or intrusion where she was no longer wanted. A call of warning. She would make that clear.

There was no answer at the apartment. When she tried the office, the answering service reported that the office was closed until Monday morning. Did she wish to leave a message? No. One could hardly leave a warning to watch out for a man with protruding yellow teeth.

She called Martin next, tracked him down at his home, and cried out her story. 'I'm sure it was George's man,' she concluded. 'George was right, the teeth are the giveaway.'

'If he's not the killer, he obviously knows who the killer is.'

'Well, he practically said as much. I wonder whether Fisher did the actual job on George.'

'I don't know. We're watching him very closely. And there are other developments out of town, which I can't talk about on the phone. Incidentally, be careful on your phone until we get rid of the bug. I'll see that it's taken care of on Monday.' There was a pause. 'I understand you're not on the case anymore.'

'That's true. I was dismissed.' A kind of defensive pride rose in her. 'Not for any professional reason. It was entirely personal.'

'I had an idea it must have been. And I'm sorry. You're a credit to the profession.'

She felt a renewed surge of tears at the praise and thanked him.

'Well, good thing you weren't hurt. That's the most important thing. But you've had a close call, and my advice is to go home, have a shot of Scotch, and rest.'

When the telephone contact was broken off, fear flowed back into the room. I need someone, anyone, she thought. Not friends, who knew nothing of all these troubles. Not

Jill. One didn't lean on a young girl, nor did one scare her to death.

But there was Peter ... And she telephoned the Waldorf-Astoria.

He sounded surprised and pleased. 'You just caught me. I was on my way to dinner with some people who flew in today from Chicago.'

'Oh.' These words, finally, defeated her. 'Oh,' she said, sighing.

'What's the matter? Are you crying?'

'No. Yes.' And again she sobbed out her story.

'My God! Did you call the police?'

'No. He didn't actually *do* anything to me. What can I prove?'

'That's ridiculous. What are police for? Call right now.'

'You don't understand! I deal every day with these things! They must get a thousand calls a minute in this city. You don't know. They're not going to bother about something that almost happened but didn't. And the man's ... vanished, anyway.' She faltered. 'Besides, I'm exhausted.'

'I'm coming right over,' he said promptly. 'Lock the office door until I come up. I'll keep the cab waiting and take you home.'

'You have a dinner appointment.'

'The hell with it! Wait there for me.'

'My phone was bugged. Can you imagine? He knew about Jill.' She had taken off not only the torn blouse but also the jacket and skirt, everything she had been wearing, as if they were defiled; she would never wear them again. Now she sat enclosed by the wings of the chair, huddled and trembling, cold even in her thick quilted housecoat.

'My God, if I hadn't found that letter! He was in such a rage, a queer, quiet rage. He never raised his voice. It was eerie. Thank heaven I found it, and thank heaven he believed it.' She hadn't stopped talking since Peter had brought her home. Her words poured out in a high, nervous voice. 'I can't get it through my head. The land is so innocent, Peter, it's lain there forever just growing trees, so quiet, with little wild things and geese coming in from Canada. So innocent!' she cried. 'And then come the two-legged beasts to fight over it, tearing one another to shreds or killing for it. Yes, beasts! I've seen plenty, you know. In my work one doesn't exactly deal with sweetness and light, but still, until you go through it yourself, you can't believe what people will do for money. The violence you read about is nothing until you become a victim, an object. . . . Oh, I can still smell him; can you understand that, Peter? He had a cologne or shaving cream I would recognize again; it had a sweetish smell – like cinnamon, almost. If those cleaners hadn't come – oh, God, do you think . . . do you think maybe he would have killed me afterward? Or maybe just slashed my face? He said something about cutting it. There was a case like that, remember? Oh, I can't believe this happened to me! It's something you only read about in the newspaper.'

With her hands around her knees she rocked, making herself small in the chair. A gust of wind-driven rain rattled the windows and startled them so that they both looked around.

'It's nothing,' Peter said. 'Only a miserable winter night, and we're facing north.' He looked large and calm. 'No one can get in, Jennie. The door's locked. I slid the bolt.'

She had to smile. 'Thank you for reading my thoughts.' With him there she felt safe. It was the second time. 'You're being very good to me,' she said.

His brows were ruefully drawn together. 'I never thought I'd live to hear you say I was good to you.'

'I didn't mean *then*. I'm talking about *now*. These last few days and this minute. You're helping me get through this minute.'

'I'm staying all night. I'm not going to leave you.'

She raised her eyes to meet a painful, troubled frown. He seemed about to speak, then closed his lips, looked away, and finally did speak.

'I haven't told you enough about the guilt I've felt.'

'Yes, you have, Peter. Don't beat your breast anymore. It's not necessary.'

But he persisted, 'I should have gone after you when she was born whether you wanted me to or not.'

When she raised her hand in protest, he resisted. 'Don't stop me. Yes, I should have. I want you to know that. And I did think about the child. But you made it so clear that you wanted nothing more to do with me –'

She interjected, wanting to hear no more, 'It's true. I did. So what use is it now to –'

'Only to unburden myself. That's the use. Maybe this is selfish of me, I don't know, but it's been bottled up, stored away in an effort to forget it or to deny it, and I want – I need, Jennie – I need to say it all.'

Things stored away, to forget or to deny. And she said, very low, 'I suppose, after all, that I hurt you too.'

He turned his hand out, palm up, in a gesture of rueful dismissal. 'A scratch compared with a sledgehammer blow. It's not enough of an excuse, the one I've made to myself, that I was very young. Not enough.'

The lamplight fell on his bent head and clasped hands, emphasizing sadness and penitence. There was something familiar to her in the posture. It took a few minutes for her to recall when she had seen him like that before. Among all the fleeting, faded images, now one returned with sudden, shocking clarity: On the last night before she had taken the plane to Nebraska, he had been sitting just like that at the end of the bed in the dingy motel, watching television.

'Jennie? It doesn't seem like nineteen years, does it? I mean, I don't feel the strangeness that I imagined I would feel. Do you?'

She turned away from the searching question, answering, 'I guess not.'

'We did well together while it lasted, didn't we?' There was something hopeful in his voice, wanting confirmation.

'That's true.'

She felt a wave of sadness at this reminder of loss. Was that what life was, a series of adjustments to loss? The optimist in Jennie refuted that; there had to be more to life. There *was* more. Nevertheless the sadness settled.

'Do you want a sleeping pill?' Peter asked.

'I never take them.' The words sounded brave.

'I thought maybe after today you'd need a little help.'

'No. But I think I want to go to bed now. Are you sure you want to stay here?'

'Sure.'

The decision satisfied her. On the surface she could maintain bravery, but still, it was good not to be alone. It wasn't natural to sleep alone; even a dog liked to be near somebody, to feel a presence at night.

'I'll get some blankets. I'm sorry there's only the sofa.'

'It's fine.' When he curled on his side to demonstrate, his knees were brought up almost to his chest.

'Shorty,' she said, looking down at him, and giggled. 'Pop asked me why you were called Shorty, and I told him because you were six feet three. You'll be miserable on that thing. You'd better go back to the hotel.'

'I'm not going back. Not after what you went through a couple of hours ago.'

She considered something. Her bed, which she had brought from her parents' spare bedroom in Baltimore, was king-size. Three strangers could sleep in it without even touching one another. And she made a hesitant offer.

'You can have the far end of my bed if you want. It does seem ridiculous for you to be cramped on the sofa. You won't be able to sleep.'

'If you really mean it, I'll accept the offer.' He sat up and grimaced. 'This is really pretty painful.'

'Then it's settled. I'll turn out the light and you can just crawl in whenever you're ready.'

'No problem.'

For a long time she stayed awake, fighting the memory of that creature's contempt and violent hands, trying to wipe out the hideous memory of what had been, what had almost been, and what would have happened next if ... if...

The night sky above the city poured its glow through the blinds, so that she could just see the outline of Peter's motionless back as he lay on his side. Wryly she thought, I was accused of being in bed with him when I hadn't been, and now I really am in bed with him. The very last time was at the motel all those years ago. We lay apart then, too, but for a different reason. He was afraid to touch me, scared because I was pregnant, I suppose, or perhaps even repelled by what was in my belly. The bitterness of that night!

But once we used to consume each other, counted the hours of longing from weekend to weekend. From one Friday night to the next was one hundred sixty-eight hours. When, during the week, we met in passing, our eyes used to speak what they remembered and anticipated.

How lovely their beginning had been! Fresh as spring all that year through, and warm with its light. There had been so much wild, young laughter between them. And she wondered now whether, if their marriage had not been blocked by other people, they would have lasted together, after all; lasted with all that tenderness and laughter.

There would have been no Jay, then. Queer thought. She would never have known his tenderness, his subtle wisdom, or his special grace. Neither would she have known nor lost him. Queer.

The sheets rustled now as Peter turned.

'Stretch out your arm.'

Across the wide bed their fingers barely managed to touch.

'I only wanted to say good night. Have easy dreams, Jennie. Try not to think about today, if you can.'

The voice and the brief touch were consolation. The sound of his breathing soothed. You're safe, she argued with herself. You're not alone. Traffic on the avenue was a distant rushing, like surf. She felt herself drift. . . .

And she dreamed. She dreamed she was enfolded, that arms enclosed her, loving, tender arms; at the same time she was saying, 'Yes, you are having this healthy dream so you won't think of how sex can be a terrifying weapon. So go on, dream, don't wake up, don't stop, it's delicious, it's wonderful.'

She was half awake. Someone was kissing her, and she had been responding.

'Darling,' Jay said.

And 'Yes, yes, don't stop me,' she heard, and started, fully awake now.

'Peter, for God's sake, what are you doing?' she cried, appalled, and sat up to slide out of the bed.

'I've been holding you for the last ten minutes. You wanted me to,' he said simply.

'I was dreaming! You don't understand,' she said, hiding her face in her hands.

'I know. And I was too. I dreamed that you wanted to be loved.'

Her lips quivered. 'This was a stupid idea. It's I who should have thought of sleeping on the sofa. It's long enough for me.'

She turned on the bedside lamp. Peter's eyes, the prominent opals with the lavender tint, were frightened and ashamed.

'Dream or not, you did want to be loved, though.'

'Yes,' she said miserably.

'But not by me.'

She couldn't answer, and he said, persisting, 'By him, still?'

'You ask too many questions. I can't answer. I don't know.'

Yet she did know. In her dream it was with Jay that she had lain, it was his face she had seen and his name she had spoken. And she knew, abruptly and sharply, that she was not ready for anyone else. Would she ever be?

The light fanned out over the carpet, over the rumpled blanket, over Peter's crestfallen, heated face.

'Only one more question,' he urged. 'Are you furious with me?'

She was painfully confused. He'd had no right to think that she would. . . . And yet, asleep or half asleep, she had lain in his arms, in the warm, tight cave. And she understood that he felt his manhood had been rejected, and she was sorry.

'You're still one of the most attractive men I've ever known,' she said gently.

'Thank you, but you don't have to say that. You're saying it because you think you've hurt me.'

'That doesn't make it any less true. You still are one of the most attractive men.' She clutched her throat and her mouth twisted. A sudden, tearful awareness of the absurdity of the situation, the scene, the picture they made, had overwhelmed her.

Peter said at once, 'I'm going to the sofa. You get back to bed.'

'I'm wide-awake. I can't go back to sleep.'

She followed him into the other room. It had grown colder because the heat was lowered at night. The wind was still rattling the windows. Now he, wrapped in a blanket, and she in the quilted robe, sat down to face each other again. After a minute Peter broke the bleak silence with another question.

'It was he who got you into the land case, wasn't it?'

'He?'

'Tom, if you like. It's as good a name as any.'

'That's why you were relieved of your job.'

'Yes. Why bring that up?'

'Just wondering. Anyway, it's as well you're out of it. The party's gotten rough and dangerous.'

'But I wanted to win that case. My heart was in it.'

'There'll be other cases. Other people too,' Peter added after a pause.

'I don't know.'

'But you've had others all these years.'

'Other cases or other people?'

'Other people, I meant. Men.'

'Yes, but this time it was different.'

'Don't people always think that?'

She smiled slightly. 'But sometimes when they think so, it really is. One person dies or – or goes away, and the other one is changed forever.'

Peter gave her a serious look, which she returned; their eyes touched. And he said slowly, 'Yes, I believe you're one woman who can be like that if anybody can.' And he sighed.

She sensed things waiting to be spoken. Perhaps he had really hoped that he and she might come full circle; hadn't Jill said it would be so 'tidy'? That she had a 'feeling'?

And at that moment he said, 'I might as well tell you I've been having some unexpected thoughts these past few days. I should have known they were unrealistic. May I tell you what they were?'

'Of course.'

'Well, then. Naturally I didn't expect an immediate miracle, but I did think that maybe there was some sort of fate, something that would in time, plenty of time, bring us together again. I'm not superstitious, you must know that, but I really did think I saw some sort of pattern in the way things have turned out with Jill, and the way you and I have come together without anger. But you don't want it.' His sigh was wistful.

'Peter ... I'm sort of dead inside, don't you see?'

'No, you're not. You're alive and in very much pain. And you don't deserve it.'

She didn't answer. For a moment he waited, then asked quite softly, almost in a whisper, 'Won't you talk about him?'

'No. I've had my message. What's finished is finished.'

'It just struck me ... how odd that both times in your life it was Jill who caused the breakup! First with me and now with him.'

'In very different ways, Peter.'

'True. But you ought to be married,' he said abruptly. 'It's time.'

She smiled at his vehemence. 'You think so? What about yourself?'

'I have been married. Three times.' He turned away, as if he was making an effort to conquer embarrassment. 'That startles you, doesn't it?'

'A little.'

'It doesn't make for an impressive résumé. Not anything to be proud of or easy to talk about.'

'Don't talk about it, then,' she said, pitying him for his confession.

'I never do. But for some reason I want you to know.' He drew a deep breath. 'The first one was my sister's friend, the one who was visiting that weekend.'

The brat who sat on the bed while I tried on that ridiculous dress, she remembered.

'We married the day after my college commencement. She was seventeen and a half. We never had anything to talk about. I bored her when I went on to graduate school.'

'Why on earth did you marry her?'

'She grew up to be a beauty. And the families . . . I don't know. We were always thrown together.'

'I see.' The hovering families – nudges, winks, hints, little suppers, and picnics artfully arranged. 'I see.'

'We lasted not quite two years.'

'No children?'

'Good God, no. The next was a studious girl from Alabama, a country girl with a scholarship at Emory. She and my mother didn't get along. She hated my family and didn't try to hide it. And my mother wasn't exactly pleased with her, I admit.'

I can imagine, Jennie thought. A chill came over her, as though again she were sitting in that vast room under the regal portraits on the wall.

'So it made things tough all around.'

She could imagine that too: Peter caught between wife and mother, when all he wanted, generous boy that he had been, was peace.

'It couldn't last. I still have a strong sense of loyalty to my family, you know, even when I don't always agree with them.'

Jennie knew. Why take a stand about Vietnam? Go along and pretend to agree. It's orderly, it's pleasant that way.

'She wouldn't live in Atlanta after her graduation, and

I wanted to. So that ended it. The funny thing is, I left for Chicago a few months afterward, anyway. Well, that was number two.' Peter stopped. 'Are you shocked? Disgusted?'

'Neither.'

She was moved by this tale of defeat, as well as by his candor. He still had his frank naïveté. In contrast and in a flickering instant, it brought to her mind Jay's reflective manner and, no matter how intent his feelings, his habit of prudence.

'What happened with number three?'

As a sudden wind shuts with one blow a door that had been wide open, Peter's face closed. She had to wait a few moments for his answer.

'Alice,' he said. 'She died.' And then, as if the door had blown open again, he almost cried out. 'She was wonderful, Jennie, really wonderful. She had a little boy. We had fun together, the three of us. Her parents took him after – after she was gone. I miss him, miss her – Well, you get over things, don't you? Or try to, anyway.'

She could say only, 'I'm so sorry, Peter.'

He gave her a quizzical look, a strange look, sad, hurt, yet with the faintest touch of humor.

'I'll tell you something. She was very much like you. Full of ideals and energy. She even looked a little bit like you.'

Again Jennie found few words, just, 'Thank you, Peter.'

She was immensely moved by his tribute and saddened by his story. Would not Alice probably have been the one who lasted? On the other hand, after two failures, and if he was still his mother's boy, she might not have been. They were so complicated, the ways in which people connected with one another; one needed more knowledge than Jennie possessed to puzzle it all out. She knew only two things surely now: that Peter was a good man and that he was not for her, in spite of what Jill or he himself might think.

'You look sorrowful,' he said anxiously. 'I shouldn't have dumped my troubles on you.'

'Please!' she protested. 'After all that's been dumped on you this week? I'm thinking, I'm hoping that something very good will happen to you.'

'Oh, plenty of good things already have! You mustn't think I'm mourning over my life. I like where I live, I've had plenty of friends, and I'm doing the work I always wanted to do. Besides, although I guess it sounds too boastful, I have to admit that I've made a rather big name for myself.'

'I know. Jill told me you're pretty famous. Her father's an amateur archaeologist, and he's been looking you up ever since she told him about you.'

'They sound like very decent people.'

'They are. You have only to look at Jill to know that they must be.'

Peter laughed. 'Don't you and I get any credit for her? Let's not be so modest.'

'Yes, yes, of course we do.'

Jennie was suddenly exhausted. This incredible day, which had begun with bitter disappointment, continued with shocking violence, and ended with a confusion of dreams had overwhelmed her.

She stood up. 'It's late. This time you'll take the bed and I'll sleep here. The sofa fits me.'

'Afraid to try me again, are you? Don't trust me?'

'It's not that. I just think it's better this way.' She kissed his cheek. 'Good night.'

In the morning she woke up late to find him gone and the big bed made. He had left a note: 'Be careful at the office from now on. Check the door at home too. I'll call you before I go back to Chicago.'

After a while, bestirring herself, she went ahead with the morning's routine, cleaned the kitchen, and washed her hair. Then came files to study, a whole day's worth of them.

Toward noon Shirley called through the door.

'Hey! You in there?'

In her new coat, with flamboyant, multistriped hoops in her ears, Shirley was dressed for a day of leisure, Jennie saw. She also caught Shirley's quick investigative glance around the apartment.

'You feeling up to lunch and an afternoon movie? I'm meeting some of the girls.'

'Thanks, but I can't. I've that whole pile of work to make up.'

Shirley, perched on the edge of a chair, complained, 'You've been behaving so mysteriously. Frankly I've been worried about you.'

'I haven't meant to be mysterious.' Jennie, shuffling papers, wished Shirley would just go away.

'Good Lord, what happened to your face?'

The bruise on her cheek was turning livid.

'I had to get up last night, and I bumped into the bathroom door.'

The other raised skeptical eyebrows, then waited a few moments, as if deciding whether or not to plunge.

'Jennie – what's happened between you and Jay? I suppose I'm prying, but after all, we've known each other for more than a few years, and I can't help but care. I *am* prying. I see I am.'

For into Jennie's eyes, in spite of the determination that had been restraining her, the tears had sprung. She bent her head over the papers without answering.

'Oh,' Shirley said. 'Oh, I'm sorry. I didn't mean –'

'Just don't be kind. And don't feel sorry for me. It makes it worse.'

At once Shirley stood up. 'I know. I won't. But please just remember that whenever you want to talk about it, if you ever do, I'm here.'

'I'll tell you sometime. But I have to learn to live with it first.'

For long minutes after the door closed, Jennie sat with her head down on the desk. How do you cope with such pain? You clamp down on it, that's what you do. So with clenched teeth and clenched fists, she conquered it, at least for the moment, and returned to her papers. Steadily, one by one, she dealt with them, compiling notes; breaking off briefly to make a supper of toast and eggs, she went back to them and was still at work when, shortly after nine o'clock, the telephone rang.

'How are you?' Jill asked.

The faintest thrill of pleasure passed through Jennie. 'Fine. And you? What are you doing phoning me on a Sunday night? You're supposed to be out having fun.'

'My boyfriend's father was taken to the hospital this afternoon. So I'm here in the dorm.' Jill lowered her voice. 'Peter called and told me what happened to you yesterday. So savage, so horrible! They ought to kill men like that.'

'Unfortunately it's not the way the law works. But I wasn't hurt. I was lucky.'

'Do you feel well enough to talk about something?'

'Oh, sure. What is it?'

'Well, I got tomorrow's paper ahead of time, and there's an article in it about an environment case, a tract upstate called the Green Marsh. That's your case, isn't it? I thought I recognized it.'

There was no longer a reason for elaborate secrecy; Jennie answered directly, 'It *was*, you mean. I've been fired.'

'Peter told me. That must hurt awfully, when you've done so much work on it.'

'What hurts most awfully is that I'm afraid the builders will get their way.'

'Isn't there anything you can do?'

'Nothing. I'm not a resident, and I don't pay taxes in that town.'

'I don't agree. You're an American citizen, aren't you? This kind of protest is going on all over the country. You can go anywhere you want and talk up. There's no reason why you can't go to that meeting and speak your mind.'

Jill was talking in her most emphatic manner, so that Jennie could visualize the wide gesture with which she tossed her hair back from her cheek, could imagine the two vertical lines of frowning concentration and her vivid glance. All this contrasted to her own weariness.

'I've lost my energy,' she said.

'Are you afraid because of yesterday? But you'd be safe in a public meeting.'

The implication of fear offended Jennie's pride, or her false pride, she thought, and she answered promptly, 'That's not the reason. I just don't have the heart for it.'

'You have to have the heart,' Jill insisted. 'You've come this far. Do you want to lose now?'

'It's not my fight anymore.'

'It is your fight, I told you! It's everybody's. My parents travel all over the Southwest, they go to every meeting, write to their senators, never give up.'

Jennie remembered Martha Cromwell's words: 'You're a spellbinder, Jennie.'

Her appeal, the one that as an attorney she had already outlined, would have been striking. It would have gone straight to the heart and conscience of anyone who possessed a heart and a conscience.

'I'll go with you if you'll do it,' Jill was saying.

It took a moment or two for this astonishing offer to register.

'You'll go with me?'

'I'd surely like to. I can afford to cut a couple of classes.'

You're a spellbinder, Jennie.

It was a wild idea. On the other hand, maybe it wasn't so wild. As a private citizen, she could be even more outspoken than counsel could be. She began to feel the stirring of excitement. There was dramatic intrigue in the undertaking.

'Jennie? Are you thinking about it?'

She conceded slowly, 'It might be interesting.'

'I should say it would be! Then you will?'

There came another pleasurable thought: This would be a chance to display her talents to her daughter. For the first time the word came unselfconsciously and naturally: daughter.

'Well, it's worth considering. Let's see, I could rent a car. We'd have to leave by three at the latest. Can you do that?'

'Earlier, if you want.'

'Three will be okay.'

Suddenly Jennie was charged with a spirit of adventure. Part of her mind, observing the rest of it as was her habit, told her that she needed something like this. It would propel her forward, to the land of the living.

Then defiance flashed a little spurt of fire: Listen, there was life before Jay and there'll be life after him. There has to be. To hell with him.

'Yes. Okay. I'll pick you up at the main gate on Broadway.'

14

On Sunday she polished and refined her brief remarks. As a mere private citizen, no longer the legal adviser, she would have to talk fast before someone cut her off. She would have to make her points clearly without sacrificing eloquence. She was working away when Peter called to say goodbye.

'I was glad to hear about your expedition with Jill.'

'It was her idea. She encouraged me.'

'I guess you two are going to be pretty solid together now.'

'I hope so. I think so.'

'Then something good *has* come out of it, after all, hasn't it? I hope it'll help a little to make up for the rest, Jennie.' And when, not knowing what to answer, she was silent, he added more brightly, 'I'll be coming back. You'll not get rid of me so easily.'

She said, meaning it, 'I'm not trying to get rid of you.'

They passed through a corridor that smelled of cleaning fluid and was flanked by doors labeled Health Department, Dog Licenses, Police Department, Traffic Violations, Tax Collector. They entered the courtroom where the town council sat on its dais with the American flag on a stand at its side.

A man who was standing against the rear wall touched

Jennie's arm, and she recognized Jerry Brian, who had 'wired' George. He was in plainclothes. 'Are you still interested?'

'That's why I'm here,' she responded.

'I thought you might be. Okay.' And drawing her away from bystanders, including Jill, he whispered, 'You won't believe it, but we've already got a lead.'

'So fast?'

'The boss has been working day and night. This fancy-looking company's got a bad reputation. Mob connections.'

'Barker Development, you mean?'

'I mean. The top honcho's built in California under another name, got in trouble, got out of it, then came East and started to look respectable.' Jennie let out a faint, low whistle. 'What kind of trouble?'

'A bomb in somebody's car. Something to do with a site they wanted to buy and the owner wouldn't sell. Something like that. Martin says they weren't able to prove it, but everybody knew it, anyway.'

'So can they prove this? About George?'

'Martin thinks so. Mind you, I'm not in on the whole picture. I'm only here tonight to keep my eyes open, see who's here. Not that we're expecting Mr Teeth to show up.' Even in the dim corner Jennie could see the young man's grin. 'I hear you got off lucky with him.'

'That I did.' She thought of something. 'And Fisher, that creep? Where does he fit in?'

'He doesn't. A creep is all he is. Small fry who happens to have a piece of land he wants to sell and gets mad at the opposition.'

'I could have sworn he was in it,' Jennie said. 'I guess I'm not so smart, after all.'

'You're smart enough. Look, it's filling up. You'd better get a seat.'

A large crowd had already taken most of them. From the rear Jennie searched the room for a pair of vacancies. Her moving eyes recognized a few faces on the dais, then flickered back up the sides of the room and caught the silver-gray heads of Enid and Arthur Wolfe. They were alone, which was to be expected, for Jay hardly would have given up a day in the office or a federal courtroom to be up here tonight. Their heads turned for only a fraction of a moment, yet Jennie was certain they had seen her. With Jill beside her, she walked in full view to the third row down front, where there were two places. If they want to acknowledge me, she thought defiantly, now is their chance. And if they should wonder about this beautiful young woman who is with me, why, I shall simply tell them who she is. I came to that point just a minute ago. I don't know how I reached it but I did, and here I am.

The Wolfes, however, made no move. What must Jay not have told them! She imagined their widened eyes, their horrified astonishment. And, vividly, she saw them in their kitchen – blue-and-white gingham curtains, African violets in red porcelain cups, the dog at their feet – having their evening tea and cake. They'd have shaken their heads, commiserating with each other and marveling: 'But she was so sincere, so frank and open!'

As quickly as confidence had risen, so quickly did it ebb. She shouldn't have come back here, abrading her wounds. The sensible thing would be to turn around and go home right now. Let someone else fight for the Green Marsh and win it or lose it. But that would be humiliation in front of Jill. Hadn't she come here in part to show off a bit before Jill?

So, waiting her turn, Jennie sat through the routine procedures, the pledge of allegiance, the minutes of the previous meeting and all the technical reports. Again the lawyers argued. Barker's young man gave a repetition of his arguments, persuading his listeners of the benefits that Barker Development was prepared to bring to the town. She wondered whether this engaging, respectable-looking gentleman with the open, confiding manner could possibly be acquainted with Robinson, also known as Harry Corrin, and decided that he probably was not, because in organizations of Barker's size and nature, it would be prudent and necessary to keep the right hand from knowing what the left was doing.

The tired, middle-aged lawyer who had replaced Jennie was a poor match for the other man. Droning statistics, he was beginning to lose the councilmen's attention; the mayor was yawning contemptuously.

Discussion eventually was thrown open to the public. Jennie waited until half a dozen citizens had expressed their opinions. They were fairly evenly divided. The council, too, she supposed was probably still evenly divided, as it had been a few months ago. So the vote would be close. She raised her hand, was acknowledged, and stood up to speak.

'My name is Jennie Rakowsky,' she began firmly. 'Some of you may remember that I've spoken here before. This time I'm here just as a citizen. I want to talk to you about Barker Development. Like all developers, they come with a fine speech, luring you with talk of jobs, tax abatements, and all the wonderful improvements they're going to bring to your town. Don't you believe a word of it,' she cried, and raised a warning finger. 'They've come to make money, that's all they've come for. They don't give a damn about anything but the bottom line. There's nothing new about these people, either. They were around back in 1890, trying to cut Yosemite National Park in half right at the start. If good citizens hadn't fought them then, we'd have no Yosemite or Grand Canyon or any other wilderness park today.'

Somebody clapped and was immediately hushed. The Wolfes were staring over Jennie's head toward the dais, or perhaps toward the ceiling, for all she knew, but someone else had applauded; it spurred her on, and Jennie began to gallop.

'We can go a lot farther back than that, to Isaiah more than two thousand years ago, or to the ancient Greeks. Plato knew that when you cut forests down, you don't hold rain, and the earth washes away to the sea.'

She had notes in her hand yet didn't need them. 'And part of your land here is wetland, a sponge to slow water that could flood your lands. It's home to wildlife, it's beauty and recreation. It's an ecosystem that took thousands of years to build. If it's destroyed, it can't be rebuilt. You know that, and these people know it as well as you do, but they don't care. That's the difference.'

Heads turned to Jennie. There wasn't a sound in the room.

'We can always save "farther out," people say. But what about when there is no more "farther out" to save? This planet's not elastic. And right now it's the only planet we have.'

She talked on. It already had been six minutes and she kept expecting to be stopped, but no one on the dais stopped her. She was aware of upturned faces, of Jill's rapt attention and the flow of her own energy.

'It's not as if this were a question of housing the homeless here. There's no real need for this construction, for condominiums and golf courses. It's frivolity – that and greed.' She paused a second. 'We all know greed when we see it. The world's full of it. People even kill because of it, don't they?'

That's for you, Robinson, she thought, and in that very

instant she caught sight of Fisher. He was sitting diagonally across the aisle in the row ahead. She hadn't noticed him before, but there he was, wearing the same black jacket with the same black, malevolent sneer on his face. Well, you fooled me, she thought. You certainly did. You didn't kill George. You're only a street-corner tough. You're not smart enough to be in on a scheme like this one. Still, you're not the type I'd care to meet on a dark night!

She recovered her train of thought; having spoken well, it was time now to stop. And she quickly concluded, addressing the rows of heads on the dais.

'We need a new way of seeing our world. I hope you've begun to see it and will agree that this application has to be refused.'

Her heart was still hammering when she sat down.

'You were perfect. Eloquent,' Jill whispered. Her eyes shone with admiration.

A surge of joy passed through Jennie. At the same time she would have liked to know what the Wolfes were saying.

The mayor then asked whether there were any more comments from the floor, and since there were none, the discussion was closed.

Now it was the council's turn to deliberate and vote. Discussion was short and offered no surprises; as at the first meeting, there were angry remarks about do-gooders who cared more for skunks and weasels than for people, remarks that brought laughter from some in the audience and applause from others. Fisher got conspicuously to his feet to show approval. The librarian spoke for preservation. The thin man who seconded him was Jack Fuller, the dairy farmer. 'You've got a fantastic memory for names,' Jay had said.

Then came the vote. One for. One against. Two against. Three in favor. Jennie leaned forward in her seat.

A heavy man wearing cataract glasses got to his feet. 'I have to say that I was, at the start of the evening, still wavering. I could see merit in voting either way. But after listening to the young woman who spoke last, I made my decision. Yes, we do have an obligation to future generations. She's certainly right. And so I vote no to the proposal. Leave the Green Marsh alone.'

'Four to four,' Jennie murmured. Jill squeezed her hand. The mayor was flushed and furious as he polled the man at the end of the table.

'Mr Garrison?'

The one with money troubles. A decent sort, Jennie recalled. But they said he could be swayed.

Now he cleared his throat, as if about to give a speech, and took on a solemn expression. Obviously he was feeling his own importance.

'I, too, was of two minds,' he began. 'There's always something to be said on behalf of conservation. But there's also much to be said for creating jobs, and certainly we can use ratables to ease the tax burden.'

Jennie groaned silently.

'It's a question of weighing the two. On the one hand –'

Oh, for Pete's sake, she cried silently, will you get to the point?

'On the other hand –'

After two minutes' worth of weighing hands, he did get to the point. 'So I vote to turn down the application. Let the state take over the land as a wilderness park.'

Jennie laughed. Her eyes filled with tears. Jill kissed her cheek.

'You did it! You did it!'

The crowd moved slowly toward the night and the dimly lit parking lot. Behind and around her in the crush, Jennie heard comments.

'If it hadn't been for that young lady lawyer, it's my opinion they'd have voted the other way.'

'Maybe so. She helped, that's for sure.'

'She swayed them: I watched their faces.'

'You could almost feel Garrison making up his mind.'

'There's a lot of anger here, though. You don't see money like that go sliding through your fingers without getting pretty mad.'

'You must feel wonderful,' Jill repeated as they drove away. 'You did it all.'

'No, I didn't do it all. I did some, and I'm happy about that,' Jennie replied.

Jay would have applauded that speech. It had been concise, it had been damn good. All my pride and all my heart were in it, she thought.

They passed through the town and were soon out on the highway. Jennie looked at the clock on the dashboard. 'Nine-thirty and no traffic. We'll be back in the city by midnight.'

Fields, divided by the road's black thread, were a black-and-white patchwork where snow had melted and re-frozen. The sky was white and calm.

'I never realized there was so much empty space in the East,' Jill remarked.

'Well, you've only been in New York. Look over there, that's the little road that leads to the Green Marsh. The lake's just half a mile in. It's one of the prettiest places you could hope to see, even in New Mexico.'

'All right, let me see it.'

'Now? At night?'

'Why not? See how light it is out? And it's only half a mile, you said.'

Jennie was moved by the girl's eagerness. 'Okay. Then we'll just get home fifteen minutes later.'

The little car bumped and slid on the ruts and stopped

where the lane became too narrow. A short walk over crunching snow brought them to the crest of the hill above the lake. It, like the land, was a patchwork of black and white. Where the ice was broken, the water glistened like black marble. A deep quiet lay on the hemlock-covered hills and on stark birches, unmoving in the windless night.

Here under the benign sun she had come upon this place and stood in the bright air, perhaps on this very spot, with his arms around her and their life lying ahead of them, as warm and gold as the sun and the air.

'Oh, look, Jennie, an owl!'

From a low branch, it stared out of round, amber eyes; then, raising its great wings, it sailed downhill above their heads, crossed the lake, and disappeared in shadow among the trees.

'How beautiful it is here! I know what you mean and why you fought for it,' Jill whispered.

And Jennie understood that she was being considerate of the silence. She had gotten the feel of the place. Her hands clasped before her, she stood and gazed at the sleeping wilderness while Jennie just gazed at her.

Then they got into the car and started back to the city. For a while they rode in silence, the whir of the tires and the thrum of the engine making the only sounds. It was Jill who spoke first.

'I told Mom and Dad everything.'

'Everything?'

'Yes, about you and the reason you didn't want to see me. Mom said I shouldn't have insisted.'

'Just tell Mom it's turned out all right.'

'Really?'

If only it were so simple, so clear a division between black and white!

'Yes. Really!'

'I just want to say one thing. Your secret – about me – would have been safe. I never would have told.'

A lump rose in Jennie's throat. 'I couldn't have lived with a lie. Gotten up every day and faced him, knowing something he didn't know.'

'It's been done.'

'But not by me.'

For the second time that night Jill placed her hand on Jennie's; the two hands rested lightly on the wheel.

What do I feel? Jennie asked herself. A flow of love, a mingling of gratitude and grief. Then she thought, silently chiding herself, Oh, we are all too self-absorbed these days! Stop all this analysis! Just take things as they come. Stop asking yourself what you are feeling or why. It does no good.

And she said practically, 'You must be starved after that hurried little supper. Let's stop somewhere for a bite.'

'I'd rather not. I didn't realize it would take so long to get back.'

'Okay, it is pretty late. Too late to go back to the dorm. You'd better stay at my place overnight. Why don't you put your head back and sleep? You've had a long day.' Looking over at Jill, she thought, I sound like a mother.

'You sound like Mom,' Jill said.

'Do I? That's nice.'

The girl slept. Rolling toward the city, the car passed landmarks that Jennie would not be seeing again: a bridge; a road-side stand where Jay always bought apples to take home. And here I am, she thought, with my child of chance, unexpected and unwanted, beside me. Her beautiful hair is a collar around her pure, sleeping face. The two of us are riding through the night.

It was shortly before one o'clock when Jennie stopped the car. The street was dark, but the windows in her apartment were all lit.

What now? Who now? She felt an urge to flee, to get back in the car and keep going.

'What's wrong?' Jill asked.

'The lights are on in my apartment. I don't think we should go in.'

'Why not?'

'After what happened at my office, can you ask?'

'Give me the outside key. We'll go up, and if anything's wrong, we'll scream, that's all, and wake the house.'

'You're making me feel like a coward. All right, I'll go, but I want you to stay down here.'

'I'll stay a few steps behind you.'

'Not a few steps! Downstairs, I said.'

'You're sounding like Mom again.'

Jennie started up. On the third landing she stopped to listen. There wasn't a sound in the house. See, she reasoned, it's just another burglary. They've somehow gotten in, taken the stereo, the television, and some clothes because there's nothing else in there to take. It's not the worst thing in the world. In this city it happens every day.

The door was ajar, and she hesitated, gathering courage. Jill reached in front of her and pushed the door open.

'Go on in, Jennie. Go on.'

At the far end of the living room two men stood up. Peter was laughing, and Jay, with reaching arms, was running toward Jennie.

'Oh, Jennie!' he cried.

Unable to absorb the reality of what she was seeing she stammered. 'W-what is it? What are you doing?'

'Oh, Jennie,' cried Jay again. He put his arms around her. 'You ought to hit me! Beat me! Throw me down the stairs! What I've done to you! What I've done!'

Through starting tears she said again, 'What are you doing? I don't understand.'

'Peter came to my office this afternoon and told me everything. Why ... oh, for God's sake, why didn't you tell me yourself?'

She hid against his shoulder.

'You could have told me,' he protested when she did not answer.

'No, she couldn't have,' Peter said.

Jay raised Jennie's head so that she was forced to look at him.

'Why didn't you?' he repeated.

Still she was unable to answer, and could only put her hand on her heart as if to cover its fierce beat.

And Peter, in whom the first laughter had died, so that his eyes were stern, said, 'I've explained the way I see it, the way it is.... She was too afraid.'

'Afraid of *me*?' Jay was bewildered. 'Not of *me*? I can't believe it.'

'Please,' she whispered.

'Darling Jennie, you should have told me at the very beginning when you first found out.'

Somehow now, Peter was taking charge. 'I'll answer for her. She was afraid of losing you. And,' he said in a roughened voice, 'as I also told you, it goes back to me. Me and my family. I've done a lot of thinking these last few days.... We marked her. After that she never thought she was good enough. This was just a repeat situation.'

'Is that the way you felt about it, Jennie?' Jay said sorrowfully.

'I guess so. Something like that,' she whispered.

'We would have lost everything if Peter hadn't come to me. The way it looked, I thought ... I *had* to think ... I went a little bit crazy, the way you'd feel if you suddenly found out that your mother was a spy for the enemy –' He broke off. 'And this is your girl?'

For Jill had been waiting, observing the scene with curiosity and tenderness.

At last Jennie found coherent speech. Proudly she said, 'Yes, this is Jill. Victoria Jill.'

'So you're the cause of it all!' Jay took hold of Jill's shoulders and kissed her on both cheeks. He looked from her to Jennie and back again. 'If this is what you can produce, Jennie, you ought to have a dozen.'

There was a swirling in Jennie's head, a weakness in her knees, and she had to sit down.

'Such a week,' she murmured, wiping her eyes.

'The worst,' Jay said. 'The worst. But what am I talking about? I've just heard what happened to you at the office. I went crazy all over again when Peter told me.'

Jennie closed her eyes to shut out the dizziness, while Jay, sitting next to her, laid her head on his shoulder and stroked her hair.

'I feel as if I'd lived a lifetime since this afternoon,' he began slowly. 'When Peter walked into my office, I couldn't believe what I was seeing.'

Peter chuckled. 'He recognized me by my hair. It's very hard to disappear in a crowd when you've got hair this color.'

'He came in and started to lecture me. He attacked me and told me I had no right to be treating you like that, that it was brutal and –'

'I must have seemed a lot braver than I felt. I really expected to be thrown out of the office. But I had to do it. I couldn't get on the plane back to Chicago and leave Jennie like that when it was my fault.'

'Not really your fault,' Jennie objected.

'Well, however you want to look at it. Anyway, I remembered your neighbor, Shirley. You'd said she knew everybody's business, so I came over here and asked her some questions – as your friend the doctor, of course. That's how I got Jay's name. It was easy.' Peter was pleased with himself.

Now Jay laughed. 'It's never hard to get Shirley talking, bless her. The trick is to stop her.'

'I knew all the time what Peter was planning,' Jill said now. 'And when we drove up and I saw the lights on, I knew it had worked out all right. I was on pins and needles all day thinking about it.'

'No wonder you were in a hurry to get back and wouldn't stop to eat,' Jennie said.

'Oh!' Jay exclaimed. 'I forgot all about today. I've been in such a condition that I didn't give a damn anymore about the Green Marsh or anything else. But Jennie didn't forget. Jennie, you went –'

'It was Jill who made me go.'

'Yes, and aren't you glad you did? She won,' Jill told the men. 'She gave the most marvelous speech, and that's what turned the vote. She fought and won.'

'Yes, my Jennie's a fighter.'

Then came Peter's voice. 'For good causes, yes. For other people.'

No one said anything for a moment. Then Jay asked somewhat uncertainly whether his parents had been at the meeting.

'They were there. But we didn't speak.' There was something she had to know. 'What did you tell them about me?'

'Only that I thought, I had reason to know, that you'd found somebody else. I was vague. I couldn't have said anymore, and they didn't ask anymore.'

'They're such good people,' Jennie murmured.

'Well. They liked you so much. But of course, when they believed you'd hurt their son, you can understand why Dad got another attorney. I asked him not to; but he wouldn't listen, he was just so hurt himself.'

'I'll make it up to them, Jay.'

'You don't have to make up to anybody for anything! And listen, the first thing in the morning, we're going for the marriage license. Forget the fancy wedding arrangements. I don't want to wait any longer than three days.' He reached out and took Jill's hands. 'I want you there too. You're Jennie's daughter, and you're going to be mine.' And very softly, so softly that Jennie barely heard him, he finished. 'I love your mother so much, Jill. And I almost lost her. Through my own fault.'

'When you come down to it, it started with me. My fault,' Jill said. 'I can't bear to think I almost ruined everything.'

'I think it's time now to stop all the talk about fault and being sorry,' Peter objected. 'Let's look to the future.' He yawned and stretched. 'It's late and I'm catching an early plane, so I'm going to say good-night.' He took his coat. 'Will I be seeing you sometime in Chicago, Jill?'

'Sure. I could change planes on the way home for Christmas vacation and have lunch with you. I'm in a hurry to get home, though, to see Dad and Mom and the kids.'

Jay was looking at her intently.

'You look puzzled,' Jill remarked with a smile.

'Not exactly. It's just that I don't know anything about you, and I want to.'

'You will. I'll visit a lot whenever you ask me. I'd love to.'

'Just "visit"?'

'Oh, were you thinking I would move in with Jennie? I never wanted that! I've got a wonderful family of my own! What I wanted,' Jill said earnestly as Jennie watched the now familiar flash of eyes and toss of hair, 'what I wanted was only to know who I am. And now that I know who I am, and love who I am,' she added, touching Jennie's arm, 'I'm at peace. Yes, I'm very peaceful.'

'Well, you can have two families,' Jay said.

Peter corrected him. 'Three. I am a family of one.'

'Can't you stay for the wedding?' Jay asked as Peter put on his overcoat. 'Only three days more?'

Peter shook his head. 'Thanks, but I'm off. A rolling stone, that's me.' He shook hands, kissed Jill, and was about to shake Jennie's hand when she got up and kissed him.

She laughed. 'You don't mind, Jay?'

'No – I could kiss him myself.'

'Please don't,' Peter said, and they all laughed, breaking the strain.

As if by common agreement, the three went to the window when he had gone. They watched him cross the street under the lamps and move toward the avenue in loping, boyish strides.

Jay said abruptly, 'I liked him.'

'I thought I hated him,' Jennie answered.

'But now you don't,' Jill said.

'How could I? He gave you both back to me.' She took Jill's hand and with her other held Jay's, which was warm and firm.

'It's been a long time, a long way,' she said.

A softness flowed in her, sweet rest, as on seeing home again after a journey. This plain little room contained a world, a full, bright, new world.

Then she thought of something.

'Hey, Jill! Aren't you the person who said she would keep the secret, who would never tell?'

'Well, I lied,' Jill said cheerfully.

BELVA PLAIN

DAYBREAK

Things haven't turned out too badly for Laura Rice.

Husband Bud is handsome and reliable. He may crack the odd racist joke, but he is a devoted and kind husband and father.

Elder son Tom is intelligent and athletic. He's picked up some funny ideas from his new college friends, but he'd do anything for his frail kid brother, Timmy.

One day, out of the blue, Laura is visited by a local lawyer with some devastating news. He represents a family from the other end of town who are mourning the death of their son. Only he wasn't really their son. For in one of those million-to-one accidents that you just read about in the papers, they've discovered that he was swapped in the hospital at birth.

HODDER AND STOUGHTON PAPERBACKS

BELVA PLAIN

WHISPERS

A dream home, a successful husband, two beautiful childen, glamorous country club parties: Lynn Ferguson seems to have it all.

Only her closest friend Josie can see below the surface. Robert Ferguson – somehow too ambitious and correct. The children – becoming increasingly difficult.

And, most worryingly of all, the tell-tale marks that have begun to mar Lynn's lovely face . . .

Belva Plain's novel, written with extraordinary understanding and warmth, faces up to a subject too long discussed only in Whispers.

BELVA PLAIN

TREASURES

A child. That was what Lara wanted. A child, and for the family to stay together.

Travel. To get away from the small Ohio town to the wide open spaces of Texas. That was Connie's urgent dream.

While for Eddy, New York beckoned. Wall Street, wealth and influence.

The day of Peg Osborne's funeral was to mark a turning point. The lives of all her three children were about to alter dramatically.

But dreams can turn sour and ambitions mislead. And tragedy, heartache and disgrace are in store before the family becomes one again and each discovers life's true treasures.

HODDER AND STOUGHTON PAPERBACKS

BELVA PLAIN

HARVEST

Iris and Theo Stern seemed to have it all: a secure marriage, four attractive children, a beautiful house filled with lovely things as well as the respect that came from Theo's work as one of the country's top surgeons.

But one outsider, Paul Werner, knew better. Watching over them with anguish, he knew of Iris's frustrations, Theo's wandering eye and affections. He saw their eldest son, Steve, bright and sensitive, beginning to rebel against the values and beliefs of his family.

But above all he knew the secret that lay buried at the heart of the Sterns' seeming security and happiness. The secret that could destroy everything . . .

'Belva Plain writes with such warmth and compassion about family life that you'll enjoy every minute of this book'

Annabel

HODDER AND STOUGHTON PAPERBACKS